THE THREAT UNSEEN

EVERGREEN
BOOK SEVEN

MATTHEW S. COX

DIVISION ZERO PRESS

The Threat Unseen

Evergreen Book 7

© 2022 Matthew S. Cox

All Rights Reserved

ISBN (ebook): 978-1-950738-56-4

ISBN (paperback): 978-1-950738-57-1

CONTENTS

SOMETHING IMPORTANT

SUNDAY, MAY 10TH

Metamorphosis had become something of a habit for Harper Cody.

The quiet high school girl people used to tease because they thought her a contradiction—an introverted redhead—seemed as distant a memory as mall trips, Starbucks, or feudalism. Well, perhaps not so much feudalism. For all she knew, it could be making a comeback somewhere in the world. She'd gone from timid to desperately trying to protect her little sister. Few things could coax the wildcat out of a shy teen as effectively as a nuclear war. From there, she'd evolved again into a militia soldier working to keep an entire town safe.

Over and over again, she tried to understand how it happened, yet no explanation made any logical sense. She'd done things impossible for her to imagine in that other life. On some level, she felt like an actor playing a tough-girl cop in some never-ending *Groundhog Day* type theater production... with an amazing special effects budget. Whenever she stopped to think about her reality, she couldn't believe who she'd become. It unsettled her to realize the idea of speaking in front of people now freaked her out more than the idea of killing a person—as long as they deserved it. Harper still couldn't shoot an innocent or defenseless person, but if a situation called for killing someone and they deserved it, the guilt didn't last too long.

A new metamorphosis took shape beneath Harper today. More specifically, it took the shape of a large horse named Two Bale, presumably because he could eat two whole bales of hay by himself. In addition to being the largest of the handful of horses the militia had, Two Bale also happened to be the most laid back. Because of this, Walter and Adriana Rodriguez—the woman who ran the Express post in Evergreen as well as managed the horses—encouraged her to take him out today.

"So weird," whispered Harper to no one in particular. "Shy geek to freaked out kid with a shotgun to militia soldier to... cowgirl. Never in a million years would I have ever dreamed this."

Instead of taking the bike out on her patrol, which she still preferred, she found herself trying to remember all the details about how to ride a living animal. A host of signals ranging from specific clicks, to words, to nudging with her knees or tugging on the reins circled her thoughts, battling for focus against her constant fear of falling or being thrown. Sure, many millions of people throughout history rode horses without a problem, but she could only think of Christopher Reeve. An injury like he suffered in a world like this would be fatal.

Also, if an emergency situation pounced on her, she fully expected her brain to eject every bit of 'horse knowledge' and leave her stranded atop a giant animal she couldn't effectively control.

Probably why they wanted me to take him out on patrol today. Do a thing often enough it becomes subconscious.

Years ago, she'd been as uncomfortable around shotguns as she was about horses. Hours and hours of practice later, she could knock clay pigeons out of the air as easily as breathe. Neither she nor her father ever expected she'd one day be firing on people. It hadn't been an easy hesitation to overcome. Thankfully, the guilt she once felt over her father's death shrank from a devouring demon sitting on her shoulders to a disapproving little gremlin in the back corner of her mind, staring imperiously down its pointed nose at her. She refused to give the bastard any satisfaction by hesitating again and getting anyone else killed.

Do I count as mentally damaged? Shooting deer for food makes me feel worse than killing Lawless.

Harper steered Two Bales around a small Honda SUV parked on someone's front yard. The little truck had weeds growing through the wheels, not having moved in almost two years. Before she arrived in Evergreen, the militia went around to collect all the gasoline they could get from every vehicle left behind. The mountain topography played weird games with the EMP coming from Denver and Colorado Springs. Here and there, bits of electronics survived while others fried. Of course, by now, any gasoline would long since be worthless. Like shopping centers, Applebee's, and dance class, cars faded into the past as relics of a former era.

With the horse, she'd been advised to avoid paved roads as much as she could since it hurt their feet. So, she'd altered her patrol route in a novel way by ignoring streets entirely. She crisscrossed among the houses, letting the horse walk at whatever pace he cared to. Being mindful of the animal distracted her more than she liked. The Express riders made it look so effortless and easy. She argued back and forth with herself between pressing on because she really should learn, and deciding it was too much of a risk. How could she effectively patrol if most of her attention focused on not falling off a stupid horse?

Walter only let me do this alone because he thinks this is the safest area. She sighed. *It isn't. Nowhere is.*

This patrol area could be argued as the safest only in the sense of danger from within. Mostly families with children lived here, close to the school. Odds were lower one of the residents would become a threat here than, say, on the west part of town where they assigned most of the young, single men and newcomers. Perhaps in a throwback to times gone by, the citizens of Evergreen maintained a guarded distrust of new arrivals until they'd lived here a while without causing problems.

It also didn't really feel right to think Walter looked at her like a kid who needed an easy-slash-safe militia assignment. Maybe some of the guys thought of her as a child at first, but none ever said so out loud. No one treated her as a kid in need of coddling. Most of the time, she even felt respected. Of course, whenever that happened, she had to fight off a wave of guilt. Whether or not she deserved their respect, part of her felt like an imposter lying to everyone. She wasn't some bad-ass wasteland Annie Oakley, ready to kick ass and take names. Deep down inside, Harper Cody remained a freaked-out teenager who wondered what the hell happened to the world.

She'd gotten so good at pretending to manage her new reality, sometimes it almost felt like she actually could handle it.

Harper chuckled to herself, entertaining the idea she truly had weathered a nuclear storm and came out stronger for it. Meandering around a quiet mountain town in Colorado on a horse certainly had to be nicer than spending eight hours a day in an office cubicle being leered at and or patronized by men old enough to be her father. She still couldn't say what she might've ended up doing with her life if the war never happened. It didn't matter at all anymore, so she'd given up trying to answer the question. Office job, waitress, or something else… who cared?

This would be kinda nice if it didn't require billions of people dying.

Two Bales decided to stop walking to sniff at a cluster of bushes. They didn't have berries, nor resembled any of the stuff Adriana told her not to let horses eat. Sitting still atop a horse scared her less than being on a moving animal, so she took advantage of the momentary security to look around at the woods and the three houses partially visible around her. Distant voices carried over the otherwise silent neighborhood, men on the farm that used to be a golf course.

The former Hiwan Golf Club covered too much land to waste, so it had been repurposed to farming in addition to the 'primary' farm. In a technical sense, the 'north farm' sat on the edge of what the militia considered to be the town's border. This made it tactically vulnerable to raids from the outside. However, in a real sense, the development didn't obey this artificial line on a map. Hilly, tree-covered ground studded with widely spaced houses went on for miles to the north and east from the 'border' of Interlocken Drive. As far as Harper knew, no one occupied any of the homes east of the road. She didn't patrol out that far, and couldn't remember ever spotting anyone moving around among the properties visible from the road.

An expanse of abandoned suburbia outside a mountain town wouldn't be much of a deterrent against potentially hostile outside forces. Denver wasn't *that* far away. When—not if—the Lawless decided to visit Evergreen, they would almost certainly come in from the east, right here. They might be stupid enough to follow Route 74 into town, exactly the way she, Madison, Cliff, and Jonathan walked when they arrived, the proverbial path of least resistance. If they didn't expect organized armed defenders, the Lawless would certainly walk in like they owned the place—and get a huge surprise. Alas, after this much time without an attack, she had to assume they played it smarter and had sent in scouts at some point. Any one of the survivors who'd trickled in over the months could have been Lawless scoping things out.

Stories also came to town. Stories about how the Lawless turned Mile High Stadium into a temple of death worthy of a *Mad Max* movie. While exaggeration was common, she trusted what Renee said. Her friend had been taken by the gang in the aftermath of the war, forced to run around looting, assaulting, and going wild—or to be more accurate, following them while they did the going wild part. Thankfully, the idiots believed Renee's lie of being only fourteen and didn't rape her. She did, unfortunately, overhear them assaulting other women as well as talking about their 'citadel.'

The stuff Renee told her she'd overheard other Lawless talking about sounded straight out of the campiest post-apocalyptic movies. Survivors of the nuclear war deemed too 'weak' to be in the gang were forced to fight against each other in a gladiatorial arena. Winners got the chance for freedom if they could survive a gauntlet—essentially an obstacle course they had to navigate while Lawless attacked them from the sidelines. Exact details varied from shooting to throwing knives to improvised bombs. Renee said they made it sound like no one ever escaped alive. The 'gauntlet' was a cruel lie to torture people with futile hope.

Her mind—and nightmares—filled in the rest.

Although she believed with a reasonable degree of certainty she'd killed the man who murdered her father, it brought neither peace nor security. The Lawless wouldn't care. So what if one girl who lost her parents found revenge? It wouldn't dissuade the others from continuing to do what they did. In fact, the remaining Lawless probably said the guy deserved it for being too weak to survive.

"Live by the sword, die like a dumbass," muttered Harper. "Or something."

She gazed to her left—generally northeast—in the approximate direction of Denver, only able to see the nearby trees and houses. A distance of only about six miles by road separated her former home in Lakewood from the stadium. Dad once loved being so close, as it made going to see games easy. Harper never really got into sports, but she didn't mind going there with him. The Lawless changed a place full of fond memories into a crucible of nightmares she dreaded, yet one more thing they needed to be held accountable for.

Alas, as she discovered when she shot the man who killed Dad, revenge offered only the hollowest of solace, one brief flicker of satisfaction consumed by the fear she might become the very thing she recoiled from. Thoughts of charging into Denver to wipe out the Lawless never made it past idle daydreams. She couldn't risk her life for a task well past justice into vengeance. Madison had recovered—as much as any child could—from witnessing their parents shot dead. Losing Harper would ruin her, perhaps irrecoverably so. No one appointed Harper the guardian of all Colorado. It didn't make her selfish to prioritize her sister over any future harm the gang might inflict. She'd pushed herself quite far beyond her comfort zone already. Much to her surprise, being on the militia, she could handle. Turning into 'Furiosa' and rampaging a swath of vengeance across the wasteland wouldn't be happening. At least, not without some other serious tragedy erasing her desire to remain alive.

She exhaled. "And on that cheery note... C'mon, Two Bales. Let's go."

The horse continued sniffing around the bush, nibbling here and there in a manner more curious than hungry.

Oh, what was it to get him walking? A click or a heel tap?

Harper fidgeted at the reins in her hand, unable to remember the command and afraid to accidentally send the horse into a spontaneous gallop. Was she supposed to lean forward? Horses could sense a shift in the rider's weight and respond to them. Or did she need to push the stirrups forward? Make a clicking noise?

Panic started to well up in her gut. If she blanked like this when Lawless or some other dangerous outsiders showed up, she could be shot, stabbed, or worse—kidnapped. As long as Madison, Lorelei, and Jonathan remained alive, Harper decided it better to be kidnapped than killed. No matter what any abductor did to her—short of murder —she had the chance of escape and going home to her family. It also tended to be much more difficult to get revenge for being murdered.

"Come on, horse. Walk." Harper bounced in the saddle.

Two Bales lifted his head from the bush, one ear twitching.

Sigh. Come on... Oh, duh.

Harper leaned forward and lightly tapped her heels against the horse's sides. At this, the horse lurched into a slow walk. His ear twitched again.

Aha! Success. She blinked. *Oh crap. His ears are flicking. Someone's coming. Or something is coming...*

The scuff of a shoe on pavement drew her attention around to the right, and eased her worries about mountain lions or bears. Blues and greys of clothing blurred past the gaps in a swath of close-spaced trees. Someone walked on the road not far from her. Harper swung Two Bales around to face in that direction and meandered up near the road without going on it. As soon as she got past the swath of trees, she recognized Krystal Tucker. The young woman had been one of the survivors Cliff found on a long patrol, a fairly routine exercise where the militia followed a perimeter a few miles away from Evergreen. She couldn't be much more than two or three years older than Harper and appeared to be carrying a bundle of foodstuffs she'd gotten from the quartermaster's. The group she'd been with when Cliff found them had four children ranging from ten to twelve years old. They'd become something of a family the same way Harper and Madison adopted Cliff, Jonathan, and Lorelei—and now Carrie and Renee, not to mention the twins.

Upon realizing the sound the horse reacted to didn't mean danger, Harper relaxed—then blinked at herself. She'd swung Two Bales around to face the road subconsciously.

Huh... maybe I might figure this out after all. She took a slow breath. In truth, she learned the stuff just fine. The problem came from fear. Horses scared her. Mom used to tease her about having to surrender her 'girl card' for not being all about horses. As a little girl, her mother had tons of figurine horses and whatnot. She considered it 'normal' for little girls to love horses.

Yeah, Mom. I'm an outlier. Shy redhead, a girl who doesn't like horses...

Harper nudged Two Bales forward, walking the animal beside the road. She struck up a casual conversation with Krystal. Other than being much cleaner, she hadn't changed much since her arrival. The woman's long, dark brown hair, slender figure, and faint hint of a Spanish accent reminded her of a slightly older, slightly whiter, version of Christina Menendez, one of her close friends from school, a girl she hadn't seen since the day before the bombs fell.

As they meandered down the road, Krystal mostly talked about the kids she'd become mother to despite being nowhere near old enough to have given birth to any of them. Rylee, the youngest, recently turned eleven. The poor girl had mood swings. One minute, she'd act like the world was normal and had always been like this, the next, she'd be curled up in the corner, sobbing for no apparent reason. The other three, Allie, Tristan, and Elliot, seemed to be doing well, happy to be in Evergreen and coping.

"Maddie was kinda like that, too, for a bit." Harper fidgeted at the reins. "Just be there for her. Kids are resilient. You could also bring her to see Dr. Tegan if you think it's not getting better. She's almost a psychiatrist."

"Almost?" Krystal laughed. "What does that mean?"

"Means she was studying it but didn't finish getting a degree because the world melted."

"Oh. Yeah, I guess. Probably kinda hard to find a legit shrink these days."

Harper smiled. "She's legit. What good is a piece of paper from the state anymore?"

They soon reached the house where Krystal lived, one of the bigger ones in the area. Neither of the men, Randall or Kip, were there at the moment—likely over on the farm for the day. No sign of kids either. At this hour on a Sunday, they'd also be helping out with lighter tasks. Survival after a nuclear war didn't get weekends off. Krystal waved, then headed up the small driveway to the house.

Harper kept riding, veering once more away from the road. Steering Two Bales seemed to be easier when she didn't really think about doing it. The hard part became trying *not* to overthink.

Her mind wandered over the conversation. Rylee should be okay. She had a decent new family and the support of a whole town. Most of the kids here reached a point of acceptance, acclimating to the new reality with aplomb. She considered 'aplomb' a 'Grace word' because she couldn't remember hearing it used in real conversation by anyone else. Grace happened to be smart and didn't suffer Harper's problem of feeling embarrassed about showing it. Harper didn't consider herself a genius, but she had to be at least above average to coast through high school on As and Bs while barely doing any work. Grace, on the other hand, could've been one of those kids who went to college at fourteen. She didn't have to hide her brain because she also looked like the star cheerleader. Ironic she happened to *be* a cheerleader. Being on that team bus undoubtedly saved her life. If Grace had been home in Colorado Springs when the bombs fell, she'd have been vaporized.

At least the kids are okay.

Watching any of them now, it would seem as if they'd grown up in a world without reliable electricity, television, or modern conveniences. Cliff compared it to his childhood in the Eighties, 'back when kids played outside' as he put it. He loved to talk about how he and his friends never had cell phones as kids. He knew when to go home because the sky started to get dark and the streetlights came on. Granted, they didn't exactly have streetlights anymore, either.

Somehow, the little ones found it possible to be happy. They played with bikes, Frisbees, soccer balls (if they could find one) sticks, and whatever else they could get a hold of. Many—including her siblings—found it exciting to roam around and explore the empty houses. So many abandoned homes surrounded 'New Evergreen,' it remained a veritable certainty that some of them contained dangerous things. Short of keeping the kids on leashes in the back yard, she couldn't do much more than tell them over and over again to be careful and how much it would hurt her if they did anything stupid and dangerous.

Thankfully, the close call they had while exploring a crashed airplane not long ago made them all hesitant to stray too far away from town—and possible help. Jonathan carried an air horn canister like the militia so he could signal if they got in trouble. This, of course, wouldn't last forever. Eventually, the air horns would run out of air. They'd need to come up with something to replace them more effective than shouting. Thus far, no one had any good ideas.

For the most part, Evergreen's younger residents took nuclear war in relative stride. The teenagers had their fair share of PTSD type issues, but no more so than the adults. Harper kept questioning her own sanity for *not* being a basket case after everything. In her effort not to overthink controlling the horse, she started to dread the idea that a breakdown stalked her and she'd so far been able to delay it. As soon as she felt truly safe and secure, she'd collapse.

Or maybe she wouldn't.

Nah. If I was going to crack, it would've happened already.

A woman in the distance yelled, scolding a small child for wandering too far from the house. The kid had to be five or younger to be home at this hour rather than on the farm. Instead of school on weekends, children helped out with light farm work until about noon. The tone of the woman's voice ignited a memory, sounding too much like Mom yelling at her and Madison for having their cell phones out during dinner.

Such a stupid, trivial thing to be mad about.

A brief spike of sorrow and longing dragged a tear out of Harper's eye. What she wouldn't give to rewind time just to see her parents again. She sighed. *No going back. Heh. I wonder what parents in the 1800s yelled at their kids about over dinner? Bart, don't play with that wooden horse at the table!*

The asinine thought chased away the sadness and let her chuckle at the absurdity of the world. She lived in a strange mix of old and new, past and present.

Yeah... I'm riding a horse, wearing Nikes, carrying a Mossberg... it's like the prop and costume departments were on drugs and didn't know what movie I'm supposed to be in.

A child's wail rose in the near distance. She listened for a few seconds. Nothing alarming. A little boy frustrated he couldn't go walking away into the woods alone. The child coughed from trying to scream, cry, and protest all at once. Harper started to smile, then cringed. The coughing reawakened her worries about the babies. Owen and Emmett, Cliff and Carrie's twin boys, both had... something. Likely a passing bug or common cold, but society didn't exactly have proper hospitals anymore. At least, if it did, they would be really far away in some other country that neither the USA nor Russia nor China considered worth hitting directly with nukes.

Assuming anything still existed at all. Cliff thought giant clouds of fallout went around the globe, ruining almost everything. Of course, he also thought they should be in the throes of an extinction-level nuclear winter event... but it hadn't happened. Getting eighteen feet of snow—in places—not too long ago had to mean something went haywire, though. The farm managers said the Earth got a couple degrees colder. Didn't sound like much, a mere couple of degrees, but they thought it could wreak havoc.

This only made her worry about the farm.

She considered experimenting with riding fast in a simulated emergency as an excuse to race home and check on the babies. Carrie,

Cliff, and even Dr. Tegan insisted the infant boys would be fine. Harper couldn't evade the dread that even a small sickness could bloom into a major problem. That Carrie had given birth and walked away alive seemed as awe-inspiring as any soldier coming home from two tours in Vietnam without missing any body parts.

Even crazier, Darci had a baby, too, whom she named Piper as an homage. Her friend believed Harper saved her life by getting her out of that Army survivor camp. She didn't fault the military for the conditions there. They tried, but with limited resources and no remaining central government, how much could they really do? Too many people in too close quarters would eventually result in problems. That Darci resorted to prostituting herself in exchange for extra food infuriated Harper almost as much as the Lawless killing her parents. Not having any specific person to blame made it worse.

Two Bales' ears twitched.

She didn't have to worry what the animal heard for more than a second.

"Harper!" yelled a child. "Harper!"

A little red-haired girl came barreling through the trees down from the road to the left. She wore one of the new dresses handmade by Renee's group, a plain-ish affair of undyed fabric. The child tripped over a root, tumbled two or three times, and somehow bounced up back on her bare feet running once again, seeming unfazed.

Harper jumped down from the saddle in time to catch the girl before she crashed into the side of the horse. The child, around six or seven years old, had a wide-eyed expression of urgent panic and didn't even appear to comprehend she'd fallen over.

"Hey… it's okay. Slow down. Take a breath." Harper brushed her hands over the girl's head, taming her wild mane while racking her brain for the kid's name. Evergreen didn't have too many people with red hair. She knew this kid came from the farm in Kittredge where escaped convicts had basically enslaved the adults, including the girl's parents.

"Not okay," rasped the kid. "Kelsey's in trouble. She did a stupid."

As soon as she heard the name, Harper remembered the sisters,

Rain and Kelsey. This girl, Rain, was the older of the two. They'd been six and four when the Evergreen Militia raided the farm, freeing their parents and others from the convict gang.

Kelsey's four... maybe five. She couldn't have done anything too *crazy, right?* "I'll help. Just tell me what happened."

Rain nodded, then decided it time to catch her breath. After a moment, she exhaled hard, then sucked in a huge gulp of air. "Kels couldn't find Mr. Fluffy Butt. She started crying. We looked everywhere, but no Butt. Kels thinks we forgot him in the bad place. Daddy said we didn't forget it and she's 'membering wrong."

"Okay." Harper tried to keep a straight face. "Who or what is Mr. Fluffy Butt?"

"A stuffed am-i-nal. I fink he's a rabbit, but Kels says he's a sheep. Mom says he's an a-pack-a."

Whew. Okay. Missing plushie. This is my kind of crisis. I got this. She smiled. "All right. Let's go find Mr. Fluffy Butt."

"No..." Rain bit her lip and ground her toes into the dirt. "Kels finks Daddy just said that 'cause he don't wanna go look. Kels is tryin' ta go to the bad place an' find Fluffy Butt. She's gone. I can't find her."

Ack! Harper's smile evaporated. The problem ballooned from a misplaced plushie to a five-year-old girl attempting to walk, alone, to Kittredge. It didn't seem even remotely possible for a child that age to accurately find her way back there. She could've gone in any direction.

"How long ago did Kelsey run off?"

"Umm. I dunno. I was feedin' chickens. Kels tol' me she was gonna go get Mr. Fuzzy Butt inna morning before I hadda go to the farm. We got to go home early 'cause we're little and it's a nice day. Kels wasn't home. I can't find her."

Harper suppressed her initial urge—to take off into the woods in a random direction and start searching. She had to keep her head on. The whole militia would need to be involved. Every minute counted. A five-ish-year-old kid could get into all kinds of trouble wandering around alone, from falling into a storm drain or ravine to being picked off by a mountain lion, a creep, or some random passerby who mistook her for an orphan. They had to find her before sundown. Good thing it seemed to be only a little past noon.

She obviously couldn't send a seven-year-old alone across town to alert the militia. However, sending her home shouldn't be a big deal. The girl lived basically down the street from here.

"Okay. We'll find Kelsey. Are your parents home?"

Rain nodded.

"Good. All right. Go tell them Kelsey wandered off, and that you found me and the militia is going to find her."

"I can't." Rain twisted side to side, making her dress flare.

Harper blinked. "Why not?"

"Because they tol' me to go play outside. Mommy and Daddy like takin' all their clothes off and wrestlin' on the bed. I'm not s'posed to go in their room when they do that. I know they're doin' it 'cause they got the door locked."

"Uhh…" Harper blushed.

"I fink Mommy's losing 'cause she's makin' a scary noise." Rain simulated the sort of moaning she must have overheard.

Hand clamped over her face to hold in a laugh, Harper merely stared at the kid until the seriousness of the moment overwhelmed the humor. "It's okay. You won't get in trouble this time because you're telling them something really important, okay? I promise you they won't be mad. You have to tell them that Kelsey is missing. And tell them the militia is going to look for her."

"Okay. I will." Rain hugged her, yelled, "Thank you!" and ran back up the shallow hill the way she'd come from.

Harper looked at the horse. She debated leaving him there and running, but she'd be much faster riding… as long as she didn't fall off.

Hell with it. We don't have time for me to be a chicken. She scrambled back up into the saddle, leaned forward, and tapped her heels against the animal's side.

"C'mon, boy. We gotta move."

THE COLLECTOR

MAY 10TH – LATE AFTERNOON

Harper trekked through the forest on the far side of Interlocken Drive.

The unfamiliar layout of trees, hills, houses, and abandoned cars raised her anxiety well past a comfortable level. Crazy as it sounded to think about, she almost knew the streets around the old Hiwan Golf Club better than the neighborhood she'd grown up in.

"I never roamed around Lakewood purposefully trying to memorize everything," she half-whispered. "We usually hung out inside or went somewhere. And... the place looks kinda different now."

She glanced left and right, not entirely sure how long ago she'd lost sight of Marcie and Jaylen, the two nearest militia people in the circle with her. Everyone on the militia, including Walter, plus just about every other person in town sixteen years old or older healthy enough for a long walk had formed a huge ring around Evergreen and proceeded to advance in an expanding circle, following a direct line away from the town center.

Voices called out at varying distances in random intervals, the searchers yelling Kelsey's name, asking if she was okay, telling her she wouldn't get in trouble, and so on. Harper shouted for her as well, every thirty seconds or so, then listened for any signs of a little kid struggling to reply. Whenever she spotted a potential hiding place like a giant outdoor trash can, recycle bin, car, or something large enough for a five-year-old to get inside, she'd pause to check it.

By everyone's—including Kelsey's parents—best estimation, the girl had been missing for about three hours. No one believed the child knew the way to Kittredge and had likely picked a direction on a whim and started walking. The only thing Harper knew for sure was that the child did not take Route 74 north out of town, since the team at the bus barrier did not see her walking on the road. Good chance she also didn't make it to Route 74 inside town and go south, since any number of people would have noticed a kid so small wandering around alone.

In fairness, children did run around without adult supervision far more often now than before civilization collapsed. However, they usually did so in packs, and kids as young as Kelsey didn't usually go wandering around far from home. Locals wouldn't pay much attention to a group of tweens, but a single five-year-old would get noticed. With the main highway being an unlikely path for the child, Harper guessed the girl had either gone east—where she searched—or west, meandering among the trees.

Kittredge sat pretty much directly east from the center of 'New Evergreen,' roughly two and a half miles in a straight line. Of course, going there in a straight line meant climbing over some serious hills. Kelsey's family lived in a house up by the golf club turned corn farm, so she'd have to go east, then south... assuming, of course, a kid her age had any idea which way to go.

She could be in any direction. Oh, please get frustrated and scared and turn around.

The words of Harper's dad haunted her thoughts from a memory of her first camping trip. She'd been probably seven or eight at the time. He told her if she somehow got separated from her parents, she should pick as sheltered a spot as she could find and try to stay in the same place, so it would be easier to find her. If a missing child kept going in circles and the searchers kept walking in circles, it would take forever to find them. Kelsey's parents probably didn't tell her that.

Once we find her, I'm gonna suggest we start teaching the kids how to react to ending up lost in the woods. She paused to check inside a big blue recycle bin at the end of a long driveway. The container, almost as tall as her chest, held so many empty plastic bottles they touched the lid.

Whoever lived here really loved spring water... and hated the planet.

She let the lid fall closed, then peered up the length of the long, curving driveway at the face of a two-door garage attached to a large —compared to hers—house. It appeared to be in decent shape despite sitting unoccupied since the nukes, or so she assumed. Circles of concertina wire decorated the top of a wooden ranch-style fence around the front yard. A mound of sandbags blocked one of two gates into the yard, the one nearest the garage doors. More sandbags formed a wall in front of the garage.

Someone had to have fortified the place after the war. Razor wire and sandbags are a bit extreme for keeping the Mormons away. She peered at the windows, all blocked off with curtains or shades. No one appeared to be peeking back at her. Both the front door and the fence gate were closed. Except for its remoteness, the house looked wonderful, the sort of place her parents would never be able to afford.

Nice place... don't like being this far away from town though.

Something about the area nagged at her. It looked a bit too well-kept to have been abandoned since the war. However, despite her standing right there in the open, no one inside the home reacted to her presence. She couldn't remember anyone claiming to live out this far that she'd seen in town. If the house contained a territorial squatter or perhaps the pre-war owner, they'd certainly be shouting at her by now to go away, opening fire, or at least making it obvious they watched her every move. For no reason she could pin down, the place made her uneasy.

Madison had been talking lately about a book Mila found... witchcraft stuff. Not that she believed in that sort of thing, but the same way watching ghost stories late at night before bed got her all creeped out, merely talking about such topics primed her brain to be scared.

Her feelings shifted back and forth from 'someone died here' to 'I'm being watched' to 'this place is too clean, something's wrong here' to 'maybe there's useful stuff inside.' Still, it would have to wait. No way could she go exploring until Kelsey was safe. She took note of her surroundings. The last little road sign she saw on the street connected to the long driveway leading to this isolated house said Juniper Court.

The loudest and most ragged voice calling for Kelsey came from her father, Michael. That Harper could still hear him when he'd gone almost due south choked her up. The poor guy took most of the blame for not keeping a proper watch on her because it had been his idea to slip into the bedroom with Amy, his wife, to have sex. He kept muttering 'she'd never run off before.'

Harper didn't blame the guy, but also hated that excuse. Just because something had never happened before didn't prove it couldn't ever happen. She stopped walking, cupped her hands around her mouth, and yelled, "Kelsey?"

Her shout set off a ripple effect in two directions as the nearest other searchers also called for the girl. Only two people to the right and left remained close enough to understand the word. The third person sounded more like a strange bird cry, their voice distorted by distance and trees.

She resumed hiking, following an annoying downhill stretch too steep to be comfortable but not quite steep enough to require actual climbing. Moving slow so she could keep looking around, Harper made her way to the bottom of a shallow area between two hills and proceeded along the incline on the other side.

Another house came into view from the woods about where the ground leveled off up ahead on her right. She approached, scanning the area for any signs of the missing child. The back door hung ajar, which presented the possibility Kelsey might've gone inside more so than a closed door. Not that the girl couldn't open doors, but it didn't seem likely she'd take the time to close it behind her.

"Kels?" called Harper.

No answer came from the house or surrounding woods.

She hurried over, crossed a small concrete patio, and poked her head in the door. The sour stink of mold greeted her. Enough dirt collected on the kitchen floor to prove Kelsey hadn't been here: no footprints. Sunlight in the living room up ahead suggested a hole in the ceiling. Harper held her breath and advanced across the kitchen for a better look. Black fuzz clung to the walls of the front room. Water dripped from the ragged edges of shredded ceiling drywall hanging from a hole big enough to drive a car through.

A large mass of mangled metal lay against the wall on her left, where it had crashed down, obliterating the entertainment center. Carpet and floor around it appeared charred. Two small fire extinguishers in the middle of the room hinted that the prior occupant of the house survived the impact. It appeared to have once been some manner of huge cylindrical tank. Even though it collapsed and twisted like a stomped-on soda can, Harper estimated it used to be about fifteen feet tall and likely eight feet or more in diameter.

What the hell was that?

The only explanation she could come up with is some manner of industrial storage tank that got flung into the air by a nuclear blast wave… and managed to fly all the way out here. Seeing another case of debris smashing into a house brought on a momentary shiver at her personal close call. If not for her parents' habit of waking up super early, Harper would've been asleep in her bed when a giant hunk of concrete landed on top of it.

"Kelsey isn't here."

She proceeded across the living room, went out the front door, and kept going east into the forest.

Soon after leaving the house, a distant air horn sounded five quick pips.

Harper stopped walking, exhaled hard, and collapsed to sit on the ground, overcome with relief. Right before the search party started, they agreed on 'five short' as a signal meaning someone found Kelsey alive. 'Four long' would've been bad news. From the sound of the horn, the child had gone the opposite direction, west. Knowing the girl had been found safe allowed Harper to laugh. The poor kid went about as directly away from Kittredge as possible.

"Heh. If I was her mom, I don't think I'd be able to yell at her... too happy she was okay." Harper raked her fingers through her hair. She smiled, thinking of Renee since her friend had recently cut it for her. The giant red mane no longer hung down over her butt, trimmed to its normal length midway down her back.

The girls—Harper, Renee, Darci, and Grace—had a little hair party last week. Darci and Renee did most of the snipping. Grace kept laughing the whole time, imagining her stuffy, uptight mother being horrified at 'some girl' cutting her daughter's precious hair instead of an expensive stylist.

Cheering finally made its way around the ring of searchers close enough to reach her ears. Marci shouted 'she's okay!'

Harper let out a 'woo!' and flopped over on her back, staring up at the perfect blue sky. Well, perhaps not quite perfect. A noticeable haze remained way up high, but other than that, it looked pretty... as perfect as it could get anymore.

A few minutes later, she'd had enough rest and scrambled upright. Based on the sun's position, she estimated the time at between two and three in the afternoon. Her patrol shift officially ended for the day, freeing her to go home. Better yet, Carrie effectively stepped in as mom. Harper didn't mind helping, but no longer faced the full burden of responsibility for doing all the things. Cliff cooked dinner and cleaned when he had the time, but the militia kept him going for insanely long shifts, often thirteen or more hours a day as he did most of the training in addition to active patrolling.

Having two parents helping her look after the kids and take care of the house took a tremendous weight off her shoulders.

Somehow, she'd found confidence. Perhaps even contentment.

Without the need to search, Harper hiked with purpose, moving at a fast pace back the way she'd come. When she caught sight of the bottle-filled blue bin again, curiosity got the better of her. *Something* about the property bothered her. She couldn't say what, but needed to know. Since Harper didn't believe in supernatural woo, sixth-senses, or ghostly whispering, it had to be something visual her subconscious mind registered as out of place.

After slinging her shotgun off its shoulder strap, she clicked off the safety and adopted a tactical stance. She once more scanned over the windows for signs of anyone watching her. The house appeared exactly the same as it did before.

Harper followed the driveway toward the front of the house, stopping at about the halfway point to take cover behind a tree. Nothing appeared to be out of place or unusual, and that bothered her. This house looked so ordinary it might have fooled her into feeling like a nutcase running around civilization with a loaded gun if not for the razor wire on the fence and the sandbags. Three outdoor trash bins stood sentinel beside the garage, positioned neatly where they probably belonged. Most every other house around here had them out on the street. It had evidently been trash morning in Evergreen when the bombs fell.

Someone had clearly been living here after that day, as the bins did not sit out at the end of the driveway by the road. Strange they left the recycle bin where they did, almost as if the person didn't realize war happened and carried on as if the trash truck showed up but the recycling crew ran late. She didn't think the house had been vacant. Unoccupied houses didn't usually have trash bins at all. Any garbage the militia cleaned up in the resettling effort got hauled out of town somewhere. She didn't know where; it happened before she arrived here.

"Hello?" called Harper. "I don't want any trouble. If there's someone in there and you don't want company, I will leave."

Sixty seconds of silence later, she swallowed the saliva building up in her mouth.

Someone's either waiting to ambush me or the place is empty.

It seemed too far-fetched to imagine anyone lived here, so close to town, without being noticed by now.

This creeps me out like those stories about strangers living in people's attics without being discovered for years.

Harper fast-walked to the next nearest tree and took cover. She scanned all the most likely points of attack if anyone inside, behind, or on top of the building intended to shoot her, finding no one.

"Evergreen militia," called Harper. "Just checking to see if there's anyone here or if they need help. If you don't want me here, just say something and I'll go away."

Again, no response came from the house.

Okay. It's gotta be empty. So weird.

She dashed out of cover and hurried to the fence. Though someone stapled razor wire along the top, they hadn't done anything about the gaps between the rails. Three wooden spars spanned between the posts, leaving plenty of room for a scrawny girl like her to slip between them. Even though the gate looked normal, she didn't trust it not to have a booby trap. No one would go to the trouble of installing razor wire and sandbags, then leave the gate defenseless. A feat of minor acrobatics would be easier and safer than dealing with any potential dangers attached to the gate.

She bent forward, stuck one leg into the space between the uppermost and middle spars, then slid through. A quick sprint cleared the front yard in three seconds; she rushed onto the porch, not quite crashing shoulder-first into the wall beside the door. Thirty seconds of silence passed. She knocked. Still no response.

Am I an idiot? No, better to treat an empty house like a live hornet's nest. Can't get killed being overly cautious.

Harper took her left hand off the shotgun and grabbed the knob, giving it a gentle turn. It simultaneously surprised her and didn't to find the door unlocked. She let go of the knob and put her hand back on the gun, staring at the inch gap between door and jamb. At least this house didn't give off a moldy stink.

No holes in the roof.

She used her foot to nudge the door open, then swept around the corner, Mossberg poised, sighting over her weapon at a living room, dining room, and hallway. The home seemed to be in relatively good condition, but messy as if a lazy teenage son had been left home alone for a month while his parents vacationed in Europe.

"Evergreen militia," called Harper. "Just doing a check. Is anyone home? I'm not here to cause trouble."

Her voice filled the room. Total silence hung in the aftermath. No one jumped in surprise, no one breathed. Even though she didn't hear any traces of life, it proved impossible to shake the *feeling* something or someone happened to be there watching her.

Ugh. I've been listening to Madison talk about that occult crap too much. It's in my head.

On high alert, Harper made her way from room to room, doing her best impression of a cop clearing a suspected crime scene. The first room she expected to be a bedroom contained a reloading bench, a shelf of plastic storage bins holding brass, slugs, and likely gunpowder, plus four refrigerator-sized gun safes.

"Wow... how is this stuff still here?" She blinked in awe. *Someone's gotta be defending it. If they catch me inside, they'll probably shoot before saying a word.*

After backing out of the doorway, she did a quick spin to make sure no one tried to sneak up on her. While she saw no one, the feeling of not being alone dogged her. The master bedroom at the end of the hall showed signs of use. Whoever slept in the bed didn't bother to make it. No way to tell how long it had been since anyone touched it. No one appeared to be hiding in the room, or the attached bathroom, so she backed out and went the other way down the hall toward the kitchen.

Harper discovered a violation of the Geneva convention in the fridge.

Barely a full second after the door opened, the greenish-black mass inside and accompanying smell of rot doubled her over. She staggered away, one arm across her face to protect her mouth and nose from the fetid air. Bile churned in the back of her throat. Whoever lived here stacked slabs of raw meat in the fridge without any sort of container or wrapping.

As soon as the phrase 'raw meat' crossed her brain, the contents of her stomach demanded freedom. Harper lurched over to the sink and threw up. Thankfully, only bile came up—no wasted food. It had been long enough since breakfast and she'd not had the chance to eat lunch while searching for Kelsey. Once the heaving passed, she instinctively tried to turn the water on. Nothing happened. This place sat too far out from the town proper to be part of any municipal water system. Either the well pump gave out, had no power, or the pipes froze and shattered during the brutal winter.

"Ugh." She spat, pulled her hair off her face, and spat again.

The strangeness of silver on the window distracted her from the miserable experience of vomiting. Duct tape covered the glass. A thick electrical cord came through a hole drilled in the lower part of the window, running along the counter to the space behind the fridge.

Did he connect it to a generator in the yard? How much gas did this dude have? She gagged. *Obviously not enough.*

She rubbed her stomach, frowning at the otherwise clean-looking kitchen. If someone really was here waiting for a good time to ambush her, they had the perfect opportunity while she'd been bent over the kitchen sink, helpless in the throes of puking. That no one did anything when she'd been so vulnerable almost convinced her she had the house to herself. Or at least if someone else happened to be here, they wanted no part of interacting with her.

Can't be anyone here. There is no food. Whatever is in that fridge is so far gone, it needs a proper burial.

As soon as her stomach settled, she recovered the Mossberg from the counter beside the sink and made her way to the other side of the house, checking a small office room and a big main bathroom before reaching a laundry room at the end of the hall. From there, a plain brown wooden door led to the two-car garage.

The near space contained hand-built wooden shelving, stocked with MREs, canned goods, military style ammunition cans, boxes of flares, some first-aid kits, and two bright yellow devices. It took her a few seconds of staring at them to recognize Geiger counters. Some of the provisions had been opened, suggesting at least one person survived on them for a while.

"Someone lived here during the worst of the chaos, keeping looters away... but what happened to them?" She whistled at the two dozen or so ammo cans, scarcely able to believe all of it remained here. "Did the militia not check houses out this far? Was the guy still living here when they came looking?"

The house sat alone in the trees, so isolated it basically had a private dirt road connecting it to Juniper Court, a trail the prior resident probably referred to as a 'driveway.'

"You know your house is in the middle of nowhere when you need to *drive* your trash to the curb."

Harper frowned. Since she hadn't been here when the militia established itself, she had no way to know the real extent of their efforts to run around scavenging all useful items from abandoned homes. In the two months following the attack, when she'd been hiding in the basement with her family, the original inhabitants of Evergreen mostly evacuated. She had trouble understanding why they did, considering the mountain topography largely shielded them from the blasts that flattened Denver and Colorado Springs. They'd even gotten amazingly lucky with fallout, which seemed to have either gone by overhead before coming down elsewhere, or taken a different route around Evergreen.

Perhaps the Army forcibly evacuated the people because they didn't know where the fallout would go, or didn't know if more nukes were on the way? Maybe people simply panicked and ran somewhere on their own? Anyone who used to live here ought to have come back by now. But, so far, only a handful of people did. Al Gonzalez, the man who returned to find his house assigned to a young couple, hadn't been here during the war, so he had no idea what happened to anyone else. Even Carrie, who'd been living in her house the entire time, didn't know. She'd kept to herself, and didn't remember seeing any Army people. Then again, she had been an emotional mess over losing her husband and basically spent months hiding in her house by herself, refusing to talk to anyone.

It's straight out of Unsolved Mysteries. "Whole town vanishes without a trace," whispered Harper.

She moved around the shelves, looking over the contents. When she spotted cans of ravioli, she resolved to take a few home. The kids would adore the reminder of more sane times.

Creak.

Harper froze, beyond grateful she hadn't yet reached for any ravioli. Both of her hands remained on the Mossberg. The noise came from beyond the shelves, in the second half of the two-car garage space. She listened for footsteps, but heard silence.

Again, something creaked.

She leaned closer to the shelf, peering over the ravioli cans at a black Cadillac Escalade in such pristine condition, she wondered if the guy who lived here bought it the same week the war happened. No one appeared to be in it, nor moving around it to sneak up on her.

Again, the creak.

That time, her eyes caught a tiny bit of motion. On the other side of the Escalade, a door appeared to lead out to the side of the house. It hadn't been closed all the way and wobbled in the breeze.

Oh... only wind.

A random absurd thought came out of nowhere. *Wind on an Empty Doorway* sounded like an album title from one of those weird alternative hipster type bands her friend Andrea loved. Harper wanted to laugh and cry at the same time, but did neither. Making sound in an unsecure environment could kill her.

Wherever you are, And, I hope you're alive and safe.

She kept watching the blue door wobble and squeak, not moving from her position behind several cases of canned ravioli. Jonathan occasionally made jokes about zombies, comparing their post-nuclear world to a video game he liked. Harper refused to play it after finding out they killed a little girl in the opening scene. It made no sense to her. In her opinion, the lazy writers had an armed soldier needlessly shoot a defenseless kid fleeing the zombie invasion purely to create artificial tragedy and set up the dad to be missing a daughter so he'd take care of the game's main character. Harper didn't much care for sad stories, especially when they were so unrealistic and forced. She figured if the game's writers phoned in the opening, they probably phoned in the rest of the game, too. Plus, too depressing.

Still, thanks to the constant feeling something else lurked nearby, she couldn't help but think about zombies as she stood there in the garage watching the door wobble. No one in her family had ever been superstitious, into the paranormal, religious, or given to any trust in stuff like horoscopes or fortune-telling. Her dad was an absolute pragmatist. He'd probably know why she felt like someone stood next to her. Maybe he'd blame it on a weird geo-acoustic phenomenon, vibrations or sound in the air beyond human hearing. Assuming, of course, he sensed it too and didn't tell Harper it existed all in her mind.

Roy Ellis, former cop, had spent many hours training the Evergreen Militia on various subjects, including how to study an environment for clues something was off. This whole house bothered her. Such a stash of food and ammunition shouldn't still be sitting there. How could the militia have missed it? If a resident lived here after the nuclear strike, especially when the newly formed militia ran around grabbing useful stuff from all the empty houses, why hadn't anyone bothered to mention a heavily armed survivalist in a home-turned-fortress?

Maybe they didn't think the guy was a threat and left him to his own devices.

Five minutes of watching a door flap about in the breeze seemed sufficient to trust a person wasn't about to come charging in at her. Harper crept out from behind the shelf and went around the back end of the Escalade. The smell of residual gasoline clung to the walls near the SUV, though any fuel would undoubtedly be rotted by now.

I've got more chance of sprouting angel wings than this truck has of starting.

A mild, but constant breeze blew past the doorway. Dirt on the floor as well as muddy spatter on the side of the Escalade facing it made her think the door had been unsecured for a while. The lack of mold invading the house baffled her.

She gently kicked it open and peered out at the woods beside the house. Going left would take her to the backyard. Going right, to the front. More sandbags formed a curved waist-high barrier by the door, offering a little bit of cover against attack coming from anywhere but the backyard.

So strange. I don't even hear birds. Do they sense ghosts, too?

Harper rolled her eyes at herself. She didn't believe in ghosts, but for the time being, had no better way to describe the bizarre mood clinging to the house. If anyone alive happened to be inside, they'd have to be in the attic or crawlspace... and had no desire to make contact with her at all. In the interest of being thorough, she exited the garage and went left to check the yard behind the building.

As soon as she rounded the corner at the end of the house, she stopped short at another confusing sight: an older-looking red Dodge pickup truck parked in the middle of the backyard. A blue tarp covered something big enough to take up the entire bed and stick a few feet out past the tailgate. The end closer to the cab came up to about even with the truck's roof. It had to be seriously heavy as it made the truck sit low on its suspension, far heavier than seemed reasonable for its size. Tire ruts traced the path the truck had taken here around the house, deep enough they remained visible after over a year.

She figured it had to be that long ago since vehicles would've stopped working around then. Even the ones in Evergreen lucky enough to escape EMP thanks to the mountains would've run out of usable gas within six months of society grinding to a halt.

Curiosity tempted her toward the tarp. Based on size and apparent weight, the object under the blue plastic covering couldn't have been easy to move. What about such a ponderous thing could've tempted a person to throw it on a truck and bring it home?

She made it three steps closer before a fluttering motion to her left made her freeze. On the other side of the house's elevated deck, a scrap of flannel shirt fabric flapped about in the wind beside a tree stump. Dingy jean legs and work boots lay beside a collection of small logs. Wedges of split wood stood in a relatively neat stack on the other side of the stump. Harper lowered the shotgun and approached.

The corpse of a man clutched a black and yellow axe with a rubberized grip and polymer handle in both hands. He'd decomposed somewhat, but not so much she couldn't tell he'd been white, and probably older than sixty. Wispy scraps of sparse beard clung to his face, making him look like a three-year-old got a hold of clippers and pranked grandpa in his sleep... and totally shaved his head. He didn't look to have been dead for *too* long, and surprisingly didn't give off too much smell.

"Poor guy... must have had a heart attack while chopping wood."

An AR15 leaned against a big toolbox beside the woodpile, exactly where it would be if the man set it down before he got started splitting logs. The weapon had advanced well into the process of rusting away to uselessness, appearing as though it sat there for a long time. She raised an eyebrow at the apparent contradiction. The corpse looked much more recent, but it also didn't make sense for him to have left a rifle rusting in the yard, or for the weapon to be positioned like he'd put it down before getting to work and having a heart attack. Also, the quantity of untouched supplies remaining in the house seemed rather high if someone had been living here up until a month or two ago.

She scrunched her nose, debating if she should go get a shovel and try to bury him or leave him undisturbed. He didn't smell much, though it would be respectful to give him a proper burial... if only so no children found the bones at some point. Sooner or later, the kids in town would get brave enough to wander out this far.

Harper glanced at the house, thinking of the garage full of food, ammo, and supplies.

No way am I carrying all that myself. It would fill that Escalade four times, and that thing's never going to run again.

Only one option made sense: return to town, tell Walter what she found, and come back out here with a team and the one former United States Postal Service truck Rafael Espinoza—their only mechanic—managed to resurrect thanks to his hand-built ethanol engine.

She decided to leave the dead man as he lay for now. Hopefully, some of the guys would take on the task of burying him. Harper didn't fancy the idea of laboring with a shovel if she could avoid it. She crossed the yard toward the pickup, intent on satisfying her curiosity about what the tarp concealed.

Feeling pretty confident no one hid in the house waiting to ambush her, she approached the Dodge casually, grabbed the tarp, and lifted it, peering under at a big dull grey cone. The front end appeared crumpled and crushed as if it had collided with soft ground at high velocity. White markings on the side resembled Russian letters.

Harper stared in bafflement for a few seconds, which rapidly turned to abject terror as her brain finally processed what her eyes tried to tell it. She blinked once, then flicked her hand open, so the tarp fell back over the warhead.

"This is a freakin' nuke," she whispered. "Uhh, I think I figured out why everyone abandoned Evergreen."

3

WHISKEY TANGO FOXTROT

MAY 10TH

Harper stood there, too terrified to move.

All the moisture retreated from her mouth. She might've peed a little, but couldn't tell. Fear gripped her as though the warhead would explode if she made the tiniest sound or motion. It had obviously been there for a while without going off. Noise probably wouldn't bother it.

After a moment, she snapped out of the paralytic fear and stared down at herself. Her legs shook, as did her hands, but at least her jeans remained dry. If she did have a small accident, it had only been a few drops.

"Wow… I thought that whole 'peeing yourself scared' thing was a movie trope." She exhaled hard. "Holy shit… this is a nuke."

She dry swallowed twice, then remembered the yellow boxes in the garage.

Still too scared to run, she gingerly tiptoed away from the pickup truck and made her way back into the garage. Part of her wanted to take off sprinting for home and tackle-hug Cliff like a nine-year-old who really needed Daddy right now. She couldn't do that, nor did she *truly* need it. Only a momentary passing bit of panic. Hell, Cliff would probably want his daddy too if he saw this thing.

A girl on a mission, Harper bee-lined to the shelf, grabbed one of the Geiger counters, and went outside. She stopped ten paces from the pickup truck and fiddled with the device until she found the power button.

The counter's needle went crazy and the device gave off a high-pitched squealing noise.

"Eep!"

Harper turned it off. Once again, her hands trembled. She stared at the now-silent device, then shifted her gaze left to the dead man on the ground. Sparse beard... no hair... falling out in clumps. "Umm... I don't think he had a heart attack."

She backed up another twenty steps, standing by the garage door and turned the counter on again. The needle spiked up to max, fluttered back somewhat, and continued flapping like a pinball game paddle. Noises coming out of the counter oscillated between squeals and rapid clicking. She took a few steps closer to the truck, and the clicking stopped—now it only squealed.

"Shit..."

Harper ran away from the yard, sprinting past the front of the house and continuing at full speed until the noises coming from the Geiger counter sounded like someone chewing on cellophane. She had no idea how to read one, but based on the change in sound and needle activity, assumed she'd gone far enough away from the warhead to get out of range of *deadly* radiation.

She kept running until the counter gave off only a steady, almost rhythmic clicking. At that point, she felt safe enough to stop and catch her breath.

"Holy shit... holy shit... holy shit," she rasped. "No wonder the house is still full of supplies."

Harper wiped her face on the back of her arm.

"How the hell did they miss that?" She shook her head, refusing to believe anyone in the militia might have known about an unexploded nuclear warhead and not bothered to tell anyone about it. "What kind of idiot finds one of those and brings it home?"

She switched the Geiger counter off to save battery power, then debated stripping where she stood in case radioactive material got on her clothes. Instead, she turned the counter back on and waved it over herself. The needle wobbled a bit unsettlingly, but nowhere near as bad as it freaked out in the yard. Even the counter itself might be contaminated since it had been sitting in the garage. Maybe the basement wall shielded it. She didn't know enough about how to use one of these devices to figure out if it could scan itself. At this distance from the house, the slow clicking didn't scare her *too* much. Hopefully, one of the doctors, or someone in town, knew how to work the thing and could tell her if she needed to spend the next two hours washing herself over and over.

"Crap. Crap. Crap." She gazed at the sky. "Please don't blow up."

Three deep breaths later, she took off running for town.

4

HOT TOPIC

MAY 10TH – EARLY EVENING

Curled in a ball, Harper sat in a chair staring at Mayor Ned, Walter, Anne-Marie, Cliff, Tegan, Ken Zhang, and Roy Ellis. The reality of what she'd discovered set in after she'd finished explaining the situation to Walter. If anyone noticed how much she looked like a terrified little girl who just crawled out of a blast zone, no one commented on it. At least, she felt like a child in that moment, helpless to do anything about a huge, deadly problem.

She almost felt ashamed of herself, but coming within inches of a device capable of instantly killing everyone in a several-mile radius went way past screaming at a spider or having a nightmare. From the looks of the faces of those gathered in the small conference room with her, the others shared her fear. Maybe she didn't really look as terrified as she felt.

Mayor Ned, Walter, and Anne-Marie had no idea an unexploded nuclear warhead sat in a truck so close to where they felt safe. Cliff brought up how Carrie had been here the whole time, though admitted she'd been rather out of sorts for the first month or so. It had already come up in conversation between them she recalled hearing someone banging on the door. She'd assumed it the Army coming to evacuate survivors. At the time, she'd been so depressed at her husband's almost guaranteed death on the East Coast, she didn't care what happened to her.

Harper suggested the original citizens who lived here probably knew about it and fled the area. The banging Carrie ignored might have been the locals, not the Army. To her, it made more sense the people who already lived here discovered the moron with his nuke and evacuated rather than the Army evacuating people from an area that escaped the worst of the strike. Evergreen had been the place everyone outside wanted to go *to*, not run away from.

For obvious reasons, Walter initially took her claim of finding the warhead with a few fairly large grains of salt. However, after she led Cliff and Roy back there to show it to them, everyone accepted the town of Evergreen had a serious problem.

Cliff confirmed the device as a Russian MIRV. It didn't seem too likely the man who collected it would've gone all the way to Denver to do so. The best guess anyone came up with was that this particular MIRV experienced a guidance malfunction, veered off course into the mountains and—miraculously—failed to detonate. She wondered if the 'tank' she'd found smashed into the other house might have been part of the missile that carried the MIRV. Perhaps the malfunction kept the warhead in its housing until relatively near the ground.

Harper hugged her legs to her chest, peering over her knees at the others talking about nuclear weapons.

"Nah, it's not *too* crazy odds," said Cliff. "Nuclear weapons, even the Russian ones, have fail-safes upon fail-safes. No one wants to blow themselves up. If you knew how many nukes *our* government lost, you'd pass out."

"Lost?" asked Ned.

"Yeah. Aircraft crashes, or sometimes even accidental deployment of live weapons." Cliff scratched his beard. "Few times, we had live bombs dropped. First one comes to mind is Goldsboro. B-52 crashed in North Carolina with two live bombs on board. They didn't go nuclear. Mars Bluff, late Fifties. Something went wrong in the bomb bay, one of the guys messed up, pulled the wrong pin and the bomb dropped straight through the closed doors. Hit a kid's playhouse."

Everyone gasped.

"Oh, shit," whispered Harper.

"It blew up, but only the conventional explosives went off." Cliff cringed. "Essentially, a dirty bomb. Scattered nuclear material around, but no fission. Amazingly, no one was hurt."

Anne-Marie blinked at him. "What does this have to do with our current situation?"

"Just saying, these devices are overengineered to be safe..." Cliff held his hands up at her as if making parenthesis. "They are many times more likely *not* to go critical than to explode. Odds are, if it was going to go off, it would've done so already."

"What kind of odds are you talking about?" Ned raised an eyebrow.

Cliff hooked his thumbs in his pants pockets. "Not really sure. I ain't a nuclear engineer. Can't give you specific numbers."

"I still want to know why that idiot brought the goddamned thing to his house." Roy shook his head. "Why? He had to know what it was."

"Maybe he wanted to sell it on E-bay," muttered Ken, to nervous laughter.

Harper almost chuckled, feeling a bit disconnected from reality. "I wanna know how he got it into the truck."

Roy gestured at her. "That, too."

"What are our options?" asked Anne-Marie. "Let's put everything down and then figure out which one sounds best."

"Evacuate." Ken folded his arms.

Everyone stared at him with varying levels of disbelief.

"After all the work we put into the farm?" Ned scowled. "We clawed our way up from a handful of survivors to damn near an established town. You want to walk away from that?"

"Hey." Ken raised his hands in surrender. "Not saying it's a good idea or an idea I like, but it *is* an option."

Beats ending up vaporized. Harper squirmed. She didn't fancy the idea of having to leave Evergreen, either. Though, perhaps they could take over one of the unused ranches to the south. "How far would we need to go?"

Cliff pursed his lips, his expression said 'how should I know?' After a moment, he exhaled. "Well... if I had to guess, that thing's probably a 750-kiloton warhead. We're looking at a complete incineration zone of about a kilometer. Maximum destructive blast wave would go about double that, so everything within about two kilos of the device would be unrecognizable. Beyond that, we can expect some degree of damage out to roughly ten kilometers. Deadly levels of radiation would spread out to anywhere between eight and twelve kilometers. The area would be fatal for weeks, and dangerous for years."

Ned twisted around to look at the map on the wall. "So, basically, we'd have to go to Idaho Springs or Aspen Park to be safe."

"Something like that." Cliff folded his arms. "But, I still think it's unlikely we'll see a detonation. If it hasn't gone off by now..."

"Assuming no one monkeys with it." Roy shifted his weight from leg to leg.

"The greater danger," said Tegan, "is the radiation. Cliff, didn't you say the shielding is cracked?"

"Yeah." He looked down, kicked a boot at the carpet, then sighed. "That sucker hit the ground pretty hard. Probably struck a nice cushiony bit of ground as it didn't bust apart completely."

"It didn't really look too damaged." Roy twisted a hand in the air like he screwed in a light bulb. "Nose end is kinda crumpled. Doesn't really look like it slapped into the ground at rocket speed."

"I found a big cylinder smashed through the roof of another house." Harper nibbled on her lip. "Maybe it was a chem tank blown here all the way from Denver, or maybe it's part of the missile. Could the MIRV have failed to launch and fallen with the rest of the thing, only popping loose near the ground?"

"With Russian shit, any sort of catastrophic failure mode is a real possibility." Cliff wagged his eyebrows.

Walter sighed. "Wouldn't it still have smashed when it hit the ground? How fast are those things moving?"

Cliff shrugged in a 'don't look at me, I am not a nuclear scientist' sort of way. "Guidance malfunction. Thing might've been tumbling or it had a drag chute. No way to know. Point is, it's a hazard."

"How dangerous?" Anne-Marie rested her elbows on the table and grabbed her face in both hands.

"This is napkin math." Cliff pulled a little notepad out of his pocket and flipped it open. "So, account for some errors in either direction. Radiation dose falls off fairly rapidly over distance from the source. Closer a person is to the thing, worse it gets. Right on top of the warhead, it threw off way more rads than this counter could keep up with. Estimating it's somewhere between 200 to 400 millisieverts per hour if you're close enough to touch the warhead. Ten steps back, it might be two thirds of that. Twenty paces away, half. I'd say no one should spend more than two or three minutes within ten feet of the thing." He turned to point at Harper. "I don't want you anywhere near it again."

Under any other circumstance, she'd have felt patronized being talked to like a little kid. However, she wanted no part of messing with a nuke. "Okay."

"Anyone under thirty should try not to go near it. Anyone under eighteen should be kept away from it entirely." Cliff tapped his foot. "I don't mean to sound overprotective, but I'm being overprotective."

"Damage from radiation can be more severe on children who are still growing." Tegan gave a somber sigh. "And they have smaller body mass, which results in a larger effective dose."

"Easy fix. We ask a bunch of fat old people to carry it out of town." Ken grinned.

His nonserious tone caused another ripple of nervous laughter.

Harper fidgeted at her sneaker laces. "It's fine. I don't want to be near it either. I mean... I'll help if I'm needed, but I'd rather stay away from it. I haven't been that terrified since the morning I thought Cliff's underpants were going to fall off him in the kitchen."

"Hey..." Cliff put on a face of mock insult.

The others all smiled at her.

Ken patted her on the arm. "I have to say I'm impressed how calm you're managing to stay, given the discovery you made."

Only because I still don't fully believe it. She gave him a 'yeah I guess' sort of stare. "Flipping out won't help. Not sure I even believe this isn't a dream. Maybe I never woke up and that giant hunk of concrete killed me. This whole thing is all some crazy post-death head trip my ghost is on."

"I haven't had anywhere near enough marijuana to think about that," said Walter.

Anne-Marie blinked at him. "I wasn't aware you indulged."

"I don't." Walter winked.

"What are our other choices?" Anne-Marie sighed at Walter, then looked around at everyone else. "I don't like the idea of leaving, either."

"Taking it apart is an option." Roy grimaced. "A bad option, but an option. You got a conventional charge in there to ram the nuclear parts together and set off the big one. If we rip the plastic explosive— or whatever's in there—out, then we just have two nuggets of plutonium to worry about and not a mushroom cloud."

"Assuming no one cuts the wrong wire." Anne-Marie let her arms fall to the table and sighed.

Cliff chuckled. "It's not like a *Mission Impossible* movie."

"Can you disassemble the device?" Walter peered over his glasses at Cliff.

"Never touched one before." Cliff waved randomly. "Give me a couple days to Google up some schematics and I'll get back to you."

Harper put a hand over her mouth to stop herself from laughing. His deadpan sarcasm hit her like a fart at a funeral. Nothing about the situation came anywhere near being funny, but the inappropriateness of his remark threatened to set off a storm of giggling.

"I've had some EOD training." Roy broke the awkward silence. "But we never looked at anything this complicated or destructive. Depending on what the mechanism is that triggers the conventional explosives, I could probably do enough damage to it so it couldn't go off big."

Cliff raised a hand at him. "Hold on, Roy. You saw the Geiger, right? By the time you got that thing taken down, you'd have sucked up enough rads to have just enough time left to walk to your grave site."

Everyone got quiet.

"He's exaggerating." Roy set his fists on his hips. "It's not *that* hot. I wouldn't drop dead right after disarming it. Though, I'd probably get three different kinds of cancer."

After letting the comment percolate for a moment, Cliff continued. "The containment housing inside the warhead is cracked... somewhere."

"You saw the break?" asked Ned.

"No. I'm making an educated assumption. If it hadn't cracked, we wouldn't be reading such high levels of radiation." Cliff almost gave the mayor a 'that was a seriously stupid question' glare, but held himself back. "Opening the outer casing will only make the radiation leak worse. Disarming this thing would require a team of like thirty technicians working in two-to-five-minute shifts only once and then never going near it again."

"It sounds like you're saying that disarming it is off the table." Ned managed a weak smile.

"That's one way to put it, yeah." Cliff shifted his jaw side to side.

"Bury it." Harper uncurled, letting her feet slip off the chair to the floor. "We should bury it."

"That's a thought." Walter perked up, for the first time in the past hour or so he *didn't* look hopeless.

"How the heck are we going to dig a hole deep enough to be safe?" Ned bit his lower lip. "We'd need to ask pretty much everyone to drop all the work on the farm and start creating a tomb..."

"And there'd be no keeping it quiet at that point." Anne-Marie cringed. "People could panic. Some would flee Evergreen. There might even be violence."

Harper slouched, feeling stupid. She stared away from the ensuing debate, not wanting to dig herself into a metaphorical pit any deeper. Walter did like the idea of burying the device. Earth offered great radiation shielding. Cliff remarked about underground nuclear tests. Devices set off significantly far underground released very little detectable radiation or destruction in the environment. Of course, that generally required depths far in excess of what could feasibly be attained using shovels. Typically, the government dug deep tunnels for it.

"Mines!" blurted Harper. "What about mines? We don't have to dig a hole if we can use one that's already there. Colorado's got a bunch of mines… somewhere."

"You're right." Walter rushed over to the wall map. "Don't think they're gonna be on this map, but I know of a few south of here. One of 'em ought to have a deep tunnel."

Anne-Marie drummed her fingers on the table. "This sounds reasonable except for one logistical problem. How are we going to move it?"

"It's already on a truck." Harper fidgeted in her chair. "The hard part's done. No idea how the guy got it in there, but it's on wheels now."

"That truck, lest anyone forget, is probably radioactive." Cliff frowned. "That close to the device for at least a year, maybe two, it's going to be irradiated."

Harper rubbed a hand down her jeans. She'd gotten lucky. A little peek under the tarp hadn't disturbed much of any dirt or dust. It had been relatively damp out there thanks to recent light rain. She hadn't picked up any significant amounts of radioactivity on her clothes. Cliff, thankfully, knew how to work the Geiger counter. Being mostly plastic except for the detector wand, it hadn't retained much radioactivity itself. The food and ammo in the basement may or may not be salvageable, though the general opinion in the room leaned toward not wanting to taking the risk—especially with the food.

"And the possibility of that Dodge starting is less than zero," added Roy.

"We don't need it to run." Mayor Ned paced around. "Harper is right. It's on wheels. A trailer would be better, but we don't have the equipment to move it."

"It's not *that* big. Eight or ten guys could lug it." Cliff fake smiled. "But there's no reason to hug the damn thing if we don't absolutely have to. Just flip the truck into neutral and tow it. Send the whole package, truck and bomb, straight into a mine tunnel."

Another debate consumed the town's senior leadership: how to go about towing a pickup truck and a nuclear bomb. No one thought Rafael's USPS truck had the power to pull it. A team of horses might work, but they'd either have to be hooked up on an extremely long chain to keep them safe from radiation or… end up being killed by it. Horses would not move fast, especially pulling a weight like that.

"The semi," said Harper, interrupting an argument a few minutes later. "Rafael's been trying to get one of the semi-trucks to run on biodiesel. The Post Office truck basically has a lawnmower engine he hand-built to run biodiesel. The semi was already diesel. He said it wouldn't take too much to convert it to tolerate the different fuel."

"He's been working on that for a year." Walter chuckled. "Even named it 'big brother'. I suppose it couldn't hurt to ask him about it. If he did get that thing running, a tractor cab would definitely have the power to haul that."

Anne-Marie stood. "Well, sounds like we have at least a starting point. I understand the danger we're in. But, please bear in mind. This thing has been where it is for as long as we've been here. It hasn't gone off yet, and it hasn't killed anyone."

Harper raised her hand.

"Yes?" Anne-Marie smiled at her.

"Sorry to be *that* girl, but it did technically kill at least one person… the man who lived at that house."

"Oh, yes… Of course." Anne-Marie bowed her head. "I meant it hasn't resulted in any injuries among our people. That poor man likely died before we settled here or we would have heard about him."

"I dunno. It's so weird." Harper squirmed. "He didn't look like he died long ago, but his rifle was all rusty."

"Corpses decay more slowly in radioactive environments." Tegan rubbed her hands up and down her arms as if cold and trying to warm herself up. "The bacteria responsible for decay die under sufficient gamma radiation. There's nothing left to advance the process of decomposition, so some bodies may achieve an almost mummy-like state of preservation."

"He was definitely decaying." She swallowed bile. "But, looked like he'd only died a few weeks ago."

Roy glanced at Tegan, then made a few faces as if thinking. "We can likely assume the radiation leaking from the warhead had something to do with slowing the visible decay. My guess is the idiot died sometime before Ned and Anne-Marie got here and started the settlement, probably after the original residents hauled ass."

"Damn fool brought it on himself," muttered Cliff. "What kind of idiot takes a damn live nuke for a souvenir?"

Harper felt a bit sick to her stomach, not at the vindictiveness, but at the thought all the food in the garage might be contaminated. Tegan's comment about radiation slowing or stopping decay made her remember something she'd seen on TV a while ago about some place that used radiation to preserve food but didn't know for sure how it worked or how it compared to being near a broken nuclear warhead. Better to err on the side of caution, especially since they had the farm.

"My point," said Anne-Marie, "is that I feel it is in the best interest of everyone here if we keep the existence of this device on a need-to-know basis. The last thing any of us want is someone deciding to play hero and trying to do something about it themselves and ending up dead, setting it off, or making things worse for everyone."

Everyone nodded in unison.

"How likely is this thing to go off?" Ken made a hammer-tapping gesture. "If something taps it on the nose, are we going to wonder why everything is suddenly bright orange?"

"Why don't we avoid tapping it on the nose?" Ned smiled. "It's sat out there for this long without anyone finding it. We have no reason to worry someone is going to stumble across it."

"No one from town, anyway." Cliff picked at his fingernails. "Saying no one found it before doesn't mean some jackass isn't gonna wander by tomorrow."

Harper smiled at him. "Yeah. Maybe we should put up danger signs or something."

"I think calm should be the order of the day." Walter knocked on the table. "We've been here five months shy of two years and it hasn't caused trouble yet. Now that we know about it, we can do something about it... but we need to be methodical and look at every angle. Roy, can you please check with Rafael about the truck? Anne-Marie and I will start looking through whatever records we can find regarding mines in the area close enough to reach but far enough away that we won't be in danger if the worst happens. Cliff, Ken, you two see what info you can get from those who lived in the area before the war, see if they know about any deep mines."

The others voiced varying levels of agreement.

"Anyone have questions?" asked Anne-Marie.

"Lots of them, but nothing anyone in here can answer." Cliff nudged Ned. "Hurry up and recruit a nuclear physicist already."

Ned gave a wheezy chuckle.

"All right then. Thank you all for gathering on short notice." Anne-Marie pantomimed smacking a gavel. "Please let us know if anything new develops. Until then, I'll call this session adjourned."

Hasn't caused any trouble... except to the idiot who brought it home. Harper stood and exhaled. *There's a nuke close enough to delete us. Yeah, I'm not sleeping tonight... or this week.*

5

KEEPING SECRETS

MONDAY, MAY 11TH

S tress proved the victor over fear.

Harper did eventually fall asleep. Despite Cliff's assurance that her clothing hadn't been dangerously contaminated, she still tossed all of it in a bucket as soon as she got home, then took a bath, too impatient to let the water warm up all the way. Scrubbing might not have been physically necessary given her fairly limited exposure, but it made her feel better.

Monday the eleventh came with another significant event to distract her from spending every waking moment thinking about the nuke: Jonathan's birthday. He grumbled a little in the morning about having to go to school, only because it cut into party time. When Madison pointed out the teacher would probably do some fun stuff for his birthday—like she did for every kid's birthday—he stopped complaining.

Trying to keep herself outwardly composed, Harper went through the motions of her usual patrol, relieved to be using a bicycle again instead of riding Two Bales. A haunting thought chased her around the entire time she spent on patrol: it wouldn't matter if she had a bike, a horse, or only her shoes. If that thing went off, she'd never get away from it.

Probably won't even have time to yell 'oh shit.'

A few hours of feeling trapped led to a state of awkward calm. She couldn't do anything about the warhead, lacking the tools or experience to dismantle it. Alone, she had no way to move it. At no point in her life up until that moment did she take the idea of ghosts or an afterlife seriously. She still didn't, but the half-serious thought that if the device *did* explode, she'd be reunited with her parents afforded her a little bit of solid emotional ground to stand on and hold everything together.

So what if it amounted to still expecting Santa Claus would bring her gifts? She intentionally tried to lie to herself so she could function. It wouldn't help anyone if she surrendered to panic. The level of calm detachment Anne-Marie held in regard to the situation left her awestruck. Evergreen's 'town manager' seemed almost ambivalent to the idea they could all be wiped out in an instant at any moment. The woman either had metaphorical balls of steel, didn't care if she died, or truly believed the warhead would not go off.

Harper had two choices within her power. One: grab her family and run for the hills. Two: cross her fingers and hope Cliff was right about the failsafe stuff. It made sense. The people who made and worked with the bombs in the military certainly did not want them going off randomly in storage. Much better to have frequent failures in the field due to excessively redundant failsafes than blow themselves up. Could be that someone in Russia forgot to pull out a pin somewhere, or put in a module required to arm the device. The thing might have been launched in an unarmed state, so it always had zero chance of detonating. She figured it would be fairly likely the people responsible for launching the weapons had probably been freaking the hell out while doing it, not believing it had really come to that. Heck knows, maybe the people doing the shooting intentionally left some of the nukes inert as an act of protest.

Or perhaps a fully armed MIRV simply malfunctioned.

Hell, the stupid warhead tolerated that jackass loading it into a truck and moving it. If that didn't set it off, sitting still probably won't. Wonder if the idiot covered it with a tarp to keep rain off it or to hide it.

Her thoughts turned to stuff Cliff told them about radiation. Specifically, he'd been warning the children—not so much Harper— that during their exploration of abandoned places, they shouldn't mess around with any old medical equipment. If they saw someone doing so, they should run away, especially if anything glowed. He shared some stories of people, mostly in other countries, who got their hands on old X-ray machines or some other kind of radiation therapy device with a quantity of radioactive cesium inside. Some guy and his friends who wanted to sell the scrap busted it open, exposing the cesium. His little daughter found the glowing powder, thought it looked pretty, and smeared it all over herself. And... well... everyone more or less got sick and died.

Harper figured the idiot she'd found dead by the wood pile probably tried to salvage the MIRV or, given the room full of reloading equipment and all those provisions, he'd been a prepper-slash-military enthusiast. He might not have intended to take the thing apart at all, merely keep it as a souvenir.

A debate about stupidity went back and forth in her mind. On one hand, the stupidity of a man who would bring an unexploded fired nuke home. On the other, the stupidity of a society that could brainwash and train its young military people to unthinkingly obey orders and push a button that had a seriously high chance of ending all life on Earth. Even if the scientists had been slightly off in their prediction or perhaps the nuclear attack hadn't been as bad as might have been, the soldiers in every country pushing those buttons wouldn't know what would happen. They had to know what they were about to do would not just kill 'the enemy,' but kill everyone they loved, too. They did not simply conduct an attack on a military installation. They fired a weapon that would incinerate the very land, killing millions of civilians indiscriminately.

How much hatred does it take for a person to be willing to burn every man, woman, and child in some other country, knowing that by doing so your own country will burn, too? She bowed her head, ashamed of her own species. It made zero sense to her how one crazy person in power could give an order that thousands of others would robotically follow without question, despite the cost.

A cloud of gloom and anger followed her for the rest of the morning.

By the time she finished her appointed shift, picked the kids up at school, and walked them home, she felt reasonably confident she acted normal. Of course, this meant she didn't. As soon as Harper went to the bedroom to store the shotgun and kick her shoes off, Madison slipped in behind her and nudged the door shut.

She double checked the safety, then set the Mossberg on its butt, tucked slightly behind the headboard of the bed. In a civilized world, she'd end up in jail for leaving a loaded shotgun out like that in a house with children. Now, a few seconds' delay in getting to it could mean someone died. True, it had been a while since any bad guys stirred trouble in town, but the minute they let their guard down, something would happen. Also, she didn't exactly have a gun safe or a trigger lock. Then again, almost every child in Evergreen had witnessed people being shot for real. She, Cliff, and Carrie reminded the kids at least three times a week not to touch firearms. None of them seemed overly curious about guns, but it didn't ease her worries.

Maybe she should make a high shelf where the kids couldn't reach it.

"Harp?" asked Madison.

"What's up, Termite?" Harper stepped on the heel of her left sneaker and pulled her foot out. She paused. *Damn. Maybe I should be gentler on these. Need to make them last forever. Renee's team hasn't figured out how to make shoes yet. When they do, it's gonna be like moccasins or some crap.*

"Something is bothering you." Madison approached and slipped her arms around in a hug. "What is it?"

Ugh. She knows me too well. "I'm not allowed to talk about it."

"Allowed? You're not a kid anymore." Madison squeezed her.

"Militia stuff. Like how CIA agents can't tell people stuff." Harper lifted her right foot, grabbed the sneaker in both hands, and eased it off. "But, I can't keep important stuff from you."

"Ack. This sounds bad." Madison stepped back, biting her lip. "You're not sick, are you?"

"No." Harper's stomach gurgled at the memory of the Geiger counter screaming. *At least, I don't think so. Was only there a few minutes. Not enough to get cancer, right?*

"Why are you acting all weird, then?" Madison also kicked off her shoes, then grabbed a comb from the small dresser. Her hair remained straight as ever, raven black, and now so long she often sat on it.

"I'm willing to tell you because I trust you and want to keep you safe. It's really scary though, so you might not want to know."

Madison stopped combing her hair, staring at her via the mirror above the dresser. "I can handle scary."

Where did this Madison come from? She's only eleven, but she sounds like she's almost grown up. "Yeah, I bet you can. At least until it gives you nightmares."

Madison stuck out her tongue.

Harper smiled. "If I tell you, you can't tell anyone else. I'm serious about that. It's super important. I shouldn't even tell you, but..."

They looked at each other in silence, an unspoken *you're the only family I have left* hanging between them. Of course, they both considered Cliff, Carrie, Jonathan, and Lorelei to be family, but it didn't quite feel the same as her actual blood family. The others hadn't been with them their entire lives.

Madison twisted away from the mirror to look at her directly. "I never told Mom and Dad about how you and your friends drank rum and watched a tittie movie."

A combination choke-laugh burped out of Harper's throat. "Uhh, that wasn't a 'tittie movie'. Just an R-rated one."

"I saw boobs on the screen. That's a tittie movie." Madison gestured at her. "You were thirteen. Would'a got in big trouble if they caught you."

"How the heck do you remember that?" Harper gawked at her. "You would've been what, six then?"

Madison flashed a knowing smile while tapping a finger to her temple. "A girl's brain is amazing at storing blackmail fuel." Her kid sister examined her fingernails. "Not that I would do something like that to you. Just saying why I remember it. You know I had ample opportunities to use it and never did."

"We didn't really drink much rum." Harper glanced off to the side. "I remember it tasting really nasty and making me feel woozy."

"Renee threw up," said Madison.

"Were you spying on us?" Harper fake glared.

"No. I was in bed, just awake. Heard her." Madison set the comb down. "I'm saying, I can keep secrets. Even juicy ones. Especially if telling it will get you in trouble."

Harper sat on the edge of the bed and patted the mattress next to her.

"Oh, a 'you better sit down first' type secret." Madison padded over and sat beside her. "This really is bad, isn't it?"

"Yeah." Harper let out a slow breath. It had been Anne-Marie to ask everyone to keep it quiet. It hadn't come from Walter, the leader of the militia and technically her 'boss' insofar as anyone in the world still had bosses. Semantic to draw a line between her asking and Walter ordering, but it might be enough of a technicality to avoid issues. She also trusted her sister. If the kid hadn't used catching her and her friends trying alcohol at thirteen against her by now, the girl could keep her mouth shut when it mattered. "You know about Kelsey wandering off, right?"

Madison rolled her eyes. "Everyone does."

"While I was out helping look for her, I found this house…" Harper lowered her voice to a bit over a whisper and explained what she'd found.

Her kid sister's eyes widened so much she almost looked like a cartoon. "Oh fuck. Seriously?"

"I just told you we're sitting within the kill zone of a nuclear weapon," whispered Harper. "I'm not going to make a big deal about the language."

"Oops," deadpanned Madison. "But crap… what are they going

to do?"

"They're working on how to move it safely."

Madison fidgeted. "Where is this house?"

Harper narrowed her eyes.

"Seriously, I just want to know where *not* to go." Madison shook her head rapidly. "I'm not gonna go anywhere near it."

She had no doubt Madison felt the same way about the warhead she did: pure terror. "It's a little over a mile east of the old golf course in the hills."

"Oh, whew. No one goes out there." Madison pretended to wipe sweat off her forehead. "Not gonna find it on accident."

Harper pulled her sister into a hug. Having her 'in the know' about the big problem helped her deal, almost like a second person bearing half the weight. Maybe she shouldn't have dropped something like that on her, but if she said nothing, Madison's imagination would've run amok and the kid would have scared herself silly as well as been worried about what had so affected Harper. She only had one genetic relative left in the world. If she couldn't be honest with her, she couldn't be honest with anyone.

"You okay?" asked Madison.

"As okay as it's possible to be."

"Why don't they want to tell anyone?"

"People have a tendency to become panicky and stupid in large groups. They're afraid someone might get hurt. Riots, some idiot going crazy, some other idiot trying to take the thing apart without knowing what they're doing... that sort of thing."

"Oh." Madison exhaled. "Like that movie with the asteroid about to blow up the planet. Government didn't wanna tell anyone."

"Right. No one could've done anything about it, so... why cause needless panic, or worse... set off the nutjobs who would run around doing whatever they wanted because there's no reason to be afraid of jail anymore."

Madison peered at her. "Can we do something about it?"

"We the town? I think so. We as in you and me? No. Not really, unless you count running away as a viable option."

"Nope. Not viable... unless we take everyone with us." Madison nodded toward the door. "We should go outside. Carrie's bringing the cake soon."

Harper took a few breaths. "Do I look okay or like I'm scared?"

"Not really scared. More worried. Like you forgot to study for a big test that's gonna make you fail and repeat the whole year. It's subtle. I don't think anyone else is gonna notice." Madison scrunched up her nose. "Cliff might, but I guess he already knows about the thing."

"Yeah." Harper let all the air out of her lungs, then stood. "C'mon. We have a birthday party to manage."

"Whoa." Madison got up. "Seems kinda weird to have a party when *that* is right outside town."

"It does, but... what good will it do us to sit around being scared? Not like we're procrastinating. They're gonna fix it as soon as it's possible to do."

"Right." Madison headed for the door. "Party face on."

———

DECEIT NEVER CAME EASY TO HARPER.

Like any relatively normal teenager, she'd told her fair share of lies... but they'd all been harmless in the grand scheme of things, kid stuff. Her first attempt to tell a significant lie failed spectacularly—when she'd been caught shoplifting in the mall. It had been a stupid dare. Pressure got to her, and she crumbled so fast the mall security guard—ironically, Cliff—never doubted her guilt. Between him being a softie and her parents not only paying for the stolen garment but buying a bunch of other stuff—that Harper had to donate to charity—the police didn't get involved.

Suffice to say, she never dared shoplift again.

A lie of omission didn't feel any easier than a lie of speaking false. *Not* telling a room full of happy children they could all be vaporized at any minute had to be a bigger deal than trying to tell a security guard she didn't steal some $24 sweater, pants, or whatever it had been. She couldn't even remember the item… only that it had cost $24. She'd sat with one wrist handcuffed to a chair in the security room for over an hour staring at the price tag while not knowing if the next time the door opened there'd be cops—and her life would be over—or if only her parents would walk in.

Much to her surprise, she kept herself outwardly calm enough to fool the kids at the birthday party. Even more surprising, Madison carried on like nothing happened. Harper hovered at the edge of the room, nibbling on cake and watching Jonathan and the kids do their best to enjoy a party in a world without television or video games. Most of the fun would happen outside in the yard later. She glanced from kid to kid, trying to guess how they'd react when or if they learned about the warhead.

Mila would probably pack up and start hiking to a safe distance. Lorelei wouldn't react much. The kid had a fearless streak, largely from not understanding danger. She'd want to play with a warhead the same way she'd not be scared of a sketchy looking man sneaking up on her with a knife or want to go hug a bear.

She'd totally be the little girl who smears the glowing blue powder all over herself, not knowing any better.

That thought made Harper scoop Lorelei up and squish hug her, clinging for about ten minutes. Lorelei didn't mind. In fact, she adored the overt show of affection.

Eva and Becca would probably have similar reactions that involved lots of screaming and panic.

Jonathan… he'd more than likely start trying to figure out a way to manage the situation. The boy had a strange habit of being scared of trivialities like hairy bugs, wasps, or ghost stories… but deadly serious things made him react analytically. Sometimes, he freaked out after the danger passed.

Harper tried to copy his ability to defer emotion. The calmer she could keep herself now, the better off everyone would be. Thankfully, she didn't feel alone in her anxiety, not the 'little kid' on the militia who couldn't be trusted with stress. Even Roy Ellis, former SWAT cop, seemed a bit fidgety. Anne-Marie probably paced in circles and had a meltdown once she didn't have to keep a brave face on for everyone as the town's manager. After the meeting, Walter went over to Earl's for a beer or two to calm his nerves, and the man *rarely* drank alcohol.

Cliff, Carrie, Mrs. Parsons, Becca's parents, and Lucas Garza hung out in the kitchen, talking.

Having a former celebrity standing around in her house seemed as unbelievable as one of her friends basically marrying the guy. He and Darci had a kid together. That so few people in town said anything about their age gap felt crazier than a live warhead being so close. Lucas wasn't *super* old, only like thirty-three or so. Harper had seen worse. One of the women who worked at Mom's place married a guy more than twenty years older than her, like fifty-five to her thirty-one. Still, it felt weird to think about Darci and Lucas as a couple. She couldn't decide if the weirdness came from his celebrity or his age.

Few could deny they'd been good for each other. Lucas had trouble coping with the end of civilization. Most people thought he simply couldn't handle not being a rich and influential person anymore in a world where money and fame meant nothing. In truth, he'd been devastated by thoughts of the scope of death around the world. The man couldn't care less about losing his fortune. As much as Harper hated to think about it, Darci ended up in bad shape mentally after the Army survivor camp. She might've been contemplating suicide at one point... but the two of them found reasons to live in each other.

Mrs. Parsons, Eva's mother, who Harper recently found out was named Lynn, still didn't seem quite convinced life had any purpose. Whispers around town said the woman only stayed alive for her daughter's benefit. She'd given birth to a baby girl last December, but didn't want to be responsible for raising a child conceived by rape within a week of her husband's mysterious murder. News she'd given the baby up came as a huge relief to Harper. She'd worried the woman might neglect the baby or worse, harm her on purpose. The Army medics at Eldorado Springs Camp refused to perform an abortion, since by the time Mrs. Parsons realized she'd become pregnant, the baby was 'too far along.' She begrudgingly agreed to bear the child claiming the baby shouldn't be punished for its own existence, but didn't want to even see it after the birth. As far as Harper knew, Tegan still looked after the baby, which she'd named Taylor. Odds seemed high Tegan would keep the kid long term and be mom.

At least Mrs. P doesn't seem annoyed to be here.

Renee, Grace, and Darci—with baby Piper in her lap—sat on the couch in the living room. Elijah, the boy Darci adopted, raced around with the older kids as they zoomed back and forth from the yard to the house. He turned six last January, which made him the youngest in the room after Lorelei, not counting the *three* infants in the house. Whenever Darci brought him over, he and Lorelei were inseparable— and often uncontainable, as if they'd drank a whole case of sugary soda.

In a stunning display of normal, the kids, the teens, and the adults all grouped in their respective clusters. Except for the lack of a blaring television, it felt like most other birthday parties she'd ever been part of.

"This cake is really good," said Darci. "It doesn't even taste like the mix was stale."

"Because it wasn't," called Carrie from the kitchen.

Darci twisted to peer over the back of the sofa at the kitchen doorway. "How the heck did you find mix that wasn't stale?"

Carrie poked her head into view. "Who said anything about cake mix?"

"Umm. How else do you make a cake?" Darci blinked.

"Oh dear. Are you being serious or teasing me?" asked Carrie.

"She's being serious," deadpanned Renee. "Darci's so bad in the kitchen she needs a recipe to boil water. She was raised on Hot Pockets, freezer meals, and ordering pizza."

Darci made a cooing noise at Piper, then aimed the baby toward Renee. "C'mon, sweetie. Throw up."

"Ack!" Renee laughed. "Don't you dare."

Piper made a warbling noise, then grinned.

"If you want to learn how to make a cake like they used to, let me know. I can teach you." Carrie smiled. "Cake did exist before box mix, you know. Now that we've got a working farm, it isn't that difficult. Just time consuming. Betty Crocker didn't make cake *possible*, she made it much faster."

"I wasn't aware we're growing sugar cane," said Renee.

"We aren't." Harper chuckled. "I think she used berries or something."

Carrie held a finger up until she finished chewing a mouthful of cake. "I did. Food coloring is not why the cake is maroon. Wild strawberries and blackberries."

"I wouldn't mind learning how to whip up a cake." Harper un-leaned from the wall and moved to sit on the arm of the sofa beside Renee. *Something to do and spending time with family, sounds like a win.*

"Sure, why not." Darci shrugged. "What kind of girl would I be if I can't bake a cake?"

"One whose diet consists entirely of Hot Pockets and microwave meals," deadpanned Renee.

Darci gazed at the ceiling. "I'd totally like legit kill someone for some pizza rolls right now."

"Ouch," deadpanned Harper. "The roof of my mouth hurt just from hearing the phrase 'pizza rolls.'"

Becca and Eva asked Carrie to include them in the cake lesson.

"I want to learn, too," said Jonathan.

"Boys don't make cakes," chirped Eva in a tone too ambiguous to tell if she meant it sarcastically or truly thought so.

"Sure they do." Jonathan shook his head at her. "Lots of fancy bakers are guys."

"Don't you gotta be French for that?" asked Cliff—in a definitely joking voice.

"Oui, oui," said Jonathan, before babbling in complete nonsense that sorta sounded like French.

When the laughter subsided, Cliff strode into the living room, scooped Jonathan up, and perched him on the recliner chair like a little king on a throne. Knowing it was Cliff's favorite spot in the house, Jonathan gave him a 'whoa, really' stare.

"I'll allow it for a few minutes since it's your birthday." Cliff winked, then handed him a cloth sack.

Black writing on the fabric read, 'this is gift wrapping.'

Jonathan laughed, then opened it to reveal a bunch of action figures, some manner of Japanese animation type robots. He cheered, hugged Cliff, and held the toys up to show them off. Becca and Eva didn't seem terribly thrilled about them, but Christopher—Jonathan's best friend—yelled, 'awesome.'

Harper gave him a small stash of comic books she'd found on a shelf in the quartermaster's 'miscellaneous stuff' area, where non-vital but 'neat' things collected on various scavenging efforts ended up.

Renee gave him a couple shirts she'd made herself as well as a pair of shorts—her first successful attempt at pants.

None of the kids brought gifts, which had been expected. Not like they could ask their parents to take them shopping anymore. For the most part, the kids didn't seem too bothered about birthdays and Christmas no longer meaning they got showered with expensive stuff.

Right when everyone thought the gift-giving part of the birthday ended, Mila ran outside without a word, then returned a moment later with a box. She sat on the rug next to Jonathan, held the box out, and smiled. "Happy birthday."

"Thank you!" He hugged her, then took the present and opened it to reveal a set of graphite art pencils. The box had clearly been opened already, some of the pencils showing use.

The room fell silent. Most everyone stared at Mila except Harper, who glanced around trying to figure out what about a set of pencils brought everything to a standstill. Eva, Becca, and Chris seemed awkward, perhaps wondering if they should've brought a gift, too. Cliff's expression gave off a sense of questioning more than anything.

"What?" blurted Mila after a few seconds. "He likes to draw."

"It's not the pencils," said Cliff.

Mila let out a small, irritated huff. "Am I in trouble for scavenging alone?"

Cliff almost smiled. "You should probably not do that, but no, you're not in trouble."

"I think they're surprised you didn't give him something... weird," whispered Madison a little too loud to be private. "You know, black, pointy, creepy, or squirming. Pencils are so... tame."

Mila laughed, then flailed her arms. "Come on, guys! I'm trying to be normal here."

Says the ten-year-old who can throw a knife into a man's eye at thirty paces.

"I love them. Thank you." Jonathan leaned over and kissed Mila on the cheek.

Renee and Grace 'awwed'.

"They're cute," whispered Carrie.

"Like a siren luring a sailor," muttered Cliff past a grin.

Carrie nudged him. "Oh, stop. She's adorable."

He chuckled. "So are sirens... until they stab you."

Infant wailing rose from the improvised crib in Cliff's bedroom at the end of the hall. He hadn't been using it too much lately, spending most nights next door at Carrie's house.

"Oh, here we go." Cliff winked. "I got it."

Harper smiled at her pseudo-dad as he hurried to collect his two sons. He didn't look much like the mall security guard who scared the hell out of her years ago. Longish, shaggy hair, a beard, and no trace of excess pounds replaced the clean-cut face and belly paunch he sported when his life had no direction or meaning. As awful as nuclear war was, it gave him purpose again. Some men simply couldn't adapt to the civilian lifestyle. This changed world suited him well: he could simultaneously have the family he never thought he'd get *and* use every skill the Army gave him.

He's so calm and happy even knowing about the warhead. Harper exhaled. *I hope it's because he really thinks it won't go off.*

The kids ran outside, screaming in delight and having a blast celebrating Jonathan turning twelve. Madison didn't exactly give off exuberance, though she managed not to seem terrified either. Harper started to wonder if she messed up by telling her, but didn't get the chance to dwell on it too long before Darci, Renee, and Grace dragged her into their conversation.

6

THE TALK

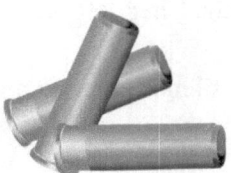

TUESDAY, MAY 12TH

I t occurred to Harper that she'd forgotten what fabric softener smelled like.

She lay in bed, awake, but didn't open her eyes. Mornings had always been the worst. When she'd been in grade school, Mom or Dad sometimes had to physically lift her out of bed to get her going. When high school started, and she got too big for Mom to pick up, the parents resorted to other means to get her going on the days she just couldn't find the energy to move when the alarm clock went off. Tickling, awful music, and sometimes lifting her mattress so she slid off to the floor.

Not that Harper hated school or didn't want to go. She just couldn't wake up so damn early.

Sophomore year, she'd done a science project about research into teenage brains and how they needed extra sleep. Apparently, some doctors figured out the traditional schedule could be harmful to teenagers… but for some reason, the school establishment ignored it and kept insisting on starting classes butt-crack-of-dawn-early in the morning.

Dad used to tease her that she'd end up working second or third shift at whatever job she ultimately found herself in. The militia didn't keep people on a punch clock. Her 'on-duty' time technically never ended. They merely expected her to patrol her sector with a reasonable degree of diligence from morning to afternoon. No one quibbled about an extra twenty or thirty minutes of sleep.

Worrying about the warhead proved every bit as exhausting as physical work. She'd passed out much faster than she expected.

Madison snuggled against her left side. Lorelei curled up under her right arm.

The peaceful morning silence came to an abrupt end with a faint, high-pitched fart.

Lorelei giggled.

"Ugh, who did that?" muttered Harper.

"Not me," said Madison in a half-awake voice.

"I didn't do it." Lorelei giggled again.

Gotta be Maddie. Lore would totally claim it. She exhaled. No point to making a big deal about it.

Seconds later, the air grew... pungent.

Oof. Maybe I should bring her to the med center. Ugh. Foul. Harper held her breath. She made no comment about the odor to avoid hurting Madison's feelings. Unlike Lorelei, who thought of farting as completely hilarious, Madison tried to pretend girls just didn't do that. Farts were, according to her, 'a boy thing.' She'd be embarrassed.

She's never been around Veronica after Chinese food and broccoli.

Wanting to be able to breathe again provided enough motivation to overcome inertia. Harper got out of bed and headed across the hall, trying not to yawn until she got clear of the blast zone. After emptying her bladder, she left the bathroom. At the same time, Jonathan's bedroom door opened. Harper didn't think much of him wandering out in only underpants—until she spotted Mila leaving the room right behind him, also with only underpants on.

Harper stopped short, staring in shock.

Both kids seemed dazed, as if they'd not quite fully finished waking up yet. Neither acted strangely, nor attempted to avoid being seen. Mila waved at her, as did Jonathan. They trudged past Harper to the bathroom and paused by the door.

Jonathan gestured. "You can go first."

"Kay." Mila scurried in and shut the door.

Jonathan stood there, waiting, and yawned. "Morning."

"Uhh... morning," said Harper, still too stunned to think.

A moment later, he peered up at her, one eye open wider than the other. "Why are you looking at me like that? Did we do something wrong?"

She blinked. "I don't know. Did you?"

Jonathan shrugged. "I slept with Mila last night."

The presence of a nuclear warhead so close to town no longer meant anything. The thought of it entirely flew from Harper's brain at the words coming out of him. She braced a hand against the wall to stop herself from fainting.

"Harp?" Jonathan tilted his head. "Are we gonna get a baby now?"

The warhead might've just detonated; Harper wouldn't have noticed. *Somehow*, she managed not to scream, freak out, or lose consciousness. Her brain wanted to ask if they used protection or if he tried pulling out like Logan did... but her mouth refused to utter such things to a twelve-year-old, especially a boy she thought of as a brother—so she simply stared at him.

"What?" Jonathan yawned again.

She fought for calm. *No. I can't leap to conclusions here. This can't possibly be what it looks like. She's ten. He's twelve. They have no idea.* "Umm, what, exactly did you guys do last night?"

"We slept together."

Harper pursed her lips. "When you say... slept together... are you suggesting something else?"

"Huh?" He scrunched up his nose. "What do you mean? Oh..." Jonathan smiled. "I kissed her before we tried to sleep."

Umm. Harper blinked. "Are you saying 'slept with her' literally meaning that the two of you both slept in the same bed and that's it?"

He nodded. "Yeah."

Harper's legs gave out. She sank to kneel in a puddle of relief. "Oh. Okay."

Jonathan tilted his head. "What do you mean 'that's it'? Were we supposed to do something else?"

"No." She patted him on the shoulder. "You did fine."

He scratched his chest. "Why do people get so weird about sleeping together?"

"Uhh, ask Cliff." She grinned. "He'll explain."

The bathroom door opened. Mila emerged, yawned, and trudged back to Jonathan's room. The boy rushed into the bathroom.

Oh wow. This is going to be a fun breakfast conversation. Harper dragged herself into her room to get dressed.

HARPER, MADISON, CLIFF, CARRIE, RENEE, JONATHAN, LORELEI, AND Mila squeezed together around the kitchen table, with Lorelei in Harper's lap due to lack of chairs. Cliff and Carrie seemed slightly surprised to see Mila there so early, but didn't say anything. Carrie 'officially' took Renee in since she'd been underage when she came to Evergreen. Now eighteen, Harper's best friend didn't technically *need* a parent, but loved having people she could go to for emotional support. The time she'd been held captive by Lawless could have been much, much worse, but it still traumatized her.

The whole 'big family' thing made Harper feel better, too.

Conversation over a breakfast of pan-toast, eggs, and fried potato slices went on normally enough until Harper decided to lob the grenade she'd been sitting on. "So, Jon slept with Mila last night."

Cliff coughed, nearly launching a wad of potato across the table.

Renee started choking. Carrie fumbled her fork but managed not to drop it. Madison looked up with a 'so what' expression. Lorelei continued eating, showing no reaction whatsoever.

Mila stared at Harper, mirroring Madison's 'so what' face. Jonathan squirmed a little as if he expected to get in trouble, but couldn't understand why. Two seconds of silence later, he and Mila exchanged a glance. She mouthed 'what'.

"Before anyone has a heart attack," said Harper, "They just slept in the same bed."

Jonathan looked at Cliff. "Harp said you'd explain why people get weird about sleeping together."

"Oh, I will, will I?" Cliff playfully glared at Harper before exhaling. "Yeah... Okay. I guess it's about time we had that talk."

"Sleepovers are fun," chirped Lorelei. "Bad mommy had boys sleep over all the time, like free or four a week!"

Cliff wagged his eyebrows at Harper. "That one's yours."

Chuckling, Harper squeeze-hugged the seven-year-old in her lap. "Right..."

7

COINCIDENTAL

WEDNESDAY, MAY 13TH

Harper walked along the street, following the kids as they explored an abandoned part of Evergreen.

They'd gone south a bit, east of the lake, past a little shopping center with a Baskin Robbins and into the forest to check out the houses in the area. Even though it hadn't been two full years since the war, it felt as if they made an archaeological expedition into a forgotten civilization. The kids wanted to go farther out than they would dare by themselves, so they asked Harper to come along after school. Multiple people had thus far accused her of impersonating an adult, so they felt safe having her around.

Going with the kids put her in a strange place mentally. She simultaneously felt like a teenage kid having fun as well as 'mom.' Since they hadn't left town—at least what used to be considered Evergreen before society collapsed—it didn't seem like a reckless undertaking. This area still did technically fit inside 'new Evergreen,' though in the dead space between 'North Evergreen' and 'South Evergreen.' Even though she carried the Mossberg, and wouldn't hesitate to use it if needed, wandering around the trees and empty homes didn't give her the same sort of anxiety it would have to bring multiple children on a dangerous trek across the wasteland.

She'd had her fill of that running with Madison out of Lakewood.

They discovered an absolutely massive house surrounded by trees off Mariposa Road. It had to be easily three times the size of her home. Whoever lived there before must have had serious money to afford it.

Naturally, as one tended to do in a post-nuclear world, the kids barged right in like they owned the place. The militia had been obliging enough to bust open the door lock, as they did with most every house within reasonable distance from the town center during the first few weeks after the bombs. Once they determined no one lived in any particular house, they raided it for usable canned goods, weapons, ammo, medical supplies, or anything they felt would be useful to survivors.

Harper parked herself in the enormous living room, half-leaning against the wall while the kids spread out and ran around. The place was so damn huge it reminded her of the sorts of homes they showed in movies or TV shows—often impossibly big or lavish for the theoretical income of the characters. An over-100-inch flat panel television sat on a sleek black entertainment center facing a massive sectional somewhere between blue and indigo. Fat watermelon-sized ceramic or porcelain lamps decorated a pair of end tables at either end of the giant sofa. Harper figured they'd either come from Ikea or cost about ten times what they looked to be worth for being 'trendy.' Jonathan thought the lamps looked like the eggs from the movie *Aliens*.

Some dirty footprints on the ground indicated someone had been here since the abandonment, but for whatever reason, didn't stick around, nor did they make a mess. Past experiences suggested it had either been horny teenagers in search of privacy or someone from South Evergreen scavenging for useful things.

Wow. This house would take a team of people to keep clean.

The kids ran back and forth from room to room, went upstairs, and ran back and forth overhead. Harper didn't feel any need to go racing about, contenting herself to keep an eye on the door and an ear on everything.

About twenty minutes or so later, the kids swarmed back into the living room. They'd apparently found a stash of board games upstairs, decided to bring them *all* down here, and set about deciding which one to try. Mila steered everyone's interest to the Ouija board... at least until she opened the box and set up the board. Lorelei thought it looked like a boring game, so she got up and resumed exploring the house.

Mila, Madison, Jonathan, Christopher, Becca, and Eva flopped on the carpet between the TV and sofa, surrounding the board. Harper couldn't help but chuckle to herself as Mila explained to the others how they could use the board and pointer to talk to dead people and 'other kinds of spirits.'

Except for no one using any electronics, the scene in front of her looked so normal she could almost pretend the world hadn't changed. She'd never been in a house this big before, nor did she know anyone whose parents could have afforded a place with a second-floor hallway-slash-balcony overlooking the living room downstairs. The elevated walk spanned the entire long width of the living room and went past it, becoming a normal hallway. From the ground floor, she could sort of see into three rooms upstairs through the bars of the wooden banister, one of which appeared to be full of electronic piano keyboards on wall shelves. Grace probably grew up in a house similar to this one, or even bigger, but they hadn't known each other back then. Her old home also likely didn't exist at all anymore. Colorado Springs got hammered worse than Denver, or so rumors claimed. She hadn't felt any urge to go down there to see for herself.

"We call out to any spirits that might be listening," said Mila. "Talk to us through the Ouija board."

Due to somewhat limited space around the board, Christopher and Eva moved back, not touching the pointer. Mila, Jonathan, Becca, and Madison had their fingertips on the planchette, all staring at it in rapt anticipation.

"No matter what happens, do *not* take your fingers off it." Mila narrowed her eyes at her friends. "If we stop touching it, the demon can get loose and cause trouble."

Becca gave a faint whimper. "Maybe this isn't such a good idea."

"You're moving it," whispered Madison.

"I am not." Jonathan shook his head.

Madison shook her head. "Not you. Becca."

"I'm not moving it." Becca shivered, eyes wide. "It moved a little but it wasn't me."

Harper covered her mouth to hold in a laugh. *What is it about tween girls and occultism?*

The shockingly ordinary surroundings brought her back to the night she, Andrea, Renee, Darci, Veronica, and Christina scared the hell out of each other with a Ouija board. They'd all been around fourteen, having a sleepover at Renee's. Most sleepovers happened there since everyone else's parents considered Renee's parents highly responsible. Also, Harper and her friends thought of Renee's mom and dad as 'cool.' Not quite as 'let the kids smoke pot' cool as Darci's father, but that's probably why they never had sleepovers at House Sutherland. Christina begged everyone not to talk about using a board, since her religious parents would've freaked out and punished her if they ever found out she'd touched one.

Mila started asking random innocuous questions to the 'spirit,' asking its name, if it died here, what music it liked, and other random stuff.

Harper tried not to snicker too loud at the memory of Andrea and Veronica screaming and clinging to each other when the lights died unexpectedly. It had been extra hilarious as Veronica was their group's resident 'tough girl' thanks to her being so into karate and sports. 'Ronnie' as they all nicknamed her, was the group's token jock-slash-extrovert. She'd adopted all the introverts.

Well, at least the power won't cut out here and make everyone wet their pants.

When the lights died back then, Harper screamed like her friends. Fear proved to be contagious, even if she didn't believe ghosts existed.

Looking back on the memory was funny. Living it at the moment hadn't been.

She gazed up at the ceiling, noting Lorelei had been awfully quiet for a while.

Quiet and seven-year-olds usually means catastrophe is in the making. "Lore?"

"Yeah?" called the girl from down the hall.

"What are you doing?"

Lorelei walked out of a doorway into the hall, naked. "Playin' dress up. I found clothes."

"You found clothes?" Harper blinked.

The little blonde girl nodded emphatically. "Yeah. Lots of 'em."

Harper chuckled. "Then where are they?"

Lorelei pointed at the door she came out of. "In there. I'm changing when you called me."

Before Harper could say anything more, the child darted into the room, out of sight.

"It's not working," said Christopher. "The thing is just kinda fidgeting around, not going to letters. You guys are doing it."

Everyone touching the planchette denied moving it on purpose.

Becca recoiled from it.

"Don't let go!" shouted Eva.

"Eeeeeee!" Becca screamed and hurriedly put her fingertips back on the plastic pointer.

"Okay, wait." Mila sat up a little taller. "Let's try to talk to the spirit of someone we know."

Madison shrank in on herself, avoiding eye contact with anyone like a kid terrified of being called on in school.

"You know that stuff isn't real," said Harper before anyone could suggest 'contacting' her and Madison's parents.

"We don't *know* that." Mila shrugged. "Maybe it is. Maybe it isn't."

Jonathan glanced at Madison, then Harper. His expression said he thought the Ouija board thing was total BS, but he said nothing, wanting to humor Mila. Becca seemed ready to scream again and run out of the room at the slightest unexplained noise. Christopher's blank expression and focused attention on the planchette made him seem totally into the idea of ghosts being real. Eva looked close to falling asleep.

"Umm." Mila looked at Madison, nodded once, then exhaled. "We can try talking to my first mom."

Relieved, Madison lifted her gaze off the rug.

"Mom? Are you out there? Can you hear us? Can you make contact with us?" asked Mila, sounding like an old 1930s fortune teller conducting a séance.

Lorelei popped out into the hall, attempting to wear an adult woman's purple evening gown. She held her arms up to either side. "Princess!"

"Very pretty!" Harper clapped.

The little one pirouetted, got tangled up in the gown, and wiped out, falling flat on her front. "Oof."

"You okay?"

"Yes." Lorelei laughed. "Dress too big."

Harper chuckled.

Lorelei crawled into the bedroom.

"It moved," whispered Christopher.

"Eeeeeeek," whimpered Becca. "It is! It's moving!"

It took a fair amount of willpower for Harper not to roll her eyes. As far as she believed, those boards were nonsense. The motion of the planchette came from the interaction of multiple people subconsciously twitching, similar to the mechanism of how when a person tries to hold their hand perfectly still, it shakes more and more the harder they try to concentrate on not moving.

"Are you Mila's mother?" asked Jonathan.

The kids all squealed as the beige plastic thing slipped sideways across the board.

"No," said Madison.

"It moved by itself." Becca sniffled. "I didn't do that."

"I didn't either." Jonathan leaned closer, as if trying to study how the plastic pointer could possibly be maneuvering around.

"Someone's pushing it." Eva curled up by the coffee table.

"Someone's gotta be pushing it. Right? It's daytime. Ghosts don't come out during the day."

"Stop moving it," whispered Mila. "Let it move on its own."

"It *is* moving on its own," whined Becca.

Mila cleared her throat. "Whoever is contacting us with the board, please spell your name."

Lorelei paraded out of the bedroom again, now wearing a black dress. She had to hold the neck closed to keep it from falling off her shoulders to the floor. On her, the hem of the skirt barely touched the carpet.

Eek. Harper grimaced mentally thinking about what the garment would look like on a grown woman. *That wouldn't cover much.*

"It stopped," whispered Becca.

"Will you spell your name for us?" asked Mila.

As soon as the question left her lips, one of the end-table lamps by the sofa exploded, spraying bits of porcelain everywhere.

Jonathan, Christopher, Becca, and Eva screamed.

Mila stared at the now empty small table, eyes wide in an expression of 'holy shit'.

Becca burst into tears.

"Someone's in trouble," said Lorelei in an unimpressed voice. "Broke a lamp."

"Ghost," whispered Eva. "Is it mad?"

Stunned, Harper stared in bewildered awe at the remains of the porcelain lamp that seemingly detonated as an angry response to Mila's demand. A man somewhere outside yelled a stream of obscenities before three loud pops went off. Harper realized what really happened to the lamp. It hadn't been the act of an angry ghost.

"Everyone get down!" yelled Harper. "Now! On the floor."

Becca and Eva, already stretched out on the carpet, didn't move, though Becca kept screaming like she thought real demons were coming after them. Mila shifted from sitting cross-legged to rolling onto her belly. Jonathan flopped on his side. Lorelei ran back into the bedroom.

Jonathan crawled to Becca and covered her mouth. "Shh! It's not a ghost. Someone's shooting at us."

Becca glared at him, but stopped screaming. When he removed his hand from her face, she whispered, "That's not any less scary."

Harper rushed to the front door, taking cover behind the wall to the right. More gunshots went off in the distance. Two or three men shouted in anger, cursing at each other in between firing. As far as Harper could tell, none of the bullets hit the house.

She risked a peek around the doorjamb for two seconds. No one appeared to be in the front yard, on the street beyond, or around the house across from this one. She couldn't see too much more thanks to the trees blocking her view. Yelling sounded as if it came from roughly 100 to 150 yards away, on the other side of trees east of the house. She doubted the men intentionally shot at her or any of the kids, and likely didn't even know they existed.

"I'm hit!" yelled Eva.

Fuck. Harper twisted to look, her heart almost stopping.

"No, you're not." Jonathan held the girl's shirt up to expose her back. "It's a piece of lamp, not a bullet."

"Ow!" wailed Eva.

"She's fine," whispered Madison. "I got it."

"Ow!" yelled Eva, even louder. "Why'd you pull it out? Now I'm gonna bleed to death."

"No, you're not." Madison sighed, holding a small sliver of white material up. "It's tiny. Like a toothpick."

Harper closed her eyes. *I can't take much more of this.* She felt like an idiot for agreeing to this exploratory hike. Needless risk. But... she couldn't exactly keep the kids locked up in a basement until they turned eighteen. It's not as if they went far away from town, either. Idiots came to them.

Lorelei, once again wearing the beige handmade dress Renee made for her, crawled out of the bedroom.

Three more shots went off. The kids twitched in time with each one.

A distant man screamed in agony.

Harper again risked a peek out the door. Seconds later, a man appeared out of the woods a fair distance past the house across the street, running away from her position. Another man stumbled, evidently wounded, onto the road behind him, attempting to chase and shoot him at the same time, but doing poorly at both. The second man wore a bright red shirt, not exactly the best thing for stealth. He chased the wounded guy, taunting him not to run since he'd only die tired.

At range, she couldn't tell who they were. No one from Evergreen officially lived in this part of town. Perhaps some guys traveling together had a nasty falling out that turned violent. Maybe some people she didn't know from South Evergreen came here looking for a deserted place to settle their differences.

Huddled against the wall, she crouched beside the door listening to the two men run off... and kept listening for a while after any detectable sound came from outside. Jonathan jumped up and ran to the kitchen, keeping his head down like ground crew scurrying over to a helicopter. It had been quiet for long enough that Harper didn't yell at him to stay on the floor, but she also didn't like him moving around just yet.

He returned with a roll of paper towels, which he proceeded to use to wipe at the wound on Eva's back. Becca and Madison each held one of her hands, telling her it wasn't a big deal and to calm down. Eva lay on her side, shirt up around her armpits. A hole about the size of a number two pencil lead along one of her prominent ribs oozed blood.

Ack. It probably stuck in her rib. "Keep light pressure on it for a while. It'll stop bleeding." Harper nodded to Jonathan, then patted Eva on the head. "It's small. You're fine. We'll go to the med center when we get back."

Eva sniffled, but seemed reassured. "Okay. If it's so small, why did it hurt so much?"

Madison held up a shard of white glass an inch or so long, triangular in cross-section, and pointy. Evidently, the lamps hadn't been made of porcelain. About a quarter inch at the tip darkened with blood. "It stuck in her like a dart. Not bad. I've had worse from Melissa's cat."

"Her cat was mean." Becca frowned. "He scratched a lot. I hope Liss is okay."

"Yeah." Eva looked down.

Madison closed her eyes as if making a wish over a birthday cake.

"Broken glass is sharp. It stuck in pretty deep. Good thing, it looks like the tip didn't break off and stay inside you." Harper glanced at Eva and Becca's feet. The two preferred to go barefoot on warmer days. Lorelei as well. "There's smashed glass all over this room. Careful where you step."

Christopher picked Becca up and carried her to the foyer. Harper did the same for Eva.

Finally, about five minutes after the last gunshot, Harper felt secure enough to get the hell out of there. Eva appeared to have calmed down. She continued to lay on the floor while Jonathan pressed a folded paper towel against her back.

"All right. Sounds like they're gone." Harper motioned toward the door. "Time to go."

Mila hurriedly packed the Ouija board, seeming intent on keeping it. Christopher grabbed the remaining stack of board games. Whatever other 'treasures' this huge house contained, they'd have to wait. Jonathan gingerly lifted the towel. Bleeding appeared to have stopped, so he smiled, tossed the towel aside, and gently tugged her shirt down.

No one protested the early end to their adventure. Mila being outwardly disappointed at the mundane explanation for the exploding lamp instead of an angry ghost kinda worried Harper. A little girl two months shy of her eleventh birthday should not be so unfazed by a bullet zinging through the room. At least Mila didn't complain out loud about the lack of obvious paranormal activity.

Harper looked over the kids to make sure she had everyone accounted for and none had any unwanted glass darts stuck in them, then took a cautious peek outside. Everything appeared calm. It had been at least ten minutes since the last gunshot, so she felt safe enough to break cover and hurry outside.

Being back in the heart of Evergreen wouldn't necessarily make them any safer from unexpected violence. However, at least there, she wouldn't be completely responsible for dealing with managing the kids, plus handling any threats. Even the most experienced people on the militia, like Cliff and Roy, preferred to work in teams.

She grumbled mentally to herself while jogging west into the trees behind the house. Things had been relatively quiet lately, so much so she'd started to forget the world fell apart. More had changed than only going back in time to an era before retail stores and reliable electricity. Society still had to work out the shock of massive upheaval in the social order. It would probably take a generation or two before things calmed down enough to expect a degree of sanity comparable to how things used to be. Until then, she had to be ready for everything from bad guys like roving Lawless, to Promise Keepers who abducted a bunch of kids to force their parents to continually supply them with food, to plain old idiots causing problems. The world would always have the odd one-offs, but hopefully, people would settle down and get used to the new reality at some point and they'd no longer have to worry about marauding gangs.

Problem being, such a settling down may or may not occur within her lifetime. Roy liked to say that humanity possessed a certain violent element that bristled at the notion of being contained by civilized society. He didn't think order would return naturally. According to him, without an organized, nationwide sense of law and enforcement, chaos would rule eternal.

Roy tended to be a cheery sort of optimist.

Evergreen offered a glimpse of hope at what could be, but that hope also came with a dangerous illusion of civilization. She couldn't really say they'd even gone recklessly far from town. The huge house couldn't be more than two football fields' distance from the lake and Bear Creek Road, which connected right to 74 and ran north into the heart of Evergreen.

Harper looked back to make sure the kids kept up.

They followed her in a single file line, but spread out, moving from tree to tree more like small soldiers than kids on a nature hike. She hadn't told them to do it, but they knew someone nearby fired a gun, so they tried to stay safe. Her heart broke a little. Kids didn't deserve to live in a warzone... but the entire world had become a warzone. When she considered how she, as well as these kids, grew up hyper-aware that a shooter might show up at their schools at any time, her heart broke a little more. None of them had ever truly enjoyed life without some degree of fear over being shot.

It could've happened anywhere. Harper exhaled and decided not to feel like an idiot for letting the kids talk her into this exploration. Chances were, they wouldn't be interested in another adventure for at least... a few days.

Soon after they reached the road circling Evergreen Lake, the kids stopped moving like a platoon of child soldiers and gathered in a cluster behind Harper, acting like normal kids out on an almost-summer day. They'd put over a hundred yards of trees between them and the house, not to mention the shooters ran in the opposite direction. Harper also felt safe enough to stop squeezing her knuckles white on the Mossberg's grip. Still, she didn't slow down.

"Why were they shooting at us?" asked Eva.

"They weren't shooting at us." Harper glanced back at the woods. "A few guys were trying to shoot each other and a stray bullet hit the house."

Becca bit her lip. "Did the demon make the bullet hit the lamp?"

"Maybe." Mila shrugged. "Can't tell."

"Just a coincidence," said Harper.

Mila peered up at her with an eerie little smile. "You sure?"

"Are you doing the creepy thing on purpose?" Eva glanced at Mila.

"No." Mila shook her head. "I'm asking seriously."

Harper squinted at the hazy sunlight overhead. *Wow, the sky still looks so dirty. How long before it starts getting cleaner?* "Two things happening at the same time doesn't prove one caused the other. I mean, it doesn't prove they *didn't*... but, you shouldn't blame everything weird on demons."

"There are so many stories about crazy things happening with Ouija boards." Christopher whistled. "My dad loves that stuff. He watches all creepy videos… umm, used to watch creepy videos all the time."

"A lot of that stuff is fake." Jonathan plucked a bit of plant matter off his shirt and tossed it aside. "We have a lot of real things to be scared of."

A lump formed in Harper's throat. *Yeah… like a damn Russian MIRV.*

8

NATURAL

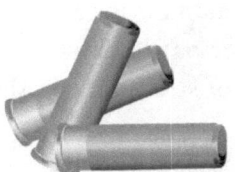

FRIDAY, MAY 15TH

The town leaders still hadn't come up with a definite plan of action regarding the warhead.

By now, everyone on the militia knew about it. Walter directed them to discourage people from going west past Interlocken Drive. For now, they used fabricated rumors of Lawless sightings in the area as a deterrent. Harper didn't feel completely comfortable lying to people, but much like the government in that asteroid doomsday movie, accepted it would do no one any good if the people panicked.

Two-person teams of militia made forays into the surrounding areas, mostly south or west, scouting out mines in which they might bury the warhead. Rafael had 'almost' gotten the semi-truck operating on biodiesel and assured everyone he could have it running in a few days. Up until this crisis, he hadn't put much time on the project as the need for a working truck cab hadn't been there. The farm eliminated the need to go farther and farther away from town in search of canned goods or other food. Having an enormous semi-trailer for long haul scavenging trips didn't make sense.

Anne-Marie preferred as distant a mine as possible for Evergreen's protection, but also wanted to make sure relocating the device would not put any other people in danger. They had to make sure no one settled close to it, which more or less eliminated any mine to the south since it would be too near the ranches where the Overton family and others lived.

Having a nuke so close became a constant, nagging weight in the bottom of Harper's stomach. Knowing it had been there likely the entire time she lived here didn't make her feel any better. In fact, if she thought about walking her patrol day after day, blithely unaware of the danger lurking a mile or so east of her, she came close to throwing up.

Thankfully, no one freaked out over the expedition to the big house. Mrs. Parsons reacted to Eva's injury about the same as a parent would react to a skinned knee or any other childhood ouchie. Granted, it *had* been minor, but still the result of a stray bullet.

Darnell and Leigh went out to the site upon Harper informing the militia about the gunfight. They discovered one corpse and a bunch of pistol brass scattered around. The dead man hadn't come from Evergreen. Worn clothing, many recent scars, and malnourishment painted a picture of someone who'd been living quite rough for some time. Curiously, Leigh made a joke about the dead guy having a blue flannel shirt on over a bright red tee. It struck Harper as too similar to the man she saw running off chasing the other guy. Blue and red? Both of them? Either they'd found a scavenger's clearing sale somewhere or did it on purpose as some kind of identity. It made her think of the Lawless and their blue sashes. Of course, two guys happening to wear red and blue clothes proved nothing more than two guys liked to dress similarly. She didn't bother to go look at the remains, content to let other people handle it. Unfortunately, she had no idea who the other men were or why the three of them had been so close to Evergreen.

Walter sent word to the south militia station to be on the lookout for potentially violent outsiders. Thus far, no sign of them resurfaced. It didn't seem like those men even knew how close they came to a survivor town. Based on what Leigh and Darnell said, the dead guy looked half starved. If they knew the town existed, why didn't they make contact and ask for food—or try to steal some?

Everything melted into a churning miasma of unease topped with a nuclear cherry.

Friday afternoon, Harper sat with Logan, his younger sister Luisa, Darci, Renee, and Grace outside the house her boyfriend claimed. He'd managed to talk Anne-Marie into letting him take the place diagonally across the yard from Harper's. Carrie owned the house directly east of hers. Logan's place touched backyards with Carrie's. A small dirt-and-gravel road led north from Hilltop Drive to the front of Logan's house, but it didn't really matter. No one used cars much lately. Whenever she wanted to go to see him, she simply cut across the combined yard space between the three houses.

The six of them sat around a folding card table playing Uno. Darci perched baby Piper in her lap and also decided to make things awkward by showing up topless. Renee ended up finding it funny more than anything. Logan played it cool, neither making a show of avoiding looking at her nor staring. Luisa couldn't make eye contact with anyone. Grace didn't seem to care, being too fascinated with the baby to bother with what her mother wore—or didn't.

"Planning to run around like that all day?" asked Renee while pondering her next move at Uno.

"Yep." Darci wagged a stuffed tiger at Piper, who cooed and tried to grab it.

"Okay, I gotta ask. Why?" Luisa asked in a voice slightly above a whisper.

"Lots of reasons." Darci made cute noises at her daughter. "I'm too lazy to keep washing shirts Piper pukes on. It's comfortable. Makes it easier to feed her. Who cares? Society collapsed. Cops aren't gonna give me shit for being comfortable. That whole bullshit about dudes can go shirtless and it's no big deal, but girls aren't allowed to is gone."

Renee whistled. "Wow. Never pictured you going from goth to hippie. I guess we should be thankful you're at least wearing jeans."

"Only because it's a little too cold for full nature girl." Darci wagged her eyebrows.

"Eeeeeeeeeee!" squealed Lorelei—as she emerged from the woods to the north and ran south along the dirt road naked toward Hilltop Drive.

Darci turned her head to follow the running child. "Or maybe it isn't."

"Aww." Renee bit her lip. "I thought she was outgrowing that. She's been good about keeping her clothes on lately."

"Trying to get her to." Harper sighed. "Tegan said I shouldn't flip out and make a big deal about it, so she doesn't develop any psychological issues."

"Bah." Darci waved dismissively. "Just let her be. It's like nature intended. Not like you have to worry CPS will show up and take her away if you don't conform to society's expectations."

Harper smirked. "Technically, I am CPS. If someone's mistreating their kids, the militia will intervene."

"If nature intended us to be naked all the time," said Renee, "we would have fur."

Grace held up one finger. "Technically, we did have fur but evolved out of it once clothing became a thing."

Lorelei came running back the other direction, still making a strange squealing noise somewhere between gleeful delight and alarm. She definitely did not sound scared.

"Yeah, but the militia has better things to worry about than Lore zooming around in her birthday suit." Renee laughed. "I mean, they let Darci do it."

"You aren't scared?" Luisa managed to lift her gaze off the table to make eye contact with Darci. "Someone might attack you?"

"Nope. If a guy's gonna do that, it doesn't matter what the hell a girl's wearing." Darci scowled briefly, then her expression shifted to concern as she watched Lorelei go back the other way. "Is she squealing in delight or horrified?"

"Can't tell." Logan twisted around to look at the child. "Sounds like she's running through a cold lawn sprinkler."

"Doesn't sound hurt." Grace set her Uno cards down and also turned in her chair to look. "Is that blood on her arms and legs?"

"Lore?" called Harper. "You okay?"

The child abruptly stopped running, turned to face them, then dashed straight over to stand beside Harper. She kept her hands up in the distinct pose of a child who'd touched something disgusting and just couldn't even. Dark orangey brown goo spattered all over her face, arms, and legs. The part of her body normally covered by a dress appeared mostly clean, save for some smears of the same substance that evidently soaked through the fabric.

"A sick man frew up on me," gasped Lorelei. "It got all on my dress."

Renee covered her face in both hands. Logan did the same. Luisa gagged.

The Mike Tyson of stink punched Harper right in the nose. The substance splattered on Lorelei smelled more like poop than vomit... though it didn't look like fecal matter.

"Ahh," said Darci in the tone of a Shaolin monk who'd reached enlightenment. "She released a squeal of existential disgust."

Lorelei fidgeted in place, staring at Harper. "I wanna bath!"

"And brain bleach," muttered Renee. "Eww, that smells..."

"Are you sure that's puke?" Logan cringed.

"Yeah." Lorelei pivoted to face him. "It came outta his mouth."

"Copremesis?" Grace blinked.

"Do I want to know what that is?" Renee cringed.

"Sounds like the name of a dark metal band." Darci bounced Piper.

The baby scrunched up her face at the smell wafting off Lorelei.

"Probably not." Logan grimaced.

Grace smoothed her hands down the front of her dress. "Let's just say it is possible for a person to vomit poo. It's a very serious condition."

"Shit coming out your mouth is a serious condition," muttered Darci. "No freakin' kidding. Gah. That's horrible. Are you serious? It can happen?"

"Yeah. It's rare, but possible." Grace ran a finger down the middle of her chest. "Mouth to butt. It's basically one long continuous tube. Certain medical conditions can, uhh, reverse the flow."

Renee dry heaved, as did Luisa. Harper nearly threw up at the mere thought... and the smell radiating from Lorelei did not help.

"But." Grace shook her head. "That isn't what happened here. Whoever this man is, he's in very bad shape. That smells like necrosis. Dead, liquefied flesh. It's not poo."

Renee and Luisa gagged.

"Oh, man." Logan winced. "That poor guy must be in rough shape."

"Bath! Now!" yelled Lorelei. "Pleeeeease!"

"Harp!" shouted Madison in the distance, further north.

She lifted her gaze, peering over Lorelei at her sister and Jonathan sprinting toward them.

Lorelei began muttering, "Bath" repeatedly in a low voice while bouncing on her toes.

"Harp!" Madison waved her arms to keep balance as she skidded to a stop beside them and gasped for breath. "We found a sick guy on the ground by the road. He's not far, and he really needs help."

Renee stood. "I'll get Lore cleaned up. You can go check on that poor guy."

"I'll come with you." Grace set her cards on the table and stood.

"Okay." Harper glanced down at the .45 on her belt. The shotgun was back in her bedroom. She probably wouldn't need it to deal with a man so sick his vomit smelled like death. "Lore, go with Renee. She'll help you get cleaned up. Logan, can you run to the med center and tell them to come out here with the 'ambulance'? Maddie, Jon... one of you wait here for the medics. The other show me where the guy is."

Madison and Jonathan did rock-paper-scissors.

"Yeah. No problem." Logan dropped his cards and jumped to his feet.

Renee scurried around the table to Lorelei.

"No hugs. I'm stinky." The girl raced off toward home.

"Amazing she didn't throw up," whispered Darci.

"She did," deadpanned Madison and Jonathan at the same time.

"We all did." Madison rubbed her belly, almost gagging again.

Jonathan cringed. "At least Lore's mouth was closed when the guy blasted her."

Harper grabbed her stomach. "Stop. Please. Just… show me where he is."

Darci smiled. "You're pretty good at this whole 'crisis managing' thing. You totally sound like a cop."

9

THE LONG SLOW DEATH

MAY 15TH

Harper followed Jonathan north up the dirt road away from Logan's house while Madison waited at the house for the stretcher crew.

The boy cut a straight-line path across the back-and-forth route of a meandering paved road, preferring to go through trees and past houses nestled in the curves of the street. When they reached Sun Creek Drive a couple minutes later, he cut right and followed the road northeast. They didn't have to go far. Mila, Becca, Eva, and Christopher stood in plain sight in the middle of the road, maybe 500 feet away.

Jonathan jogged along, clearly in a hurry.

Harper and Grace followed him. The other kids stood back from something on the side of the road like cops wary of an explosive device. As Harper got closer, the recognizable form of a man in filthy dark grey pants, black work boots, and a plain white T-shirt became apparent, slumped over on the dirt. Relatively short black hair clung in blotches to his head around multiple bald spots. He appeared to be of Hispanic descent, somewhere between thirty and forty. The poor guy also looked ready to die at any minute.

Dark reddish-brown fluid formed a puddle on the ground by his face. A saturated wad of fabric—no doubt Lorelei's dress—lay in the road a short distance away, surrounded by a halo of impact splatter.

Despite being barefoot, Grace didn't hesitate to approach the guy, stepping in some of the mess to do so. Eva and Becca covered their mouths and looked away, whispering 'eww' repeatedly to each other.

Christopher blinked. "That's just nasty."

"What happened?" asked Harper.

"We found him." Christopher pointed. "He was like that the whole time. Lorelei crouched by his face to say hello and he just totally power-washed her with puke."

Jonathan closed his eyes, seemingly fighting off the urge to vomit again. "I think he tried to talk and just hurled instead."

"Where does it hurt?" asked Grace.

"*Si,*" wheezed the man. "*Hay dolor. Mucho dolor.*"

"He said he's in a lot of pain." Christopher crept closer, stopping where the toes of his sneakers came within an inch of the spatter on the road. "I don't know too much Spanish. My grandma spoke it, but I only picked up a little bit."

Grace gingerly looked the man over. "Can you tell him I'm an apprentice doctor?"

"Umm. I don't know how to say that." Christopher scratched his head, then spoke hesitantly, as if unsure he used the correct words. "*La linda chica rubia quiere ser doctora.*"

The man managed a smile and wheezed, "*Si esta es la última cara que veo, estoy lista para morir.*"

"No idea what he just said. Too fast." Christopher flapped his arms. "He looks happy, though. Umm, wait. I don't mean happy... like he's glad you're here."

"What do you think's wrong with him?" asked Harper.

"Umm." Grace opened the buttons on the man's shirt, looked over his sunken chest, then closed the shirt. I don't see any external injuries. "But... this discharge smells so bad. It's probably cancer or internal gangrene resulting in necrosis. Maybe radiation sickness. It's a bit beyond me right now. Reading giant books only helps so much without seeing things for real."

Harper attempted to talk to the man via Christopher translating. The guy didn't understand much English beyond 'hello' and 'byebye'. Unfortunately, the boy's Spanish vocabulary consisted mostly of things his grandmother might've said to him and didn't include many words useful in describing a post-nuclear-war environment.

"They're coming," said Mila—miraculously not making it sound ominous.

Harper glanced away from the man, back down the road.

Madison, Logan, Darnell, and two of the guys from the farm hurried over with one of the town's 'ambulances': a trailer formerly used by a landscaper to haul lawn care equipment. Tying a mattress to it turned it into a medical transport.

Harper stepped back and let Grace direct the guys on how to move the poor guy. They soon got him positioned on the mattress and hurried off toward the medical center. The trailer-bulance didn't handle going off road too well, especially while being pulled by people rather than a pickup truck.

Once the group with the sick man had gone far enough away to be out of earshot, Harper looked at the kids. "If any of you got any of that guy's vomit on you… I want you to go scrub with soap."

"Maybe some specks on my arm." Madison glanced at her right arm. "I was right next to Lore when he exploded."

"Is it gonna make us sick?" asked Mila.

"Not sure, but it can't be healthy." Harper ushered the kids away from the spot.

"What about Lore's dress?" asked Becca.

"Burn it." Mila simulated a flamethrower sound. "It's the only way to be sure."

Harper stifled a laugh. "As much as I hate to waste clothing, I don't think there's any saving it."

"Yeah." Jonathan grimaced. "It's completely soaked. Good thing Renee made her a few."

AFTER CHECKING ON LORELEI AND MAKING SURE MADISON WASHED HER hands—and arms—Harper headed over to the medical center. She found the deathly ill man in one of the treatment rooms with Dr. Khan and Al Gonzalez. Marcie, Ken, Fred, Leigh, and Walter congregated in the hallway outside, soaking up the news. Harper stood unobtrusively off to one side, listening in.

Al happened to be quite fluent in Spanish. He talked to the man while Dr. Khan examined him. Between overhearing their conversation as well as the chatter among the militia people, one heck of a story came out.

The man, Oliverio, had made his way north from Mexico on foot over the past several months. In between periods of being in too much pain to talk, he told Al he'd come from Mexico City and described a horror-on-Earth down there. As far as Oliverio knew, Mexico had not been struck directly by any nuclear weapons. However, a massive wave of fallout from the attack on the US washed over them. Rather than billions being vaporized in an instant, it sounded as though the majority of the population faced a slow, withering death from radiation, starvation, and the violent, chaotic breakdown of an infrastructure wholly unprepared to cope with eighty percent or more of the population needing intensive medical care at the same time.

Oliverio described riots, shootouts between gangs, police, and ordinary citizens. He'd seen thousands of people rotting in the streets, screaming in pain as the skin fell off their bodies. He mumbled something else, then lost consciousness.

Everyone fell quiet, looking at Al expectantly.

"He said it would have been kinder to have the fireballs." Al bowed his head. "They didn't suffer the same kind of EMP problems we did. There are pockets of civilization left where the bodies aren't piled up so high to make a person sick from simply breathing. Many people didn't believe the danger, the fallout. They kept living where the ground killed them."

"It's not still glowing down there, is it?" asked Leigh.

"No. Doubtful." Walter pursed his lips. "At least, it's no worse than anywhere up here where a nuke went off. Probably isn't totally safe yet. Everything I've been able to find about the predicted aftermath of a nuclear war said the largest danger of fallout radiation would abate after five years."

"Only three to go." Ken set his hands on his hips.

"Something like that." Walter exhaled. "Depends on how thick it came down. Lot of variables. The good news is, we're not facing a planet poisoned against human existence for thousands of years. Hollywood took that a little too far. Course, I wouldn't want to go setting up a homestead in any craters, but outside of ground zero points, things ought to be relatively livable pretty soon."

Despite the horrible and depressing tale Oliverio brought with him, his story stirred a current of hope among the militia. No EMP hit Mexico, which meant they had a significantly better chance of maintaining modern technology in whatever pockets of civilization survived the chaos and mass radiation deaths. No guarantees, but it offered a bit of promise for the moderately distant future.

Dr. Khan gave Oliverio a shot, then exited the room.

"How bad is he, doctor?" asked Walter.

"Cancer. It's all throughout his body. I can't say with a hundred percent accuracy what kind of cancer it is, or where it started since our fancy diagnostic equipment—that we didn't even bother moving to this building—consumes more power than our present grid can support. Sadly, there is nothing we can do for him but spare some morphine. Even before, at this advanced stage, it would only have been palliative care. Not that we have any, but chemo would only finish him off at this point." Dr. Khan glanced back at the man. "I can't explain how he managed to walk this far. He's been sick for months, at least for the disease to be this progressed."

"Poor bastard." Ken looked down.

"Is he contagious or radioactive?" asked Walter.

"No." Dr. Khan tugged the door mostly shut. "Neither of those. He is in a great deal of pain and may or may not survive through the night. All we can do now is give him fluids and keep him comfortable."

Al clasped his hands. "Oliverio knows he is going to die soon. He wanted me to tell everyone he apologizes for bringing the burden of burying him here."

Harper had never seen the man before, but the idea that he apologized for being a burden on total strangers in death choked her up. What could possibly have driven him to leave home and wander aimlessly? Did he know months ago he would die soon and want to spare his family the task of burial? Had the poor man intended to die alone somewhere so he wouldn't inconvenience anyone?

Desperately needing to be with her family, Harper slipped away from the medical center and ran home.

AN EXPENDABLE LUXURY

SUNDAY, MAY 17TH

A week after coming face to face with a nuclear warhead, Harper could barely contain her frustration.

She kept going back and forth between setting it aside as an omnipresent dread in the back of her mind and wanting to run over to the town office and start shaking Anne-Marie by the shirt collar until someone did something. The problem simultaneously demanded immediate action as well as careful planning, a true CF as her dad would have said. Mom hated that word, cluster-f. Mostly, she hated the f bomb and all of its variants. Surprisingly, she didn't mind it if Harper or even Madison said 'shit,' 'ass,' or any of the other lesser swear words.

Harper felt like using all of them.

Being frustrated didn't help anyone. Screaming wouldn't be of any use, either. Feeling like a useless teenager with no valuable skills only added to her discontent. So what if she could nail a six-inch target at long range with a shotgun reliably? Yes, she did have a somewhat rare skill that resulted from hours and hours of practice. Unfortunately, marksmanship did no good against a nuclear warhead.

To vent her frustration as well as prepare for the future, she channeled excess energy into archery practice. Wanting to avoid any risk to the kids or other bystanders while working on longer ranged shots, she headed back up to Sun Creek Drive, which offered a nice long straightaway unobstructed by trees, houses, or people. No need to walk all the way over to the spot they found Oliverio. She set up her target at around 120 feet—roughly forty paces from the baseball sized rock she used to mark her shooting position. The nice thing about the compound bow, she didn't have to worry about using up all the ammo. While the weapon might someday break, it would likely outlast the gunpowder in her shotgun shells. This, of course, also depended on how often violence found her.

Target shooting used to be fun when she trained to compete. Training to fight took *all* the joy out of it. Bit by bit, she'd gradually been getting used to the feel of archery. Given the choice, she'd still much prefer to take the Mossberg into a bad situation. However, the day would come when she had no more shells and Dad's semi-automatic shotgun would be reduced to a piece of wall art, something to remember him by.

She fired a few arrows at the target, hitting with all of them though nowhere near a bulls-eye. Nailing a four-foot cube wasn't terribly difficult, way easier than shooting a person taking cover behind a car or wall. She had to get better, had to be able to reliably hit a spot the size of a basketball. At least sticking arrows in the target prevented them from shattering on impact with the pavement or making her run all over the place to collect them.

In between shots, she daydreamed about being a little old lady reading a book in a chair and glancing up at the 'old' shotgun, maybe reminiscing about the 'crazy days' when civilization failed. Her imagination kept shifting gears between a nice future where civilization returned and no one needed to carry guns with them everywhere, and one where her great grandkids, all of six years old, grabbed their crude metal spears and crawled out from the bunker to forage for food.

Who am I kidding? I'm not going to get old. Be shocked if I make it to fifty.

Madison emerged from the woods, hands stuffed in the pockets of her jean shorts. Her kid sister wore a black T-shirt too big for her, bearing the image of a scary looking man in a black leather jacket with white face paint and blackened eyes under the words 'Dimmu Borgir.' Neither Harper nor Madison had the first clue what language it was or what it meant, though she suspected it to be a heavy metal band. They had never heard of them, but despite the creepy dude, clothing had become too precious to refuse for something as silly as 'scary artwork.'

"Hey, Termite. What's up?" Harper lowered the bow and looked back. Her sister being out here alone worried her. "You okay?"

"Yeah. Mostly." Madison punted a small stone off the road into the weeds. "Just the paralyzing terror of a you-know-what being so close."

"Wanted to talk about it? That why you snuck off alone?"

Madison pulled her hands out of her pockets, hugged her, then stepped back, smiling. "I didn't sneak off. Just, you know. Happened to be alone. Beck and Eva are home. Lore's pestering Carrie. Jonathan's drawing."

This happened every now and then. Madison rarely initiated activities, which sometimes resulted in her ending up being the 'fifth wheel' who sat alone until someone noticed she looked bored or sad. At least she no longer worried the other kids avoided her on purpose. At long last, Maddie seemed to have found a good place to be mentally. Without the pressure of all the after-school activities and clubs Mom insisted on, she'd mellowed out in spite of the world burning itself to a crisp.

"Ahh. Okay." Harper pulled her last arrow from the quiver, drew it back, took aim, and released.

Thwunk. It struck within eight inches of center. *Getting there. Now all I have to do is be able to hit that close twice in a row... then on every shot.*

"Can you show me how to shoot that thing?"

"Sure." Harper smiled, her mood instantly better. It had been a while since they had sister time, just the two of them. "Be right back. Grabbing arrows."

Madison waited by the big rock while Harper ran down the road to the target, collected eleven arrows, and returned. She handed the bow to Maddie, gave her a few pointers on how to hold it, how to keep her left elbow stiff, and how to use the sights. Before handing over the first arrow, she ran back to move the target closer, starting her off at fifty feet.

For the first two shots, Harper grasped the bow on top of Madison's hand and aimed for her so she could see approximately how the target looked past the pink and purple aiming posts. Naturally, the first arrow missed entirely and skipped down the street. The second one landed short, bounced off the road, and hit the target at an upward angle, albeit cracked in half.

"Oops. Sorry, I broke one." Madison cringed.

"It'll happen. These are just practice arrows, anyway. I'd never use them in a real situation. We can make arrows way more easily than new gunpowder or bullets."

"Kay." Madison grunted while pulling the string back. "This is tough."

"I won't do what Cliff did."

Madison shifted her gaze to Harper. "What did Cliff do?"

"When I said the bow was hard to pull back, he talked for like half an hour about English longbows."

"Dork," muttered Madison. She shifted her gaze back to the target. "What's an English longbow?"

"A longbow... from England."

"Dork," said Madison. A second later, she let the arrow fly, hitting the target about two inches above the road. "Well, that's progress." She faced Harper. "What, exactly, is a longbow from England and why did he talk about it so much?"

"Medieval weapons, like from *Lord of the Rings*. Just wood and string. They were so hard to pull back, archers had to be like football player huge and many of them suffered bone damage in their shoulders throughout their lives."

"Yeah okay." Madison loaded another arrow. "I totally see how that's relevant."

"He was calling me a wimp for complaining about pulling a compound bow." Harper folded her arms, chuckling. "Or telling me I have it easy thanks to modern technology, so I shouldn't grumble so much."

"Fine, but I'm littler than you, so I can bitch about this being hard."

"Bitch away." Harper laughed.

"Commence complaining in three... two..." Madison fired again. The arrow missed completely, going left of the target—and way down the road.

"You're anticipating letting go and twitching right before you shoot. Just let the string roll off your fingers."

"Okay." Madison nocked another arrow but didn't draw it. "Why did Cliff and Carrie get weird when you told them Jon and Mila slept together?"

Harper bit her lip. "Because..."

"Obviously, saying 'we slept together' means something else to grown-ups than just sharing a bed."

"Yeah. It does." Harper looked down, kicking the toe of her sneaker at the road.

"Can I get the deets?"

Good question. She's eleven. Not a little *kid. Don't need to go into grisly detail, but it's probably not a bad idea to tell her about stuff. Hell, having some facts might protect her.* Harper shifted her jaw side to side, trying without success to figure out if the world had become less safe or paradoxically *safer* for girls. Some random creep catcalled her when she was only twelve. In a world without organized law, she really could just shoot any jerk who used 'hey Red' on her. She wouldn't, though. Not unless they got physical. Merely saying dumb things didn't deserve wasting ammunition. As long as they stayed in Evergreen, the odds of someone being a creep to Madison were significantly lower than if no war happened and they lived in Denver surrounded by thousands of total strangers.

In a small town where everyone basically knew everyone, creeps had short lifespans… unless the entire town was evil. Thankfully, they didn't face such a problem here. Still, though, outsiders could arrive at any time and no one would know what to expect from them.

The world hadn't exactly been an awesome place to be a young girl before the war. *I can't even say the only difference is they don't have to worry about prison now.* She'd once heard that less than ten percent of men who assaulted women ever faced legal consequences. Her parents often said that rape was the only crime where the victim was made to feel more shame than the criminal. At least they didn't have to worry about that anymore. No legal system—or slimy defense lawyers—existed to publicly humiliate any woman or girl who dared come forward about an assault. They also had a Deacon. He'd been in prison for bank robbery at the time of the war, and freely admitted to it, as well as to one of the first things he did when the walls collapsed was to take an axe to the skull of a kid-toucher. If anyone in Evergreen dared lay an unwanted finger on any kid and Deacon found out about it… the militia would probably find something to distract their attention temporarily elsewhere and pretend nothing happened.

Regardless of the safety of a small town, this changed world still offered many different opportunities for Madison to be in danger, and the most likely scenario wouldn't be an outsider or a *Mad Max* leather-clad raider. It would be a boy she knew who wouldn't take no for an answer.

"Okay." Harper exhaled. "Up to you. Do you want to stay innocent a bit longer or know the truth?"

Madison pulled the bowstring back and took aim. "I haven't been innocent since those assholes killed Mom and Dad right in front of us." She loosed the shot, hitting the target two inches away from bullseye. "I can't afford innocence."

Harper blinked. "Holy shit. Nice shot."

Madison's serious expression faltered to an awkward smile. "Total luck. No way could I do that again. I'm not a badass, I just play one on television. Seriously, though. We both had to grow up too fast."

"Fair point. All right." Harper sat on the road.

Madison sat next to her, bow across her lap.

Deep breath. "So, you know how there's girls and boys…"

11

OUTLAWS

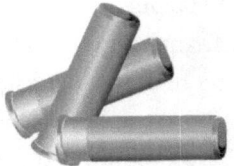

MAY 17TH

After the most hilarious, awkward, and emotional conversation of her life, Harper walked with Madison back to their house. Madison carried the giant foam block target over her head in both hands.

"Eww," said Madison.

Harper chuckled.

"Eww."

Harper snickered.

Madison narrowed her eyes. "Why are you laughing at me?"

"Because I thought boys were 'eww' at your age, and I didn't know one-fiftieth of what you now know about... things. Boys will stop being 'eww' eventually. It'll make sense to you then. Don't waste time worrying about it yet."

"Ugh." Madison sighed at the clouds. "That's not why I'm saying 'eww.'"

"Then why are you saying 'eww'?"

Madison gasped. "They use it for *peeing*. Eww!"

"You know... I never really figured out why it isn't disgusting."

"It *is* disgusting." Madison shivered.

"Trust me, you won't be thinking about what else they do with it when you're old enough."

"Eww." Madison made a face.

As they got closer to home, Jonathan and the other kids came into view, kicking a ball around the grassy area in between the three houses. The instant Madison saw her adopted brother, she burst out laughing.

"Dare I ask?" whispered Harper.

Madison dropped the foam target to hold her mouth shut for a moment. "Umm, it's nothing bad. It's just hilarious that Jon thought if he and Mila only slept in the same bed, a baby would spontaneously appear in nine months. I'm so tempted to borrow a baby and prank him."

"Heh." Harper almost laughed. A burst of happiness came over her so intense she couldn't resist the urge to squish-hug her sister. *Maddie is finally okay. That's her sense of humor back.*

"Love you, too," rasped Madison, overacting a voice as though all the air got crushed out of her.

Harper let go, smiled again, and resumed walking. Madison grabbed the target and hurried along beside her. Once they reached Logan's house, which sat at the northeast corner of their combined backyard spaces, Madison tossed the foam aside and ran over to join the soccer game. Harper kept going to her house. She went inside to put the bow and arrows back in the closet, then took a seat on the little concrete porch to watch the kids and simply enjoy the happy moment.

Sure, they might be mere seconds away from ceasing to exist if that MIRV went off, but the warhead didn't even intrude on her thoughts for now.

Her sister's (admittedly unserious) idea to prank Jonathan with a live baby was so 'pure Madison' she couldn't decide between screaming in joy or breaking down in relieved sobs. Her sister really had become herself again.

Jonathan, Mila, Becca, Eva, Christopher, plus Rylee and Elliot (who must have happened by and decided to join the game) more or less played soccer in the combined backyard space between the three houses. They'd used scraps of white fabric tied on as headbands to identify teams with Jon, Mila, Eva, and Elliot on the headband team. Amazingly, Lorelei kept her dress on, though she didn't appear to care whatsoever for teams... chasing the ball and kicking it toward whatever goal happened to be closer to her at the time. The other kids gave up shouting at her that she technically belonged to the 'no headband' team and tried their best to play around her interference.

With the four-on-three imbalance, Madison ran in to join the team without headbands, making it a four-on-four match (with Lorelei serving as an environmental hazard). The little blonde girl seemed to be having a blast, squeal-giggling almost constantly as she ran around in pursuit of a ball everyone else tried to keep away from her—unless they thought she'd try to kick it into the goal they wanted to score on.

Harper settled into a plastic chair, grateful for the happy time and not having to worry about cooking dinner tonight. Carrie handled it some days, Cliff others, Harper filling in whenever needed. Eva jogged by, lifting her shirt up to wipe sweat off her face. The eleven-year-old's ribs looked too prominent, seeming even more so in broad daylight from the front than the other day when she'd taken a glass shard to the back. The poor kid had been near starved in the Army camp at Eldorado Springs. She'd gained weight since then, but seemed to have lost some of it. To Harper, she appeared *too* skinny. Maybe she'd been this thin the whole time, and it just hadn't been noticeable under a shirt, but Harper couldn't shake the worry Mrs. Parsons might be having emotional problems and neglecting her. Eva finished wiping her face, let the shirt fall back over her stomach, and raced after the ball, seeming as happy and into the game as any other kid there... except for Lorelei.

Lore was an endless font of giggles. No kid in Evergreen could compete with her for happiness.

Harper decided to invite Eva to have dinner with them whenever she wanted to, and also to go check on Mrs. Parsons soon.

The idea barely finished crossing her mind when a burst of gunfire went off in the distance to her left. All the kids dove to the ground, Rylee clinging to the soccer ball. Madison scowled at the gunfire the way she used to make faces at Mom whenever she nagged her to do some chore in the middle of watching a movie or playing a video game.

A firecracker like quality to the shooting put the likely location of the violence far enough to the west that Harper didn't feel the kids faced immediate danger. After another barrage, an air horn blast, one long blart, the 911 signal, rang out.

No shit there's an emergency. Harper exhaled hard. "Guys, go inside and stay low until the all clear."

Carrie came running out the back door of her house, carrying a hunting rifle. "Kids, over here. Harper's gotta go help out."

The stream of children running for the house swerved and headed for Carrie's place instead.

"Stay safe and kick ass," yelled Madison as she ran by.

Harper raced to the bedroom, grabbed the Mossberg and her hip bag with extra shells, then sprinted out the front door to the bicycle leaning against the house. Gunfire continued coming from the west along with another wave of air horn calls. She slung the shotgun across her back on its strap, jumped on the bike, and zoomed down Hilltop Drive toward Route 74.

The shooting sounded as if it came from southwest of the quartermaster's building, probably all the way at the end of Elk View Drive, basically the western edge of town. The land farther west from there was more or less all forest for a good swath.

Harper pedaled hard, standing on the bike. Darnell and Private Hooper flew down Route 74 from her right, also on mountain bikes. They passed the end of Hilltop Drive before Harper reached the end and turned left to chase after them. Private Hooper and his superior, Sergeant Clarke, had come up from the Army camp at Eldorado Springs as part of a trade arrangement. The Army helped out the militia by giving them the services of two soldiers in exchange for whatever food could be spared from the farm. It probably meant something both men much preferred to be here than at the camp.

She rode straight over the scrub grass at the end of Hilltop Drive, powering over the berms and up onto Route 74. She kept going straight across the highway, up another hill, then swerved left to follow the street into a small pocket of residential housing. These buildings housed people who didn't have kids young enough to need school, the earliest arrivals to Evergreen after the war. Walter lived in one of the larger houses on Elk View, which he shared with a few other guys.

She trailed Darnell and Hooper around a corner where the street intersected Elk view, following it to the right. Going straight west through trees, backyards, and around houses wouldn't be faster on a bike. At this distance, voices joined in the gunfire. Some screamed in panic, some shouted commands, and a few crazy ones whooped and hollered like morons.

What the hell was that?

A moment later, they rounded a leftward curve near where she remembered Elk View coming to a dead end. Cliff, Roy, Sadie, and Deacon took cover behind a house on Harper's right, snapping off shots from their rifles down a small spur of road leading straight west. The pavement ended after maybe 200 feet, where it met a hiking trail going into the forest.

Darnell and Private Hooper ditched their bikes and ran up behind the other militia. Harper did the same, five seconds later. She swung the Mossberg off her back into a ready grip. Since the guys had all collected on the left side of the house closest to the small spur road, she went the other way, intending to cover their flank in case the enemy decided to sneak around the house and surprise them.

She pressed her shoulder against the house, took a breath, then chanced a quick peek around the corner to the west, scanning for anything moving. The woods appeared empty and quiet, so she held still, aiming generally at the opposite corner of the house, ready to acquire and shoot at anything threatening.

"Clear," said Cliff. "Moving up."

Harper swallowed a bit of saliva. As the other militia migrated out from behind the house and made their way down the small spur road, she went forward, circling around the house on the north side. Every nerve, every sense she possessed raced on high alert, no thought or emotion in her head other than 'stay alert; identify before shooting.'

When she reached the end of the house, she spotted a man wearing bright red and blue clothes running away in the woods. She took aim, but... too far away, too many trees between them for her to waste buckshot. One of the other militia—she couldn't tell who with a house in the way—fired a few 5.56 rounds after the man, but missed. Scraps of bark and splinters went flying off a tree near the man, who howled in fear and dove out of sight.

Whoa. Since when did we adopt a 'no survivors' policy?

"Clear," echoed Roy. "Stay alert, but I think they had enough."

Harper lowered her shotgun—a little—and made her way south, past the west face of the house, to where everyone else congregated at the end of the road spur.

Three unfamiliar men lay dead and bleeding amid armloads of stuff, mostly vegetables or other food. Their clothes looked like something from a 1980s punk music video, clearly trying to match in terms of bright red and blue however they could. One man had fallen thirty feet down the hiking trail. The other two didn't make it off the road. The two close enough for her to see had been armed with a Remington hunting rifle and an M1 Garand.

A sense of being horrified that her militia gunned down some guys just looking for food began to rise in the back of her mind, but evaporated as soon as she turned to look east. A fiftyish woman, two boys about seventeen or so, and several older men gathered around the bodies of their relatives or friends. She counted four dead, at least out in plain sight, and five or so wounded, mostly older residents who would be home in the middle of the day as opposed to working on the farm.

Deacon and Roy went into the woods after the attackers.

Harper stood there, not entirely sure what to do with herself. While grateful she hadn't needed to kill anyone, she couldn't deny anger toward the kind of people who could open fire on a bunch of sweet older folks who'd have likely been happy to share food if asked.

Cliff approached Mr. Hedley, the only non-militia local in sight not presently in the middle of a grief-stricken breakdown. The seventy-one-year-old looked like a skinny version of 'hipster Santa Claus' to Harper with his short hair, long, narrow white beard, and suspenders. However, his M4 rifle wasn't standard North Pole issue. While the militia rounded up military grade weapons for use defending Evergreen, they'd evidently let him keep that one.

Harper decided to add herself to the conversation, if only because it gave her an excuse not to look at dead bodies. "Are you okay, Mr. Hedley?"

"Fah. You're old enough ta pick up a rifle, you're old enough ta call me Wilkins." The elder nodded at her. "I'm fine, just pissed off."

"What happened?" asked Cliff.

"Them fools showed up and started kickin' in doors, grabbin' stuff, and makin' a right mess. Didn't take long for shoutin' and cussin' to turn ta shootin' and more cussin'. Ada went after one with her pan and the sumbich shot her. Bastards weren't ready for me, though. Ain't nothin' deadlier n' an old man with a gun who don't got much time left and don't much care."

Cliff almost chuckled, but forced a serious face back on. "How many did you see?"

"Six. Maybe seven. Two dead in the house. Rest o' them bastards hauled ass. You an' Roy got here pretty quick. Ya saw the rest."

Deadlier than an old man who doesn't care if he dies... Harper sighed out her nose, trying not to feel bad for him. Wilkins didn't seem suicidal, only old-school. The sort of 'women and children first' kind of old school guy who'd think it better an old man like him dies to protect younger people who had more time left.

Men from the farm, along with Annapurna, Dennis Prosser, and Tegan arrived with two 'ambulances.' Harper and Cliff left Wilkins Hedley to stand watch and helped out moving the wounded onto the former landscape trailers. Tegan declared Betsy Petersen too injured to move and got to work on the sixty-something woman right where she'd fallen on her porch.

As the farm workers pulled the ambulance trailers away as fast as they could safely go, Harper turned to stare west into the trees.

Roy Ellis stepped up beside her. She hadn't noticed him return in the midst of loading wounded. "That look you're wearing. Don't tell me you're disappointed the gunfight ended before you got here?"

"No. I'm disappointed this bullshit happens at all." Harper scowled. "Where do they keep coming from?"

"All over." Roy waved dismissively. "Ex-cons, paranoid militia nutjobs, desperate survivors who don't trust outsiders, random psychos... the whole lot. We're basically in the Wild West all over again."

She glanced down to ensure the Mossberg's safety was on, then slung the shotgun over her shoulder. "Think they'll come back?"

"I suppose anything is possible. We don't know much about them yet." Roy spat to the side. "Looks like they're a gang of some kind. All wearing the same colors. No telling if all of them showed up or if we just met a scouting team. They didn't seem organized. No plan. Just a bunch of idiots running into a town to raid it."

"Ugh." Harper set her hands on her hips. "Great. Just what we need. As if we didn't already have enough doom hanging over our heads. Same blue and red like the guys who started shooting east of the lake the other day. Think we have another gang to worry about on top of the Lawless now?"

"Seems." He patted her shoulder. "Wouldn't worry too much about these guys. They practically shit themselves when old Wilk opened up on them. Don't think they expected resistance, or at least as much as they got."

"They killed four people... probably more than that." Harper glanced over at the flurry of activity on the porch. "Betsy doesn't look too good."

Roy glanced down. "Didn't say they weren't a threat. Said they were idiots and we don't need to panic. Only time they hit anyone is if they were close enough to punch them. Just shooting wild. That guy right there with the Remington looked like he forgot how to work the bolt in the heat of a gunfight. If the rest of them ever come back, keep your head on and keep distance. Use cover. I kinda doubt they'll be back after having their whole squad mostly taken out by one old man... but if they do, it probably won't be a frontal assault in the daytime again."

"Okay." Harper scanned the woods. "I sense increased patrols in our future."

"Hah." He winked. "Didn't know you were psychic."

12

NOT QUITE FUTUREPROOF

TUESDAY, MAY 19TH

T he morning's militia briefing went almost exactly as Harper expected, with Walter assigning extra patrols along the town's western border. Most everyone believed the raiders' primary goal had been food. After going over all the witness accounts, it seemed as though they attempted to intimidate the older residents into letting them loot and run off, and hadn't been prepared for anyone standing up to them. They shot Ada Gardner, a sixty-six-year-old grandmother, after she bonked one over the head with a pot, then killed Ellery Dominguez and Shirley Addison, who happened to be nearby at the time, seemingly out of spite.

Perhaps they hoped that such a show of brutality would make everyone give up and back off, but it had the reverse effect. Old Wilkins Hedley charged at them, shouting and firing, dropping the men who killed Ada and Shirley where they stood and chasing the others out into the street. The raiders took cover behind houses, dead cars, and one brick porch, engaging in a gunfight with Wilkins for a minute or two until Roy and Cliff—who patrolled quite close to that area—arrived and joined in. Evidently realizing they were about to be severely outnumbered, the remaining five raiders broke cover and hauled ass, only two making it away into the forest alive.

Roy and Deacon followed them enough to make sure they didn't simply wait nearby to come back as soon as the heat died down. They didn't make contact with them nor see any signs of a campsite.

Harper escaped any additional patrol detail. Walter didn't say anything to her about why. She assumed because she patrolled the area where most of the families with children lived and they wanted her there since the residents were used to and trusted her. They also added Josh Webb and Tyreek Dawson to her sector, to pick up patrol after her shift ended. Ken or Marcie would join Harper for the next week or two, ensuring that anyone on patrol had at least one partner. If the raiders didn't show up again within that time, things would go back to normal.

The worst part of the briefing came when Marcie Chapman brought up the 'what if' of those raiders discovering the warhead. Specifically, she worried they might try to threaten the town into giving them food or they'd set off the bomb. Roy didn't think it a likely scenario, citing their idiocy. If they could even tell what the thing was, he doubted they would be able to set it off. Even if they could somehow find a way to set it off, doing so would incinerate them, too. Dennis Prosser said if they were as dumb as Roy believed, they might not realize it would kill them as well. Or worse, they might be desperate enough not to care.

This led to debate going around as to whether or not the militia should shift from a purely defensive force to sending out teams on 'hunt and kill' missions looking for the rest of them. Ultimately, Walter decided against that for now.

Since someone else brought up the warhead, Harper asked about progress on disposal. Unfortunately, no decision had yet been made. Bringing it to a mine still sat at the top of the list of good ideas. Problem being, no one really felt comfortable disturbing the device, worried that moving it might make it go off. Cliff attempted to reassure everyone on the militia that it would not spontaneously detonate simply from being jostled around in transit. It had already survived impact with the ground at several hundred miles per hour, then been moved onto a pickup truck and transported to the house where it sat ever since.

That it presented a radiation hazard simply to be near it did not exactly encourage people to undertake transporting it anywhere. Sadie brought up the idea of going to nearby military installations or maybe power plants to see if any protective clothing might have been left behind. Her suggestion started to gain momentum until Private Hooper said military bases likely would have been targeted for direct strikes.

So, again, nothing had been done about the warhead other than more talking.

She paused outside the HQ building to let a heavy sigh go. *Yay. Society is coming back. Government just talks without doing anything.*

In fairness, a little progress happened. Scouting teams had been going to check the viability of some abandoned mines in the area. Technically, *any* mine counted as abandoned now, not only the really old ones. They searched for a site that met two ideal parameters: deep enough tunnels to contain a blast and an opening large enough to accept the entire pickup truck.

"Harper," called a woman over a loud rattling.

She turned to look.

Elizabeth Trujillo, the town quartermaster, approached pushing a shopping cart loaded with random pieces of metal scrap, mechanical parts, and wire spools.

"Morning," said Harper. "What's up?"

"Wondering if you could do me a small favor." Elizabeth stopped beside her, quieting the noisy cart. "Since you're already just walking around all day,"—she winked—"I was hoping you might be willing to run this stuff up to Jeanette. That's pretty close to where you're going, right?"

Jeanette Ortiz, the town's senior electrician, had appropriated some tennis courts roughly a thousand feet north of Hilltop Drive and a short distance south of the former public works garage for the solar panel farm. Not like anyone had interest in playing tennis nowadays.

The electrical team also took over the public works garage. Proximity explained why Harper's house enjoyed reasonably strong, and reasonably steady electrical power. The focus hadn't been on giving power to the militia's homes, rather the medical center in the former La Plaza Office Park professional building. They just got lucky happening to be on the same circuit of existing wiring.

"I go a bit farther north for patrol, but I go right past it to get there." She smiled. "Sure, I can run this over to Jeanette on my way."

"Thanks." Elizabeth fist bumped her. "Be careful out there, okay?"

"Always."

They chatted for a little while, mostly Elizabeth asking after the babies and Carrie. Harper passed along that Owen and Emmett appeared to be recovering from whatever sickness they had. Elizabeth also assumed it an ordinary cold. Harper almost asked her if she knew whether or not Mrs. Parsons picked up food regularly, but decided against starting rumors. Better she pull Eva aside somewhere they could have a private conversation. She'd known Madison's friend since before the war, and the girl didn't seem to be acting like her mother neglected her intentionally. Could be she's worried and not eating as much as she should despite having food available. Or, maybe the kid had become so active running around with her friends she burned more energy than took in.

Worrying about Eva seeming a bit too skinny gave Harper something to focus on besides a nuclear bomb she could do nothing about.

She said farewell to Elizabeth after assuring her the babies were doing well, then pushed the surprisingly heavy load down the road from the quartermaster building. A shopping cart loaded with metal and mechanical junk kept her on paved roads. She went left along Bergen Peak drive, taking it to the intersection by the bus barrier. The easiest route would be to go straight across 74 onto Lewis Ridge Road and follow it to the municipal garage. Odds were, Jeanette wanted this stuff to make more windmill generators, so it would end up at the garage anyway rather than the tennis courts south of there.

Cameron and Sadie waved from the top of the buses as Harper

went by. She returned the wave, continuing east across the highway and down the road. Two more tennis courts sat to her right, near the old Wendy's. They, too, had been repurposed to solar panel farms as the combination of flat open space and tall surrounding fence made for the ideal solar farm location. Jeanette's people spent months going around the unoccupied parts of town and scavenging panels off the roofs of homes no one lived in anymore.

Harper had no idea how long panels would last, but it definitely wouldn't be forever. The change to wind generation sounded like a better idea. While a mechanical generator attached to a big fan would probably wear out and break more quickly than a solar panel, fixing them and making new ones was significantly easier. No one in town, or perhaps the entire world now, had the expertise, materials, and equipment needed to make new solar panels.

The municipal garage building came into view up ahead. A nice brown wooden fence—like might be around someone's backyard, ran along the edge of the road. The roof of the garage building rose about half a story over the level of the road she walked on. She figured the fence existed more to keep people from falling down the fairly steep hill on the other side rather than for security. Brownish grey metal roofing and a long, narrow strip of windows along the top of the garage made her imagine a giant robot peeking its head over the hill.

Fourteen or so windmills set up in the lot around the garage gave off creaks, squeaks, and whirring noises. Voices from the electrical team echoed inside the building over the occasional bit of hammering.

A few hundred feet of walking later, the wooden fence to her right changed to a multicolored stone wall that curved inward toward the property gate. Harper leaned back, fighting gravity trying to pull the cart down the hill into the lot. Too late, she realized she'd become a spaceship that strayed too close to the event horizon of a black hole. The hill would claim the shopping cart no matter what she did as she lacked the strength and body mass to hold it back. Harper ended up skidding along on her sneakers as the weight of the scrap metal and other junk pulled her along. She did manage to keep it from accelerating so fast it careened into one of the windmills set up in what used to be a giant parking area for the town's fleet of street maintenance vehicles.

A couple of guys who happened to be out working on the windmills came running over and helped her drag the cart to a stop. The black guy looked about twenty and grinned at her in a way like he tried not to laugh. His associate, a short but muscular man with a big 'Mario mustache' chuckled and said something in Spanish.

"Sorry… what?" asked Harper.

"Close call," said the older guy.

"Oh. Yeah." Harper stared at the cart. "It didn't really seem all that heavy until I started going downhill."

"Heh. Ain't that always the way." The younger guy grinned. "Everything's fine 'til it goes downhill. What's all dis?"

"Elizabeth sent it over. Said Jeanette's expecting it?"

"More parts for the generators." The older man grabbed a spindle of copper wire. "Need way more than this, but every bit helps."

Before Harper could reply, a heavy thudding *boom* shook the whole garage. Both men twitched. Harper dove to the ground. Seconds later, smoke began leaking from one of the open windows near the warehouse roof. Upon realizing something exploded and no one attacked them with a cannon, she scrambled to her feet and ran toward the building. The men followed.

Multiple voices shouted inside, asking what blew up, who did what, and various forms of 'oh shit.'

Harper skidded to a stop in one of the big, open garage doors. Six people, including Jeanette, had formed a circle around a scrawny adolescent boy who lay flat on his back, arms and legs out in an X. A few feet away from him, a panel on a big electrical cabinet hung open. One of the circuit breakers inside appeared to be on fire. Smoke, or perhaps steam, wafted up from the boy's afro. It took Harper a second or three to recognize Terrence (formerly T-Bone).

"Dammit." Jeanette crossed her arms, her expression simultaneously angry and horrified. "I told him to make sure the shit was off before he touched anything."

Shock. His heart stopped. Harper bolted over to him. *He's not gone just yet.*

She slid to a halt on her knees and checked for a pulse, pressing her fingers into the fever-hot skin of his neck. No pulse, but she dismissed it as her doing it wrong or being in too much of a hurry. Without wasting another second, she started rescue breathing and chest compressions.

In the midst of her third set of rescue breaths, Terrence opened his eyes.

Overjoyed, Harper pushed herself up away from his face and again checked his neck for a pulse. That time, she felt one.

He coughed, then peered blearily up at her. "Bet that's the first time you kissed a black guy."

A chorus of relieved noises and a few whistles came from the ring of people surrounding them.

"Jesus," muttered Jeanette. "I thought he was dead."

Harper grinned at him. "You're not a *guy* yet. What are you, twelve?"

"Might be thirteen. What day is it?" Terrence struggled to sit up.

She rested her hand on his shoulder. "Don't. We gotta get you to the doctor."

"Cool. Cool. I'm just gonna lay here then."

"Where does it hurt?" asked Harper.

"Hand, mostly. Arm."

The index and ring fingers of his right hand looked a bit too thick, likely swollen. Fortunately, it didn't seem as if he'd been hit with extreme voltage. She didn't see serious burns. This was, after all, only windmill and solar power. Still, it apparently packed enough of a wallop to be potentially fatal.

Jeanette dragged a large cart over, similar to the ones people used to move lumber around at Home Depot. After loading Terrence on it, Harper, Jeanette, and a guy named Bill Gonsalves, who used to work for a power company in West Denver, hurried him out the door, pushing the cart down the road toward Route 74.

"Stay awake, okay?" asked Harper.

"I ain't that messed up." Terrence chuckled. "Feel dizzy and like the shit got kicked out of me, but I ain't sleepy. Sorry, Miss Ortiz. Thought I hit the switch first."

"It's okay, Terrence. We'll go over it again when you're ready." Jeanette patted him on the hand. "I'd much rather you do things slowly and safely rather than rush and… something happens."

Upon arrival at the medical center, they lifted Terrence—not a difficult task as he remained rail thin—and carried him inside. Lumber carts did not handle wheelchair ramps terribly well.

Jeanette told Dr. Khan the boy accidentally completed a circuit with his hand in a capacitor cabinet and went flying about ten feet. Everyone thought he'd been killed instantly, mostly due to the tremendously loud boom and the smoke coming off his hair.

Harper bit her lip. "I didn't feel a pulse at first but did CPR and stuff and he woke up. I… probably just missed it."

Terrence, stretched out on the exam table, reached up and squeezed her hand. The look on his face said he totally believed she'd brought him back from the dead. Maybe she did. Maybe she didn't. Either way, it took everything she had not to freak out.

"How long was he unconscious?" Dr. Khan lifted the boy's shirt and listened to his heart with a stethoscope.

"Uhh." Harper fidgeted. "I got to him maybe fifteen to twenty seconds after the bang. One set of rescue breaths, one set of chest compressions, two more breath sets and he woke up."

The doctor nodded once, listened for a moment, then let the stethoscope drop against his chest. "It doesn't take a whole lot of current to stop a heart. The good news is, the rhythm sounds normal now."

"Did she bring me back?" whispered Terrence.

"It's possible." The doctor thumbed the boy's right eye open wider and peered into it. "The shock might have stunned your heart into an abnormal cadence that may or may not have resolved by itself. It's also possible it did stop and she gave it a nudge."

Harper covered her face in both hands. How could *saving* a life get her choked up so much more than killing people? She hadn't even taken the CPR class at school seriously. Just something to do because it sounded noble and fun. She never expected to actually need it. Thankfully, Roy had been conducting refresher training with the militia. She probably learned more from him than the gym teacher.

"Cool. Cool." Terrence exhaled. "Far as I care, she kept me alive. Ain't know what to say but thanks. Don't seem enough."

"It's fine," stammered Harper. "Just glad you're okay."

Not too long ago, she'd caught Terrence and his two friends trying to break into the quartermaster's to steal food. They'd walked all the way to Colorado from like Chicago or something with a small group that dwindled along the way until only the three boys remained. Since they'd only been kids trying to survive, the town welcomed them rather than treated them like raiders or thieves. She and Terrence had one thing in common—the Lawless killed their parents. In his case, just his mom.

She stood there, holding his hand for a while as the doctor and Jeanette talked. Dr. Khan recommended the boy get a couple days of bed rest and drink plenty of water. The shock seemed to have hit a 'goldilocks range,' being powerful enough to mess with his heart but not so potent as to char the skin off his fingers. He did have some blackening at the tips, but it would heal.

In a crazy twist of fate worthy of a Hallmark movie, Katherine Bowden ended up taking Terrence and his two friends in. Her biological son, Noah, who turned fourteen a few weeks ago, had become best friends with the three boys who broke into their house and stole food and a handgun. Upon learning a trio of desperate kids did it—and not some crazy wasteland wanderer—Katherine went from frightened to full 'mom mode.' She had a house big enough for four teenage boys, so it worked out.

Katherine arrived, somewhat out of breath, about twenty minutes after they got Terrence to the medical center. She remained upset, but did calm down quite a bit when she saw him awake and smiling.

Wanting to give them some privacy and evade any more embarrassing praise, Harper took the opportunity to slip out into the hallway. Unless raiders attacked the medical center, she couldn't spend much more time not being out at her patrol area.

Jeanette happened to be heading for the door at the same time. They fell in step with each other on the way up Route 74.

"Nice work, kid."

Harper bit her lip. "Thanks. I feel obligated to say I'm eighteen and not a kid."

"You're a kid." Jeanette chuckled. "To someone my age, anyway."

"Oh, come on. You're what, thirty?" Harper rolled her eyes. "That's not old."

"You either have a great memory or that's a good guess." Jeanette smiled. "I feel forty."

"We all do… except maybe the little ones." Harper kicked a pebble off the road. "How's it going with the power? Stable? Or… should we get ready for going full 1800s."

Jeanette laughed. "I wouldn't go nuts making candles just yet. Migrating over to windmills is definitely going to keep us electrified more reliably than the panels. Won't be as stable as the way things were before, but we should at least have enough juice to run the big fridges for years."

"Cool. At least until they crap out."

"No worries." Jeanette twirled her hand around in a 'no big deal' gesture. "We'll just head over to Walmart and get new ones when they die. Oh… wait." She snapped her fingers in fake disappointment. "Guess we won't."

Harper cringed. "Umm. What are we going to do when the freezers and refrigerators stop working?"

"Not gonna be too much we *can* do except, I suppose, make sure there aren't too many leftovers." Jeanette wagged her eyebrows. "Probably go really old school at that point. Hand out stuff that won't spoil like vegetables. Meat, fish, or anything else'll probably wind up being community cookouts. If we lose the ability to put ninety percent of a deer on ice, we're going to have to eat all of it in one sitting. That's gonna take more than one or two families. Suppose there's making the meat into jerky, but we don't have that much salt."

"Yeah." Harper shook her head, unsure if she should laugh or be worried. "The future is sounding weirder and weirder."

13

THE SADS

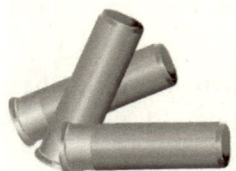

MAY 19TH, EARLY EVENING

The first phase of Harper's plan worked perfectly.

She'd invited Becca and Eva over for dinner, an event that happened somewhat often before the world exploded. Of course, back then, the invitations included Melissa as well. No one had any idea what happened to Madison's other friend. Having zero information left the door open for hope at least.

Harper played it casual, going through the motions of a normal dinner with the family. She had, however, confided in Cliff, Renee, and Carrie that Eva looked too thin and worried there might be some problems going on at home for her. No one presently in Evergreen other than Eva and Harper saw Mrs. Parsons at the Eldorado Springs camp—not even Darci, despite her having lived at the camp for a while. The poor woman had it rough, to say the least. She'd given up on life. Whether or not she hadn't killed herself because she had Eva to take care of, or she lacked the motivation to do it, Harper couldn't say. Right after she found them, Harper worried the woman might hurt herself once they got to Evergreen and felt Eva would be safe there without her. But... so far, she hadn't.

Mrs. Parsons didn't seem happy, but she no longer made random comments about how life had no purpose or meaning.

Tegan suspected Eva's mom had some issues, mostly from what she said about the baby. While no one could expect a woman to be all rainbows and unicorns about a baby conceived from rape, not even wanting to see or touch her own child after the birth raised some red flags.

Attitude wise, Eva seemed normal, or as normal as any kid could be after living through a nuclear war. She had become a bit clingier than before toward Madison and Becca, her friends from a sane world. No surprise there.

Harper watched the girls during dinner, paying specific attention to Eva. She ate, but not enthusiastically. Madison, having evidently overheard her talking to Cliff and Carrie, urged her to finish her portion. It didn't take much prodding.

After dinner, the kids began to filter outside to play in the last hour or so of daylight. Harper sat on the tiny back porch—basically a block of concrete with steps.

When Eva went by, she tapped the girl on the arm. "Hey, can I talk to you for a sec?"

"I didn't do it!" Eva stopped short, wide-eyed.

Harper chuckled. "You're not in trouble. Just want to make sure everything's okay."

"Oh." Eva looked down, twisting her big toe into the dirt. "Why?"

"Are you getting enough to eat?"

"Yeah." Eva rubbed one hand up and down her arm. "Sorry."

"Why are you apologizing?"

"I know you think I'm too skinny." Eva sank to sit on the lowest step. "I don't finish my dinner all the time. It's not my mom."

Eep. Guess I'm not the first person to ask about this. "Is your mom okay?"

"Kinda. She's sad all the time. I am too. I miss my dad."

"I'd love to tell you it gets easier, but it doesn't. Just... with time, it dulls. Only hurts when you think about it."

"Yeah." Eva looked up, pulled her mouse-brown hair out of her eyes, and sighed. "I'm not sad about the war. I mean, well... I am, but it's not why I'm sometimes not hungry. It happened and we can't change it. I'm sad because Mom is sad and I don't know how to fix her."

Aww. Harper let out a heavy breath. "Your mom loves you, even if she might not say it out loud so often."

"She kinda does." Eva reached down to tease her fingers at the grass between her feet. "Say it out loud, I mean. She's mad at a baby. How can someone be mad at a baby? It's too little to do anything bad."

"Eva, look at me."

The girl lifted her gaze to meet Harper's.

"You know she's not really angry with the baby."

Eva sighed. "Yeah. I know what happened. She's mad at the man who hurt her. The baby reminds her of everything... even me being so skinny cause we had no food."

"You're getting thin again."

Eva stared down.

"I wish I knew how to fix your mom. I have some ideas, but they might not work." Harper gave Eva's hand a squeeze. "I do know that if you get sick, it's going to make her feel worse."

"Yeah, I guess. How do you eat when you're sad? I just... don't feel hungry."

"You could try being angry with the man who hurt your mom."

Eva shrugged. "Why? They shot him already."

"Just to trick your stomach." Harper grinned. "Tell your mom you're worried about her. Make sure she knows you're happy she's here to take care of you."

"Okay." Eva sighed. "I'll try. And I'll try to eat all the food."

"Don't eat *all* of it." Harper winked. "Leave some for the rest of us."

Eva started to roll her eyes, but ended up almost smiling. "Dork."

"Yep. I am a dork."

"Harp?" Eva stood. "Thanks for being worried about me, too."

"You bet." Harper hugged her. "If you ever need to talk about anything, I'm here, okay?"

"Kay."

Harper smiled. "Okay. Go on and play before you run out of daytime."

14

PITCHING IN

THURSDAY, MAY 21ST

Learning that Mrs. Parsons hadn't been underfeeding Eva or neglecting her eased more weight off Harper's mind than she realized the worry caused. Before starting her patrol shift, Harper stopped in to talk to Mrs. Parsons to get a feel for her mental state.

While by no means even close to a psychiatrist, she felt her duty to the town as part of the militia went beyond simply being around in case bad guys needed to be shot. She often did everything from helping an overwhelmed parent take care of little kids for a while to running errands, attempting to pitch in with home repairs, or whatever didn't feel too far out of her skill set. She would not, for example, attempt to work on a fuse box or windmill generator.

Eva's mother did seem depressed. Harper hadn't exactly spent a lot of time around her in the world before the war. The mother of her little sister's friend took up minimal space in her thoughts back then. However, she'd seen the woman enough to notice she was definitely less animated and tended to stare at the floor all the time. For the most part, she seemed okay, merely sad. Nothing came up in their brief conversation to make Harper worried to the point of doing anything.

As Harper went to leave, Mrs. Parsons raised a hand. "Harper?"

"Hmm?" She stopped halfway out the door to look back.

"I... umm." Mrs. Parsons exhaled hard, then fidgeted, looking around as if she'd misplaced her phone. "We're almost out of food. I've been meaning to, well... would you mind going with me?"

The woman appeared frightened to leave the house and ashamed to admit it.

Oh, wow... Eva was covering for her mom. She's not too sad to eat. They really don't have enough food. Or maybe it's both.

"Sure. Happy to. Whenever you need."

Mrs. Parsons managed a nervous smile. It took her a minute or five to summon the nerve to go outside. Harper swung the Mossberg off her back to carry it in a ready position. At that, Mrs. Parsons calmed visibly.

They walked down the road in silence for a few minutes, turned at the intersection, and headed toward Route 74.

"You must think I'm a bit foolish. Old enough to be your mother and here I am hiding behind you for protection."

"I understand. And no, you're not foolish." Harper walked at an unhurried pace, watching the woods on either side of the road.

Mrs. Parsons kept quiet for a moment. "Well, maybe I think I'm foolish. But I still can't do it."

"Do what?" Harper squeezed her jaw.

"Just go places alone."

"What you went through... it's hard to cope with." Harper gave a somber chuckle. "Sometimes, I wonder how I'm not hiding under my bed all day long."

"Oh, dear. Did someone...?"

"No, thankfully. Not for lack of trying, though. Had guys try to grab me a few times." She held up the Mossberg. "If I didn't have this..."

"Still, it couldn't have been easy to shoot people. I..." Mrs. Parsons fidgeted at a jade-and-bronze bracelet around her left wrist. "Weren't you the kid who couldn't step on bugs? I remember Eva saying something about that. She couldn't believe you picked up an insect with your bare hand."

"Yeah. Is it psychotic that I feel worse about killing bugs than shooting bad guys?" Harper glanced over at her. "I mean… it took me too long to get over that. My dad is dead because I was such a wimp."

Mrs. Parsons raised both eyebrows, what little color she had in her face drained. "What happened, hon?"

On the rest of the walk to the quartermasters, Harper explained about her first two months after the bombs… and the day the Lawless found them. Mrs. Parsons covered her mouth and gasped when she learned Harper and Madison witnessed both of their parents killed. "… and it just kinda all became about keeping Maddie safe. She didn't deserve any of what happened. I figured I'd already broken, killed people. She's still a kid so, whatever I had to do to make sure she was safe, I convinced myself to do it."

"I should be stronger for Eva, but I've never touched a gun."

They trudged up the hill off Route 74, crossed the other road, then entered the quartermaster's building. "You don't need a gun to be there for your daughter. You just need to be there for her. As long as you don't feel comfortable outside, please just ask me to walk with you. I don't mind."

"Thank you. Your parents would be so proud of you."

Harper looked down, but smiled. *Yeah, I guess they would be.*

FIFTEEN MINUTES LATER, THEY LEFT THE QUARTERMASTER'S WITH MRS. Parson's allotment of food for the week and headed up Route 74, taking the easiest path north.

The door to the medical center opened. Annapurna backed out, pulling one end of a legit stretcher like from a real ambulance. Harper slowed to watch, curious who'd be coming *out* on a stretcher. When the opposite end came into view, she realized the person had to be dead because they'd been wrapped completely in fabric, covering the head and face. Some of the injured from the shooting the other day were in bad shape. Betsy didn't make it, but she'd died within two hours.

Deacon pushed the stretcher from the head end. He and Annapurna brought the remains out onto Route 74 and started south.

Harper stepped aside to give them room, asking, "Who?" when they passed by.

"Oliverio," said Annapurna. "He passed sometime last night."

Even though she didn't know the guy, the sight of his body being taken to the graveyard affected her more than she expected. She bowed her head out of respect, standing still until they'd wheeled him a reasonable distance away.

"Who was Oliverio?" whispered Mrs. Parsons. "I don't recognize the name."

"A man we found the other day. He was in bad shape. Wasn't from Evergreen."

"Oh. I see. Do you know what happened to him?"

Harper resumed walking. "Cancer."

She told the story of finding him, as well as the information he'd passed on about the conditions in Mexico. Neither Harper nor Mrs. Parsons spoke again for the last few minutes of the walk back to the house.

Upon reaching the front steps, Mrs. Parsons turned to face her. "Well, I should like to ask you something, Miss Harper."

She finally looked up from the ground. "Okay."

"Next time you walk with me, can we please talk about something less somber?"

Harper smiled. "Sure. No problem."

FOR THE NEXT FEW HOURS, HARPER WALKED HER USUAL PATROL ROUTE after catching up with Marcie.

It was strange, but not in a bad way, to have a 'partner' on patrol. While it made sense to have militia going in pairs, it also thinned out the areas they could cover. To come close to the same level of availability across town, they either had to spend more hours on duty or shrink their focus to smaller regions.

Walter implemented a compromise. A handful of militia who didn't have families volunteered to stay on longer per shift, and they limited patrols in less populated or critical areas. No one had seen any sign of the 'blue and red' group since their initial deadly raid. Losing five men from a seven-person raid hopefully shocked some sense into the survivors and they wouldn't try again. If they did, they'd most likely be sneaky and come in at night.

Eventually, time came to meet the kids at the school, escort them home, and go about the rest of her day.

Marcie walked with her to the school. Being one of the militia without any family, Marcie would be patrolling for another four hours before calling it a day.

A rush of children emerged from the school, ranging in age from six to sixteen. The usual crew of Madison, Jonathan, Lorelei, Mila, Becca, Eva, and Christopher stayed in a tight group as they walked over to Harper.

Madison had an unusually surly expression. The others all seemed normal. Harper gave her a raised eyebrow, but said nothing.

"What?" muttered Madison, sounding a bit on the pissy side.

"You look upset." Harper tilted her head. "Want to talk about it?"

Madison let out a drama queen worthy sigh. "You're going to insist, so why are you even asking?"

"Whoa." Harper leaned back. "You can say you don't want to talk about it. I'm not gonna interrogate you."

Mila, Becca, and Eva all glanced at Madison, seeming surprised at her mood.

Harper gave her space, continuing to walk with them across the old sports field behind the school and into the strip of forest between it and Route 74.

"Sorry." Madison leaned over backward, staring up at the sky. "I'm just being selfish."

"How?" Harper put an arm around her shoulders. "You haven't done anything but make sour faces."

Madison flailed her arms. "School's almost over for the year and I miss having summer vacation. They're gonna make us work on the farm again, and I'm annoyed. Child labor sucks."

The others mostly laughed. Becca's expression said 'ugh'.

"You like animals, right?" Harper exhaled in relief. *Good. Nothing serious.*

"I know." Madison wiped a hand down her face. "I said I'm being selfish. Doesn't make sense for me to be this upset about stupid summer vacation. We have to farm or we're gonna starve. Maybe I'm PMS-ing."

"Ack!" Harper overacted cringing. "At eleven? I really hope not."

"Maybe nuclear war pissed off my ovaries," deadpanned Madison.

Lorelei peeked up. "What's a ovaries?"

Eep! "Something girls have that boys don't," said Harper faster than the speed of logical thinking.

"I 'fought that was brains," said Lorelei, her face completely straight and serious.

"Oof," whispered Mila.

She must have heard that from her bio mom. Harper winced.

"Hey!" yelled Jonathan, half smiling. "Not nice."

"Uhh, she's not wrong… mostly." Madison flapped her arms. "If we had a woman president, we wouldn't have had a war."

Harper ruffled Lorelei and Madison's hair simultaneously. "We can't really say that. No one knows who started it."

"Exactly." Madison thrust a hand out for emphasis. "If we had a woman president, we wouldn't have shot first."

"Unless they were PMS-ing," whispered Christopher.

Mila thumped him.

"Ow." Christopher rubbed the back of his head.

Harper chuckled. "If some other country shot first, it wouldn't matter how aggressive or peaceful our president was. They had some rules or something. If nukes came at us, we'd have to fire back. Not really a decision."

"Someone's gotta know who shot first." Jonathan stretched.

"What difference does it make now?" Becca rolled her eyes. "Can't un-nuke everyone."

"If I ever find the old president, I'm gonna kick him in the balls," said Eva. "Twice."

Madison huffed. "Okay. Fine. I'll try not to think of the farm as forced work. We're all pitching in to help out so we don't starve."

"That's not tricking yourself." Mila poked her. "It's true."

"Yeah, but it makes me sad to think we could starve if something goes wrong." Madison hooked her thumbs in the pockets of her jeans.

Harper squeezed her sister's shoulder. "We're not *that* close to starvation anymore."

"No, but we're also not too far away from it, either." Madison frowned. "Cold snap, or weird radiation weather, or the animals get sick... something could happen."

"Hey, stop that." Mila fake glared. "I'm the gloom queen. You're stealing my lines."

Jonathan, Becca, and Eva laughed.

"Harp?" Madison peered up at her. "When am I gonna start PMS-ing?"

"No idea. I was thirteen. But... we aren't eating tons of processed food loaded with artificial growth hormones anymore."

"Okay, Dad," droned Madison.

Their father used to always complain about stuff like that. Harper laughed... then stared into space, surprised at herself. Talking about Dad didn't make her interminably sad. She'd actually laughed.

"Well." Harper rubbed her chin. "I suppose any time between twelve and fifteen or so, your uterus will betray you. They say lots of stress can make it take longer, so maybe not until you're in your thirties."

Lorelei gasped. "What if she hides from the uterus so it can't find her?"

Harper and Madison laughed so hard they had to wipe tears. Becca and Eva giggled.

Mila scowled. "It's *so* not fair we have to deal with that and boys don't."

"Yeah, true but..." Madison held up one finger. "Boys have to deal with being boys. I think we have it easier."

"Oh, ouch, yeah." Mila winced.

"Hey!" yelled Jonathan.

DOCTOR ROWLAND

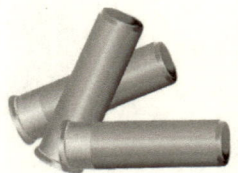

MAY 21ST

When the group reached the fence overlooking the highway, the kids scrambled over it with well-practiced ease. Except for Lorelei, who waited for Harper to pick her up and lift her over. The girl *could* climb the fence, but she saw an opportunity for a hug and took it.

Harper handed the Mossberg over the fence to Jonathan to hold while she climbed. The boy held it in both hands, almost like a samurai receiving a gifted sword. Some people would squirm at the idea of a twelve-year-old holding a shotgun, but Harper had been younger than him when Dad started teaching her. Of course, he'd never have let her carry a loaded weapon around. Even on the competition courses with multiple shooting stations, the guns waited for her at each bench.

"Someone's coming," whispered Mila. "Up the road."

All the kids turned to look north.

Harper jumped down from the top of the fence, looking up the road while collecting the shotgun Jonathan held out to her.

A lone man limped toward them on an improvised crutch. He

looked a bit on the older side, with white hair and a short beard the same shade. The man wore a beige wide-brimmed hat, dirty white shirt, and beige khakis. Sunlight glinted off a machete dangling from his belt, the naked blade wobbling in time with his stride. A black compound crossbow with neon green accents clung to his back on a strap, neither cocked nor loaded. Behind him, a child's wagon trailed along on a rope tied around his waist. The 'cart' held a collection of small backpacks like the ones Harper and her friends used to use for schoolbooks plus three plastic gallon bottles partially full of water.

Blood marked his shirt and pants here and there, evidence of prior injury. He had a few bruises on his face, a cut lip, and bandaging around his right knee.

None of the kids seemed afraid of him, more curious or concerned.

The man smiled and raised his left arm in greeting, though remained too far away to bother speaking.

Harper stared at him, taken by the odd sense she recognized him from somewhere. Despite his various weapons and injuries, he didn't feel threatening. A smile and harmless act didn't prove anything. Even a kindly looking old guy could be a monster in disguise. She liked to think her gut would warn her in that case. Here, she got no 'bad vibes.' Other than being sure she'd seen this guy somewhere before, she mostly wanted to run over and check on him out of concern.

Lorelei darted forward, arms wide. Madison and Jonathan reacted fast enough to catch her before she got more than three steps away.

"Aww…" Lorelei stood there, not even trying to struggle. "He needs a hug." She made an 'uh oh' face, then flashed a cheesy, apologetic smile. "Sorry. F'got I'm sposed ta ask if it's okay first."

"The guy looks familiar," said Harper in a low voice.

"He looks like the crazy doctor from *Jurassic Park*." Jonathan chuckled. "He's even got the same hat."

Harper almost laughed. *Holy cow. He does!* "Wow. Yeah. You guys hang back here. I'm going to go talk to him."

The kids mostly nodded. Jonathan and Madison kept holding Lorelei by the arms. Harper moved to the middle of the highway and walked toward the man, keeping the shotgun sideways. Mila trotted after her.

"What are you doing?" whispered Harper.

"Giving you some backup." Mila tilted her hand just enough to reveal the black leaf knife concealed under it.

"I think I can handle an injured old guy."

"Uh huh." Mila smirked. "That'll be on your grave stone. 'Thought she could handle an injured old guy alone.'"

Harper sighed. Mostly because this man didn't look like a threat, she decided not to argue the point. Besides, as weird as it sounded to think about, Mila could really help tip things in their favor if this encounter turned violent. It didn't make much sense to her how a guy Cliff considered an incompetent fool could have trained a then-nine-year-old in only a few months to such a degree of lethality. Maybe the real mastermind was still out there, some CIA spy or Special Operations soldier. Even with cruel, abusive training methods like Mila described… someone would need to actually *be* a dangerous killing machine to be able to teach it. The so-called 'Shadow Man' turned out to be an idiot.

"Hello there," called the man once they got close enough to where he didn't need to yell.

Harper approached to within ten feet, so she didn't have to raise her voice. "Hi. Are you okay?"

"I've been better. Considering everything, I can't complain too much." The man gave a wheezy chuckle. "Wouldn't suppose you kids have any water to spare? I'm nearly out."

"Yeah. We can get you some water, but not on us. It's back in town." Harper twisted left and nodded in the direction of Evergreen.

"Excellent. Lead the way then, if you would. I…" He stared at her, head tilted.

Men had stared at Harper somewhat frequently ever since she'd been about twelve. She'd gotten fairly adept at telling the difference between the creepy stares and the bewildered 'holy crap did that little girl just hit all twelve targets' stares she got from men at the shooting range. Some guys couldn't handle watching a 'little kid' tear up the range. Or they thought it the greatest thing ever to see a child sharpshooter. This guy's stare was neither creepy nor impressed/disbelieving. He gave off the air of a grandpa who just forgot what he wanted to say.

"Sir?" asked Harper. "You okay?"

"Oh, yes. I… just couldn't help but think I've seen you somewhere before."

"You watch YouTube?" asked Mila.

"Not in a while. I've been having the darndest time finding good WiFi these days." The man chuckled.

She relaxed a bit. "Yeah. You know, I kinda think I've seen you somewhere, too. What's your name? I'm Harper Cody."

"Jerry Rowland," said the man. "Or, Dr. Rowland, but… who cares about that anymore?"

"You're a doctor?" Mila raised both eyebrows. "Do you wanna stay here? You can live in our town."

Dr. Rowland chuckled. "Not that kind of doctor, I'm afraid. I've a useless scrap of paper with my name on it that says I know a lot about chemistry and physics. Or, I *had* a scrap of paper. No damn idea where it got off to."

Oh shit! Harper let the Mossberg hang on its strap and covered her mouth in both hands. No wonder she recognized the guy. She'd sat in his classroom for not quite a full week before the bombs fell. The eccentric physics teacher everyone at her high school adored. Rumor said that some student years ago said he looked like the guy from *Jurassic Park* and he decided to run with it, even buying the same hat. The guy might've even had a prop cane with the mosquito in amber, though if he owned one, he'd lost it in the chaos of war.

"I was in your class." Harper couldn't explain why seeing him kicked her emotions into a spiral like a five-year-old meeting Santa Claus. It had to be seeing someone she knew before who not only survived, but had *not* turned into a jackass like the Starbucks barista who went raider. "Physics. Senior year… all of what, four days?"

Dr. Rowland sighed. "Something like that. Damned fools. May the fleas of a thousand camels infest the nether regions of whoever hit the button."

"What does that mean?" whispered Mila.

"It means I wish great discomfort and anguish upon them." Dr. Rowland smiled. "And yes, I think you are right, Miss Cody. Shall I assume you did not complete the reading assignment?"

Harper couldn't help but let out a sad laugh. "Sorry. No. I didn't have time."

She waved for the other kids to come closer. Madison and Jonathan released Lorelei, who came charging in like a tiny blonde missile. Harper caught her around the chest before child-to-elder impact could take the poor guy off his feet.

"Be gentle." Harper let go and patted her on the head. "He's hurt."

"Okay." Lorelei stepped over and cautiously hugged him as if he'd been made out of cotton candy she didn't want to squish. "Hi. I'm Lorelei."

Mila held out her hand to shake.

Harper blinked, not having noticed the moment when the girl put the throwing knife away.

"Hello, child," said Dr. Rowland.

"I'm Mila."

Jonathan seemed the most guarded until he received a friendly smile and handshake from Dr. Rowland. Harper didn't know what, if anything, to do about it. Even this long after the war, he still braced for abuse from strangers who blamed Chinese people for what happened. She couldn't fault him. An angry mob killed his parents for no reason other than being Chinese. Harper totally understood his emotional response. At least she could blame a specific group for what happened to her parents—The Lawless.

"Are you out here with all these kids by yourself?" asked Dr. Rowland.

"No… We live in Evergreen now. It's turning into a real town." Harper shouldered the Mossberg on its strap and started walking down the road. "C'mon. I'll show you in."

"Grand." Dr. Rowland lifted his pipe crutch and hobbled after her.

The kids fell in step around them. Eva and Becca snooped over the contents of the wagon. The teacher either didn't notice or didn't care to shoo them away from his possessions.

"How did you get hurt?" asked Eva.

Becca tugged at the rope tethering the wagon to the man's waist. The knot, apparently intended to be easy to undo in a hurry, came open. She and Eva pulled the wagon along.

Dr. Rowland appeared grateful for the help, walking with noticeably less pain on his face. "A series of chance encounters with rather desperate ruffians over the past few weeks."

"Lawless?" asked Madison. "Did you kill any?"

The question appeared to shock him. He gave her a pitying look for a second, then shook his head. "I'm not sure what a lawless is."

"A gang. They're mostly in Denver and the surroundings." Harper frowned. "They wear blue sashes or headbands."

"No…" Dr. Rowland grunted in pain, favoring his knee. "Didn't see anyone in Denver when I passed through. Granted, I did not stay long. Downtown areas are dangerously irradiated."

Harper shivered. She'd been back and forth to the downtown area a few times. "Eep! I've been there a few times. Am I gonna get sick?"

He looked over at her. "How long did you spend there, and how long ago?"

"Couple hours, I think. Maybe six months ago. Not that long."

"That shouldn't be enough to cause problems." He winced again when putting weight on his right leg. "It will be another four-to-six years before I'd consider it safe to live there long term."

"Not hundreds?" Becca scratched her head.

"No. Well, not unless a nuclear reactor melted down." Dr. Rowland whistled. "That's a different situation entirely from a weapon. Much dirtier."

Harper shifted her jaw side to side, worry and annoyance battling for prominence in her thoughts. "So, you were in Denver and didn't see anyone? Like not at all?"

He shook his head. "I did not. It's disturbingly quiet there."

"Are there gonna be three-headed coyotes?" asked Jonathan.

"Heh." Dr. Rowland chuckled. "Maybe. Never know."

Becca and Eva gasped. Jonathan, Christopher, and Madison laughed. Lorelei appeared oblivious to the question. Harper had a feeling he teased the kids about three-headed animals. She started thinking about Denver, the Lawless... her half-baked crazy idea to fly down there and go on a rampage to wipe them out. It had been nothing more than an idle revenge fantasy she'd never have acted on, something to daydream about to make her feel better.

Hearing her former teacher talk about Denver as a ghost town raised the dark specter of hope that perhaps someone had done what she only fantasized about.

"Where did you come from?" asked Eva.

"Now there's a question with many possible answers." Dr. Rowland gave a pained chuckle. "Ahh, damn this leg. To answer your question, I shall assume you are not asking in a philosophical sense where we came from and are rather curious about where I've been since the fools tried to end the world."

"Yeah. That." Eva nodded.

"Spent most of the time at home. Had a house in a nice little development in Littleton, northwest of Louviers. Some great thinker decided to plop down a pleasant patch of suburbia in the middle of nowhere. We avoided a direct hit but had a bit of a fallout issue. Spent a good couple of months in my basement. Those hydroponic units were quite an investment."

"Hydroponics?" asked Jonathan. "Are you a doomsday prepper or did you like pot?"

Dr. Rowland wagged his eyebrows. "The latter."

Harper laughed.

"You'll like it in Evergreen." Mila smiled. "Darci and Lucas grow a ton of weed now."

"It has numerous medicinal applications." Dr. Rowland nodded knowingly.

Uh huh. Sure. Harper smiled, not really caring. Pot seemed far less harmful than alcohol. She'd never heard of anyone getting high and starting a bar fight. The militia had to break up brawls at Earls two or three times a month. She still didn't want to use it herself, but had no issue with other people doing so.

"Why did you leave home?" asked Becca. "Did you get attacked?"

"Yes." He grumbled. "The problem with humans is we have a bad habit of gathering in tribes. Not all the tribes play nice with each other. A dozen or so of us were making do with a bunch of small gardens and a stash of canned goods. Couple weeks ago, this pack of idiots rolled in and started taking whatever they wanted and trying to kill anyone who stood up to them."

Harper frowned, thinking of the 'red and blue' idiots. "Wonder if it's the same guys who showed up here a few days ago."

"Oh, dear. I hope not." Dr. Rowland glanced at her.

"Six or seven of them walked in. Two got out," said Harper in an uncharacteristically cold tone. "I doubt they'll come back. We have an organized militia."

"Grand." He gestured off to one side. "First sign of civilization I've seen since leaving home. Even the Army camp looked deserted."

"Army camp? You went all the way to Eldorado Springs?" Harper raised a hand toward the bus barrier across the road up ahead, waving slightly side to side as a 'no threat' signal.

"No. Wasn't Eldorado Springs." Dr. Rowland stopped walking, leaning most of his weight on the pipe crutch. "Moment, kiddo. Leg's not cooperating. The Army camp was south of the Chatfield Reservoir. Looked like an emergency medical station. Whole mess of huge tents, bunch of Humvees and a few excavators. Abandoned. Oddest thing. Looked like everyone just left in a hurry. Might've been a fallout issue."

"Looted?" asked Harper.

"Not sure." Dr. Rowland resumed limping along. "Didn't go in. Leg isn't in the mood to climb fences right now. Though, to be fair, my legs haven't been in the mood to climb fences for thirty years." He laughed.

"Hey, Harp," called Sadie in greeting from atop the bus. She held a sniper rifle up, rested against her shoulder. "You good?"

"Hey." Harper waved at her. "Yeah. Heading over to the medical center."

Dr. Rowland studied the two buses parked nose-to-tail across the highway. "Hmm. They'd better move those before they get tickets for obstructing traffic."

Harper, Sadie, and Mila laughed. Jonathan scrunched his nose as if to say 'no one gets tickets anymore.'

"What's this you said about a medical center?" Dr. Rowland ambled around to face Harper.

"We have real doctors here." Harper took his arm to help him walk. "I'd say we ask every new arrival to get checked out first, but you kinda look like you need a doctor for other reasons."

"Indeed." He wagged his eyebrows. "Also, would not mind a bit of the leaf if you can get in touch with that friend of yours."

"Sure. Let me help you over there first and then I'll go see if I can find Darci." She guided him around the side of the buses. "Med center is just over here."

16

HOUSE CALL

FRIDAY, MAY 22ND

Harper sat in the big conference room down the hall from Anne-Marie's office, on a blue-cushioned chair. Several rows of identical chairs held the entirety of the 'north' militia. Walter Holman called for a briefing again, and spent the first fifteen minutes talking about three main topics: the 'red and blue' gang, the warhead, and Dr. Gerald Rowland.

Walter confirmed there had been no further sightings of the 'red and blue' raiders, and if that trend continued for another four days, they'd be reverting back to their normal patrol patterns. No one raised objections. Everyone sounded confident the handful who survived wouldn't dare come back.

Private Hooper raised a hand, then asked how they should respond if one of them came back in peace, looking for food or a place to stay.

A not-quite argument broke out with about two-thirds of the militia in the room thinking they should be turned away or shot where they stood. They had, after all, been responsible for the deaths of six residents, all 'vulnerable' older people. A few, like Deacon and

Jaylen Bailey said they ought to at least be talked to. Maybe they'd been forced to join the gang and weren't dangerous.

Walter instructed that if such an eventuality occurred, to bring the individual in for questioning.

As far as the warhead problem went, he shared that the scouting teams had discovered two, possibly three, mine sites with the potential for 'reasonably safe' disposal of the MIRV. Harper kept her head down, staring at the bluish-grey carpet between her sneakers. Half of her hoped they didn't ask her to be part of the team to escort the weapon out of town. The other half figured it wouldn't matter if she happened to be right next to the thing or a mile away. If it went off, she—and everyone she loved—would be dead, anyway.

The topic of Dr. Rowland came up only due to Harper having passed along his story of finding an Army medical camp south of Chatfield Reservoir. Her former teacher pointed out the spot on a map in an apparently empty portion of land south and west of the reservoir, near Route 121.

It got more attention than likely worth due to his mentioning a fence he couldn't climb.

"I'm thinkin' if this camp had been looted already," said Walter, "the gate would've been open, and he'd have just walked right in. Good odds there's some medical supplies thereabouts we can make use of."

"That close to Denver, why didn't the Lawless hit it?" asked Dennis. "Them bastards are everywhere."

Harper looked up from the floor. "Yeah. Any medical station like that would've been set up within days of the attack. I don't think there's much chance of finding useful stuff there. Even if the Lawless didn't go that far south, someone else would have to have looted it by now."

Everyone murmured amongst themselves in thought.

"He also said it looked like everyone just picked up and left." Harper rubbed a few more sleep crumbs out of her eyes. "If that's true, something had to make them leave. What could possibly make the Army abandon a whole camp?"

"Funding dried up," muttered Cliff. "Or they ran out of coffee."

Dennis and Roy laughed.

"Damn, I'd legit shoot someone for a fresh cup of coffee." Darnell closed his eyes and inhaled, as if smelling it. "Why ain't we growin' any?"

"Probably because it needs a tropical climate." Harper scratched the back of her head. "And maybe because we didn't have coffee seeds for the greenhouse."

"If you could snap your fingers and either get rid of that warhead or have all the coffee you could drink, what would ya do?" asked Fred Mitchell.

The non-serious vote went twenty-to-three by show of hands in favor of coffee, with Walter abstaining. Cliff jokingly shot Harper a 'you can't be serious' look when she voted for getting rid of the nuke.

"Hey." Harper perked up. "Speaking of nukes... could we ask Dr. Rowland about it? He might know what to do."

Cliff drummed his fingers on his knee. "There's a big difference between a high school physics teacher and a nuclear physicist."

She folded her arms at him. "Do we *have* a nuclear physicist?"

Cliff grinned.

"I suppose it might not hurt to ask him." Walter pursed his lips. "How do you think he will react, Harper?"

She shrugged. "I had the guy's class for four days. Don't really know him, but everyone always said he's a really cool guy. I think he'd try to help." *The laid-back attitude makes so much more sense now that I know he smokes pot. Should probably bring a peace offering with us when we tell him there's a live nuke a mile away from town.*

LATER THAT AFTERNOON, HARPER WENT WITH WALTER, CLIFF, DENNIS Prosser, and Dr. Rowland out to the house where the nuke lived.

The teacher traded his pipe crutch for an aluminum cane taken from the senior care center. He still seemed to be in a moderate amount of knee pain, but between the urgency of a nuclear device and a visit from Darci the Weed Faerie, he readily agreed to hike out to examine the situation.

Cliff insisted that Harper stay a few hundred feet back. She didn't object. She'd gone with them to act as a liaison of familiarity between the militia and her former teacher. Also, since she'd been the first to discover it, she felt an odd degree of personal responsibility about the problem.

On the walk out there, Cliff and Dr. Rowland discussed the Geiger counter readings Cliff got when he came back out here to verify after Harper reported the find. The militia hadn't accused her of making it up. They would have sent people to check on a claim like that no matter who reported it.

Upon getting close enough to see the house through the trees, they stopped. Cliff and Dr. Rowland put on lead aprons taken from a dentist's office and removed all metal objects from their person. Harper waited with Walter and Dennis while her new dad and former teacher approached the house, each of them holding one of the Geiger counters found in the garage here.

No one said a word.

Harper counted time in her head. After her best guess at 136 seconds, the men reappeared at the corner of the house, walking at a quick but not panicked pace. Dr. Rowland's facial expression made him look like a young boy on a wonderful adventure.

"How bad is it?" asked Walter.

Dr. Rowland glanced at a little notepad in his hand. "The radiation shielding around the fissile materials within the warhead is indeed broken. My suggestion is that exposure to a distance of twenty feet or less to the device be limited to no more than two minutes at a time with at least a seventy-two-hour interval between exposures, if at all possible. Dose rates fall off somewhat sharply with distance. Working between twenty and sixty feet should be limited to no more than ten minutes at a time with a similar break interval. Beyond sixty feet from the device, it should be safe to work for a reasonable time given adequate precautions."

"Definitely Russian." Cliff rested his fists on his hips. "Shocked it didn't blow up on the launch pad."

"Huh?" Harper blinked. "Why would it blow up on the launch pad?"

"I'm making a sarcastic comment about their outdated technology, shoddy maintenance, and general lack of care about everything." He sighed hard out of his nose.

Harper helped Dr. Rowland out of the lead apron. "Would it make a difference if we wrapped these around the bomb?"

"It might." The physics teacher smiled at her. "If we had about fifteen of these vests and a whole crate of duct tape, we could create radiation shielding exceeding Russian specifications."

Cliff laughed.

"What do you think is the best way to handle this?" Walter shifted his gaze left, at the house.

"I shall assume you do not have access to appropriate tools or storage vessels." Dr. Rowland brushed his hand down his sleeves as if chasing away dust. "Attempting to disassemble the warhead would not be wise. It would lead only to increased contamination that would be worse than if it had gone off."

Harper cringed. "They're thinking about dumping it down a mine shaft somewhere, truck and all."

"Ahh, yes." Dr. Rowland smiled. "That is not a bad idea. Please take extreme care with transporting the thing."

"Umm." Harper leaned back. "Is it gonna go off if we bump it too hard?"

"Considering the amount of damage it sustained, the odds of a proper thermonuclear detonation are pretty low. The tube separating the main fissile payload from the secondary is undoubtedly warped."

"I don't know what that means." Harper chuckled.

Dr. Rowland held his hands up as if illustrating a pipe. "That device is what's known as a 'gun type' fission bomb. There is a small charge of normal explosives near the nose that fires a mass of fissile material down a channel, or 'gun,' into a larger mass of fissile material.

When both masses combine, they go prompt critical and result in a thermonuclear reaction."

"But if the pipe is bent, the two masses won't collide," said Harper.

"The secondary mass will break apart. Some of it will undoubtedly reach the primary mass, but not enough to cause criticality. The conventional explosives will simply scatter plutonium all over the place and make a huge radioactive mess." Dr. Rowland gestured around. "A nuclear detonation consumes the majority of the radioactive isotopes, leaving behind much less of a hazard than an undetonated device breaking apart."

"How feasible would it be to disable those charges?" asked Walter.

Dr. Rowland patted Cliff on the arm. "You'd have to ask a bomb guy about that. I don't know too much about explosives. I *do* know that it would probably require working in close proximity to radioactive material for too long to be healthy."

"Right, so we just move the whole damn thing." Cliff shifted his stare to Walter. "How are we coming with that truck?"

Walter nodded once. "Last I checked with Rafael, he said he was close. Just working out some formulation issues with the fuel. Wouldn't want the motor conking out halfway there."

"My opinion is you should proceed with your plan to relocate the device." Dr. Rowland wagged his cane at them. "Gently."

17

A NEW OLD PROBLEM

TUESDAY, MAY 26TH

A few days after Walter, Anne-Marie, and Mayor Ned made the decision to check out the Army hospital camp described by Dr. Rowland, a team of volunteers set out from Evergreen, riding in the former United States Postal van Rafael modified to run on biodiesel. They had an effectively renewable source of fuel from farm waste, though the truck—and anyone who spent more than a few minutes inside it—smelled like oily stale corn chips seasoned with a light dusting of cow manure.

It managed a modest thirty-fiveish miles per hour. Not fast by Harper's memory of cars, but definitely better than walking, bicycling, or riding horses. Also, if the Army camp happened to contain any useful supplies, the truck would let them carry significantly more of it back home than they could manage otherwise.

Going near Denver, even the outskirts, once filled her with dread. Today, she couldn't wait to see it. Dr. Rowland claimed to have walked through the city and not seen a single person. The idea that the Lawless might be gone proved intoxicating. She wanted to see it for herself. If it proved wrong, she felt sure she could resist the temptation to start a gunfight.

Rafael drove the truck. Leigh Preston sat in the passenger seat, AK-47 across her lap, the barrel pointing up to the right out the window. Deacon rode in back with Harper, Ken Zhang, and Sergeant Clarke. Though he'd been active-duty Army at the time of the war, the sergeant's motivations and loyalties proved ambiguous. He'd said more than once they'd lost contact with any sort of central command. Short of hopping on a horse and riding across country to the Pentagon, they had no way to know how much remained of the former government. For the months he and Private Hooper had been in Evergreen with the militia, the two men seemed mostly focused on simply being helpful.

Some among the militia worried they might be spies, taking stock of Evergreen's usefulness in case the Army wanted to roll in and take it over. Given the stories Harper brought back of the conditions in the camp at Eldorado Springs, most locals didn't look fondly on the idea. Thus far, neither Army man had said or done anything to make her personally suspicious they had ulterior motives.

Sergeant Clarke did insist on going with them today. Not like a triage camp would have sensitive military technology he'd want to hide from civilians. More likely, he either had friends there or shared in Harper's curiosity as to what would've made the military abandon the place.

They followed Route 74 north out of town, then west past Kittredge—which remained empty—and east past Idledale toward Morrison. Harper zoned out, losing her sense of time and awareness while her thoughts circled around the warhead. Waiting was intolerable. Eight people... or maybe five plus Deacon, could lift the thing. This postal truck could carry it... maybe. Slap a bunch of lead aprons on people, transfer the warhead to this truck, and drive it wherever.

She came back to the here and now somewhere on Route 470, based on the conversation going on up front between Rafael and Leigh.

"What'chu think, boss?" asked Deacon, eyeing Sergeant Clarke. "What are we gonna find there?"

"Probably a whole bunch of empty tents and some folding tables." Sergeant Clarke chuckled. "National Guard set up a bunch of stations around the area to manage the wounded. This is probably one of those."

"You don't know for sure?" asked Harper.

"Nah. I'm not NG. Not like they gave every soldier a list of every possible camp. From the moment Command picked up those birds coming in, everything became a barely controlled shit show. Most of us held it together, but when you know the world is going to end in half an hour, it doesn't seem quite so important to follow orders." He rolled his eyes. "NG tends to do its own thing, anyway. It's a damn miracle whenever they got anything right. Guys get a taste of civilian life and they get in the habit of cutting corners, getting lazy."

Harper chuckled, not because she found it funny, but because Deacon laughed and she didn't want to seem out of place. "Can I ask you something?"

"Sure." Sergeant Clarke glanced at her. "But I'm too old for you."

"Hah." She smiled. "Not where I was going. When I was first trying to get out of Denver, I saw some guys in camo chase down these people and basically like arrest them. Were they real soldiers or like a gang kidnapping people?"

Sergeant Clarke pursed his lips in thought. "Ehh. Might have been National Guard going after looters."

She stared. "Really? Looters? The whole damn city is on fire and they're arresting looters? Who the heck would steal televisions and crap after nukes fell? And... those people didn't have anything. They were just running away."

"I did say National Guard. Not the sharpest knives in the drawer." Sergeant Clarke tapped a finger to the side of his head. "Course, they also might not have truly understood the scope of what just happened. I dunno. Might've been deserters going crazy. Maybe those people tried to grab weapons from a military checkpoint. Too many variables."

"So, you think they were real soldiers?"

"Anyone could put on camo." He shrugged. "When was this?"

"Two months after the strike." Harper idly tapped her sneakers together.

Sergeant Clarke scratched his eyebrow. "Could've been legit. Might have also been some nutty militia. Maybe some no-go's cracked and went nuts."

"No gos?" Harper shifted her weight to the right, trying to let blood flow back into the half of her butt that had fallen asleep.

"National guard." He winked. "N.G. No go. Also, because they stay home in country and don't go where the real issues are."

"Joke's on them." Deacon exhaled into a whistle. "Real issues came ta us."

The truck slowed.

"Got some people up ahead," said Leigh. "Gonna check it out."

Harper, Deacon, and Sergeant Clarke readied their weapons. As soon as the USPS truck came to a stop, Deacon yanked the rear door open and jumped out. Harper waited for Sergeant Clarke to get out of her way, then rushed after them. Leigh opened the passenger door, but stayed behind it for cover.

A short distance ahead on the highway, a group of people had come to a stop, staring at them. A brown-haired man in his early thirties held the hand of a woman around the same age. His ragged polo shirt, longish hair, and wild beard made him look like an office worker who'd been marooned on a desert island for months. The woman appeared equally unkept, her dense black hair unevenly cut around shoulder length as if she'd done it herself with a knife. A pair of children huddled close to them: a boy about ten who resembled a smaller version of the man without a beard and a girl a couple years younger with long jet-black hair. The couple had no weapons. Mom wore a man's button-down shirt with jeans a bit too big on her, and sneakers. The kids both had adult-sized T-shirts on like dresses, the boy barefoot, the girl in pink flip-flops.

Five adults surrounded the apparent family: four men and a woman in armor cobbled together from military vests, police tactical gear, knee pads, shoulder pads, and random bits of scrap metal. They'd painted it white and emblazoned red crosses on both shoulders as well as the chest. While no two suits looked exactly the same, the general theme was a definite attempt to match. At the back of the formation, the woman and one man carried rifles. A guy in the front held a long wooden pole with an axe head on the end. Both other men, standing on either side of the family, carried weapons similar to medieval broadswords, but obviously made from scrap metal.

The way the five armored people stood around the family struck Harper as not quite right. Perhaps it came from the grim expression on the woman, the desperation in the man's eyes, the fear on both kids' faces, or simply the way the armed group had arranged themselves around the people with the rifles in the back. She couldn't help but think it looked like a prisoner escort.

"That don't look like no Red Cross," whispered Deacon.

"Pretty sure they're not supposed to be medics." Ken whistled a note of disbelief. "But hey, if you're going to jump off the deep end, at least have a theme."

Harper walked forward. Deacon and Sergeant Clarke moved up on her left and right side. They came to a stop fifteen feet or so in front of the truck, still about twenty feet from the people. The armored group appeared unsettled at all three of them carrying firearms... or perhaps at Deacon's size.

"Hi," called Harper. "Nice to see people out here."

"Greetings, child." The man with the pole-axe took a few steps closer. "What are you doing out here in the wasteland?"

She tightened her jaw. Her gut said something here was wrong. Even if she fully trusted these people, it would be foolish to talk about their plan to investigate a potentially large stash of medical supplies. Otherwise benign survivors might get jealous and attack them for medicine. But this crew? They didn't seem benign. "Checking the area, trying to get an idea of the damage."

"It is not safe out here, child." The man eyed her shotgun. "We are on our way to Safe Haven."

"We know it's not safe out here." She hefted the Mossberg. "But we're ready for problems. Thanks for the concern."

He bowed his head slightly without breaking eye contact. "You should come with us. You will be protected within Safe Haven."

He keeps saying that weird. Is 'safe haven' the name of a specific place to him?

The two guys with swords crept closer. One ogled Harper's weapon like he wanted it.

"Who are you?" asked Sergeant Clarke. "What unit are you with?"

"We are not the military of the failed society." Pole-axe guy smiled a plastic smile. "We are a reawakening of man's covenant to God. We are the Knights Templar."

Oh, no. Not more religious crazies. Harper winced mentally.

"Right," said Sergeant Clarke. "Well, if that works for you folks, more power to ya."

"You should come with us to Safe Haven," said the dark-haired sword-bearer. "There you would have no worries."

"We've got a place to go already. Just out on a scouting mission." Harper subtly shifted her thumb closer to the safety. The vibe coming from the group turned on a dime. She had the distinct impression they intended to *insist* everyone go with them.

The little girl bolted out of her flip-flops, sprinting toward Harper and the others. She ducked around the blond swordsman, who clumsily missed grabbing for her. "Help! They're gonna hurt us!"

Both 'templars' with rifles raised them as if to shoot the child in the back before she could get away. The unarmed man—likely her father—whirled around, pouncing on the guy with the rifle, trying to wrestle it out of his grasp. The woman Templar shifted her aim off the child to him.

Harper and Sergeant Clarke fired at the woman at the same instant she snapped off a shot at the dad. Pole-axe guy started after the little girl, but skidded to a stop as soon as Deacon stomped toward him. The child zoomed around behind the big man and clung to his side.

Buckshot went exactly where Harper wanted it to go—striking the woman in the face. Spurts of blood flew from her back, trailing after Sergeant Clarke's bullets. A single shot came from the USPS truck a half-second later, sending the helmet flying off the Templar rifleman wrestling with the unarmed man.

Screaming, the boy and his mother ducked to the ground where they stood, her shielding him as best she could.

Both Templars with rifles fell dead to the pavement. The dad staggered sideways, hand clamped over his right bicep.

A tense silence fell over the highway. The two sword-wielding guys backed up.

Harper pointed the Mossberg at the nearest man holding the pole-axe. "Stay away from the family or you'll learn what buckshot tastes like."

"Nah, don't shoot 'em." Deacon loomed forward. "I'd much rather twist they heads off."

The three remaining Templars, armed with a pole-axe and crude swords, did not seem terribly interested in continuing a fight against five semi-automatic firearms.

"*He* sees your iniquity," yelled the pole-axe guy. "Judgement will come for you."

"I'm 'bout ta judge that fancy axe straight up yo ass." Deacon took another step toward the man.

"Uhh, guys?" called Leigh. "Are we supposed to just shoot psychos in preemptive defense of innocents or is that bad?"

At that, the three Templars ran off the road to the east, sprinting across the grass to an off ramp they followed downhill before disappearing behind a brown-and-beige Holiday Express building.

"Was that a serious question, or did you just say that to scare them away?" asked Ken.

"Second option, but I probably wouldn't have felt too bad about shooting them." Leigh clicked the safety on her AK.

Mom stood and rushed over to her husband.

"Dad's bleeding!" yelled the boy.

The girl burst into tears.

Deacon plucked the child up into his arms and carried her over to her parents, stopping to pick up her flip-flops on the way.

Harper and Sergeant Clarke followed. Rafael drove the USPS truck forward at roughly walking speed.

"What the heck happened here?" Deacon set the girl on her feet beside her parents, then handed the child her shoes back.

"These crazy sons of bitches showed up out of nowhere," said the man. "They basically told us we were going to join their cult, or they'd kill me and take Melanie and the kids, anyway."

"They burned our little house." The girl bowed her head, sniffling as she stepped into her flip-flops.

"Everything we had, which… wasn't much." Melanie stared off into nowhere. "The bombs lit our real house on fire. Had to leave so fast, we lost everything. Spent a while roaming around. Couple weeks back, we found a nice little RV. Been living in it, scavenging whatever we could find from wherever."

Sergeant Clarke examined the man's injury, which appeared to be a deep graze with powder burns on the outside of his bicep. "C'mon back to the truck. Got a first aid kit in there, can rig a bandage on this."

"Sounds good. Thanks." He offered a hand. "Grant Anson. This is my wife, Melanie. The kids are Brandon and Zoey."

"With a y," whispered the girl, almost as a reflex.

"They didn't even let Zoey keep her teddy bear." Brandon glared. "They made her leave it in the trailer when they burned it."

Zoey sniffled and wiped her nose on the back of her arm.

"What the hell did they do that for?" Harper gawked. "Just to be cruel?"

"They called it a false idol or something crazy like that." Grant whistled in disbelief. "I think they were too close to a nuclear detonation and their brains got microwaved."

"Heard some rumors about them." Melanie rested her hands on the kids' shoulders. "Been going around by us. Some people livin' in other trailers or RVs nearby said they heard tell of these nutballs grabbing anyone they can get a hold of who can't fight them off."

Great. Just what we needed... another group of insane bandits. Harper exhaled.

"You said you got a safe place to go?" asked Melanie. "What is it?"

"Town. Evergreen." Ken smiled at her. "You folks are welcome to come with us if you have nowhere better to be. Couple hundred people. Proper militia, school with real teachers, two actual doctors. Farm's in good shape, too."

Melanie shot her husband a look that said, 'we are going with them.'

"Sounds good." Grant squeezed her hand. "I should've listened to you about the settlement. Not sure why I had a bad feeling about them."

Melanie kept staring at him.

"To be fair, I had a much worse feeling about these idiots." Grant kicked the dead rifleman.

The family followed Harper and company around to the back of the USPS truck and got in. Deacon dragged the three bodies off the road, returning to the truck a few minutes later with two hunting rifles, a few handfuls of bullets, and three candy bars. He handed the chocolate bars to the family, then put the weapons and ammo in a footlocker near the truck's rear door.

Rafael resumed driving.

Sergeant Clarke got started on bandaging Grant's arm.

"We're not heading directly back to Evergreen," said Harper. "We were on the way to check out a place that might have medical supplies."

"That's fine." Grant winced. "I don't really want to think about what waited for us at that Safe Haven place. A long ride with a detour is a trade up."

18

TRIAGE SITE DELTA

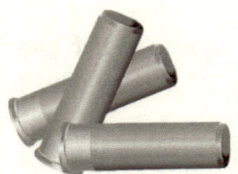

MAY 26TH

Riding in the mostly empty back of a former Postal Service truck did not make for luxury.

Not only did the 'seats' consist of bare steel floor, a few spots had protruding metal bits left over from the shelves once used to hold bins of mail. The vehicle was about the size of a minivan, but almost no consideration went into the design in regard to comfort. Cliff said something about 'made as cheaply as possible by the lowest bidder using parts sourced from the cheapest vendor.' Of course, he also said the same thing about all government vehicles up to and including combat aircraft and tanks.

Harper did not love sitting so close to a giant plastic jug of fuel. However, Rafael assured her that biodiesel would not burst into a fireball if shot. The worst-case scenario would be getting splattered with oily gunk that smelled so bad six showers wouldn't get rid of it. Unpleasant, but she'd take funky over burned.

Grant and Melanie Anson seemed to recover from the shock of their kidnapping within a few minutes, at least enough to engage in a normal-sounding conversation with Harper, Deacon, and Sergeant

Clarke. They lived in Aurora before the war. After narrowly escaping the city alive, they'd wound up taking refuge in Flagler with about twenty or so total strangers. It didn't take long for supplies to run out in a small town, or for a group calling itself 'The Renegades' to drive them off for fear of violence. Grant described them as a bunch of 'angry white supremacists overjoyed the government was gone.' In the months since they'd left Flagler, they led something of a nomadic life until discovering a handful of other survivors who'd made a village out of a campground in Daniels Park. They'd been there for just over eight weeks before the Templars showed up.

Zoey shifted around, hugging everyone. The girl didn't speak again, but the tightness with which she clung to Harper for a while made no secret she'd expected the Templars to do bad things to her family.

Harper figured they had worse plans than death for a little girl, probably raise her to be just as crazy as they were, then order her to be someone's wife.

Her brother, Brandon, kept staring back and forth between Harper and Deacon. The ten-year-old looked at Deacon the way any boy his age might gawk at a pro wrestler they'd seen on television if meeting him in person. When he looked at her, the boy got this starry-eyed puppy crush expression.

He's happy to be safe. And he's only ten. Ignore it. Don't be awkward. He's not thinking that, *I'm a superhero to him or something.*

The ride got bumpy all of a sudden. Gravity stopped working as the truck hit something and caught some air, then came down hard on decidedly rough terrain, hitting bump after bump.

Zoey, already clinging to her mother, screamed but didn't go anywhere. A bounce flung Brandon off the wheel well he'd been sitting on at the opposite wall. Deacon made a one-handed catch, almost palming the boy's entire chest.

Grant went down hard on his right shoulder, screaming, "Ffffaaaargh!"

Ken bounced off the floor, flipped over, and came down on top of Grant, both men grunting a heavy 'oof.'

Melanie slipped forward, ending up flat on her back with Zoey on top of her. Sergeant Clarke got launched straight up. He smacked his head on the roof, then fell on top of Melanie and her daughter, but managed to brace his hands on either side of her to avoid crushing them too much.

Harper's face bounced off the sloshing fuel tank, then smacked into something warm and relatively soft. It took her a moment to realize she'd flown into Deacon's other hand. He'd caught her before she smooched the steel floor.

"What the hell are you doing up there?" bellowed Clarke, stuck in an almost push-up pose over Melanie and Zoey.

"Just a little bump," yelled Rafael, before laughing.

"You call that little?" Deacon whistled. "Try not to hit a big one, then."

Sergeant Clarke rolled away from Melanie, bracing himself against the wall. "Little bump, he says. Haven't had a ride this rough since—"

"There are kids here." Ken groaned.

"A ride this rough since training new privates how to operate Humvees." Clarke shook his head. "Get your mind out of the sewer, son. Some o' them boys never even touched a motor vehicle before."

"Slow down!" shouted Leigh. "Be careful."

"Slow?" Rafael chuckled. "We *are* going slow. This thing only goes up to thirty-five."

If he rolls this truck over, we're screwed. She smiled at Deacon and scrambled to get her legs under her, sitting back on her heels. *Wait, no. He could probably lift this truck.*

Everything got quiet except for the purring rumble of the little biodiesel motor and the squeaking of the suspension. The USPS truck rocked and wobbled like a small boat on choppy waters. Frequent steering back and forth kept everyone swaying around. The frequent clank of rocks striking the undercarriage confirmed they'd gone off road.

What the hell is going on? Harper crawled to the doorway separating the cargo area from the two seats up front. Out the comparatively large windshield, she had a great view of dirt and scrub grass. They drove toward a large collection of green Army tents. Most had white squares with red plus signs all over them, denoting them as medical.

Harper pushed herself up to stand, gripping the frame of the doorway for balance. "Wow. It's really here."

"You didn't believe your old teacher?" Leigh peered up at her.

"I did, just… what I mean is, I didn't expect it to look like this." She gestured at the windshield.

"Like what?" Rafael eased on the brakes, slowing the truck to about jogging speed.

Harper surveyed the camp, looking for the right words. A tall chain link fence made of multiple portable sections formed a barricade between them and eight or so huge tents. It looked as if the Army set the place up and left. "Intact."

"Intact?" repeated Rafael.

"Yeah." Harper shifted the Mossberg strap higher on her shoulder. "I figured someone would've torn the place up already. Kinda feels like the Army just evacuated it a day ago."

"You folks mind waiting in or near the truck?" Sergeant Clarke glanced back and forth between Melanie and Grant. "We're just going to check on this site to see if there's any salvageable medical supplies or anything. Won't be long."

"No problem." Grant fussed at the bandage on his arm.

Deacon opened the rear door and stepped out. Sergeant Clarke followed. Harper scooted forward, going out the passenger side door after Leigh. Ken exited the rear door, then wandered around the driver's side, giving Rafael a dirty look over the rough ride.

"Yeah, yeah, sorry." Rafael chuckled. "When we get back home, I'll install seat belts."

"Maybe some seats." Ken wagged his eyebrows.

Brandon jumped out the rear door, walked two steps to the side, then lifted his T-shirt dress up to pee. He kept peering back over his shoulder every few seconds, his eyes wide and fearful. The boy clearly didn't want to go too far away from adults who could protect him and didn't care at all about privacy. His expression looked almost exactly the same as Madison's when they'd been on their own before finding

Cliff and Jonathan. Her kid sister refused to ever be more than arm's reach away from her, even to go to the bathroom.

Harper clenched her jaw. *Poor kid. At least he's still got both his parents.* The thought carried no jealously, only happiness for him. *Better hurry this up so we can get them back to town, fed, and cleaned up.* She approached the gate. A simple chain and padlock secured it. The others collected around behind her. Since no one said anything, she swung the Mossberg off her shoulder and brought it up to take aim at the lock.

"Hang on. Save the ammo." Deacon walked up beside her. "Let me try this first."

She peered up at him.

He spun his rifle over and hammered the stock down on the padlock. After a few glancing blows, the fourth smack popped the hasp out of the lock. Deacon grinned, then unwound the chain and tossed it aside.

Harper started to walk in, but Sergeant Clarke cut her off, taking point. Grumbling, she entered the camp following him, Deacon, Ken, and Leigh behind her. He might've thought it a bit of necessary chivalry for the actual Army soldier to go in first instead of a civilian teenager. Or, perhaps he exercised whatever sense of authority he derived from believing the United States Army still existed as an organization.

Huh. For all I know, maybe it does. Not like we've had much contact with anyone more than ten miles away.

They approached a row of house-sized tents and filed into a gap between the two nearest ones. Three green-painted excavators sat a fair distance off to the left by the edge of a massive, rectangular hole. Bodies littered the open ground in front of the tents. Harper gawked, but her initial horrified shock rapidly gave way to vengeful indignation. All eleven or so corpses wore the blue sashes of the Lawless. They'd apparently been killed in the midst of a gunfight. Three lay out in the open, the others draped over coolers, tables, a loose giant excavator tire, and the back end of a Humvee. Curiously, none of the dead had weapons lying near them. The corpses appeared relatively recent, but so pale they seemed fake, like wax figures taken out of a museum.

"Uhh…" Harper bit her lip, bracing for a stink that didn't come.

"You all right, hon?" asked Deacon, close behind her.

"Yeah. Lawless. Screw 'em." Harper turned in place, looking around at the scene of a shootout that played out an unknown amount of time ago. "I'm guessing they lost."

"Well, they dead." Deacon chuckled. "That be a good clue they didn't win."

Harper flashed a weak smile. "No, I mean… there are no bodies from whoever they got into a fight with. Also, no guns. The winning team must have collected the weapons and their own dead."

Deacon raised his eyebrow. "Oh, yeah. You right."

"If you like that," said Ken in a raised voice from off to the left. "You're going to hate this."

Harper glanced at him. He stood with Sergeant Clarke by the edge of the hole. She started walking toward them.

"Wait." Ken raised a hand at her like a crossing guard telling people to stop. "That's a pit of nightmares. Be real sure you want to look."

"I'm not a child," muttered Harper to herself, then raised her voice. "What's in there?"

"Bodies," said Sergeant Clarke. "Hundreds of them."

Can't be any worse than having a damned nuke lurking outside town. She kept going and risked a brief peek over the side.

The pit, roughly sixty feet long, twenty feet wide, and at least fifteen deep, contained an uncountable number of dead bodies. Gaps between the corpses showed the dead at the bottom had been placed in orderly rows, wrapped in body bags or linen… then more corpses stacked on top of them. Toward the top, all care had been dispensed with. People, still in whatever clothing they died in, had been haphazardly tossed into the hole like trash at a landfill. A handful of corpses at the top of the pile looked like soldiers in full camo uniform.

Eerily, almost none of the dead appeared to have decomposed much. No one she looked directly at suffered obvious bullet wounds, though many had been disfigured by horrible burns and grotesquely swollen limbs. A few naked corpses appeared to have patterns seared into their skin, detailed enough to be recognizable as having come from fabric.

For a moment, she wondered if they'd stumbled across a movie set and discovered a pile of silicone dummies. There didn't appear to be any commonality to the dead, no single group had been singled out for death. Just... citizens. Old, young, all ethnicities.

She cringed away before her gaze could linger on any kids that might be in there.

Ken put an arm around her back. "You okay?"

"Ask me in an hour. That's kinda shocking."

"Told you not to look." He gave her arm a little squeeze.

"Yeah. I know. But, I'm not a kid anymore."

Ken let his hand drop. "It's got nothing to do with being a kid. A sight like this can break even the toughest guy. Think I'm gonna be paying Earl's a visit when we get back home."

"Are they real?" Harper looked out at the dead Lawless. "The bodies look weird."

"I can't imagine why—or *how*—anyone nowadays could fake something like this." Ken exhaled hard. "But, yeah, they do look weird. Maybe it's just dry here."

"Shit." Harper cringed as realization dawned on her. "We need to hurry up."

"Why?" Ken raised an eyebrow.

"Dr. Rowland said Denver's too radioactive to live in for at least like six more years." She stepped away from the mass grave without looking at it again. "Remember what Dr. Tegan said? Radiation can kill bacteria. Look at those burns, that swelling. The patterns of fabric scorched into their skin from a nuclear flash. Those people died of radiation sickness. This place is probably hot."

"Shit," whispered Ken.

"Dammit." Leigh backed away from the hole. "Yeah. Harper's right. Surprised those poor people aren't glowing. We gotta get out of here. No wonder the place is untouched."

Harper fast-walked back toward the tents. "Radiation didn't kill the Lawless. They've definitely been shot. There must have still been some Army people here when they showed up. We're not going to drop dead in two minutes. Let's time it for five more minutes and take a quick look around for medical supplies?"

Sergeant Clarke emerged from one of the tents on the south row, grinning while fiddling at his wristwatch. "Sounds good. Okay, everyone. You heard the lieutenant. Five minutes and we're out. Split up and check the tents."

"Umm." She blinked. "I'm no lieutenant."

He grinned. "You're barely out of high school and talk like you know what you're doing and people are supposed to listen. Close enough."

His tone carried only gentle teasing, so she sighed to herself and ignored the sarcastic rank.

Harper chose a tent at random in the north row and walked toward it. She scowled at the dead Lawless. *Rowland said it's deadly to live here long term. These bastards haven't found us in Evergreen yet... and last winter was really bad.* She went past the tent to peer toward the ruins of Denver through the 'alley' between it and the next tent. Could the Lawless possibly be extinct? They certainly seemed to be dumb enough. If they hadn't attacked Harper's family, she might still be living in her basement in Lakewood. How much protection did it afford them from radiation? *Ironic as hell if being chased out of Denver saved our lives.* Too many variables went into it. Without the Lawless attacking them, they'd probably have run out of food fairly soon and done the same thing as Grant Anson and his family... started wandering. Though, they had already heard rumors of Evergreen. Perhaps they would have gotten there, anyway.

"Bah," she muttered. "Too many what-ifs not worth thinking about."

She reversed to the tent flap she'd gone past, grabbed it, and paused to yell back over her shoulder at the others. "Don't take anything metal. Especially gold."

"If this place is like Chernobyl," said Leigh, "We should just get the hell out of here right now."

"Chernobyl's far worse," called Sergeant Clarke from inside another tent in the opposite row. "That's more like a dirty bomb to a factor of a thousand. When a nuclear weapon goes off, most of the bad shit inside it gets burned up. Ground zero is deadly for a while, but the radioactive byproducts of a thermonuclear detonation decay exponentially. They resettled Hiroshima like a decade later and it's fine. Pripyat is *still* toxic."

"What the heck is a Pripyat?" asked Leigh.

Sergeant Clarke laughed. "The city near Chernobyl."

We shouldn't laugh here. Harper glanced at the pit. *It's a graveyard.*

She ducked into the tent. Fifty military style cots stood in neat rows, all empty. The air smelled of canvas, sweat, and a cloying, awful —but fairly weak—odor somewhere between feces and rotting meat. A stack of green cargo crates in the middle of the tent caught her eye. Perhaps they contained medical supplies.

Before she could take a step closer to potential loot, she spotted something else of great concern in the back corner on the right—the barrel of a combat rifle pointing at her. She froze, shifting the focus of her eyes past the tip of the weapon to the shaggy, bearded face of a frighteningly thin black man holding it. His eyes twitched with an almost manic quality, as if his sanity came and went from moment to moment. The guy wore a camo uniform under a heavy Army-issue coat. He looked like the 'crazy homeless Vietnam veteran' character from a movie. He sat in a damaged wheelchair next to a metal desk in an area of the tent sectioned off from the beds as an office.

Two millimeters stood between Harper and eternity. If the man's finger moved even a little bit, a 5.56 bullet would rip most of her brain out of her skull. No possible way could she get the Mossberg off her shoulder in time to matter. The man's eyes widened slightly.

"Don't shoot," whispered Harper as she slowly held her hands up. "Please."

THE LAST SURVIVOR

MAY 26TH

The man stared at her for an eternity of five more seconds.

Harper held completely still, except for a bit of shaking in her hands.

"Oh, you're a kid." The man raised his head from the rifle's sights but kept pointing the weapon at her. "I'll lower this thing if you aren't here looking for trouble."

"No trouble." Harper offered a wary smile. "We aren't here to cause problems. Heard about this camp and we came to investigate."

The man lowered his rifle an inch or so, not quite aiming at her, but it wouldn't take much for him to change his mind. She still couldn't make a move for her shotgun. He'd kill her before she even got both hands on it. "Had some problems with the last set of visitors. You don't seem like you with 'em." He coughed, wheezed, then coughed again so hard it made Harper's chest hurt.

She breathed out long and slow. *Please don't be crazy.* "Them? The Lawless? Absolutely not. We're survivors. Got an actual Army sergeant with us."

"Meh. Army ain't no good for no one now. Them bastards didn't help us when we asked." He grumbled.

She looked over his camo uniform, raised an eyebrow, then let her hands drop. "You're not Army?"

"Relax, girl. I ain't no threat to you. Dick fell off last month." He chuckled.

Harper gasped.

"Aww, just being a smartass." He wheeze-laughed into another coughing fit. "Sorta teasing ya. Darn thing didn't fall off, but for damn sure don't work no more. Aww hell." He pivoted the rifle sideways and rested it across his lap. "I don't have much time left, anyway. If you're a devil with a pretty face, it don't much matter. I'm gonna be dead soon."

Harper closed her eyes and let the terror of the past minute or so melt out of her muscles. "I don't want to hurt you."

"That's good." He coughed again. "Though, maybe I should ask you to. Only gonna get worse from here on."

"What do you mean?"

He scratched at his chest. "I got six dozen types of cancer and who knows what the hell else. Only reason I'm still using up oxygen is all the preservatives in the MREs. Damn cancer can't even digest that shit."

She considered unslinging the shotgun, but it might make the guy panic and start shooting. He didn't seem crazy, at least not *too* crazy, and certainly looked like death warmed over. Without the immediacy of a gun pointing at her face, her brain soaked in more details. His cheeks appeared sunken in, his hands bony. As her eyes adjusted to the dim light in the tent, she noticed his hair looked thin and even missing in clumps. Not quite what she expected from either radiation poisoning or cancer.

Duh. Cancer patients lose their hair because of chemo, not the cancer itself. She took another step closer, eyeing the boxes, which appeared to be cases for MREs.

"You're not Army?" she asked, barely over a whisper.

"Nope. Nash—" His voice broke over a lump of phlegm. He

slumped forward in his seat, thumping a hand into his chest while coughing.

Harper just stood there, not sure what—if anything—she could do for him. Asking 'are you okay' felt stupid. Clearly, this man was not 'okay.'

"Ugh. Damn cancer." He spat a brownish wad onto the dirt. "I'm National Guard. Or was. Shit's gone. Name's Jeff Myrick."

"Hi. I'm Harper."

"Nice ta see there's some people left out there who ain't either nuts or dying." He wheeze-laughed. "What's your story, hon?"

She explained briefly about a survivor town in Evergreen, meeting Dr. Rowland who mentioned seeing this camp, and them coming out here to check. "Mostly hoping for medical supplies but I didn't expect much."

"Good instincts, kiddo." Jeff winked. "We used it all up. Even ended up cannibalizing bed linens for more bandages. All goddamned useless. Just about everyone still died."

"What happened here?" Harper decided not to get any closer. This guy, seemingly friendly as he was, might have had something more contagious than cancer.

"They sent us out here—the ones of us who survived to show up anyway—to set up a triage camp, takin' care of anyone who made it out of the city." Jeff nodded toward the beds. "We got all sorts of people comin' in. Mostly burns and broken bones for the first day or so… then the radiation sickness kicked in. Poor bastards flooded in way past what we could handle. Major Deakins lost his damn mind. Started treating the civilians like horses too busted up to save and just started shooting them where they stood."

Harper gasped. "Oh, no…"

"He figured they were walking dead."

"Zombies?" blurted Ken, as he entered the tent. "You sayin' there's zombies out here?"

Jeff glanced down at the rifle in his lap. He seemed to briefly consider picking it up, then resigned himself to whatever fate Harper and her friends had in store for him.

"Relax. He's not the enemy," said Harper, a hint of anger in her voice.

"I know that." Jeff shook his head. "The damn Russians shot us."

The word 'Russian' filled her mind with an image of the dormant MIRV, just waiting for the right time to pop its horrible surprise. "You knew?"

"Command mentioned it. They knew where the missiles came from." Jeff doubled over in a bad coughing fit.

Ken hurried to his side as if to clap him on the back, but hesitated. "Good grief, man. You're just bones."

Coughing mutated into chuckling. Wet chuckling. "I know. Appreciate the thought, but I'm about ready to drag myself over to that giant hole and dive in. Ran outta food couple days ago. Sorry to disappoint you folks, but there ain't nothin' here for you to scavenge unless you're after a couple hundred pounds of canvas and a whole shitload of contaminated cots."

No thanks. "If we knew Russia nuked us, why was everyone attacking anyone they thought looked Chinese?"

Jeff frowned. "Wasn't common knowledge to civilians who did it. Besides, people are stupid. Large groups of panicking people are even dumber. Humans are irrational critters."

"Do you know why they hit the button?" asked Ken.

"Can't rightly say. Command don't tell grunts that much, and they tell the Guard even less. If even they knew what happened for real. Alls I heard is we got word by Chain of Command that the Russians hit the button and some of their shit didn't work right. One went stray, landed in India or some shit like that. They blamed Pakistan and fired back. All hell broke loose. Shit, far as we know, it might've been a rat chewin' on a wire that launched the first one."

Her heart sank. "Wow... so it really was the whole world?"

"Just about." Jeff scratched at his beard, a piece of which came off in his fingers. "Except for I guess places like the Amazon jungle or crap where there ain't no big cities or politics. Damn sure bet North Korea used the launches as an excuse to go batshit crazy and invade the south or maybe nuke them, too. Anywhere not directly lit on fire melted in the radiation clouds kicked up after. We had contact with a couple of poor fuckers holed up at a NOAA station. They were tracking radiation clouds migrating around the globe. Made Fukushima look like nothing."

"So, where did the zombies come from?" Ken backed up two steps from the guy.

"Ain't no zombies, fool. Walking dead is what we called the poor souls who soaked up so many rads they were doomed but not dead yet. Deakins figured it a kindness to just shoot them before they got all swole up and bleedin' from every damn hole. Severe radiation sickness is a god-awful way to go. Wasn't nothing anyone could've done to save them. Those first couple weeks, Denver practically glowed at night."

Harper squirmed. "Ugh."

"Problem was, he didn't bother to make sure anyone got dosed. Just assumed they all did." Jeff spat another brownish wad to the ground. "We had a bit of a personnel restructuring at that point. Most of us objected to the major's command style."

"You shot him?" asked Harper.

"Not me personally, but yeah. Soon as he pulled a gun on this little boy, Jacqueline had enough and blew his brains out right there."

Harper winced and looked down. "Was the boy okay?"

"Dunno. He and his dad took off after that. Didn't trust us. Can't blame them." Jeff coughed hard. "They're probably dead now. Heck, we're all gone already, just don't know it yet. Like them walking dead. Maybe you got irradiated, maybe you didn't. Planet's gone to shit. Fallout everywhere. We're screwed." He fell quiet for a moment, then started to explain to her about how the camp was set up hours after the bombardment ceased in order to deal with the wounded survivors… as if he hadn't already told her that.

"Do you know why the bodies look so weird?" asked Harper, interrupting him.

"They all irradiated." Jeff shook his head. "Bunch of contamination in that hole. Bacteria can't survive there. Decomposition is a product of bacteria people have inside them. Normally, it's beneficial to us, but once we die, they start eating us. Can't do it if the rads killed them off."

She glanced backward at the tent flap, then at a metal camp stove beside Jeff. Scraps of bedding lurked among the ashes. "How long ago did the Lawless attack?"

"What the heck is a Lawless?" Jeff wheeze-coughed. A trickle of blood ran down over his chin.

"The dead guys outside with the blue sashes on."

"Oh, them fools. Uhh, not sure. Time's a bit fuzzy when you sit around alone all day. Happened before the snow. Was just me and Carlos, and Wilbur, and... oh what the heck was her name? Real badass chick. Damn. Can't think of her name. See her face, though. Maria? Or something like that. Jacqueline? We held them bastards off. Or. Wait. No. Wilbur died... Deakins' people. We had a bit of a civil war, ya see. Old commander Major Deakins was a crazy asshole. He snapped, started shooting the civilians."

"Yeah," said Harper in a gentle voice. "You told us already."

"I did?" Jeff blinked. "Strange. I don't remem—"

He stared into nowhere, his face frozen in a wide-eyed mask of total confusion.

She waited for him to collect his thoughts and continue. But after almost a full minute of no change in his expression, it dawned on her the man hadn't simply paused, lost for thought. National Guard Sergeant Jeffrey Myrick died right in front of her, in mid-sentence.

"We should get out of here," whispered Harper.

"I agree." Ken backed toward the tent flap.

She glanced at him. "What's more respectful: leaving him here or carrying him to the grave and dropping him in?"

"Hard call. They're both kinda bad, but I suppose a grave is technically better than just leaving him here."

Harper swallowed saliva. She summoned up the nerve to get close and checked him for a pulse. The smell wafting off him at that distance nearly took her off her feet. A choking miasma of vomit, urine, feces, and whatever decay came from the cancer eating away inside him nearly made her throw up on the spot. *Somehow,* she fought it back and kept a—mostly—straight face.

"Yes, he's gone." She backed up a few steps so she could breathe. "He tried to protect innocent people. We should at least bury him as respectfully as it's possible to."

TICKING DOWN

MAY 26TH

Sergeant Clarke had been the one to push the wheelchair to the grave pit, sparing Harper the need to look in at the hundreds of dead faces again. Despite the huge mountain of dirt on the far side of the pit and several military excavators, no one tried to turn one on and fill in the grave. Chances were, the fuel inside the machines had denatured and wouldn't work. That, and the area—especially the body pit—presented an unknown radiation hazard. Clarke insisted they clear out.

Harper hated being right. She figured there wouldn't be anything useful at the camp. Though she hadn't been *completely* accurate. The trip proved slightly useful in minor ways if not for medical supplies and food. She learned officially the nukes that rained down on her home came from Russia. It didn't prove China hadn't fired, too. The chaos that National Guard soldier described made it sound like everyone went crazy and any nation with nuclear weapons fired them in a panicked frenzy.

The horror of irradiated survivors flowing out of Denver—so many gravely wounded and doomed innocent people—went way beyond her ability to process. It overwhelmed her to the point she didn't feel much, like reading about the atrocities of World War II in school. Millions of dead was a statistic one could file away as information devoid of emotion. One person you knew who died, that's a tragedy. This close to Lakewood, odds were high she would have known or at least met some of the dead in the mass grave. People she'd seen in passing, store clerks, teachers, other parents... possibly even the friends she hadn't seen since the strike.

If Andrea or Veronica or Christina were dead, she hoped they got vaporized right away and didn't endure anything horrible. Naturally, she'd prefer they lived, but... life wasn't a Disney movie. That she'd found Renee and Darci alive already defied the odds.

She replayed the journey with Maddie out of Lakewood in her mind up to finding Cliff and Jonathan at the flooded mall. The poor kid had been terrified when he saw her at first, and swam away. Harper fumed at the senseless anger directed at Chinese people. Russia had been antagonistic with the US for a long, long time. Many of the movies her Dad loved depicted them as the bad guys. She'd learned about the Cold War in school. What the heck made people around here forget about all of that and target Asians? Had something gone by on the news she didn't pay attention to? Did panicking people simply stop hiding their racism and lash out at everyone who didn't look like them?

Jonathan's parents died because people are vicious and stupid.

These questions, she'd likely never be able to answer. Being furious about what happened to Jonathan wouldn't help. A catastrophe like nuclear war could bring out the best in humanity as easily as it showed people at their worst. If Jeff Myrick had been right about a stray Russian nuke hitting India and setting off a retaliatory strike on Pakistan without any effort being made to verify what happened... it didn't bode well for humanity.

Cliff said the MIRV in their proverbial backyard was Russian-made. That tracked with what the National Guard soldier told her. Still didn't offer any clue as to who shot first or *why* anyone shot at all.

More shit that doesn't matter. It happened. Who cares who did it at this point?

The reconnaissance trip to the abandoned camp left her fidgety with anger she had no outlet for. She couldn't vent her rage on the people who killed Jonathan's parents. She couldn't do anything about the bomb sitting right outside Evergreen. Her gaze fell on the Ansons. Zoey clung to her father. Brandon sat next to his mother, letting her hold him like a live teddy bear.

Can't do much about a lot of things, but I can try to make life easier for people like them.

She shifted left so she could peer through the little doorway at the world outside the windshield. Highway scrolled by, a seemingly endless, empty ribbon of pavement dotted here and there with the occasional abandoned car or mangled chunk of debris flung from miles away. She watched the road until her neck hurt, then un-twisted herself to sit with her back against the partition separating the cargo area from the driver's compartment. The Anson children appeared relaxed, hopeful, almost even happy.

That guy was wrong. Harper exhaled out her nose. *Humanity is in trouble, sure, but we're not finished.*

She thought of the town of Fairplay, where everyone acted like Wild West cosplayers. It would've been nostalgic and a bit funny if not for the guns being real.

Great. Now we've got nutjobs running around pretending to be medieval knights. Okay, humanity is in a weird place right now, but it's not screwed.

Ken broke the silence, starting to talk to the family about Evergreen and what to expect when they got there: visit to the medical center, meeting the mayor and Anne-Marie, being assigned a house and so on. The family seemed grateful and receptive to the notion of settling in. All four of them, especially the kids, had enough of the nomadic life. When Harper told them about other kids they could hang out with, Brandon and Zoey cheered.

"It's kinda hard to believe, honestly." Grant raked a hand up over his wild hair. "A whole town?"

"Started off as just a bunch of survivors," said Ken. "More people kept showing up. More of the right people, that is. Farmers, a teacher, a couple electricians, a few ex-cops and a civil engineer or two. I mean, sure, we had some desperate times, but we're looking fairly stable now."

"You got any skills?" asked Sergeant Clarke.

Grant laughed. "Nothing that'll matter anymore. Used to be a software engineer."

"I worked as a branch manager for a bank." Melanie pressed a hand to her forehead. "Masters degree in accounting and it's all I could find."

"At least you don't have to worry about those student loans anymore," deadpanned Harper.

Ken's expression hardened. "Sorry to change the subject to unpleasant matters, but... do you have any idea where those idiots were taking you?"

"East." Grant shifted his weight. "Somewhere east. They didn't tell us exactly."

"You were heading north when we found you," called Leigh from the front.

"You heard the way that guy talked." Melanie rolled her eyes. "Those dumbasses probably said East but went north. Or maybe they wanted to go downtown first and then east. All they said was 'Safe Haven.'"

"Probably what they call their settlement." Sergeant Clarke absentmindedly opened, resealed, and opened a Velcro pocket on the side of his camo pant leg.

"Are the bad men going to find us?" asked Zoey.

Deacon lightly punched his right fist into his left palm. "I hope they do."

Brandon grinned at him.

"I kinda doubt it," said Sergeant Clarke. "But if they do, they are going to regret it."

"You'll be safe in Evergreen." Harper smiled despite feeling like a liar, thinking of the nuke. "Or at least as safe as is reasonably possible these days."

Grant, Melanie, and the kids all returned her smile.

She tried not to feel like a monster. Cliff and Dr. Rowland both seemed quite confident the MIRV wouldn't go off... or at least wouldn't go thermonuclear. It might explode and scatter radioactive material around its area, but that kind of detonation wouldn't immediately kill everyone. Whether or not Evergreen could manage a cleanup of such a dangerous mess or would ultimately have to uproot and go elsewhere, she couldn't say. Fear that radiation from a 'dirty bomb' blast so close by would get into the groundwater and poison the farm kept her fidgeting for the remainder of the ride back to town.

However irrational it might be, she still feared the thing might detonate big.

Well, if it does... I won't have to worry about feeling like I lied to this family.

WORST CASE SCENARIO

Heavy, overcast clouds hung in the skies over Evergreen.
Harper stood outside the school, waiting for the kids to come swarming out the doors.

All sense of time came from best guessing. The town lost power during the strike, and didn't get it back for months… not until Jeanette and her team started cobbling together solar panels. A few 'probably accurate' wind-up style wristwatches offered the only clue of the previous time system. People in Evergreen made do as best they could, guessing at the time based on daylight or the sun's position. Of course, without day jobs or corporate employers, it didn't really matter if things happened to be off by an hour or two in either direction.

A breeze kicked up, sending a spiral of dirt and old leaves swirling along the curved road passing by the school's front doors. The absence of a line of buses and parents waiting in their cars seemed unusually profound in that moment. Harper found herself confused at their absence. How had she wound up standing alone outside the school? Where had all the other parents gone?

In the midst of her 'oh yeah, we had a war' epiphany, the front doors burst open.

Madison led the charge of kids freed from the drudgery of learning inside on a nice day. She spotted Harper and came running over, beaming a huge smile as she ran across the concrete area in front of the school.

The instant Maddie's sneaker hit the road, a blinding white flash devoured the sky in the distance behind the building. Madison, seemingly oblivious to the light, continued running toward her. Other kids behind her turned in response to the flash, started screaming—and began to disintegrate where they stood.

Violet Olsen, the teacher, shrieked as she burst into flames. The woman collapsed amid a futile effort to push the smaller children back inside the door.

Little bodies turned to silhouettes, faint glimpses of bones hanging in the air for a split second before blowing away as dust on the breeze. Harper grabbed Madison by the hand and sprinted away from the building. They sheltered behind the nearest, fattest tree in sight seconds before a deafening roar went off.

The ground and sky traded places in a blurry tumble. Harper bounced over and over as the blast wave threw them into the woods. Madison's hand slipped out of her grasp. She banged her head on the ground. It didn't hurt. Impact with a tree should've smashed every rib in her chest, but somehow only knocked the wind out of her.

She slapped into the dirt on her chest, slid a bit, then came to a stop against a fallen, burning tree.

Harper tried to scream for Madison, but her voice couldn't compete with the ongoing roar of a nuclear fireball. Hot, hurricane-force winds ripped over her. She shielded her face with one arm and sat up, desperate to find her little sister.

Everything around her had become flat, open wasteland. No school ruins, no forest, no hills, blank and empty as a dry lakebed. Only a mushroom cloud in the distance offered any change of scenery. Intense warmth blanketed her from the direction of the rising mushroom, a hair short of painful. She sat on the ground, staring in mute horror at the orangey-red-black plume billowing upward.

A blizzard of ash began to fall around her, swirling and whipping in the heat-fueled wind.

Madison lay on her back a few feet away. After a few seconds, she sat up, looked over, and droned, "Here we go again."

Unable to believe what just happened, Harper looked toward the school... or where it had been, squinting at the glow of the Sun come to Earth. The building disappeared. The tree the two of them sheltered behind remained. Had it not been there a second ago when she looked up? It didn't even appear to be on fire.

"How did that tree stop a nuclear bomb?" rasped Harper.

"It didn't," deadpanned Madison.

"What?" She whipped her head around to stare at her little sister. "Are we dead?"

"No, silly. We're dreaming." Fire erupted all over Madison, racing down her arms. Skin melted off her hands in seconds. Black char crept around the sides of her face. "Ow. This hurts."

Madison's charred head fell off, tumbling forward.

Harper screamed—and sat up in bed.

The ghost of her scream echoed. She couldn't tell if she'd really screamed out loud or her voice never left the nightmare. Sweat trickled down her face.

Madison, beside her in the bed, whimpered something unintelligible and clamp-hugged her, trembling. A tiny bit of moonlight made it in the window, enough to at least see her sister's face and chase away the awful image of her burning alive.

Her voice crashed into a wall of emotion, feeble as a hamster trying to batter down the Hoover Dam. She wrapped both arms around Madison and held her tight, at the edge of tears. Madison made no effort to remain outwardly stoic, crying, and sniffling.

Lorelei, on Madison's left against the wall, remained sound asleep.

A few minutes later, Madison quieted. Harper relaxed her embrace and held her sister out far enough to look into her eyes.

"You, too?" whispered Madison.

"Yeah."

They stared at each other for a moment, then asked, "Nuke?" simultaneously.

Harper nodded once. "Sorry."

"It's okay. I would've had nightmares about something else if you didn't tell me." Madison put on a fake brave face. "I have nightmares all the time. What's one more?"

She's joking about it. Harper exhaled out her nose, relieved. *Not a big deal. She's okay.*

"Let's get rid of it." Madison pulled her hair off her face. "The city council is gonna argue forever."

Harper shifted to sit cross-legged, rested her elbows on her knees, and grabbed her face in both hands. "We can't move something like that by ourselves. It's too dangerous to even get close to it for more than a few minutes."

"Are we gonna leave?" whispered Madison.

"Nope. This is home. We've all put too much work and sweat into this place to just give up because of some stupid missile."

Madison gave a nervous chuckle.

"We'll fix it... somehow. Just need to figure out the best way to do it."

"I dreamed everyone died but us," said Madison in a distant tone.

"Same."

They sat together in silence for about a minute, then sighed together. At that, Madison covered her mouth to hold in a giggle.

"What's funny?"

"We're doing the same thing. Like, sighing at the same time." Madison made a goofy face. "Stupid, but it made me laugh."

Harper smoothed her hands up over her hair, gripped the back of her neck for a few seconds, then let them flop into her lap. "Yeah."

Another moment passed in silence.

"Just a dream." Madison wiped her face.

"Just a dream." Harper put an arm around her.

"It's because of what happened to us, right?" Madison leaned against her. "Just you and me running away from the bad guys and not knowing if anyone else was still alive."

Harper took a few deep breaths, trying to calm down. "Yeah. Probably where the nightmare came from. Or at least the part where it's just us left. It's weird we both had the same dream."

"Was it exactly the same?" whispered Madison. "We were playing in the yard. You were sitting on the porch watching us. For some reason, I don't even know, I ran over to you like I wanted to ask you something... then the bomb went off and everyone else disappeared in a bright light."

"Ugh." Harper squeezed her close. "Not quite the same. I went to pick you guys up at school. Bomb went off just as everyone came running out the doors. So freaky."

"Yeah." Madison poked her in the ribs. "Weird *you* had a nightmare. I always have them."

"You haven't had one in a while, though." Harper rubbed a hand up and down Madison's back.

Madison yawned. "Yeah, but... we haven't had a nuke sitting right next to us before."

"It's been there the whole time... we just didn't know about it."

"Uhh." Madison gave her side eye. "That doesn't really help me relax. I appreciate this whole new 'be honest with Maddie' thing you're doing, but sometimes maybe I don't need to know stuff."

Harper chuckled. "Are you being serious or sarcastic?"

"Mostly sarcastic." Madison smiled. "I'm okay. Are we going to try to sleep again?"

"Still deciding." Harper stared into the dark room for a moment, then felt a yawn coming up. She guessed it had to be approximately two hours from sunrise due to the state of her bladder: not quite full enough to make her run to the bathroom, but too full to get comfortable if she tried to go back to sleep. "Yeah, should at least try to sleep some more. Gotta pee first."

"Me too."

"Kay. Let's do that." Harper extricated herself from the covers and stood.

Madison scooted away from Lorelei and jumped out of bed, following her across the hall into the bathroom.

Her sister pushed the door shut and turned her back. "You can go first."

Harper sat on the toilet, head in her hands, and tried to force the images of Madison on fire out of her mind. She'd rather have had a nightmare where all the dead bodies started climbing out of the mass grave after her than see her sister burning alive. Unfortunately, she couldn't choose her nightmares. She could, however, choose not to let them dominate her mind. Exactly the way she'd set aside her panic when the Lawless chased them across Lakewood, she acted as if the dream didn't bother her much, hadn't been as bad as it was. Madison needed the reassurance.

Once they finished using the bathroom, they hurried back to bed. Madison snuggled in beside her, not *too* clingy, but holding her hand. The last time her sister had a bad nightmare, Harper lost all circulation in one arm... so definite improvement.

She smiled at the ceiling. *We're gonna be okay.*

22

NINETEEN

TUESDAY, JUNE 2ND

Harper found herself awake, proof the nuclear warhead decided to behave itself for now.

"Ugh," she muttered to no one in particular upon realizing the date. "June 2, 2020, twenty-one months after dumbasses lit the world on fire."

It wouldn't bother her if no one made a big deal about the day, but she knew better than to expect her family to ignore it. Madison appeared to be faking sleep, quasi-clinging to her left side, face mushed into Harper's shoulder. Lorelei—*not* faking sleep—had somehow wound up backward in bed, mostly under the blankets with her feet sticking up, one beside Harper's head on the pillow.

She would have needed to be blindfolded, dumb, and not have any sense of smell to fail to notice Jonathan slipped away for a few hours yesterday next door to bake the cake for today. Carrie conducted a handful of sessions with the kids since his birthday, which resulted in various forms of baked treats.

Today would be Harper's second birthday without her parents. Surprisingly, she didn't dwell on that fact beyond taking note of it.

Lorelei's foot proved too tempting a distraction away from bad thoughts. She reached up and tickled the defenseless sole.

Lorelei didn't react.

Harper lifted the bedding and peered down underneath to make sure the girl was still breathing. She appeared to be fine, merely sleeping hard as she usually did.

"Whoa," whispered Madison. "How'd she get upside down?"

"She's not upside down. She's backward." Harper pondered. "Wouldn't upside down be lying on her stomach?"

"No, this is a bed. It's like standing up... sorta." Madison yawned, stretched, then sat up. "Her head is where her feet should be, so she's upside down."

"Okay. Works for me. She's upside down." Harper chuckled.

She got out of bed, repositioned Lorelei the right way around, then hit the bathroom before returning to get dressed as Maddie staggered across the hall. Once changed, Harper peeled Lorelei out of her nightgown, then dressed her like a toddler while she remained fast asleep. The girl adored dresses, which made life easy, not only in putting them on her while she slept, but making new ones as well. Renee had a much simpler time crafting dresses than pants with legs.

Harper scooped Lorelei up and carried her out to the kitchen while Maddie got dressed.

It surprised her—somewhat—to find Logan there already in the midst of cooking breakfast: scrambled eggs, fried potatoes, and as close as they could get to bacon using deer meat. Harper brought Lorelei over to the counter and waved her face over the serving plate of veni-bacon.

The girl sniffed twice, then opened her eyes. She gazed around blearily, noticed the food, and tried to bite a piece. Harper lifted her away, laughing.

"Hey, no fair." Lorelei yawned again.

"Morning, kiddo." Harper set her on her feet, then kissed her atop the head.

Lorelei reached for a piece of 'bacon.' Harper didn't stop her. Grinning, the child 'stole' a strip and scurried to the table to sit.

"Hey there." Logan slid up beside Harper, one arm around her back, and kissed her. "Can I say it?"

"Never ask a woman such a vague and dangerous question." Harper winked. "But, in this case, since I know what you're talking about, sure."

"Happy birthday." He kissed her again.

"Thanks." She wrapped her arms around him, letting the kiss last a while.

Lorelei 'snuck' past them to nab another piece of 'bacon.' Harper grinned at the child seeming to think she genuinely got away with not being noticed.

Right as she and Logan began to change from a fairly innocent good morning and happy birthday type kiss to something a tad more energetic, Cliff walked in carrying the babies. Harper jumped like a teenage girl caught making out with her boyfriend. She spun to face her 'dad,' mentally preparing to deny wrongdoing—then noticed he had a gas mask on, which made him look like a bug-eyed alien.

"Gah!" yelled Harper, startled at the bizarre sight.

Logan cracked up.

"We should be thankful," said Cliff, his voice muffled.

"For what?" asked Logan.

The nuke didn't blow up yet? We survived the war? We're still alive? Harper bit her lip.

Cliff handed one baby to Harper, freeing up a hand he used to peel the gas mask off. "Thankful the Russians didn't drop goddamned diapers on us and used something tamer, like nuclear weapons instead."

Harper blinked. "Did you seriously put a gas mask on to change diapers?"

"Got the tools. Why not use them?" Cliff tossed the mask onto his favorite recliner, then shifted the infant into a cradling grip with both arms. "Mind feeding Emmett? Carrie's busy with woman stuff."

"Umm. My boobs aren't open for business." Harper chuckled to herself.

"Dammit. That's not what I..." Cliff fumbled for words, seeming more than a little embarrassed. "Are we out of formula already?"

Harper rocked her littlest brother. "They only gave us one can, and it's in the other house for emergencies if Carrie has some issues producing or the babies have issues with her milk."

"Well, you know I didn't mean for you to literally feed the boy." Cliff exhaled. "I... Carrie's doing stuff. She'll be here soon. Just... hold him. Keep your shirt on."

Snickering, Harper carried the baby over to the table and took a seat. *She's doing something for 'the birthday' and he doesn't want to ruin the surprise that's not a surprise.* She smiled down at the baby. "I think this is Owen. You've got Emmett."

Cliff raised an eyebrow. He looked at the baby in his arms, at the one Harper held, then back again. "Are you sure? They look the same to me."

"They're identical twins, right?" Logan scratched his head.

"Yeah." Cliff moved to stand beside Harper so the babies would be next to each other. "Honestly, I think they keep trading names back and forth. Probably won't know which one's which until they're old enough to tell us."

Harper made baby noises at Owen. "This one feels like Owen."

"What do you mean 'feels like'?" Cliff sniffed the hair of the baby he held. "This one smells like an Owen to me."

"Hah." Harper had no idea if Cliff really couldn't tell the babies apart or clowned around. She also couldn't say *why* she felt certain she held Owen.

Madison and Jonathan breezed in and sat at the table. Logan transferred the big serving plates to the table. Renee came in via the back door, grinned in a 'yes, you know exactly what's going on just pretend to be surprised' sort of way, and sat in the chair next to Harper's.

Her best friend wore one of her earlier attempts at dressmaking, an incredibly basic, plain thing that made her look like a Depression era foundling in a flour sack.

"'Nay." Harper held the baby out. "Is this Owen or Emmett?"

"Owen, why?"

Harper stuck her tongue out at Cliff. "See?"

"How do you girls tell them apart?" Cliff teased his index finger around the baby's mouth, overacting a gasp of pain when the infant bit him.

Renee cooed at the baby. "I dunno. I just know. This is Owen. You've got Emmett."

Carrie entered, carrying a suspicious giant Tupperware box, which she slid onto the counter, acting as if Harper didn't see it. "Good morning."

"Identify the baby." Harper held the infant up.

The little one reached for his mother and began making noises.

"Owen." Carrie took the baby from her. "Someone's hungry."

Emmett fidgeted in Cliff's lap, making a repeated 'Meh' sound.

"He's either trying to say 'mama' or he's expressing his thorough state of being unimpressed with the universe," muttered Harper.

Carrie sat beside Cliff, pulled her shirt open, and attached an infant to each breast.

"You can really tell them apart?" Cliff raised both eyebrows.

"Yeah. You can't?" Carrie grinned.

"How." Cliff leaned closer, overacting 'studying' the babies. "They look the same to me."

"Mother's intuition, I suppose. I just know." Carrie leaned up and kissed him.

BREAKFAST WENT BY TOO FAST. TIME WITH FAMILY MEANT EVERYTHING to Harper.

She escorted the kids to school, Logan going along, then proceeded to follow her usual patrol route. Logan kept walking with her.

"Spending the whole day with me?" she asked, smiling.

"I could. Probably get yelled at but, it would be worth it."

Harper idly kicked at a pebble or two on the road. "They're not going to do the birthday thing until later. We can wait for you to finish on the farm."

"I'm not showing up just for the cake." Logan grinned. "Though, it is a big plus."

She laughed. "Yeah, it's been a while, hasn't it?"

"You know I'm never going to say no if you want that... but spending time with you matters the most."

Harper sighed wistfully. As much as she felt it possible to do, she loved Logan. Neither she, nor Renee, Darci, or Grace could truly tell if she fell in 'high school girl' love with him or something deeper. After what happened with Tyler, she tried to forget boys existed at all... but then Logan showed up and, well... she couldn't stop thinking about him. She wanted sex as much as he did, much to her surprise. Only bad part, sex had become like playing Russian roulette with a giant revolver that had a baby in one chamber. No matter how careful they tried to be, every time they did the deed, she risked her life.

Perhaps she feared it too much. After all, humanity existed long before modern medicine and enough women survived childbirth for the species not to die off. It's not like having a baby would destroy her future career and education. Her parents would've been shocked and likely not happy if she got pregnant at nineteen had the world not been destroyed. She had no doubt they'd eventually have come around and helped her. Maybe she'd have put the baby up for adoption. Becoming a stay-at-home mom dependent on a man for survival never appealed. So, yeah, if she got pregnant at this age in a normal world, it would've been adoption time. Or... maybe her parents would've taken over as primary caretakers. A girl at school a year or two ahead of her faced that situation. Rumor had it the parents planned to tell the baby the girl was his sister, not his mother.

They'll end up on Jerry Springer in twelve years... if TV was still a thing.
She chuckled.

"Hmm?" Logan glanced over at her. "What are you laughing at?"

Harper explained where her thoughts went.

"Oh. Uhh... well, I wasn't thinking we should have a kid. I mean, if it happens, great. But... we should probably wait."

"Yeah." Harper breathed a sigh of relief. *Wow, he's not freaking out because he thinks I want a baby. I don't want a baby. I have enough children to take care of already.*

"If you ever want an excuse to take a long vacation from militia work…" He winked. "Let me know and I can arrange it."

Harper cackled. True enough. If she got pregnant, she'd be off the militia for a while… at least until the baby no longer needed milk. Or maybe not quite that long. She'd definitely be sidelined for the last half of pregnancy plus several months. Would Walter tell her to stay at home if she had an infant? None of the women on the militia had become pregnant yet, so she had nothing to base her assumptions on.

They walked hand in hand for about ten minutes, Harper drifting between getting cute with him and trying to stay focused on her job.

"I'm in the way, aren't I?" Logan squeezed her hand.

Harper made a noncommittal noise.

"That's a yes." He chuckled. "It's fine. You have serious stuff to do. I shouldn't distract you. Someone might get hurt, and you'd blame yourself instead of me."

She stopped walking. "That's not… okay, maybe it is fair, but it sucks to say out loud."

"Don't worry. It's not like we're trying to avoid getting fired from Wendy's." He snuck a quick kiss. "You're keeping people safe, and I'm helping keep us all from starving. Bit more important than the paycheck from a summer job."

"Yeah."

"See you later on?" He took a step back, still holding her hand.

"I better see you later on." She fake glared. "It's my birthday. And I think I know what I want from you for my birthday."

He raised both eyebrows, acting as if he'd totally forgotten to get her a gift. "Umm, you do?"

"I do." She leaned toward him, attempting her best sexy eye flutter. "And it's *not* a baby."

Logan fanned himself.

"The boy isn't as dumb as he looks." She winked.

"Today's gonna be so long..." He staggered off like a lovestruck Disney prince.

Harper sighed, smiling to herself and watching him vanish into the trees. Part of her felt a bit crazy for allowing herself to get so... horny given the current dangers surrounding Evergreen. However, she *was* eight—no, nineteen. Teenage hormones surged regardless of what the world did. And, honestly, if she had to stop enjoying the life they still had, what would be the point of working so hard to stay alive?

Perhaps shooting people hadn't been the most drastic change in her personality. The girl, once too shy to feel comfortable around boys in a swimsuit, now had to force herself not to chase after Logan and throw him to the ground right there next to South Hiwan Drive. Her racy daydream lasted only seconds before the fear of being caught dumped a bucket of metaphorical ice water over her head.

Almost a year ago, she'd investigated noises coming from an empty house and caught Beth and Jaden in the act. Barging in on the two of them naked had probably been more embarrassing for her than them. Beth still had trouble looking at her without blushing or being awkward. Craziest part of the whole thing was how the two lovebirds remained together. She'd interrupted more than a lustful teenage hookup. Maybe she and Logan had something real, too?

Ever since Luisa arrived and started living with Logan, it became more difficult to find private time together. They couldn't exactly do the deed in that house whenever they wanted. If his younger sister wasn't there to catch them, they had a yard full of children who would certainly come running if they heard any weird noises... or a Lorelei who could randomly just decide she wanted to find Harper at any moment without warning. The girl loved to show off anything curious she discovered: rocks, bugs, sticks, old toys, pieces of plastic, whatever.

The girl's basically a raven. Collects shiny stuff and brings it to me.

They couldn't do it in Harper's house either, for most of the same reasons, plus the sheer wrongness of having sex in the same bed she shared with her sisters. Even though Cliff spent nights next door in Carrie's house more often than not lately, using his bed also felt wrong. They had to get creative in search of privacy, drifting farther and farther out across town in search of unoccupied houses they could borrow for an hour or three, or wander off into the woods.

Harper exhaled, smiled, and resumed walking her patrol. Logan was right. She had to stay focused. Not much to do about the warhead, but she did worry about the red-and-blue gang as well as the psycho Templars, or whatever other lunatics might be out there. The breakdown of society meant the complete lack of organized law enforcement. Anyone could do anything and not have to fear the police coming after them. Well, mostly. In Evergreen, they'd have the militia to worry about. It ended up almost being worse than before. Very few residents liked the idea of 'wasting food' on someone who just sat in a jail cell all day without contributing to the survival of the town. While a person might end up in the old sheriff's office jail for a few days over minor things like a bar fight at Earl's, serious crimes would be punished with exile or execution.

To distract herself from such sobering thoughts, Harper recalled a conversation she had with Darci a week or two ago. She and Lucas had gone west through the woods to Bear Creek Road, specifically the creek that paralleled it, to go skinny dipping and make love in the woods. They'd done it in the water, relaxed naked on the grass beside the water, did it again, then went for a nudist hike, even checking out this weird house right beside the creek with a big, round, elevated patio type affair on the second story. The idea of her friend and Lucas just roaming around bare-assed and exploring someone else's house like that made her blush. It also excited her in a way. She and Logan had messed around out in the forest before, but they hadn't left their clothes off any longer than necessary. Going house exploring nude? No. That went past her comfort zone. Darci could have her 'last two people on Earth' fantasy.

More people than only her friend and her husband challenged old norms. Some of the younger residents, Lorelei especially, gave up on swimsuits at the golf club pool. A few adults did, too, but only in the evening after the kids went home. Darci even walked into town with no clothes once or twice to pick stuff up from the quartermaster. The girl couldn't even blame it on being too high to realize she'd left home like that. After having Piper, she'd been abstaining from weed until she stopped breastfeeding. Despite her friend's epic slackerdom, she'd been crazy dedicated to her daughter as well as Elijah, the boy she and Lucas took in. Of all her friends, Harper would've chosen Darci to be the absolute *last* one to have kids or get married. Though, honestly, despite her friend's gothy gloom and persistent air of 'life sucks, why bother,' she had a huge heart and had always been the first one showing up to help any of them with anything.

Harper chuckled to herself. Darci off weed for any length of time rivaled nuclear war in terms of shocking changes. Kids were exhausting, especially infants. Likely, her slacker side hooked up with her hippie side and decided to entirely dispense with the labor required to maintain clothing as long as the weather didn't demand it.

A few residents complained about her showing up at the quartermaster's in her birthday suit, but what could the militia really do about it? They weren't about to put someone in jail for not wearing clothes. It certainly didn't rise to the level of demanding exile. It also wasn't as if Darci ran around getting in people's business, being lewd, crass, and teasing them. She simply existed in her natural state—as she put it.

Harper suspected her friend had some notion she gave the patriarchy the finger, but it didn't make the idea of her friend streaking Evergreen any less squirmy. Somehow, Darci's story of her woodland tryst with Lucas clung to the back of Harper's mind. By the time she reached the end of her patrol shift, she'd made the decision to ask Logan out to Bear Creek tonight or tomorrow. She'd never want to get caught in town without clothes, but just the two of them in the woods did sound exciting in a taboo sort of way. Not *too* big a deal if someone caught them out there. Being off in the woods with her boyfriend (looking for privacy) had a completely different energy than casually strolling naked down Route 74 without a care as to who saw what.

Harper never really felt the stereotypical teenage compulsion to drink beer or wine. She tried it once or twice but not to excess. Drugs, however, she avoided. 'Going wood nymph' with Logan for a while tickled her sense of adventure the same way she imagined the kids at her school who snuck off to go drinking felt. They'd messed around a few times outside already on the spur of the moment. A longer, planned, 'adventure' sounded like fun.

Screw it. We could die at any second if that bomb goes off. I'm going to live a little.

ONCE HER PATROL TIME ENDED, SHE PICKED THE KIDS UP FROM SCHOOL.

She walked them home—right into the 'surprise' birthday party she expected. Harper's incredibly fake attempt to act surprised became comedic, so she ran with it. Logan arrived a few minutes later. The fourteen-to-sixteen-year-olds showing up at the farm told him school ended for the day, which meant Harper would be going home. Younger kids had the option to help on the farm or have free time for now, but in another week after school officially stopped for the summer, they'd be on the farm all morning, too.

Jonathan had indeed baked the cake, which turned out good, tasting almost exactly the same as the one Carrie made for his birthday. He also gave Harper a drawing of her as a shotgun-toting superhero ala Black Widow. She loved it for two reasons. One: he'd drawn it. Two: this illustration didn't make her cry in front of everyone like the one he gave her last birthday did.

Renee gave her a handmade dress. Grace gave her an Aragorn Funko Pop she'd found in the quartermaster's 'miscellaneous' room. Madison got 'revenge' on her for her last birthday gift by giving Harper a box of pads. Or, so she thought at first. The box didn't contain pads, rather a couple of weird-looking small pie-faced cloth dolls with simple black rings for eyes. Each had a 'skirt' made from a hair scrunchie, one green, one pink, and one blue. The three five-inch figures resembled the creepy, haunted things that tried to kill people in a low budget horror movie... yet somehow remained endearingly cute.

"I made them," said Madison. "Might as well learn to sew, right? And no, it's not because I'm a girl. It's fun."

"Those things are definitely going to come to life at night and try to kill someone," muttered Cliff.

Harper bit her arm to stop from laughing.

Madison raspberried him.

"They're adorable." Harper hugged the creepy little dolls. "I'm gonna put them on the dresser so they can watch over us while we sleep."

Madison stared at her.

"Even if Dad's right," said Jonathan, "they're like small Australian wildlife. Cute, and definitely *wants* to kill you, but can't because they're too small."

"Sounds like Mila," deadpanned Renee.

Jonathan blushed a little.

"Yes, yes." Mila examined her fingernails. "I have numerous weapons, the deadliest of which is my apparent harmlessness."

Everything got quiet.

"Wow, guys." Mila rolled her eyes. "I'm kidding. Mostly."

Chuckling spread around the room, gradually turning to laughter.

Carrie gave her a little unicorn music box.

"Oh, wow. Where did you find this?" Harper held it up.

"I've had it since I was little. Figured I'd give it to my daughter, but I never had one... until now."

Harper bit her lip. "I feel guilty."

"Don't." Carrie winked. "If Cliff does it to me again and we have a girl, you can give it to her."

Cliff put on an air of fake nervousness.

Everyone laughed.

A bunch of kids hopped up on cake zoomed out into the backyard and got to kicking the ball around while screaming off excess energy. Luisa joined them, seeming happy. She didn't really make much effort to find friends her age, not that Evergreen had a ton of sixteen-year-olds. It worked out in a way, as she was old enough to be a responsible babysitter to help Carrie and Harper wrangle the smaller ones.

Harper spent the afternoon hanging out with her friends and Logan. Lucas Garza showed up for a brief period with baby Piper and Elijah. The boy joined the other kids out in the yard while Darci fed the baby in the living room.

Eventually, it got late enough that Darci and Grace had to leave. Darci needed to take Piper home for a nap and Grace needed sleep for another long day at the medical center. Becca, Eva, Christopher, and Mila also said their goodbye-for-nows and went home. Harper found herself sitting on a metal folding chair in the backyard with her family, plus Logan. Jonathan went inside to draw for a while before they ran out of light. Madison plopped on the ground by Harper, leaning against her. Cliff reclined in a beach lounger, both babies asleep on his chest. Carrie sat next to him, she and Renee talking about random bits of local gossip as well as the clothing making endeavor.

Harper smiled at the look on Cliff's face. The man gave off a sense of being way out of his element, 'trapped' under two infants, but she knew he did it for laughs. The man adored where life took him. Looking at the twins made her start worrying about leaving the Mossberg in the bedroom. Bad enough they had Lorelei, and sometimes Elijah, around. No amount of telling the kids not to touch guns would make her feel safe.

However, until she felt totally certain random idiots wouldn't come out of the woods and cause trouble, she needed to keep the weapon handy enough to get to fast in case of emergency. She pondered asking Cliff to install a high shelf in the bedroom, somewhere she could put the shotgun out of reach of children but still be able to grab it in a hurry. She lost herself in a fondly wistful daydream of all the gun safety talks Dad gave her over the years. If he was alive to see her leaving the Mossberg simply tucked behind the headboard of her bed while fully loaded, he'd have flipped out.

What would work better? Height or concealment? Maybe both?

"What's on your mind?" asked Logan. "You look troubled."

"Just thinking about this crazy world we ended up in." She gazed at the darkening sky overhead. "Worrying about leaving guns just sitting out around kids."

He whistled. "Yeah, that's a problem. Maybe we could take the attraction out of it by teaching them how to shoot? Kids that play with guns do it mostly because they find something the parents keep hidden. It's taboo, so it becomes appealing. If we put it right in front of them, it loses that mystique."

Cliff glanced over at him, one eyebrow up.

"Really?" Harper chuckled. "Would your answer to underage drinking be to give six-year-olds beer so they know what it tastes like?"

"Hah. No. It's not really the same situation, though. Drinking beer at that age could hurt them."

Harper twirled a lock of hair around her fingers. "We don't have enough bullets to let kids shoot at targets for fun. Maybe it's not really worth me worrying about. By the time the twins are old enough to get a hold of a weapon, we probably won't even have bullets left."

"I suppose. Though I hope we do." He squeezed her hand. "If only because it means we haven't had to use them."

"Yeah. Me too." She leaned against him. "I really wasn't sure what turning nineteen would feel like, but... this isn't it."

"That's the sneaky thing about getting older." Cliff gently patted both sleeping babies. "One day, you're a kid. Then you blink and realize you've been an adult for a while and didn't even know it. Aren't sure how it happened."

"Yeah." Harper kept watching the clouds go by overhead. No one treated her like a child anymore. She didn't look like one or even feel like one. At some point over the past year, her sense of responsibility got in the habit of kicking teenage laziness and recklessness in the head—not that she'd ever been too reckless. The last time anyone truly treated her like a child, she'd been sixteen, working retail over the summer, with a total jerk for a manager. He'd talked down to her like he scolded a ten-year-old. Back then, she kept quiet and took it. Now, she'd have told him to go eat a dick... or something equally colorful.

Great self-confidence program. Guaranteed to work or your money back.
Only costs a few nuclear bombs.

Despite the morbid thought, she wanted to laugh.

As the evening deepened, she got a little cute with Logan, but
didn't do anything too embarrassing given that her 'parents' were
right there. Madison watched as if tuned into a television show,
amazingly not making faces or saying 'eww.'

Much to her chagrin, Lorelei and Madison got a bit too clingy and
happy for her to dislodge a guilt boulder and slip away with Logan.
Before he went home with Luisa for the night, she whispered to him
about wanting to do something fun, exciting, and a little risky
tomorrow.

"I can't wait. Might not sleep tonight." He kissed her.

She stared into his eyes for a long time until he finally flashed a
rogue's grin and made his way across the yard to his house. Harper
stood there watching him until he disappeared through the doorway.

Eighteen and owns—more or less—his own house. Wow, the world is
crazy now.

HARPER, MADISON, AND LORELEI SETTLED INTO BED AFTER A NICE—NOT
relaxing—bath.

One could not relax in a hot bath with a hyperactive child
splashing and laughing. Another oddity of this new world. Sharing the
tub with her sister and Lorelei had become normal, as if they'd done
so their entire lives. When the electricity or water heater decided to
be flaky, taking a bath meant having to carry buckets of hot water into
the house. Even when everything worked as well as possible, the
comparatively low power of their new grid resulted in the water
being 'kinda warm' out of the tap. For a proper bath, Harper would
mostly fill the tub from the faucet, then add two or three buckets of
boiling water to bring the whole bath up to a comfortable level. Far
more than simply hopping in the tub and turning faucets on, bathing
had become a fair amount of work, so the sharing came as much or

more from efficiency rather than Madison still being too frightened to be alone.

Lorelei *adored* bath time. Whether the girl simply had been too young to remember, so traumatized by the war she forgot most things before it, or her mother really had been *that* neglectful, she apparently never had a bath at all until her arrival in Evergreen. Bath time represented three of Lorelei's favorite activities: playing with toys, playing in water, and being with her family.

Now dry, Harper melted into the bedding and closed her eyes, trying not to feel frustrated at the inability to satisfy her hormonal desires tonight. She didn't begrudge the girls the time they wanted to spend with her on her birthday, but she would *definitely* find a way to be with Logan tomorrow.

"Harp?" asked Madison a few minutes later.

"Yeah?"

"If you, like, want to marry Logan and sleep in his bed, it would be okay."

"Are you trying to kick me out?" Harper chuckled.

Madison laughed and clung to her arm. "No. I still want to share a bed with you because it makes me feel safe. Just saying, if you *really* love him and really wanted to, I could deal. I've still got Lore to squeeze like a teddy bear."

Lorelei giggled.

Madison started squirming and giggling, too. "Stop! Harp! She's tickling me!"

This could not go unanswered. Harper also began tickling Madison.

Her sister squealed... and promptly retaliated against both of them.

All three of them seemed to have enough at the same time. They declared a truce and settled back down.

"Why are you smiling at me like that?" Madison narrowed her eyes.

"Truth?"

"Duh. Yes." Madison poked her.

"I'm happy you're coping with everything."

"Ooh. Seriousness bummer." Madison stuck out her tongue.

"Sorry." Harper chuckled. "But truth."

"Yeah... well, I'm trying. Sometimes, I really do miss stuff like Starbucks or pizza. Or movies."

"Me too." Harper closed her eyes and drew a deep breath in her nose. "Maybe we'll get back there someday."

"Ya think?"

"Who knows?" Harper yawned. "I mean, it's not like people would have to come up with crazy ideas to invent things like the first person to invent them did. We know about cars and computers and airplanes. Should be faster to reinvent things, right?"

Madison stretched. "Yeah. Can we shoot anyone who wants to make bombs again?"

"That sounds like a plan." Harper snuggled into the pillow. "Don't get your hopes up too high. I'm talking about us maybe having a place like Starbucks again when we're little old ladies."

"It's fine," said Madison in a sleepy voice. "I actually kinda like this world. Not so crazy all the time. Go to school, oh that's over, rush to gymnastics, oh that's over, time for dance class, oh wait, it's Saturday, gotta go to test prep, or whatever."

"You really don't miss video games?"

"Okay, maybe a little." Madison gave a drowsy chuckle. "Night, Harp."

"Night, Maddie. Night Lore."

"She's already out," whispered Madison.

"Swear that kid could sleep through a bomb going off."

Madison jabbed a finger into Harper's side. "Let's *not* test that."

"Ow." She cringed. "Yeah. Bad phrasing there."

"Just a little. If they don't get rid of the bomb soon, can you please start kicking some asses?"

Harper exhaled. "Yeah. Just promise me you stay far away from it, okay?"

"Swear. I'll just nag you."

"Deal."

23

AWKWARD TIMING

G rass caressed Harper's nude body.

She curled up against Logan, basking in the afterglow of long-awaited pleasure. Sweat trickled down her face, dribbling onto his chest. Tickles all down her back and legs could have been sweat, weeds, or bugs. She didn't care enough to check. A few weeks of wanting sex but never quite being able to find the time to slip off somewhere with Logan made the past hour or so much more amazing. He'd even found a condom somewhere. Not having to worry about accidents intensified the experience so much, she forgot all about having to wait so long.

They'd gone a bit south from the heart of 'New Evergreen,' west of the lake down by Bear Creek Road, where the water ran close to the street, occasionally swerving under a small bridge or two. The strange two-story brown building with the rounded second-story patio sat a short distance east from the clearing. Harper had no desire to go exploring abandoned buildings, at least not without getting dressed first. Before they dropped to the grass at the edge of the forest, she and Logan had run around the woods like a satyr chasing a nymph from one of those Shakespearean plays she once had to learn about in school.

Despite being afraid someone would catch them at any minute, she'd found the escape and freedom of it a welcome break from the constant weight of survival. Maybe Darci had something after all, though Harper remained far too embarrassed to traipse casually about town even topless, much less with nothing.

Logan talked about being happy with her, how she'd been the reason he kept hope alive when he believed he'd lost his entire family. She became a little self-conscious since she didn't regard him as the main reason she'd survived her grief. He did, however, surprise her in that she'd fallen in love with a boy—something she didn't really think would ever happen to her even before the war. That post-nuke, post-Tyler, she'd slid past all her reservations, rocketing down a rollercoaster of emotion straight into his arms had to mean something.

She'd told him as much before and said it again as they lay there under the early June sun.

"We should probably think about heading back to town before they send out a search party," whispered Harper.

"Ugh. I suppose." He caressed her cheek, tracing a finger along her jawline. "You sure I can't convince you to run off with me and spend the rest of our days out in the woods?"

She chuckled. "You've been hanging around Darci and Lucas too much. Maybe the four of us should just start up a hippie commune." Harper paused to glance up at his face. "Are you being serious?"

"Depends on your answer. I'd be game if you are, but I'm mostly kidding." He gave her a quick kiss. "Probably would get awful cold in winter."

"It's kinda fun on a summer afternoon. Though, I think the excitement is mostly coming from feeling like we're doing something we'd get in trouble for."

"I don't think anyone is going to yell at us for being naked outside." Logan stretched, drawing in a deep breath. "Except those sour old ladies who make faces at Darci."

Laughing, Harper sat up. "We shouldn't be trying to rush humanity into the 'spears-and-loincloth' age if we can avoid it."

Logan rolled onto his side, head propped up on one hand, elbow in the grass, reclining like a Greek statue. Over a year of farm work definitely had an effect on his physique. "Less thinking 'spears and loincloths' and more 'pot, skinny dipping, and sleeping under the stars.'"

"Never figured you for a hippie." She admired the view, tracing her gaze along his sweat-shiny body.

"Neither did I. I'd be adapting to my most preferred environment."

"Oh?" She raised both eyebrows. "What is your 'most preferred environment?'"

Logan rolled onto all fours, leaned closer, and kissed her on the lips again. "Wherever you are."

Harper returned the kiss. Eventually, she came up for air and made eye contact. "Swim? We should rinse off before heading back."

He grinned.

She scrambled to her feet and ran; Logan chased her across the little clearing to the creek beside the road.

Harper stifled a nervously excited squeal as she navigated the rocks forming the bank. Being outside, naked, right beside a road almost made her forget about the war; she briefly worried a car might come by at any second. As fast as she could go without slipping, she rushed down into the shockingly cold water.

She hadn't quite regained the ability to move when Logan embraced her from behind. Something in the creek water made their skin as slippery as if they'd smeared baby oil all over themselves, perhaps algae or moss. After a few minutes, she sorta adjusted to the cold and paddled around a bit. The creek didn't have much space compared to the pool, but it had enough room to feel like swimming. It didn't take long for innocent skinny dipping to turn into another chase, then kissing while they lay half submerged in icy water.

Eyes closed, lips locked, Harper drank in his presence. *We should stop before it goes too far. He only had one condom.*

"I love you, Harper. More than I imagined it could be possible to love someone." Logan leaned his head over and kissed the side of her neck.

Desire and caution got into a fistfight. If she didn't stop him soon, they'd make love again in the water… and they'd both be too into it to be careful. The timing didn't feel right for her cycle, but knowing her luck, she'd walk away from the creek with a serious nine-month problem.

Oh. I don't want to stop, but we really should.

"We… should…," rasped Harper in a breathless whisper. She opened her eyes—and spotted three men close to the creek edge watching them, one with a crossbow pointing their way. "Shit…"

Logan leaned back to give her a cockeyed look. "Uhh, what?"

She didn't have to say anything. The instant he saw the expression on her face, he whirled around.

Three men wearing mismatched clothing in bright red and blue had come out of nowhere, sneaking up on them while they'd been making out. The man on the left had a dark tan complexion, thick unibrow, and features she assumed Middle Eastern or maybe Greek. He also lazily held a crowbar with dried blood on the hook end. Crossbow Guy seemed to be the oldest, definitely into his forties. A dark blue polo with a yellow corporate logo peeked out from under his red flannel shirt. The man appeared biracial, tall, scrawny, probably not *too* physically powerful. The last guy, the youngest of the trio at maybe thirty, tossed and caught a large Rambo knife. He looked like the slightly uglier cousin of the blond preppie jerk they put in every college comedy movie… a decade after he graduated and the business he inherited from his parents failed.

Crowbar Guy and Knife Guy leered at her.

Crossbow Guy didn't ogle her. He did, however, point his weapon more or less at her face. "Get out of the water."

Harper peered past his legs at the pile of clothing she and Logan left over by the edge of the woods, maybe forty feet away on the other side of open grass. Her jeans and shirt covered her .45. The pile remained undisturbed, giving her hope the men had apparently not discovered the weapon. Spending a few hours in an uninhabited part of Evergreen—without technically leaving town—sounded safe enough. She'd perhaps foolishly left the Mossberg at home. Or, maybe doing so turned out for the better. Certainly, these three guys would've spotted a shotgun leaning against a tree and taken it. If nothing else, leaving it home stopped the idiots from using it against her.

"We should kill the boy," said Knife Guy. "Don't like the way he's lookin' at us. Gonna be trouble."

Harper glared at him, too angry to care she had nothing on. She side-eyed Logan and mouthed, 'Run.' He kept staring at Crossbow Guy as if trying to melt the man's skin off with eye power alone. She again focused on the small lump of clothing in the distance. A close-in hand-to-hand fight against three men probably wouldn't go well for her, especially considering a knife and crowbar against her hands and feet. The crossbow had one shot. She felt confident in her ability to sprint to her gun before the man could reload. Problem being, he still had that one shot. What if he didn't miss? The red-and-blue gang demonstrated horrible marksmanship on their last raid, which Cliff blamed on fear. Specifically, fear of being shot at. They would not be afraid of two unarmed people waist-deep in a creek with no clothing or weapons. How long had they been watching Evergreen, waiting for someone to be dumb enough to wander off alone?

Damn cowards.

Logan moved to the edge and climbed over the rocks. He palmed a jagged tennis-ball-sized stone, keeping it in his hand hidden behind his butt as he stood.

Harper clenched her jaw and stood out of the water. Being brazen might help save Logan's life. If these idiots stared at her, they'd be slow to react to anything he did. Much to her dismay, her boyfriend didn't seem too keen on running. If she added a little crazy to her brazenness, it might throw the idiots off guard even more.

"Go ahead and just shoot me." Harper stopped moving, still up to her shins. "I'm not going with you."

"Relax girl." Crossbow Guy kept his weapon trained on Logan. "We're not gonna touch you. Only need us a nice hostage these townies won't wanna lose. You're gonna stay with us for a while, making sure they give us food. Got my word, no one's gonna lay a hand on ya."

Yeah, sure. And I'm gonna sprout wings. She clenched her hands into fists, feeling stupid for allowing herself to relax enough to put so much distance between her and a weapon. Even in the super unlikely event this guy could manage to control his associates and none of them would rape her, they still intended to keep her hostage and extort food from Evergreen... just like that crazy 'Promise Keeper' militia did with those children they locked up in the old jail.

She weighed the idea of going with them against trying to fight. Resisting could get her and Logan killed right here and now. If she let them take her, she might be able to escape when they let their guard down. However, anything might happen to her between when they took her captive and when—*if*—she managed to get away. She couldn't trust her life to fate. While she might survive a period of being held hostage, she didn't want to roll those dice. These losers wanted easy prey, or they wouldn't have snuck up on two apparently unarmed teenagers. Even if she couldn't get to her gun, putting up too much of a fight might make them cut their losses and flee. Even if they overpowered them and kidnapped her anyway, she wouldn't feel like an absolute moron for just giving up.

Also, they hadn't gone *too* far from town. If she screamed loud enough, odds were high someone from the militia would race out here to investigate. She didn't necessarily have to kick three men's asses... merely stay un-kidnapped for long enough that help could arrive.

Three-on-two didn't seem terribly bad odds. Of course, it could instantly become three-on-one if Crossbow Guy shot Logan and didn't miss. Another fact to consider: her boyfriend wouldn't give up, even if she told him to. That meant Harper couldn't give up, or it would be a three-on-one fight Logan would *definitely* lose.

Hell with it.

Harper stepped up out of the water and stood before the three red-and-blue gang members, holding her head high. Knife Guy seemed annoyed at her defiance or lack of embarrassment. The other two did indeed stare at her as she hoped they would. She could be mortified later. For the time being, she weaponized nudity.

Logan fastballed the rock he'd grabbed into Crossbow Guy's face. The stone struck the man's cheek with a dull, fleshy *thump*. He reflexively squeezed the trigger, launching the bolt a few inches over Logan's shoulder. Screaming like a barbarian, Logan hurled himself at Crossbow Guy in a berserk flurry of punches. The man backpedaled, flailing his arms and nearly falling over.

She bolted forward and left, trying to scoot around Crowbar Guy and rush to the clothing pile and the handgun under it. The man grabbed her around the middle, but his hasty one-armed grapple slipped off her wet stomach. She twisted out of his grasp, but only took one more step before he dragged her to a halt by a fistful of her hair.

Harper yowled in pain as he yanked her backward to fall on her butt.

Knife Guy waved his weapon at Logan. "Stop! Get off him!"

Logan continued pummeling the snot out of Crossbow Guy, his incompressible roaring filled with a frightening amount of rage.

Harper rolled onto her knees, twisted around, and rabbit-punched Crowbar Guy in the nuts. He let out an "Oof!" then doubled over, grabbing his groin in both hands, releasing both her hair and his crowbar. She shoved herself into a sideways roll out of his reach, then scrambled to her feet.

Knife Guy reached around behind his back and pulled a handgun. Logan grabbed Crossbow Guy by the shirt and threw him at Knife Guy. The men crashed chest-to-chest and fell in a heap. Harper sprinted across the grass, bee-lining for her clothing pile.

Bang!

At the sound of a gunshot, she reflexively ducked and swerved left toward the closest tree cover.

Bang! Bang!

Distant snaps came from ahead of her where the bullets struck wood.

Harper dashed for the woods, not caring about anything more than putting something solid between her and an idiot with a gun. She made it to the forest edge without taking a hit, scooted around the widest tree in sight, and pressed her back against the coarse bark. Stars danced in her eyes; she gasped for breath.

Seconds later, Logan tried to round a nearby tree, wiped out, and tumbled over a few times before scrambling on all fours to crawl behind a different tree twenty feet or so deeper into the woods from where she stood. Two more gunshots kicked up the dirt on either side of him, so close, she screamed.

Elation at making it to cover without being shot lasted all of half a second. *Bastard's not shooting at me. They want me alive.*

"Son of a bitch is fucking dead," grumbled Crossbow Guy. "I'm gonna feed him his own dick."

"What now?" whispered Logan.

She couldn't see him through the tree he sheltered behind, but he didn't sound hurt, merely out of breath. "They're coming."

"Yeah, I know."

Harper looked down at herself. Water, sweat, and mud ran in narrow rivulets down her stomach and legs. A few bits of grass clung to her. No blood, at least. Months of hand-to-hand practice with Cliff blurred across her mind. Many of the grappling techniques he showed her involved grabbing the opponent's clothing. *They're going to have a hard time controlling me... as long as I can keep them off my hair.*

Rapid footsteps approached, along with plenty of cursing and growling. Crossbow Guy had definitely reloaded by now. The men would be on her in seconds. She had no time for an elaborate plan. Her decision boiled down to two options: run like hell and try to get to town for help or try to get her gun. If she ran for town, she and Logan would end up on the highway without tree cover. Even these idiots would probably manage to hit Logan if they had an unobstructed shot. She didn't want to ask herself if she could leave him behind and keep running.

Decision made. Stand and fight.

I should avoid close combat if I can. Training only does so much. I'm still not going to overpower them. While she knew a myriad of different strikes to sensitive places that could tip the odds in her favor, she didn't like her chances against three armed men without even a knife. She also much preferred the advantage afforded her by the gun hidden under her shirt.

Honor is for samurai movies, not surviving a nuclear wasteland. They want me alive... and they're getting closer. I gotta go right now before there's no room for me to get around them.

She let out a scream part desperation, part war cry in hopes they'd realize the sudden motion came from the girl they wanted to kidnap and wouldn't shoot her, then rushed out from behind her tree. The red-and-blue gang stopped short, five or six paces away from where she'd taken cover. Crowbar Guy ran after her. Crossbow Guy stood in place. Knife Guy kept advancing toward Logan, handgun raised.

She swerved left, easily staying out of reach of the man coming for her. Hands up to shield her face from a stray branch or two, she leaned into a sprint, heading for her stuff, keeping only a few strides ahead of the guy on her heels.

The *thwack* of a crossbow firing echoed off the trees. Bodies collided with a jarring *thud,* then hit the ground. Men grunted and cursed. Harper jumped over a root and risked a quick look back. Crowbar Guy thundered along close behind her. Further away, Logan tangled with the other two men in a rolling brawl on the ground.

Harper pulled a hard turn around a tree, taking advantage of being lighter and more agile than the man chasing her. He stumbled off to the side in a wider arc, struggling to stay on his feet. She pulled ahead, clearing the last few yards to the pile of clothing, then flung herself forward to seize the fabric pile in both hands an instant before the man fell on top of her. Harper clutched the bundle tight to her chest, reassured by the hard metal 1911 inside it. The man's weight squished her left hip painfully into the dirt. A wash of horribleness surrounded her: a nauseatingly sweet trash fragrance mixed with the essence of woodsmoke and a serious amount of body odor. He smelled like he'd spent the past ten months sleeping in a giant dumpster and burning garbage to stay warm.

He slid his left hand under her stomach, forcing his arm between her and the ground. Most of her attention remained on the crowbar in his other fist, which he pressed into the dirt in a clumsy attempt to push himself up and drag her into the air. He seemed unwilling to let go of the weapon to grab her with both hands, but he also didn't brandish it at her... yet.

She squirmed in an effort to get away. Unfortunately, while pinned under a 200-pound man, she couldn't move. Harper clung desperately to the gun inside her wadded-up shirt, her only hope of avoiding whatever horrible fate these men would inflict on her. Knowing she had no chance of pushing this guy off or physically overpowering him, she tried trickery. If she could only buy herself enough room to move, she could give him one hell of a surprise.

"Okay," rasped Harper as she stopped struggling and lay still. "Okay. You got me. Just... please let me put something on first."

"Nah, I like the view just the way it is right now."

Grr. I knew it. Bastards. She wriggled her right hand up into the shirt bundle and gripped the .45 by the handle. "But you said you weren't gonna do that."

He laughed, warm breath puffing at the back of her hair. "Said we weren't gonna touch you. Didn't say nothin' about lookin'."

She squeezed the fingers of her left hand through the shirt around the holster's clasp.

A gunshot went off not far away.

The man twitched in startlement. He pushed himself up a bit, loosening his hold around her waist, and started to twist toward the noise. Harper rammed her head backward, smashing her skull into his nose. He cried out in pain, reflexively jerking back from the hit, giving Harper the chance to squirm around onto her back.

Blood dribbled from his nose, pattering on her chest. He grabbed the front of her throat and squeezed. "Bitch!"

Harper stared into his rage-filled eyes and pulled the trigger. The .45 she'd pressed against his body went off with a muted *whud*. A spray of blood flew out of his back. He squeezed his hand around her throat tighter. She fired again. His hand lost strength. Growling, she shoved upward, tossing the man partially onto his knees, and yanked the gun out of the shirt and holster. Now able to see where she aimed, she fired twice more into his chest at point blank range. Warm blood splattered all over her face and torso.

With a final gurgling wheeze, Crowbar Guy collapsed to one side.

"Shit!" yelled Knife Guy, who stood alone in the woods not far from her. He looked as if he'd been run over by a car. Blood and dirt covered his face. His nose appeared to be smashed to one side, and he might've been missing teeth. That he remained standing with a gun in hand, but Logan didn't seem to be anywhere, turned her blood to ice.

Harper and Knife Guy fired at each other within a quarter second, her shot going off ever so slightly faster. A burst of splinters landed on her head from where the incoming bullet struck the tree above her. Her shot punched a hole in the man's upper left chest. He spun with the impact, pirouetting around onto his knees with his back to her. She fired again, putting a round into the back of his left thigh. Knife Guy screamed in pain, fell hard to that side, and began to rock back and forth on the ground while howling.

Logan flew out from behind a tree near where the man collapsed, crossbow held high in both hands. He raced over to Knife Guy and smashed him in the head with the crossbow hard enough to snap the fiberglass body—then hit him twice more before seeming to notice the weapon broke. Harper kept pointing the .45 generally at them, finger off the trigger. Logan dropped to one knee, grabbed Knife Guy's pistol from his limp hand, and point-blanked him in the back of the head.

He knelt over the corpse, breathing hard. Blood smeared his face and chest, splatter from the fight as well as his blood oozing from various cuts and stab wounds.

"Lo… are you okay?" Harper's voice, barely over a whisper, sounded so vulnerable it pissed her off. He either didn't hear her or didn't pay attention. She swallowed saliva and tried again in a louder, more stern voice. "Logan."

He turned his head to look at her.

"Are you okay?"

"I... think so." He twisted to his right, raised the gun, and shot twice more at something out of sight behind the trees.

Harper dropped her shirt on top of her jeans, then frowned at the blood all over her. "Why do I feel like I'm in a Tarantino movie?"

Grunting, Logan pushed himself to his feet and hurried over. "Are you okay?"

"No." She shook her head. "I'm pretty shaken up."

"You don't look it." He grasped her by the shoulders, staring into her eyes. "Are you being sarcastic or doing that disassociating thing?"

"I'll get back to you on that." She gingerly hugged him. "I'll deal. Not the first time someone's tried to kidnap me since the world went to hell. Probably won't be the last... at least until I'm an old lady no one wants."

"You'll never be an old lady no one wants."

"Yeah, you're right. We'll probably die before we get old."

"Stop." Logan touched foreheads with her. "I meant, even when we're old, I will still want you."

She teared up a little. "I think... maybe we should stay in town for a while. Better the kids catch us than something like this happens again."

"I dunno about that." Logan set his hands on his hips and grimaced. "This was *way* less awkward than Maddie or Lorelei walking in on us."

"Can we maybe not include naked gunfights in future couples' activity?" She pressed a hand to her face. "What the hell is wrong with me? I just killed a guy and I'm making a stupid joke."

"Shock, probably." Logan brushed her damp hair off her face.

"Yeah. True." She glanced at the gun in her hand, flicked the safety on, but didn't put the weapon down. "Give me a minute to rinse the blood off and get dressed before you hit the air horn."

"No need," said Dennis Prosser from not too far behind her and right. "We're here already."

Harper froze. Silence fell heavy over the area, except for the soft crunch of approaching footsteps. She would either look up, see Cliff, and drop dead of embarrassment, or not see Cliff and merely implode into a tiny little speck of matter like a black dwarf star. The Evergreen Militia had a bunch of former cops. Once word got around of this, the naked jokes would be endless.

Worse, Dennis lived really close to them, basically directly behind their house on the other side of a fence. She had to see him every day. *Is this what Beth felt like when I caught her in that house?*

Dennis approached them, not looking at her, rather staring at the corpse of Crowbar Guy. "Heard the shots. Came running to check it out. Sorry we didn't get here any faster. You two went a ways down the road."

"They obviously wanted some privacy." Roy Ellis grinned at her. Unlike Dennis, he didn't avert his gaze, nor did he excessively stare at her. He rather acted normal… as if Harper and Logan stood there fully dressed and not covered in blood. "You guys okay?"

"Logan's hurt." Harper brushed her fingers over his chest.

"Guy had a knife. Think it's mostly shallow cuts. They sting a bunch, but I wouldn't call it pain." Logan chuckled. "Neither one of them wanted to get near me."

Roy laughed. "We had a guy one night, high as hell, on PCP or something. Bare ass naked. Giant hardon. Machete. Running down the street barking at people like a goddamned dog. None of the guys wanted to get within twenty feet of him, and it wasn't the machete they were worried about."

"Wow." Logan whistled. "What did you do if the cops didn't want to touch a crazy dude?"

"Taser." Roy winked. "Works every time. So, looks like you two got caught with your pants down."

"Little more than just their pants down." Dennis, still not looking at her, snickered.

Harper couldn't decide what embarrassed her more: Dennis obviously keeping his back turned out of respect—or Roy acting like she didn't stand there naked. He'd been in the military as well as the police, so likely thought little of changing or showering with 'the guys,' but it seemed highly unlikely there had been women in the same shower room. Still, his attitude part way between a big brother about to tease her for an embarrassing situation and a fellow cop trying not to make a scene out of it left her focused mostly on her anger at the idiots who attacked them rather than getting self-conscious at her state of dress.

"What happened?" asked Roy.

If his goal was to make her blush, she wouldn't give him the satisfaction. Cops liked to tease each other, after all. At least, she felt nothing but protectiveness from him and Dennis. Maybe if she forced herself to act casual and not mortified, the jokes wouldn't happen. "Logan and I, well, you can guess what we were doing out here. We went for a swim and these three idiots showed up. Said they were going to take us hostage and make the town give them food. Same crap like the Promise Keepers. Do these jerks have like a 'how to be a wasteland bandit for dummies' book?"

Roy scowled. "Just three?"

"Yeah. Only these three." Logan offered the handgun to Dennis. "Here. I don't have pockets right now. It's out of ammo, anyway. If they had any friends, they stayed hidden."

Dennis approached Logan, took the weapon, and looked him over. "Some of those might need a stitch or two. Harper, are you hurt?"

"Just a few scratches. This blood is not mine." She headed for the creek, still naked, still with a .45 in her hand. "Gonna wash it off."

"All right." Dennis followed her, making it a point not to look directly at her. "We got your perimeter."

Thank hell no one has a working cell phone anymore. There won't be pictures. Grumbling, she hurried into the water, having decided the best way to deal with the awkwardness would be to end it as fast as possible. Dennis and his AR-15 stood guard over the creek for the two minutes or so she rinsed off using one hand—since the other kept the .45 out of the water. While she cleaned up, Roy checked over the three bodies. A blast of icy water to the face when she dunked under to rinse off the last of the blood almost gave her an instant headache.

She emerged from the creek and forced herself to walk at a normal pace over to her clothing. If she acted at all as embarrassed as she felt, she worried a storm of teasing would chase her for years. Sure, there would likely still be jokes, but if the guys didn't think it bothered her, they'd stop.

Logan, who'd opted not to jump in the creek with multiple open wounds on his chest and arms, held her jeans out. "Guessing you're not going to want to air dry first."

She took them. "You guess correctly."

24

RETURN TO SANITY

Miracles theoretically came in many forms.

Not that Harper believed in supernatural effects, gods, faeries, ghosts, or miracles. However, she couldn't help but be astonished that no one made fun of her for what happened Wednesday. Of course, Walter—and by extension the entire militia in the north—knew what happened. The official story said only that she and Logan slipped away for a romantic moment in the woods and came under attack.

Cliff, being about as fully adjusted into his role as 'Dad' as could be, hadn't commented about it beyond making sure she was okay. He exuded awkwardness the whole time, but also a barely held back rage. She had no doubt he'd spent the past day scouring the area around Evergreen for any sign of remaining red-and-blue gang members. There obviously had to be more if those three were going to hold her hostage in trade for food.

She'd gone through the expected 'holy shit I killed someone' shivers soon after returning to town. It didn't last long. By now, she'd learned how to cope with necessary killing. Within four hours of the attack, she'd put it in a mental box and dealt with it. Logan got a few stitches. Harper held his hand as Tegan worked to clean the slashes and cuts. Her boyfriend made more noise in response to isopropyl alcohol than he did at being stabbed. Thankfully, he'd suffered only superficial injuries that appeared far worse than they were.

Harper lay on the floor in her bedroom, propped up on her elbows like a teenager. In front of her on the carpet sat her remaining ammunition and the notebook she would have used to take notes in physics class. It happened to be one of the things Cliff brought back in the trunk when he'd paid a visit to her old home.

She finished tallying ammo—178 shotgun shells remaining, sixty-six .45 rounds. The day she would retire Dad's Mossberg marched inexorably closer. Harper flipped two pages back to look at the doodles and such surrounding the notes she'd taken on her third or fourth day of senior year. The last day she'd been there. The last day the world had been a normal, civilized place.

It felt like an eternity ago.

"I'd have been out of school by now, anyway." She shut the book. "At least they blew up the world before I had to lose my mind cramming for the SATs."

She repacked the ammo, stuck it in the closet with the notebook, then got up to hit the quartermaster's for their food allotment.

Cliff entered the front door as she reached the living room. His expression appeared neutral, but his eyes held an intensity that said he had a specific reason for being there. Also, he wore a full camouflage getup with tactical vest, Special Forces hat, face paint, and utility belt. A Colt M4 carbine hung across his chest on a strap. He totally looked like one of the commandos from *Predator*.

He's been out there all night. He's just now getting home. Holy shit, did he go hunting those jerks?

"You okay?" asked Harper.

He reached into a pocket on his tactical vest and pulled out six empty 5.56 brass, which he held up in a row to show her. "Fine."

It took her a second to catch his meaning. "Red and blue?"

"Not anymore. Mostly just red now." He rotated his hand, letting the brass clink together loose in his palm. "Tracked them to a campsite near Elephant Butte. Didn't look like they'd been there for too long. You, uhh, want these?"

She walked over and hugged him. "Nah. I'm okay. Are you?"

"Quite." He smiled, finally breaking the stoic 'terminator face'. "If you're heading downtown, let Walter know I am going to bed."

"All right." She stood there, watching him trudge off to Carrie's house, M4 carbine rattling against his vest. It sounded psychotic to say 'hey, Dad, thanks for hunting down and killing the guys who tried to kidnap me', so she didn't say it. However, she couldn't deny it made her feel safer.

TWENTY MINUTES LATER, HARPER STOOD IN LINE BEHIND JEN OLIVER, Mason Pruitt, and Therese.

Jen's son Daxton had come along to help carry stuff. The now-thirteen-year-old had shot up in height, almost as tall as her. He still had a boyish face, which only looked even more childish when he spotted her and beamed. The boy credited Harper with saving his mother—and a bunch of other people—from bad conditions at Kriley Pond, no matter how many times she told him *he* saved them. A twelve-year-old boy had to be quite brave to risk hiking off alone chasing a rumor to find help in Evergreen.

Some of the people working in the room, as well as others waiting behind her for their food, seemed to give her strange looks. It might've been nothing; however, she couldn't help but worry word of 'the naked gunfight' had reached the far corners of town. Doubtful anyone on the militia would spread the story. Her subconscious mind read imagined meaning into their expressions.

Doesn't matter what they think. We didn't do anything wrong. Not like I pulled a Darci.

While looking around trying to figure out what people might be thinking about her—despite telling herself she didn't care—she spotted Dr. Rowland in line behind her. As soon as she made eye contact with him, he smiled.

"Afternoon, Miss Cody."

Is he being polite or still treating me like one of his students? "Hi. Afternoon, umm, Mr., uhh, Dr. Rowland."

He waved dismissively. "I think we can leave the formalities of a dead society in the past. Though, if you insist on calling me 'doctor', I'm not going to tell you to stop."

She smiled, but it turned somber. "Dead society? Do you think it's gone?"

"My dear girl, that would entirely depend on what you define 'it' as. Are we discussing the simple capacity for humans to be civil to each other, or are we going into corrupt kleptocratic oligarchical governments doing the bidding of corporations? Perhaps you refer to feudalism, warring tribes, or some point in between all of it?"

"Umm." Harper blinked. "Whoa. I was really just kinda wondering if people would ever go to the movies and Starbucks again... and maybe not have to constantly worry someone's going to try to kill them, or they'll starve to death if too many little things go wrong in succession."

He stroked his beard. "Ahh, simple requests then."

"Heh." She backed up two steps, moving with the line as Jen Oliver and Daxton collected their stuff and walked away from the table.

Dr. Rowland made a series of funny faces over a moment or two as if thinking caused pain... or he tried to amuse one of the little kids watching them. "Well, assuming nothing goes calamitously wrong with the Earth, I believe there is a reasonable chance society could recover to some degree of normal within fifteen to twenty years. I'm talking about a sort of 1850s type of civilization without ocean travel. Given the number of people likely killed and the loss of expertise, it may take more along the lines of fifty to seventy years before we, as a society, regain the ability to construct any form of sailing ships or robustly engage in long distance trading."

She tapped the toe of her sneaker into the floor repetitively.

"That's kinda reassuring, I suppose. No wild gangs of leather clad freaks racing across the desert in hopped up dune buggies then."

Dr. Rowland laughed. "I should sincerely hope not. Though..." He held up one finger. "It may be possible someone who survived the war and happened to be fond of those movies would attempt to create that lifestyle."

"Funny you should say that..." She told him about the 'Templars' they ran into while checking on the medical camp.

He sighed. "There are always those who feel like it is their duty to fill a power vacuum using whatever nonsense they can come up with to scare or intimidate people into compliance. Wouldn't be the first. Won't be the last."

Therese got her food and walked off, smiling and waving to Harper as she went by.

Harper returned the friendly gesture, then sighed at her former teacher. "My friends think I'm being too optimistic and we're going to be stuck in the 1800s for the rest of our lives."

"One advantage to low expectations is that you might be surprised happily." He grinned. "It's quite likely there are some traces of our government left. They had all those fancy bunkers and whatnot. We're just not seeing it much out here since it's so remote. Now, you could accuse me of being overly optimistic, but I think you'll probably live to see somewhat of a return to sanity. You might not be too spry anymore by then, but I bet you'll see it."

Harper folded her arms. "Got my license only a couple of weeks before cars stopped being a thing. It would be just my luck that I'm too old to drive by the time they come back. Ugh. That sounded funnier in my head. No, I'm not seriously salty over not being able to drive. So trivial compared to everything else."

"Did not think you were being serious there." He winked. "I do hope that when society gets around to repairing itself, we get things better the second time around. We sure had our fair share of problems."

She tensed her jaw. What she wanted to say next, she shouldn't blurt in a room full of people. So, she continued to talk with him about his predictions for society rising from the ashes while they both collected their allotment of food from the quartermaster people. He'd already acclimated himself to the way things worked and—shockingly—would soon be teaching science to the older kids.

Once they walked outside and had some space to talk in private, she spoke in a low voice, "About making things better... we really should do something about that hot potato before it decides to get angry."

"Oh yes. You don't need to tell me that. I am well aware." He adjusted his grip on the cloth sack of vegetables. "I still don't believe the device is capable of functioning as designed due to the damage to the channel. The two plutonium modules wouldn't collide properly to result in a critical mass."

"Right. I remember. If it went off, it would just blow up and spray radioactive crap everywhere." She sighed into her bag of food. "That might actually be worse for us than a quick incineration. That poor man who arrived from Mexico lived through some really awful things."

Dr. Rowland's face became a pained grimace. "I can only imagine what they went through down there. Try to stay calm. Your best minds are working on it."

"Is the mine idea good?"

"It's perhaps as good as we can get, lacking the means to transport the device to a proper disposal facility." He whistled innocently. "I suspect any such *proper* disposal facilities would likely be short staffed these days and not operational."

"Maybe you could visit Mayor Ned or Walter and help them figure out if any of the mines we're scouting out are suitable to contain that thing."

"Certainly. I'd be happy to offer whatever assistance I am able to. If there is a suitably deep hole, even if the device were to miraculously detonate in a thermonuclear reaction, the contamination could be mostly contained to the immediate area."

She overacted a sigh of relief since she didn't have a free hand to 'wipe sweat' from her forehead. They talked about the bomb for another few minutes until she had to veer left onto Hilltop Drive and he kept going straight.

Harper hurried home to put the food away.

She had a mission now.

WALTER HOLMAN LOOKED UP FROM A DISORGANIZED PILE OF MAPS spread out over the conference room table when Harper rushed in.

"Sorry." She skidded to a stop by the table, hands clenched in fists. "Can we talk?"

"Of course. Are you all right? Heard about your incident over by Bear Creek."

She blushed. "It's not worse than any of the other times I've had to shoot people."

"That doesn't tell me if you're all right or not." He walked around the table and rested a hand on her shoulder.

"I'm fine. Freaked out in the moment, but I'm good now."

"Did they…?"

"No. The man who tackled me might've been thinking about it, but he didn't have the chance to even grope me."

Walter exhaled, then smiled. "Good. Sorry if that's awkward for you. Either the subject matter or my seeming protective."

"I'd rather my boss be protective than a jerk." She smiled. "So, umm. How is the disposal effort going?"

He pointed at the maps. "We're scouting out a number of possible mine sites far enough away to be safe, but also within a reasonable distance. Rafael is confident his large truck will be able to handle the strain of towing that load. Our main concern is radiation exposure among whoever is going to be escorting it to its final destination."

"Yeah, that makes sense. We need to get rid of it soon."

Walter raised both eyebrows. "Why the sudden urgency?"

She folded her arms. "I had a nightmare about it going off."

He almost chuckled. "Are we psychic now?"

"No." She slouched. "Just worry on top of PTSD on top of anxiety. I'm simply being a teenager who 'wants it now' and can't wait."

"I understand." He patted her arm. "Believe me, I understand. I'm not happy about that particular guest visiting so close either. Well, I *am* happy that it didn't work properly. Not entirely sure where it was supposed to land. Your father seems to think it might have been intended for us. It couldn't have landed *that* far away for the fool to collect it and bring it home."

The idea had already occurred to Harper that the MIRV warhead with a guidance malfunction should have vaporized Lakewood, mostly due to how her old neighborhood didn't seem anywhere near as damaged as other places. If not coming down directly on top of her, she wondered if it would have fallen close enough to her old home for her not to exist anymore. Considering the way Cliff talked about the 'quality' of Russian weapons, it wouldn't surprise her if multiple duds rained down all over the country. The warhead giving her nightmares now might not have been the one with Lakewood's name on it, but another like it could easily be sitting somewhere else like it... or broken apart, effectively becoming dirty bombs.

Dr. Rowland did call it 'freakish luck' that the warhead they found hadn't been more damaged, or entirely smashed into pieces. It must have hit something incredibly soft and dense, like a giant pile of aerated soil. Or perhaps she'd been right about that cylinder and the MIRV remained stuck inside the rocket carrier until the last few seconds before impact with the ground.

"Yeah. Umm, Walter, I'll go with the team if it'll help speed things up."

He paused, stared at her like a grandpa whose granddaughter just asked him if she could go join the Army at age thirteen, then walked over and gripped her by both shoulders. "Absolutely not. You're too young."

She fidgeted.

"This isn't me being condescending. I said the same to Ken. To Cameron. To Leigh." Walter gave her shoulder a little squeeze, then let go. "Anyone under forty isn't going near that thing. According to the doctors, radiation has a more pronounced effect on young people."

"I'm sure they meant children. I'm not growing anymore." Harper idly scratched at her arm. Merely saying the word 'radiation' made her feel spidery tingles… the same way saying 'spiders' or 'bugs' made Renee squirm.

"Still. Humor me? You have those kids to look after." He smiled. "How is Maddie doing?"

"Great. Amazing even. She's basically back to her old self with a bit more sarcasm."

"Wonderful." He ambled over to the maps. "I am asking everyone, and that includes you, who has too much future ahead of them to take a step back and not risk radiation poisoning. We're going to move that thing out of here as soon as we can do it safely."

"Wilkins?"

Walter coughed.

"He did. Didn't he? The old guy volunteered?" Harper whistled.

"Well now, uhh…" Walter glanced down, tapping his knuckles absentmindedly on the desk. "Yeah, he did."

"I feel bad."

"Don't. It's his choice, and he's got a lot less future ahead of him than you have ahead of you, even if this whole bomb thing ends up not hurting anyone. It's a simple matter of his already being seventy."

Harper looked down. It made sense. She also couldn't claim to truly want to go near the warhead. It scared the hell out of her way worse than those red-and-blue guys or even the Lawless. A person could not reason with a fission bomb or an invisible killer like gamma waves. Maybe it made her into a scared little kid, but she wouldn't object to staying out of this one.

"Okay. I guess I'll deal with being benched for the kids' sake." Harper flashed an impish smile. "But if the old geezers chicken out, let me know."

25

THE WANDERING WINSLOW

SATURDAY, JUNE 6TH

Harper sat on the deck behind Lucas Garza's house, the Mossberg balanced across her lap.

She'd stopped in for a quick break near the end of her patrol shift. With the exception of those who primarily worked on the farm or the militia, the residents of Evergreen still tended to think of the weekend as a day off. Consequently, Renee and Grace had free time to come hang out as well, and happened to be there before Harper arrived. The kids played at home under Carrie's watch. Today and tomorrow would be their only true summer break. Starting Monday, they'd all be expected to pitch in on the farm from morning until lunchtime.

Darci reclined on a cushioned outdoor chaise lounge, wearing only an assortment of cheap wooden necklaces and bracelets. Baby Piper rested in a playpen they'd taken from one of the other houses nearby. Harper still couldn't quite believe a whole baby had come out of her stick-thin friend. It didn't seem physically possible.

Lucas, off in his enormous backyard behind the deck—surrounded by marijuana plants—presently engaged in a play-swordfight with little Elijah who'd turned six last January. Their 'pirate battle' went somewhat beyond play-fighting with a child, in that Lucas didn't randomly tap their toy weapons together. He genuinely taught the boy the basics of how to handle a sword. Turns out, the man not only had played a pirate in movies and television, he'd truly learned sword-fighting 'to be authentic.' The former actor had evidently put on a pair of shorts earlier when Renee and Grace showed up, sparing Harper the awkwardness.

Renee maintained a constant mild blush and tried not to look at Darci.

Rather than let rumor sneak up on her, Harper told her friends about what happened at Bear Creek. She mostly wanted to make sure Renee, Darci, and Grace didn't do the same sort of stupid thing she'd done and wander off too far. Not that she expected it of Renee or Grace, but Darci and Lucas often went on long walks into the woods in search of beautiful scenery for lovemaking. Cliff might've gotten the last of the red-and-blue idiots, but the Templars were still out there somewhere, and any number of other idiots as well.

Once the warning passed, Darci teased Harper a little, trying to get her to admit it had been fun to 'embrace nature,' then told her how much more wonderful it felt when smoking weed. She spent the next few minutes talking about how super-baked she planned to get as soon as Piper no longer needed breast milk. Harper still couldn't quite get past a lifetime of being told 'drugs are bad.' The thought of smoking pot made her squirm. Renee called her 'weird' for being willing to get naked out in the woods and have sex where anyone could see them, but thinking pot was somehow more taboo than that.

One joke led to a series of back-and-forth quips, eventually ending with Darci daring Renee to either sunbathe nude or smoke a joint. Grace pointed out it would be bad to light marijuana on fire around her and Piper. Even if it didn't get into her system from ambient smoke, smelling it might prove too tempting. At that, Darci sighed, picked up her baby, and held Piper high over her head.

"See the great sacrifices Mommy makes for you?" Darci flashed a series of goofy faces at the baby.

Piper cooed and waved her arms around.

Harper fidgeted. Dares had been something of a thing among her and her friends ever since they were like eleven. One simply didn't refuse a dare—or walk into Mordor. A dare had been the reason she foolishly tried to shoplift from the mall, though it hadn't been one of her good friends to do it to her. Her *real* friends kept dares to harmless, often embarrassing, things everyone could laugh at and no one would end up talking to cops about. It always started the same way. Now that Darci dropped the dare gauntlet at Renee's feet, it would invariably make its way around to her. At some point in the next ten minutes, both Renee *and* Darci would dare Harper to hang out naked for a while or smoke. Darci might not have cared too much about daring her friends to fling off their clothing while Lucas happened to be right there in the backyard, but it bothered Harper. If she knew Renee at all, she guessed her friend might opt to strip if it had only been the girls somewhere by themselves, and likely would choose pot with a man around. Not only because the guy was in his mid-thirties, but... also a celebrity for whatever worth such a thing still had.

Had it just been the girls somewhere secluded, Harper would definitely choose to sit around naked for a while over smoking. It wouldn't be the most embarrassing thing her friends ever demanded she do on a dare. The time Renee, Christina, and Andrea dared her to sing *Under the Sea* out loud in the mall was *way* worse. *I'm nineteen, why am I still afraid of bad stuff happening if I don't do a dare? Why are dares such a serious thing for us? Ugh.* A sigh slid across her thoughts. She wanted to make her friends happy, always had. As long as a dare didn't hurt anyone, she couldn't say no. Her weird compulsion to follow through with dares came from the desperation of an introvert not to alienate one of her few hard-won friends, not any fear of supernatural nonsense punishing her for reneging on a challenge.

"Okay, fine. Since there's a medical reason not to light up now, it's not a fair dare." Darci lowered Piper onto her chest and wrapped a fold of blanket over the baby. "Rain check. This dare will resume once the little monster is on solid food."

"Besides." Renee gestured at Harper. "We need time to scavenge up some good sunglasses. If you're going to dare Harper to hang out naked, we'll definitely need eye protection. Or do it inside."

Harper grinned while picking at her eye with her middle finger.

"Girl, you seriously need some sun." Grace whistled.

"This is *your* guys' idea." Harper examined her fingernails. "If you ever manage to convince me to go all hippie with you out in the woods, any retinal damage you suffer from looking directly at me is entirely your fault."

"Sun doesn't help." Renee gave her a pitying look. "She goes from snow white to lobster red with no space in between."

Darci raised an eyebrow. "Okay, so the dare is on hold. But I still challenge you to make a decision now. Nature or joint?"

"Nature," said Renee.

"I'll try the pot." Grace flashed an uneasy smile. "Much rather have an edible than smoke."

The three of them stared expectantly at Harper.

She picked her thumbnail at the crosshatch pattern on the Mossberg's pistol grip. Being around Darci when she got into full hippie mode felt awkward enough. Would it be less awkward if everyone flung off their clothes or would that make it worse? Either way, it couldn't be as mortifying as speaking (or singing) in public. *Live a little, right? Might be hilarious.* Also, as she proved yesterday, not having anything on didn't necessarily interfere with her ability to defend herself. Getting high would definitely leave her too disoriented and sluggish to react to bad situations. Darci had a tendency to grow it strong.

"Nature," said Harper without looking up.

"You seriously hate weed so much you'd rather be naked?" Darci tilted her head.

Harper kept picking at the shotgun's grip. "Hate isn't the right word. I'm more afraid of it."

"It's not going to rot your brain out and fry it like eggs. That's bullshit propaganda." Darci rolled her eyes.

"Marijuana leads to harder drugs and a life of crime," said Renee in a mimicry of a serious man's voice.

Grace laughed so hard she choked. Renee leaned over and swatted her on the back a few times.

Darci frowned. "Marijuana leads to snacks and long naps."

"No, it's not that." Harper moved the shotgun off her lap, rested it against the empty chair on her left, then leaned forward, arms draped over her knees. "I'm scared of letting my guard down, being vulnerable. If I'm too high to stand up, I can't shoot straight or react to danger. I really don't know if I'll ever be able to fully relax again. Every time I think we might be safe, *something* happens."

Darci rocked and bounced Piper. "Someday, you will be able to relax again, once we get our collective shit together enough. You literally fight for a better future. I do it by refusing to let the world break me. Yeah, maybe something bad will happen to me when I'm too mellow to handle it. But, even if some jerk kills me, he won't win. This world won't win. I'd be dead on my terms. Not living in fear."

Piper gave an almost worried sounding coo.

"I don't think she wants to lose her mama." Grace stretched forward and gently patted the baby on the head.

"There's a big difference between not living in fear and doing stupid things." Harper exhaled.

"Wow, so Logan killed two of them?" whispered Renee. "That's so romantic."

Harper gave her side eye. "How the heck is killing someone romantic?"

"I made a career out of making killing people look romantic," called Lucas from the yard. "Granted, it was pretend killing, but no one was supposed to believe the men I cut down limped off and got better."

Harper and her friends laughed.

"I mean..." Renee thrust her arms out to either side. "You said he went full Conan mode, right? He didn't care what happened to him and just wanted to protect you. That's romantic."

"He's really lucky." Grace whistled. "He didn't have a weapon or anything?"

"Yeah." Harper paused. "Well, he did grab a big rock."

"How biblical… naked dude beating another dude's head in with a stone." Grace snickered.

Renee bit her lip. "Is it weird I kinda want to watch that? I mean like, not for real killing. But as a movie. Two buff guys going at it in the buff."

"The idiots who attacked them had clothes on." Grace gave Harper side eye. "And I'm sure Harp didn't care how hot they were, or not. Life isn't a Boris Vallejo."

"What the hell does that mean?" Renee blinked.

"He's a painter." Darci waved her arm around as if swinging a sword. "I think he did the Conan stuff. Or was that Frazetta? I don't remember. Gah, I was so high in art class."

"You remember more than I do." Renee laughed.

"Are you saying Logan's hot?" asked Darci in a teasing voice.

"He is, but…" Renee fanned herself. "It doesn't have to be him."

Elijah darted by and zoomed through the open sliding glass door into the house. Once inside, he flopped on the floor to play with his large assortment of various toys.

Lucas strolled up the deck steps and leaned against the railing at the top. "I think it might've been the Celts who did that on purpose."

"Bashed guys heads in with rocks?" asked Darci.

"No." Lucas chuckled. "Well, they probably did that, too. I meant they ran into battle buck ass naked as an intimidation tactic. There is something quite unsettling about a raging barbarian charging at you with an axe while his junk is swinging in the breeze."

Harper didn't know whether to blush, laugh, or try to shrink into a little place where no one could see her. Logan certainly had gone full barbarian. The war—if she could even call it that—changed people. A former high school hockey player snapped and fought tooth and claw to protect the girl he loved. Renee didn't even hesitate when agreeing to honor a dare to get naked and hang out at some undetermined point in the future. Harper didn't know Grace prior to the nukes, but seriously doubted the girl would have ever touched weed if society hadn't collapsed. The genius cheerleader princess didn't dare do anything without being told to do it by her wealthy parents, not even choosing a potential career. Even before the world collapsed, Darci used to sleep naked; her friend warned her years ago not to barge into her bedroom for early weekend wakeups—unless she wanted to see things. Nuclear bombardment erased whatever tiny scraps of care she once held for decorum. Darci had gone full boheme.

We could all die tomorrow. She's not hurting anyone. We should be happy for whatever time we've got left.

Maybe one day, Harper would cave in and try weed. Her friends might be right. Could be, pot would help her relax. She didn't feel overly stressed out or like she suffered PTSD, but she did acknowledge the constant pressure to stay aware of her surroundings.

If I ever feel like I'm losing my grip, losing the ability to handle things, maybe I'll try it. But... not now. I'm strong enough.

"I should get back out there. If something happens and I'm goofing off with my friends, I'd never forgive myself." Harper stood.

"No problem." Darci smiled. "Come back to hang out when you can, okay?"

"Sure." Harper hugged everyone, then made her way around the house to the road.

FOR THE LAST HOUR OF HER PATROL, HARPER THOUGHT ABOUT LAWS.

In a modern world where no one considered the ready availability of food to be a big deal, crimes of varying severity could be punished proportionally by incarceration. The Evergreen Militia faced the problem of jail becoming a vacation. Sure, being stuck in a small room sucked, but it's not like they missed out on TV, the Internet, video games, night life, or whatever. Sitting in the sheriff's department holding area basically let a person sleep all day and get food without having to help sustain the town.

All sorts of laws no longer really proved workable. Tons of them didn't even apply anymore, like tax evasion or jaywalking. Theft almost didn't exist either, since no one really owned much of value. With very few exceptions, everyone in town had basically stolen a house. All the clothing they wore had either been looted from abandoned stores or made here. All the food they ate got handed out for free. No one cared about money. Nothing valuable—like electronics, computers, cars, and so on—worked. A person couldn't steal an item no one owned, anyway. So, there everything sat.

Kids drinking beer underage, Darci going nudist in town, minor fights at Earl's bar... a whole bunch of little things that would have gotten people arrested before no longer mattered at all. She still couldn't believe Renee chose 'nature' instead of pot. Then again, the two of them had always been weird about drugs. As tweens, they looked down on the older kids who smoked pot as losers—as if eighteen-year-olds would give a crap what little kids thought of their life choices.

Eventually, Marcie came by to take over the patrol route. They had a brief conversation about all the nothing that happened so far that morning. Quiet route, no one in trouble, no external threats.

Harper headed west toward the farm to either collect the kids or hang out with them until they finished whatever chores they had to do. The younger the kid, the lighter the work. Other than Madison's momentary fit of drama, the kids rarely complained. Crazy how even the small ones knew their lives depended on the farm. Crazier still to think that a new generation already started who would have no idea what the pre-nuclear world had been like. Dad once teased Harper with a tape cassette and a pencil, asking if she knew how the two items related to each other. She hadn't a clue. The idea Emmett, Owen, or Piper wouldn't know what McDonalds was, or Starbucks, or even movies made her feel old the same way Dad claimed to be ancient when she'd been baffled at the tape cassette pencil relationship.

While crossing Route 74, she spotted a pair of horses pulling a train of three U-Haul trailers toward town. A man sat on the roof of the lead trailer like a Wild West coachman. He appeared to be in his early fifties, weathered and tanned. His long hair almost reached his waist, mostly grey with bits of brown striped throughout. An assortment of hip satchels, pouches, and knapsacks hung off his belt and shoulder.

Much like the man driving it, all manner of assorted junk—chairs, boxes, lamps, and so on—hung on rope nets rigged to the sides of each trailer. More stuff had been piled up on top of the second and third trailer. A small wooden garden shed sat atop the lead trailer, probably where the man slept at night.

"What the hell am I looking at?" She stopped in the middle of the highway and watched him ride up to the bus barrier.

Annapurna and Cameron raised their hands in greeting at the man, who seemed friendly.

A few minutes of inaudible conversation later, they waved him around, giving him the okay to enter town. Once it seemed unlikely the odd man would be a threat, Harper resumed walking to the farm.

ONCE THE LAST OF THE KIDS—AT LEAST THE ONES SHE HAD responsibility for—finished their chores, Harper led the brood down Route 74 into town. Madison, Jonathan, and Lorelei all looked as if they'd been caught in a wicked sandstorm. Despite it only being about two in the afternoon (give or take an hour), the older two appeared ready to sleep. Lorelei chattered on about her day, meeting the chickens, talking to the cows, and so on.

They wandered off the road to go around the end of the bus barrier, then back onto the highway. Annapurna sat in a chair by a folding table against the nearer bus, scarfing down a late lunch of fried potato wedges and meat that might've been chicken, rabbit, or raccoon.

Harper waved. "Hey, Anna. What's the deal with the U-Haul guy?"

"Trader," mumbled Annapurna around a mouthful of food. She finished chewing, took a gulp of water, then waved generally down the road. "Said he's going from town to town trading stuff. Basically, a mobile store."

"Umm. Did anyone bother to tell him money isn't a thing anymore?" Harper laughed.

"Does he got toys?" asked Lorelei.

"Does he *have* toys," whispered Madison.

Lorelei blinked at her. "I dunno! That's why I'm askin'!"

Madison facepalmed.

Jonathan and Harper chuckled.

"Might check it out when my shift's over." Annapurna shrugged. "If there's anything left."

"If there's anything worth taking at all," added Cameron from on top of the bus.

"Fair point." Annapurna grinned. "Looked like mostly furniture and junk."

"Good stuff is probably inside the trailers, so no one takes it." Jonathan yawned.

Madison made a noise of modest interest.

"Okay." Harper waved at Annapurna and resumed walking south.

The man with the trailer wagon had come to a stop on the side of the highway a little past the quartermaster's, pretty much in line with the place that used to be a boarding kennel for dogs. In the time she'd been waiting for the kids on the farm, the guy set up his wares at the base of the hill separating Route 74 from Bergen Peak Drive, which paralleled it. A small crowd of about fourteen people—many of whom worked in the quartermaster's building—gathered around to pick through an assortment of stuff set out on long folding tables.

Madison and Lorelei rushed forward to check his wares out.

Jonathan peered up at Harper. "Umm. How's he gonna sell stuff? No one has money."

"Bartering. We'd have to give him something he wants in trade."

"Oh. Uhh, better keep an eye on Lore. She'll trade her dress for something shiny."

Harper laughed, mostly because the boy wasn't wrong. "Yeah."

They hurried after the girls, shadowing them as they perused the merchandise the guy collected. The tables contained glassware, figurines, some dolls, some toys, lots of knives, tools, clothing, shoes—though mostly little kid sized ones—and a bunch of random kitsch like porcelain dragons or kittens. Unsurprisingly, he didn't have any electronics, phones, or items likely to have been rendered useless by an EMP wave.

Predictably, Lorelei gravitated to the section of tables with the dolls and toys.

Harper hovered nearby, observing.

The merchant introduced himself as "Alexander Winslow, or the Wandering Winslow if you prefer" to anyone who started a conversation. In the midst of talking to Michelle Butler—Mila's new mom—he explained that he'd come to an agreement with Elizabeth Trujillo in regard to trade for food. While he would consider personal trades with individuals, the townspeople here could take items they wanted or needed and the town would essentially pay for it in vegetables or other food.

Mila, who'd meandered a short distance from her adoptive mother, picked up a series of knives in turn, seemingly testing their balance by tossing them up and catching them before putting them down. Alexander kept glancing away from Michelle at the girl, his expression growing more and more alarmed. Harper resisted the urge to laugh.

The seventh knife Mila picked up had an all-black coating and looked like something from a military surplus store. She tossed it up and caught it by the handle, which caused Alexander to rush three steps to his left to stand on the opposite side of the table from her.

"Careful, sweetie. These are sharp."

"I hope they're sharp. They wouldn't be very useful if they weren't," said Mila in a flat tone. "This one's got good balance. Can I have it?"

Michelle fidgeted. The poor woman still hadn't quite gotten used to the idea the girl she agreed to take care of had such a lethal hobby. "You need to be careful with it."

"Uhh…" Alexander picked up a pink-haired doll. "Are you sure you wouldn't rather have something nice like this? Tell you what. You can have the doll as a gift instead of the knife."

Mila narrowed her eyes at the doll, then looked up at him. "I'll bet you I can take fifteen steps back, throw this knife, and put it in the hole of the 'A' in U-Haul behind you. If I hit it, I get to keep the knife *and* the doll."

Winslow raised his right eyebrow, dropped it, then raised his left. He appeared ready to say 'you have to be joking,' but instead asked, "What if you miss?"

"Didn't think of anything. You can come up with something if you want, but it would be a waste of your time. I won't miss." Mila stared blankly up at him.

"Do you really need *another* knife, hon?" asked Michelle. "You have so many. And I'm sure this nice man doesn't want a hole in the side of his trailer."

Mila held the weapon up so her mother could see it. "This one's balanced, *and* it's got a real handle. When I'm older, I could use this one without having to throw it. The other ones are *only* for throwing."

"All right, fine, dear. But... I still want you to run away and hide from any bad situation where you aren't absolutely forced into defending yourself." Michelle sighed.

"Thanks, Mom. And, you can hug me if you want. I don't hate it." Mila smiled.

Mr. Winslow gave them a 'this kid is weird' stare, then put his merchant smile back on.

Content, Mila clutched both doll and knife to her chest, loving them equally.

Lorelei squealed when she found a plastic unicorn toy with a rainbow mane. It had a few scuff marks and dirt on it, but she didn't care.

Winslow looked over, saw her, and sighed in relief.

"Can I have this?" Lorelei ran over to Harper with the toy unicorn.

Harper nodded.

"Of course, sweetie." Winslow jotted her name down on a spiral notebook next to 'plastic unicorn toy, small'.

Jonathan and Madison continued looking over the stuff, neither of them yet finding anything compelling enough to ask for.

Winslow drifted off to the right, toward the end of the trailer wagon, eyeing the M4 rifle slung over Ken's shoulder. His attempt to bargain for the weapon led nowhere, the gun being far too valuable to Evergreen's defense for Ken to part with it. Their conversation drifted from guns—which Winslow complained about becoming rather rare lately—to his travels around the region. He'd evidently been to the area down by the Overton ranch as well as Fairplay and a handful of other small towns as far away as Nederland, which apparently also had a sustaining farm.

As soon as Winslow mentioned arriving here after scavenging around Denver, Harper shifted from idle eavesdropping to paying serious attention.

"Did the Lawless give you much trouble?" asked Ken.

"Not sure what you mean. Lawless?" Winslow scratched at his scraggly, brown hair.

Ken began explaining about the gang from Denver. Harper slipped into the conversation, proud of herself for neither swearing nor getting emotional. The more Winslow talked about spending four days roaming around the various parts of the city without meeting a single soul, the more restless Harper became. She had to know if it might be true. Could the threat of the Lawless be gone for good?

Taken by that idea, she drifted away to collect the kids. Jonathan scored a large eleven-by-seventeen-inch sketch pad. Madison didn't find anything interesting enough to ask for, and surprisingly didn't seem upset to walk away empty handed. Winslow kept talking to Ken about how he planned to spend a few days here before moving on, but he'd be back eventually. He planned to keep making regular circuits among all the survivor towns in the area.

Harper headed down Route 74 to Hilltop Drive, her thoughts swirling around one driving idea.

I gotta know.

A TRACE OF NORMAL

JUNE 6ᵀᴴ

Later that evening, Harper nibbled on grilled fish and corn.

Space around the table had become somewhat cramped. Logan and Luisa got into the habit of joining them for dinner. He spent most of the day on the farm and didn't feel right asking Luisa to cook for him, since he wanted to protect her as a big brother and not feel as if she'd become a servant. It didn't bother him if she helped prepare food for everyone, as that felt like distributing responsibility rather than merely a role reversal where the little sister took care of him. Shared meals tended to happen more often lately, especially for dinner. People who lived near each other gathered to stretch food out, avoid leftovers they couldn't preserve, and socialize.

The farm didn't have quite so many cows they'd gotten back into the habit of butchering them for food, though the day would come in a few years once the population grew enough. Luisa gradually warmed up to everyone. Though she still tended to be quiet and not *start* conversations unless alone with her brother, she didn't mind responding to other people talking or spending time with Carrie or Renee and the 'clothing people.'

In between wondering how much contamination and bad stuff the fish she ate absorbed, Harper's thoughts drifted to her parents and the Lawless. She kept seeing Winslow's face in her thoughts telling her he'd spent multiple days in Denver without seeing another living person.

The kids finished eating and raced back outside.

Luisa grasped her plate, glancing at Carrie in a silent offer to help clean up.

Like a meditating monk, Cliff leaned back in his chair, eyes closed, rubbing his belly.

Logan mimicked the pose.

"I see you," muttered Cliff. "Don't think this old man is blind. Food comas don't make me any less dangerous."

Logan chuckled, but stopped parroting his posture.

"That Winslow guy said he was in Denver for almost a week and didn't see anyone." Harper pushed an empty corn cob back and forth across her plate, trying not to think about what the cob would be used for next. "I want to go look."

Cliff opened his eyes. "You do realize, that's not a smart idea."

"It might not be a stupid one either." She let the fork fall from her fingers; it hit the plate with a soft clank. "The guy has three big trailers loaded with stuff. He also doesn't have a gun. Why didn't the Lawless take everything he has? Dr. Rowland also said he went through Denver and didn't see anyone."

"Okay, so that's two people." Cliff tapped his fingers on the table. "Chances are it's likely true. You have a good point about the guy's junk."

"What guy's junk?" asked Renee in a distracted tone, as if she hadn't been paying attention. "What happened?"

"Actual junk." Cliff palmed his face, wiping his hand downward until he rested his chin on it. "The merchant guy with all the crap in trailers."

"Oh." Renee laughed.

"Wow, you need it bad." Lorelei walked in from the hallway, the swoosh of a flushing toilet echoing behind her. She carried her new rainbow-maned unicorn toy in one hand, not having put it down for more than a few seconds since she got it.

Cliff let his hand fall limp on the table, staring in disbelief at the seven-year-old.

Carrie covered her mouth.

Renee blushed.

Harper tried—and failed not to burst out laughing.

Unfazed by anyone's reaction, Lorelei crossed the kitchen and went outside to join the other kids playing.

Cliff kept staring at the spot where she'd been.

"She has no idea what 'it' means." Harper laughed into a sigh. "Just something she probably heard her mother say."

Lorelei poked her head back in. "Are you gonna tell me?"

"Tell you what?" Harper twisted around to look at her.

"What *it* is?" Lorelei smiled innocently.

"Yes." Harper nodded.

Cliff raised an eyebrow.

"What is it?" Lorelei flashed a cheesy smile.

"Ask me again in five years and I'll tell you."

Lorelei pondered. "That's a really long time. But..." She grinned, then chirped, "Okay" before darting away from the door into the yard.

"Five years? Twelve?" Carrie bit her lip in an 'I dunno' manner.

"Yeah. Gotta be fair." Harper slumped forward on the table, resting her chin on her folded arms. "Had the talk with Maddie. No gory details, but she knows."

"You did not." Cliff whistled.

"It just kinda happened. I mean, she's twelve. That's not a *little* kid. And, I figure it'll only keep her safe if she knows what to be wary of."

Carrie grimaced. "Bit earlier than I would have done it but, I suppose you have a point. Poor kid's been through enough."

"Uhm," said Luisa in a mousy half whisper. "I'm going to be seventeen next month. Is someone going to explain anything to me?"

Logan shot her a 'you're not serious' stare, then squirmed in his seat.

Cliff tried not to look at her, fidgeting a fork between two fingers. "That's one for Carrie, I think."

"Really, hon?" Carrie blinked at her.

Luisa lifted her gaze out of her lap. The earnestness in her expression faded to a smile. "No. I'm teasing. I know enough about enough."

"You do?" Logan blinked. "But you've never dated a guy for more than two weeks."

"Knowing and doing aren't the same." Luisa examined her fingernails. "We used to have internet. I had questions."

As if sensing taboo topics in the air, Madison, Jonathan, and Lorelei came running back inside. Thankfully, they didn't stand around the kitchen to eavesdrop and went straight to the living room, where they discussed which board game to grab. Still, nothing sensitive could be discussed in the kitchen without them hearing.

"Okay then." Cliff slapped the table. "Umm. So, Harper. You're serious about wanting to go to Denver?"

"Yeah. Maybe it's silly, but I need to see for myself that they're all gone."

"No maybe about it." Cliff shifted his jaw side to side. "It *is* silly."

"Last winter was really nasty." Madison drifted back toward the kitchen, leaning on the wall. "They probably all froze to death. Those morons didn't have a farm."

Cliff rubbed his beard. "Yeah. Good chance they didn't make it through that snow. Or, maybe they dispersed before the storm. Might'a even killed each other. Who knows?"

Ugh. What is wrong with me? Harper stared at the dead corn cob. "It's dumb. You're right. I should let it go."

"Let it go! Let it gooooo," sang Lorelei, before going into a fully committed rendition of the song while dancing around the living room as Elsa.

Madison gazed upward in the same 'please help me' way Mom used to do whenever she got frustrated. "Harp! See what you did? She'll be on that song all day now."

Everyone sat in silence, listening to the child sing. After a few minutes of nonstop singing, Madison began bonking her head on the wall.

"At least she's on key." Luisa grinned.

Cliff exhaled, then looked over at Harper. "If you truly need this, we'll do it on two conditions. One: I'm going with you. Two: we get the nod from Walter and bring a proper team."

"Ell emm ayy oh." Harper sighed. "A proper team for what? Soothing my insecurities? He's not going to give the go-ahead for an expedition to Denver just to make me feel better."

"That's a chance I'm more than willing to take." Cliff laughed.

Harper couldn't help but laugh along with him. "Okay. You guys are right. It's not a great idea. If he says no, I promise I won't run off on my own."

Madison stopped bonking her head and faced the kitchen. "Can I go, too?"

"No," said Cliff and Harper simultaneously.

Jonathan raced around behind Lorelei, swinging a blanket to simulate a magical gown following her as she danced and sang. It seemed the boy hadn't forgotten *everything* he'd learned in dance class, even though neither he nor Madison had mentioned it in over a year.

"Maddie?" Harper got up and walked over to her sister. "After what happened last time, I thought you accepted that you need to stay safe."

"I did." Madison smiled. "If the Lawless are all gone… it *is* safe."

Harper hugged her. "Fair point, but we don't know for a fact that's true. And Denver is still kinda radioactive. We can't stay there long. You're too little to risk exposure."

Madison fake sighed. "Okay. You're right. I'll stay here. Just be careful."

"I will. Cliff's gonna be with us. And besides, Walter is probably going to say no."

"Umm." Madison narrowed her eyes, nodded to herself, then held a finger up. "If you come back safe, I'll volunteer for extra farm work."

Cliff scratched his head. "What good will that do?"

"I really don't wanna shovel horse poop and stuff." Madison flailed her arms. "Like, *really* don't. I'm jinxing myself to do something horrible, so bad luck comes after *me* in a mild way instead of going after Harper in a bad way."

Luisa walked around the table and reached for Cliff's plate.

"Yanno." Cliff stood, took his plate, and the stack from Luisa. "I got the dishes, kiddo. Go have fun." He nodded at Madison. "Kid's getting as creepy as Mila ever since they started reading that crazy book."

"It's not a crazy book." Madison folded her arms. "It's witchcraft."

"Relax, hon." Carrie hugged him. "That sort of thing is normal for girls her age."

Harper raised an eyebrow. "I never played with witch stuff."

"Which stuff is that?" asked Logan.

"Ugh." Harper sighed. "Not which... *witch*."

Logan scratched his head, pretending to be confused. "I'm lost."

She fake glared at him. "Witch... as is in pointy hat, rides a broom?"

"More like lights a bunch of candles, says creepy stuff, and sits around in the dark screaming at every unexplained noise." Renee pointed at Harper. "We messed around with Ouija boards at Darci's. That counts as witchcraft. Sure, you never wore pentacle necklaces or tried to 'cast spells' but we totally did have an occult phase."

"*Everyone* messes around with a Ouija board sometime between twelve and fifteen." Harper rolled her eyes. "That's not a 'girl thing' and it's not witchcraft."

"Oops." Luisa flashed a weak smile. "I guess I missed my window. Never touched one of those boards. You really shouldn't play with things like that."

"Oh, good grief." Harper exhaled. "You believe that stuff, too?"

Cliff carried the stack of plates over to the sink. "Can't say what it is exactly, but it's not *not* witchcraft."

"Whatever it is, it's gonna work." Madison huffed.

A LITTLE OVER AN HOUR LATER, THE DISHES SAT CLEAN AND PUT AWAY. The sun started to go down. And Lorelei still hadn't stopped singing *Let it Go*, though she no longer belted it out at full volume. Madison had thrice gone on a hunt for duct tape.

"You guys ready?" Renee closed the book she'd been reading and sat up on the sofa.

"Ready?" Harper peered at her. "For what?"

"The movie?" Her best friend gawked. "How could you forget about that?"

"Umm." Harper shrugged. "I can't forget about something I never knew. What the heck are you talking about?"

"Oh right." Cliff sprang out of his recliner and bellowed, "Kids, c'mon."

"Is anyone going to clue me in here?" asked Harper.

Renee laughed. "You remember the trader guy, right?"

"Yeah." Harper closed her book and set it on the end table. "What about him?"

"He had a bunch of DVDs in his junk." Renee stood.

"That had to hurt." Cliff cringed as if someone hit him in the groin.

"Not that junk." Renee stuck her tongue out at him. "The town traded for them. We got one of those office projector thingees? You know the things they used to put a computer screen on the wall?"

"Oh, wow. Really?" Harper gawked. "It works?"

"So does the PlayStation we found here." Jonathan pointed at it. "When the power's in a good enough mood. It's usually a little weak, so the stupid thing won't turn on."

Carrie peered over the top of her book. "I thought those projectors took a lot of power."

"No idea." Renee shrugged. "They set it up outside the Safeway, since it's got white walls. Just waiting for the sun to go down."

"Neat." Harper climbed over the back of the sofa. "Let me just grab my sneakers."

She rushed to the bedroom, pulled her shoes on, and grabbed the Mossberg... just in case. Since the attack at Bear Creek, she'd become hesitant to go any distance from home without it. She hurried back to the living room, then followed her entire family plus Logan and Luisa down Hilltop Drive to Route 74. People meandered along ahead of them, the whole town coming together for the first ever 'movie night'. The weather appeared to be in a good mood, at least. A surprising number of people Harper didn't recognize joined the crowd, no doubt from South Evergreen, which as yet still did not have electrical power.

They all gathered in the parking lot at Safeway where a whole mess of folding chairs stood facing a blank, white wall. Terrence, and a few people from the electrician team, puttered around with a projector unit and a laptop computer on a cafeteria table.

Mayor Ned stepped out in front of the wall once the stream of people arriving seemed at an end. "Hello everyone. I hope you're all enjoying this fine early summer evening. Our plan is to show something for the little ones, take a bit of a break, then put on a film that's a little less child friendly for the adults willing to stay up a little later than normal. Luck, technology, and electricity willing, that is."

A few people clapped.

"Oh, may I ask everyone to please turn off your cell phones during the picture." Mayor Ned smiled.

The crowd laughed.

Since it had become dark enough to see the Windows desktop on the Safeway wall clearly, Terrence loaded a disc and started the movie *Zootopia.*

"Aww," whispered Lorelei. "Not *Frozen?*"

"This one's cute, too." Madison poked her.

Harper settled in, leaning against Logan, holding hands and sneaking a bit of making out in between peeks at the film. The moment felt too wonderful, too perfect. Harper gradually stopped making out with him and just sat there, staring past his face into the distance over the store's roof—more or less in the direction where the unexploded nuclear warhead sat. She half expected to see a blinding white light at any second.

A bright flash and *bang* went off under the table holding the projector; everything went dark.

Harper screamed. It took her brain a few seconds to realize the flash had been *much* weaker than a nuclear detonation. She slouched against Logan, shivering away the last vestiges of 'we almost just died' fear... and feeling like an idiot.

The crowd gave off a combined "Aww!"

"Not even halfway into the movie," said a child a few rows away. "Can they fix it?"

"You okay?" Logan squeezed her. "What's got you so wound up all of a sudden?"

She rested her head on his shoulder, mouth by his ear, and whispered, "Can't talk about it here. If you can keep a secret, I'll tell you later."

"Okay. Are you sure you're okay?"

"Yeah. Just nerves. Scaring myself." Harper exhaled hard.

"Workin' on it," yelled Terrence.

Whispered discussion came from the dark ahead. Someone up there lit a candle, holding it so the electricians—and their apprentice, Terrence, could try to determine if the issue had been a fuse, a blown power supply, or a melted wire. A few minutes later, the picture came back up.

The crowd clapped.

Madison leaned close and whispered, "This feels so weird."

"Hmm?" Harper glanced at her. "What does?"

"This." Madison gestured around. "Watching a movie seems so normal, but also strange. Maybe it's because we're outside, using an abandoned grocery store as a screen, but it feels like we're not supposed to be able to have modern stuff anymore. Are we cheating?"

Harper gave her a one-armed squeeze. "We won't get in trouble for enjoying this stuff when we can... before every bit of tech craps out."

"Ugh. Yeah." Madison slouched. "It won't last long, will it?"

"Probably not." Harper bit her lip.

Cliff, in a folding chair behind them, leaned forward and whispered, "They only got forty something movies. You'll get sick of watching the same ones over and over before the laptop craps out."

"The bulb in that projector will die before we get tired of the movies," whispered Jonathan. "Those things don't last long."

"Watching movies makes you sick?" Lorelei gasped.

Cliff, Harper, Madison, and a few people near enough to overhear, chuckled.

"Not sick like that." Cliff ruffled the girl's hair. "If you watch it too much, you won't want to watch it anymore."

"Oh, no." Lorelei shook her head. "I can watch *Frozen* over and over and over. Do they have *Frozen*? It's my favorite."

"Please no," whispered Madison to no one in particular.

"Yeah." Cliff let out a resigned sigh. "Six copies of it."

"Yay!" Lorelei thrust her hands into the air.

"Ugh." Madison hung her head. "She's gonna wear them all out."

27

INEVITABLE

HOUR ONE - SUNDAY, JUNE 7TH

Harper couldn't believe Walter said yes.

He also caught wind of the rumors of Denver being empty and decided it would be valuable intelligence to get confirmation that a significant threat looming over Evergreen for the past almost two years was gone. Also, they had the additional task of visiting a handful of hardware stores and any other place likely to contain materials useful in the construction and maintenance of wind-powered generators—if it turned out to be true, the Lawless no longer presented a threat. Walter didn't want anyone getting killed for electrical power. He considered it a 'nice to have' rather than a requirement.

If it proved true that they had free run of the Denver area without the need to worry about a literal army of lunatics, it opened many possibilities for scavenging. Their third objective would be to raid dentist's offices or hospitals in search of lead-lined aprons from the X-ray rooms. An expedition to relocate the MIRV would run far more smoothly if everyone participating in it had some radiation protection. Given that *aprons* tended only to cover one side of a person wearing it, everyone would need two at least.

It made sense why Walter agreed to the trip, even if his rapid agreement shocked her—as well as Cliff, who almost certainly only wanted to ask Walter to have someone else tell Harper no.

Their team—Harper, Cliff, Deacon, and Tyreek Dawson, from the militia, plus Lonnie Blanchard, Jeanette, and Rafael piled into the USPS truck. Lonnie brought his sniper rifle, the same one he'd used in the standoff he had with Harper and the others some months ago from the roof of a grocery store. The sixty-one-year-old decided to help out the militia here and there, though didn't officially join due to his age. He did pull shifts on the bus barrier, as that duty tended to favor snipers. He and Cliff got along great as they'd both been special forces. Before the war, Tyreek had been a corrections officer at the SuperMAX prison. He'd happily come back to Evergreen after the militia raided Kittredge and killed off the convicts who held him and several other people captive as slave labor.

They drove north up Route 74 to Route 70, taking the highway east toward Denver. Riding in a biodiesel-powered Postal truck beat walking or bicycles for speed, even if the puttering thing didn't move terribly fast for a car. It almost got up to fifty on downhills.

It felt like a long time since Harper had been to the city, yet she remembered every abandoned car on the road they swerved around. Madison's promise to volunteer for extra work at the farm as a jinx hex or whatever she called it to keep her safe got her thinking about daring herself to do something unpleasant. Volunteering for farm work wouldn't be that bad. Surrendering Dad's Mossberg to the militia would feel like she betrayed her family. Besides, she didn't want to quit and didn't have anywhere near the same kind of skill with a rifle as she did with a shotgun. In order for a jinx to work, it would have to be something she *really* didn't want to do but would still do under pressure. Unfortunately, the only severely unpleasant thing she could come up with that wouldn't hurt anyone, she would absolutely hate doing, and would be able to do without guilt would be to pull a Darci and streak town. Of course, she could sing Disney tunes in public, but the nudity would be less mortifying.

She vetoed the thought.

I'm being an idiot. There's no such thing as hexes or jinxes.

Her nerves prickled at the ends, though she couldn't call the emotion fear. It didn't exactly feel like excitement, either. It had to be the same emotion relatively new soldiers went through on the transport taking them to their second or third combat mission. Somehow, Harper dreaded what would happen, couldn't wait to get going, wanted to go home, and wanted to kick Lawless ass all at the same time.

Jeanette and the others pored over a small map of the city as well as a business directory, plotting out their route and stops. Between her and Rafael, they could identify a wide range of potentially useful items to be repurposed into windmills. Also, if anything happened to the truck, Rafael could hopefully get it moving again.

Harper sat with her back to the wall, sorta-leaning on Cliff, and kept her head down, trying not to think about anything. It bothered her *not* to be guilty over leaving Madison back in Evergreen. Yes, her sister would worry about her. But, Maddie had her head screwed back on right. She could handle it. Besides, this trip had to be the safest foray into Denver yet: a full team, including Cliff and Deacon, *plus* the Lawless may not even exist anymore.

That just means I'm going to die. She exhaled out her nostrils. *Anything that feels too easy is going to be the opposite.*

The vibration in the floor and the constant swaying and bouncing tried to lull her into a nap, but couldn't dent the swirling mess of anxiety and anticipation in her head.

Finally, after about an hour, the truck slowed to a stop.

"Point A," said Rafael, meaning they'd arrived at the first identified store.

Harper felt like a character in a military video game doing a mission involving multiple waypoints. Everyone put on dust-filter masks Jeanette brought from the public works garage, the sort of thing guys cutting concrete might wear on a construction site. Figuring the Denver area remained radioactive enough to the point they couldn't safely spend more than a few hours there, they decided it would be dangerous to inhale radioactive dust. Since they had the masks, might as well use them. Harper grinned to herself while putting it on, thinking of Cliff using his military gas mask for diaper detail. She imagined him making a joke about 'baby butt fumes' being deadlier than gamma radiation.

"Point A," echoed Cliff.

Lonnie climbed up to sit in the chair bolted to a round opening in the roof, Rafael's best attempt to make a sniper's roost. As the older man settled in to cover the team—and defend the truck—the others got out. The illusion of 'normal' she'd been feeling in Evergreen lately shattered in the face of the vast, obvious destruction over the Denver area. The city she once called home looked like scenes on the evening news covering a massive earthquake in some other country or films she'd seen in history class documenting the bombed-out cities from World War II.

Harper looked around at a landscape she didn't fully recognize. They'd stopped outside a Home Depot. A few hundred feet to her left, stood a Kohl's, its façade scorched and peppered with hundreds of holes, far too big to have come from bullets. The Home Depot had similar holes, likely from concrete fragments flying at crazy speeds on a blast wave.

The team walked over a short distance of debris-strewn parking lot to the sidewalk outside the store.

"Ick," said Jeanette.

Harper glanced to her left. A badly decomposed body lay on the ground at the base of a tall light pole in the parking lot below a still-intact noose made of electrical wire. The remains appeared to have been decapitated. *Decaying... nice. Not too much radiation here then.* She winced. *Ugh, what the hell is wrong with me? My reaction to seeing a dead guy shouldn't be 'oh cool, he's decaying.'*

Cliff approached the corpse, sinking to a squat a short distance away and examining the area.

Compared to the mass grave pit at the abandoned medical camp, a single body didn't bother Harper as much as she expected. The exact moment when she'd become jaded enough at the sight of dead bodies for her reaction to change from stereotypical teen girl screaming to thinking 'poor bastard' escaped her. She also walked closer, but stopped a few feet behind Cliff.

"Poor son of a bitch." Cliff shook his head. "Hung himself... and stayed up there until the cord tore through his neck."

Tyreek made a gurgling noise, rubbing the front of his neck. "Aww, man. What a way to go."

"Damn," muttered Deacon, his impossibly deep, bass voice vibrating in Harper's ribs.

"You sure he hung himself?" asked Tyreek.

"Fairly sure, yeah." Cliff gestured at the body's right arm. "Hands aren't tied. If someone else killed him, he would have had to be unconscious before they hauled him into the air." He pointed at a shopping cart not far away. "Probably stood on that and kicked it out from under himself to get the drop."

Harper looked at the corpse's wrist—and gasped at the sight of a purple-and-white fabric bracelet. "Oh... shit."

Cliff peered back at her.

She moved up, circling around to stand by the dead man's feet. The black coat, the white—formerly—shirt, the pants... it had to be him. His severed head and scraps of neck lay on the ground not far away from the rest of the body. Decomposition made it impossible to recognize by facial features, but the overall size and proportion of the corpse looked about right. Half of her wanted to cry. Half of her wanted to spit on the remains and say the world would be a better place.

"Gonna fill us in or keep us in suspense?" asked Cliff.

"It's Tyler," rasped Harper. "I—I'm pretty sure it's Tyler."

"Oh." Cliff stood.

"Who the heck is Tyler?" Tyreek walked closer. Any interest he may have had in going through the corpse's pockets died with a grimace.

"You're right. He probably killed himself." Harper closed her eyes. "Tyler had serious mental issues."

"This is what happens to anyone who breaks my daughter's heart," deadpanned Cliff.

Harper let out a slow exhale. "I'm sorry."

"You have a big heart, kiddo." Cliff patted her on the back.

"I feel as if I am missing some critical details here." Tyreek chuckled. "Considering my name starts with T-y, and this dead guy here also has a name starting with T-y, I am concerned."

Jeanette and Rafael chuckled.

"It's complicated." Harper looked down, fidgeting her thumbnail at the Mossberg's textured grip. "This guy was in Evergreen for a while. He's the one who found Lorelei almost starved to death in an alley somewhere and saved her."

"And was also batshit nuts," muttered Cliff. "Tried to kill Madison."

Tyreek raised both eyebrows. "Whoa."

"Yeah." Harper repetitively tapped the toe of her sneaker into the pavement. "He really believed the government put microchips in our heads to control us and he wanted to cut the 'chip' out of Madison's brain."

"Good for the sumbitch then," called Lonnie from the truck not far away.

"I did this to him." Harper closed her eyes for a moment, then gazed down at the remains.

"No, his issues did it to him. Or the lack of meds." Cliff tugged on her arm. "C'mon. Let's get moving. Remember what your teacher said. This place is still hot. Don't want to spend too long here."

Harper hugged him.

He put an arm around her and held on. "You know it's not your fault. People like him weren't going to last long in a world without medicine. Don't blame yourself."

"Yeah." She exhaled.

"You good?"

"Mostly." She let go and raised the Mossberg in a ready grip. "I don't know why I'm upset. He almost killed Maddie. Scared the living hell out of her. I should've shot him."

"Nah, you're too human for that. You had a gun on a man who posed no threat to you. Killing him would've been an execution. Gotta cling to that, or you turn into the sorts of bastards who run around wearing blue sashes."

Harper nodded at him, then closed her eyes. *Tyler, wherever you are, if ghosts are a thing, I'm sorry life gave you a shitty deal. I kinda understand you didn't really know what you almost did to Maddie, but I'm still kinda mad at you for not telling me you had issues.* "Goodbye, Tyler."

After one last look at the rotting corpse, she followed the others into the Home Depot.

TWO SMALLER HARDWARE STORES AFTER THE HOME DEPOT, THEY pulled up to the broken remains of St. Joseph's Hospital. This long after the strike, they didn't expect there to be any useful medicine left, so rushed in only hunting for lead aprons from X-ray rooms. The word 'Lawless' appeared in spray paint all over the walls, outside and in. So much dried blood splattered in the hallways, Cliff wondered aloud if they used the hospital as a real-life version of a video game like Doom where they hunted people through the hallways. Harper not knowing what *Doom* was struck Cliff's funny bone, and kept him chuckling to himself the entire time in between muttering, 'Damn, I'm old.'

Hurrying through the carnage-strewn halls, Harper couldn't help but think of the last time she'd been here, the time they found Renee. Her best friend wore the blue sash of the Lawless, but merely tried to keep her head down and hide. The gang found her and forced her to join them.

"What?" Cliff glanced back at her.

"What, what?" She blinked.

"You just growled a little."

"Oh. I did? Sorry. Didn't even realize. Was thinking about Renee.

Last time we came here." She smirked. "At least that idiot Zach isn't with us."

"Fuckin' moron," muttered Cliff. "Pardon my French."

They scored five lead aprons and made their way back to the truck, tossing their loot atop boxes of copper wiring and various bits of machinery taken from the hardware stores.

"On to point D." Rafael started the engine.

"See anything, Lonnie?" Cliff hopped in and pulled the rear door down, closing it.

"Negative contact. It's a ghost town." The elder rotated in the roof port. "Ain't seen a damn thing. Not even birds."

Deacon drummed his fingers on the floor. "Them birds can smell the radiation, I bet. Let's get a move on."

28

THE SOUND OF SILENCE

HOUR TWO - JUNE 7TH

The street somewhere in Downtown Denver resembled a Lego diorama in the aftermath of two Great Danes playing.

All the conversations Harper ever had with Cliff about nuclear bombs came back to her thoughts. This location had to be in 'the first ring' around the blast. Ground zero, or 'the orange spot,' represented the area directly under the thermonuclear fireball where nothing remained, only flat ground. The first ring contained the worst destruction where all but the most hardened buildings would be destroyed and anyone who happened to be in it at the time of the blast faced a near-guaranteed chance of death. The second ring encompassed the area of moderate destruction. Non-reinforced buildings may or may not survive. People had a passable chance to survive if they could find some cover. The third ring indicated the areas likely to suffer more damage from flying debris than the actual blast wave, though would still see every window shatter as well as more flimsy structures toppling over.

The size of each ring varied depending on the power of the warhead or bomb.

Finding one unexploded Russian MIRV made a good case that this area had been peppered mostly with similar weapons. Cliff said something about it having a 750-ish kiloton yield. Harper didn't really know exactly what that meant other than she'd only heard of 'megatons' before in regard to nukes. Kilo was smaller than mega— and the entirety of Denver had not been reduced to glass. Certainly, nuclear weapons did exist out there so powerful the 'orange spot' could wipe out the whole city.

They probably used the big ones on places like D.C, or New York City, or Hollywood... anything government related or so 'American' they wanted to send a message. No one thinks about Denver unless they're going skiing or cracking jokes about never-ending road construction.

"Well," she whispered to no one. "They finally stopped working on the roads all the time."

Lonnie perched atop the USPS truck, surveying their surroundings through his rifle scope. Tyreek stood opposite her in front of the truck, watching the road east. Harper covered the west. The Mossberg hung across her back on its strap. She held Cliff's AR-15 for the moment, since if anything happened out here, it would likely occur beyond the reach of buckshot.

Everyone else crawled through a gap in the debris to enter a partially collapsed electrical supply store. Jeanette hoped to find copper wire, solder, connectors, all sorts of stuff they could use to keep Evergreen lit up at night.

The soft sound of Harper's breathing played accompaniment to the distant, ethereal song of the wind in the various ruins. Denver used to have a small area of high rises in the central business district. Russia put an 'orange spot' there. A few mangled concrete-and-steel skeletons still jutted into the air, though most simply disappeared. The warhead hadn't been *too* massive. Her old home in Lakewood was roughly five and a half miles in a straight line from central downtown. Assuming Cliff had been right about a 750-kiloton bomb, the outer edge of the second ring (heavy damage) reached into Lakewood. Her former home sat square in the area where anyone exposed to the light at the time of the blast would have third-degree burns over their entire bodies.

Harper shivered slightly at the thought of a 'megaton' weapon hitting Denver; she and her family would have been killed instantly, basement or not.

Where she stood right now, no one likely survived. People caught outside at the time of the blast would've vaporized. She let out a sad sigh, thinking of little Emmy. The poor girl had been eight when the war happened. Harper didn't know the entire story of why a kid her age happened to be out of the house so early in the morning. By pure chance, at the time of the blast, Emmy happened to be walking behind a big, concrete building, four or five steps behind her parents—who were exposed past the corner. Her parents and several other people around them evaporated right before her eyes. Sure, Madison had awful nightmares but Emmy *still* sometimes woke up screaming in fear that the 'sky fire' was coming for her.

Looking at all the devastation made Harper feel grateful, as well as guilty. She'd ask why fate let her survive and others didn't, but... it would be pointless.

As Forrest Gump said, shit happens.

The oppressive quiet began to play with her mind. Here and there, she thought she heard people crying out in pain or panic. An imaginary horn blared, then sirens. Had Mila—or Darci—been here, they might have said she heard the ghosts of those killed, or picked up on an imprint left in the world from the emotional energy released when so many lives vanished. Darci loved occult stuff. 'Stone tape theory' or some nonsense like that.

Harper didn't believe it. However, not believing creepy stories didn't make her immune to the effects of standing more or less alone among the tomb-silent ruins where she knew a hundred thousand people or more died. Her imagination teased her.

She peered up.

No airplanes. The sky is so blue. No power lines. No billboards.

Even though Lonnie and Tyreek weren't far away, she couldn't see them and neither man made a sound. Harper felt like the only person left alive on Earth.

Her gaze fell on a mangled bus stop roughly a block away. Bizarrely, it made her think of Tyler.

How many people like him went off the deep end when they couldn't get meds? She glanced down at Cliff's rifle. *Should I have shot him? Would it have been kinder?*

The scope of the destruction spreading out in every direction from where she stood chipped away at hope. Dr. Rowland saying society would bounce back in fifteen years seemed silly to think about. It would take thirty years alone just to clear away the debris of Denver. Maybe he didn't mean 'society as it had been exactly before the nukes.' America started off as a network of small towns. Could enough remain of the government to manage a return to normal someday? Would the people even want to still be 'America' now? Harper and the militia wiped out the Promise Keepers, but there certainly had to be more groups like them out there... people who just couldn't wait for the government to collapse so they could be 'free' to fill in the power vacuum.

A frighteningly real chance existed the next few years could see anything from multiple independent towns fighting each other for power or a sort of lesser Civil War where the old US Government had to re-conquer territory away from wacko militias. She felt reasonably sure Walter and the others would be happy to support the original government. Most of them used to be cops or military beforehand. To them, it would be a return to normal.

Ugh. Even if the government did survive, what if it's the worst parts? The corrupt bastards who valued money over anything else? She flicked the fire selector back and forth from safe to single shot repetitively. *We might be better off without it.* A theoretical future played out in her head, taking on a distinctly cartoony tone. Some corrupt senator abandons all pretense of respectability and becomes a warlord-in-an-expensive suit. Like a *Mad Max* movie, she pictured some guy with perfect hair and perfect teeth in a $20,000 Armani suit sitting on a throne of scrap metal. Or, maybe it would be less silly: stern-faced military soldiers ushering in a new government that ruled with an iron fist. Compared to either of those, she'd *much* prefer the original government.

Maybe... just maybe... old Uncle Sam might crawl out from under the crumbled ruins of a high-rise tower, dust himself off, and start limping back to normal.

She stopped flicking the fire selector, leaving it on single for now.

Would I give up this life for the relative safety of how it used to be? When she first arrived in Evergreen, she didn't trust anyone else to protect Maddie, not even Cliff. She'd long since come to trust him like a father, but still, she didn't want to hang up her gun and just be a normal citizen again. Much better to have control over her fate. The old world she grew up in had been—reasonably—safe but also incredibly sexist, jaded, rushed, insensitive, impersonal, oversaturated with technology, superficial, focused on immediate gratification and worship of shallow celebrities.

In many tangible ways, her new reality felt better than the old one, even if it offered far, far less security and almost no medical care. If society ever did bounce back, she thought it would take significantly longer than a mere fifteen years. Dr. Rowland's estimate sounded too optimistic. Perhaps if everyone still alive all worked together without any problems, it might happen in fifteen years. But... some people out there would resist a return to the old government, and expecting various disparate groups of humans to seamlessly work together for the common good amounted to lunacy. *Most* people might tolerate that for a while, but there'd always be someone like the Lawless, or the Templars, even before factoring in the kind of evil that made people hate each other over stuff like skin color or what country their ancestors came from.

Harper frowned. *It's stupid romanticism. Humanity was better off before. This isn't freedom. We're surviving, not thriving.* She sighed. *And I'm being a maudlin dumbass. Why am I obsessing about shit I can't change? It's too damned quiet out here.*

She looked to her left at the opening in the debris everyone climbed through. As soon as her attention focused on it, the sounds of voices, rummaging, and chuckling reached her consciousness. Faint, but definitely there. Reassured nothing bad happened to the team inside the building, she resumed watching her 180-degree field of responsibility.

Well, on the positive side. We are not *seeing gangs of marauders raiding towns on dune buggies and keeping harems of young women like on* Mad Max. Sure, she'd seen cases of kidnapping, slavery, and assault… but it had hardly become the 'norm.' They didn't exist in a world of tiny post-apocalyptic villages living in constant fear of massive groups of marauders in assless chaps on spiked dune buggies who simply tolerated random kidnappings and attacks as normal.

She smiled. *Maybe there is hope.*

Another thing she noticed the absence of: Lawless. They'd been in the Denver area for about two hours at this point and had not yet seen even a rat moving. Her old teacher's opinion on the radioactivity of Denver held scarily true. The longer she stared at the empty ruins, the more likely it felt everyone had been right. Radiation levels this long after the strike probably wouldn't cause significant issues from limited exposure, but *living* here? Yeah. Definite problem.

They either left or they're all dead. I don't believe they just haven't noticed us yet.

Harper bounced on her toes like a kid needing to pee. "Hurry up. We shouldn't stay here long."

"I see nothing," said Lonnie.

"Not that. I'm worrying about rads." Harper paced. "The longer we stay here, the more dangerous it is."

"Spose, yeah." Lonnie's 'turret chair' squeaked, then he shouted, "Y'all just about done in there?"

Jeanette poked her head out the opening in the rubble. "Just about. Deac is shifting some old shelves pinning a whole bunch of copper wire. We hit a good score here. Working on getting it out."

Harper leaned against the rear door of the USPS truck, staring down the street. The absolute desolation started to bother her almost *more* than running into Lawless. Still, if they really had disappeared for good, she wouldn't complain at not getting the chance to be the one to finish them off.

Dead is dead, don't care how it happened. The world is better off without them.

Clattering came from the hole. Cliff emerged, hauling a wooden crate with plastic corner caps. "Harp, mind the door?"

She spun around, grabbed the rolling door at the back of the truck, and flung it upward. "Almost done?"

"Yep. Just got a couple boxes to load and we'll be going." He smiled. "How's it been out here?"

"Quiet." She huffed. "Almost too quiet."

29

ACCEPTANCE

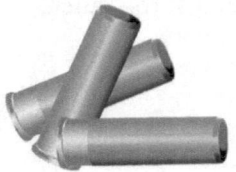

HOUR THREE - JUNE 7TH

Harper helped load, ferrying a few cases of plastic connectors or other things light enough for her to move by herself. Soon, everyone piled back into the USPS truck. They still had enough room not to be squished, though with the fruits of their scavenging taking up space, conditions had become a bit more friendly.

Since the truck didn't move too fast and it got a bit warm, they left the rear door open.

About fifteen minutes after leaving the electrical supply place, the surroundings fading off behind them seemed less smashed up—and more familiar.

Harper sat up. "Uhh, guys? Can I ask something?"

"Go for it," said Deacon.

"So, like, you know this trip was my idea and one of the reasons I wanted to come here is that I had to see for myself the Lawless were gone."

Everyone murmured agreement in one form or another.

"Considering one of our, umm, 'mission goals' is me burying some demons, would you guys mind if we made a couple extra stops?"

"What are you thinking?" asked Cliff.

"It's stupid and pointless, but I wanted to check on where my friends lived."

Deacon shook his head. "Oof. Heavy. You sure you wanna see?"

"Yeah. I am." Harper exhaled. "I'm not saying we tear the places apart, I'd just like to see them one last time."

"Where they at?" called Rafael.

HARPER BALANCED ON HER FEET UP FRONT BETWEEN RAFAEL AND Jeanette.

She directed him where to turn, leading the group around her old neighborhood in Lakewood. They reached Darci's house first... or rather, the blank lot where it had been. The house itself sat about a hundred feet away from the basement pit, smashed into another house and collapsed like a stepped-on paper drink carton.

Darci said she'd been in her bed in the basement and woke up to find the house above her missing, so Harper expected what she saw. It still felt beyond surreal to see a house she'd so often hung out at destroyed to the point of being unrecognizable. Worse, Mr. Sutherland's body probably remained somewhere under the wreckage. He'd been asleep in his upstairs bedroom at the time of the blast. She didn't want to disturb anything. Darci's basement bedroom had been totally exposed to the elements ever since the attack. Nothing there would be of any use.

"Okay..." Harper bowed her head in a moment of respect for Darci's father, then nodded. "I'm good."

From there, she led them to Andrea's house. Despite being only three blocks away, the place looked untouched. Its position among other buildings and scorched trees shielded it from the detonation. The only damage it sustained came from wind, rain, and mold getting in through the blown-out windows.

She had to have survived the blast. Harper bit her lip. No guarantee Andrea and her parents survived the aftermath, but the condition of their home made it seem likely they made it past the detonation.

"Just a second, please," said Harper.

She hopped out the passenger side door and sprinted over the little lawn to the front door. It had been left unlocked, but closed. Harper opened it, leaned in, and yelled, "Andrea? Mrs. Orton? Mr. Orton?"

No one replied. Nothing made a sound.

"Figured," she muttered to no one. "Had to try."

She backed up, closed the door, and ran to the truck.

"Sorry, kiddo," said Jeanette.

"It's okay. I wasn't expecting to find them here."

Rafael resumed driving. "What are you expecting?"

"Feel free to tell me I'm being stupid, but... I had to know if they survived the attack."

Cliff poked his head in from the cargo area. "You know Darci is okay. If you saw her house like that, and didn't know where she was, would you think she made it?"

"Ugh." Harper stared at the roof. "You and your logic."

He chuckled, gave her a back pat, and retreated to sit on a box of copper wiring. "It's fine. It'll drive you nuts if you don't look. Peace of mind is worth a few minutes."

Next, they stopped at Veronica's home.

Some charring covered the northeast face of the house. As with Andrea's, every window had shattered. Unlike Andrea's, when Harper stepped inside to call out for survivors, she discovered the interior to be an utter disaster. Someone—quite likely Lawless—had blown through like a tornado, slicing up the furniture, ripping art off the walls, breaking anything breakable. It looked like two gangs of graffiti spray paint artists got into a *Mortal Kombat* brawl.

Most horrifying of all, she discovered eleven corpses piled up in the kitchen. They hadn't decayed too much, which worried her about radiation levels. Fortunately, none of them looked familiar. No one she knew. Suspended decomposition and their frightened or agonized facial expressions made the ghastly sight so over the top the corpses didn't even seem real.

Veronica had family in Oregon. Maybe they tried to go there and left right after the bombs?

She stared at the dead bodies fighting off the worry Veronica, her little brother Germaine, and her parents might be lying in similar piles somewhere else. Not finding them dead didn't prove they were still alive, but it at least allowed her to continue to hope.

These people had to be victims the Lawless just stashed in this house for some reason.

She backed up, turned on her heel, and ran to the truck. Hope, even false hope, gave her the strength to keep her emotions in check.

"You okay?" asked Cliff. "Got a look on your face."

"Some dead bodies inside. Ronnie and her family aren't there." Harper leaned on the wall separating the driver compartment from the cargo area, and bowed her head. "Lawless used this house as a... I dunno. It's all torn up. Pile of bodies in the kitchen. They didn't decompose very much. I... I don't even want to think about what kind of craziness happened in there."

"The worst face of humanity." Cliff gazed off out the open rear door. "You get some people convinced they're going to die in hours from radiation and they'll go completely wild because they don't give a shit anymore. A man who always had thoughts about murder, rape, whatever else... all of a sudden, he doesn't have to worry about prison anymore, or even consequences. If he's going to drop dead in a day or two anyway..."

"I know." Harper wiped her face.

After pausing in silence for a little while, Harper asked Rafael to stop by the house where Christina Menendez lived. Four blocks east and north, closer to Denver, made the difference. The house—as well as most of the others nearby—had burned to the ground. No larger structures or anything else shielded them from direct line-of-sight to the fireball. Only scraps of the thickest wooden parts and the charred husks of large appliances remained on the concrete slab.

The fire had likely been immediate and intense. Whether or not

Christina and her family got out of there alive hinged on if they'd been awake at the time. Too little remained of anything here to even go exploring in search of bodies. She wouldn't be able to recognize burned bones apart from bits of former house. Better to tell herself Christina got out and escaped somewhere to safety, even if it happened to be a lie. As much as it looked like her friend burned to death in seconds, what Cliff said about Darci's house gave her hope.

Without a word, she returned to the truck, taking a seat once more in the cargo area.

"Did you find what you hoped to find?" asked Cliff.

"No. My friends weren't home." She swiped her hair out of her face. "Kidding. I didn't expect to find them. Sure, I had unrealistic fantasies that one of them might just be sorta hanging out and we'd have this happy Hallmark reunion, but I didn't really think it would happen. Still, finding nothing is better than finding them dead."

"I hear that," whispered Deacon.

He rubbed her back.

Harper leaned against him. "Weird."

"What is?"

"I figured I'd be a mess." She pursed her lips, took stock of her emotional state, then sighed. "But I'm not. Just kinda sitting here in a 'yeah, that figures' state."

"That means you've either mourned them already or still believe they're alive somewhere." Cliff let his head rest back against the stack of boxes.

She half smiled. "Maybe both."

30

THE BELLY OF THE BEAST

HOUR FOUR - JUNE 7TH

Harper tried not to squeeze the Mossberg too tight.

They approached four hours in Denver, still without any contact, yet the most harrowing part of their mission stood in front of her. Rafael stopped the USPS truck outside Mile High Stadium. Every time she called it that, Cliff or Deacon corrected her by saying *new* Mile High Stadium. Apparently, the original one got demolished in 2002 when she'd been one year old. She couldn't care less about semantics. This had been the stadium she knew for her entire life.

They didn't need to spend a great deal of time here, nor did they have to lug anything heavy. Their mission here involved only one thing: intelligence gathering.

The Evergreen Militia had little contact with the Lawless beyond several skirmishes in the midst of scavenging runs. Since they hadn't taken prisoners, almost everything they knew about the enemy came from Harper, Renee, and a handful of others who'd survived-slash-escaped Denver. Come to think of it, the last person to arrive in Evergreen with any stories about Lawless trying to kill or kidnap them had been a fairly long time ago, before the last winter snowstorm.

On one trip into the city, Harper had a brief conversation with a boy named Steve Pratt, who had been in her class all through high school. He'd been a willing member of the Lawless last time she saw him and had the honorable distinction of being the only person wearing a blue sash she *didn't* want to shoot at before saying a single word. In fact, she'd let him run away.

Renee spent weeks as a semi-captive, sometimes being treated like a kidnap victim and sometimes being treated like a kid who needed protection. Some of the guys hazed her for being too nice, too soft, and they pretty much all tried to goad her into doing the same crazy, violent shit they did. Renee had, by far, offered the most intelligence about the Lawless, having lived among them.

It all sounded so psychotic. People who, mere months earlier, had been ordinary office workers, students, mechanics, retail workers, or whatever banded together and cut loose to do whatever they wanted, whenever they wanted to whomever they wanted. Like Cliff said, some people only avoided doing bad things because they feared punishment. Renee talked about several guys she'd been around who used to be low-level corporate workers. They roamed Denver hunting for anyone they thought might have been wealthy or part of 'upper management' and tortured them to death, smashed expensive cars, set fire to executive offices and so on.

About the only positive thing Renee had to say was they generally didn't hurt children. Not that too many kids remained in Denver by the time the Lawless formed. In the five or six weeks it took the Lawless to organize into an actual gang from multiple roving bands of rioting idiots, most people evacuated the area.

Except for morons like us who hid in our basements.

Renee mentioned the Lawless established a headquarters of sorts at Mile High Stadium. She talked about how they had a leader who sat on a throne, made a crown out of a football helmet, and forced people the gang abducted to do heinous, awful things for the gang's amusement. Thankfully, Renee had not been to the stadium herself;

she'd only heard others talk about it. They described forced gladiatorial fights as well as a 'gauntlet.' According to the stories, someone who survived the gladiator pit but refused to join the gang had a chance at freedom if they ran the gauntlet... though few made it.

Harper didn't know what to expect inside this place. Her mind had gone full *Mad Max* with hanging cages, spiked everything, blood all over the place, and crazy murder buggies. That they had parked so close to the place and hadn't suffered so much as a thrown rock helped ease her nerves. She'd made this stadium out to be the absolute heart of all evil, a palace of suffering she would never want to be near, and yet... it greeted her only with tranquil silence.

The last time she'd been here, the world still worked. Sports never mattered at all to her, but Dad loved coming here. She loved spending time with him, so tolerated the white noise of 'sportsball' in the background as she and Mom called it... though, she did sometimes check out players' butts.

"Looks clear," said Lonnie from above the roof. "Ain't got nothing moving."

"All right." Cliff checked his rifle. "I'll take point. Single file. Deacon, Tyreek, Harper behind me in that order. Harper, you got rear. Try not to put any buckshot in our asses."

She chuckled and made sure her dust mask sat properly on her face.

Like a Green Beret jumping out the door of a landing helicopter, Cliff leapt out the back of the USPS truck, swung his rifle up, and moved toward the stadium entrance. Deacon and Tyreek followed, as did Harper. She shuffled along in a backward walk, covering the area behind them. It almost struck her as funny to watch Deacon sauntering along as casually as a big guy on his way into a convenience store to grab ice for a summer cookout right behind Cliff who'd gone full tactical.

Fortifications made of dumpsters, small cars, benches, and even big concrete planters created a kill box in front of the stadium doors. The obstructions forced anyone approaching to move in a serpentine path while totally exposed to any defenders in an elevated shooting platform. Somehow, the Lawless managed to get one of those enormous drop-off construction dumpsters way up off the ground to hang off the wall above the entryway on a whole mess of chains.

It didn't have any bullet dents. In fact, none of this junk looked to have seen combat. If the Lawless prepared for attack from a rival gang, some remnant of the police, or even the Army, it never materialized.

Promise Keepers, my ass. Harper scowled. *Those jerks should have been up here taking care of the Lawless, not abducting little kids to ransom them for food. They didn't deserve to call themselves a militia.*

Cliff reached the end of the kill box. He pulled a scrap of chain off the door handles, shoved one door aside, then stepped into the entry foyer. The stink of corpse mixed with mold. After a ten second pause to listen to the distant clatter of wind rattling unseen debris, he advanced.

The size of the stadium made everything echo.

Once inside the building, Harper faced forward. If anyone rushed up behind them, she'd hear them open the door and would have time to swing around. The stadium didn't match her Hollywood end-of-the-world expectations. It more or less looked normal, but extremely messy, as if every fraternity in the western United States got together for one hell of a party here and no one bothered to clean up.

Cliff headed across the foyer, down a hall, and through a series of doors, a stairwell, and another hallway. They ended up in a 'staff only' area full of maintenance equipment and trash. Another few doorways and a long, blank hallway later, they emerged directly on the field in the arena outside. Concrete boulders dotted the seats around the stadium, some having left crush trails where they tumbled down to ground level.

Deacon, Tyreek, and Harper filed out of the hallway and spread out in a line, taking in the scenery.

Several hundred cots covered the majority of the field, set up in rows under a mismatched collection of collapsible outdoor canopies in varying sizes. Some of the canopies appeared to have collapsed—probably from the massive snowstorm. It looked far too organized for the Lawless. Harper suspected within the first week or two after the strike, the local authorities tried to turn the stadium into a temporary shelter.

Wait, no... that would've been stupid. Radiation? The authorities would have tried to evacuate everyone as far away from ground zero as possible.

Near the left end of the field, a platform held a tattered reclining chair 'throne' six feet off the ground under another portable canopy. Anyone sitting in it would have a great view of the improvised boxing ring nearby. The Lawless used sign posts, chain link fence, and tons of sharp metal scrap to create a fighting arena.

From about the twenty-yard-line and further right, an obstacle course went all the way to the wall at the edge of the field, over it via a collection of folding ladders, then up through the seating area to the roof. A cluster of fat, knotted ropes suggested anyone hoping to get out of 'the gauntlet' alive would have needed to climb from the topmost seating row, up a rope, to the roof... likely while being shot at or having things thrown at them.

"Wow... it's less *Mad Max* and more *Jackass*," whispered Harper.

As the bizarre details soaked in through her initial shock and disbelief, she noticed many of the 'blankets' or unidentifiable lumps on the ground were, in fact, dead bodies. A quick count surpassed forty and kept going. From the looks of things, the majority of the Lawless died in their beds. The position of other bodies not in one of the cots hinted at an internal conflict. People lay dead over whatever objects they'd taken cover behind during a gunfight. One corpse, in particular, stood out from the rest. A huge linebacker sized dude hung upside down by a chain around his boots out the window of one of the expensive box seating areas above the fifty-yard line. He'd been stripped naked except for a black motorcycle helmet adorned with metal spikes.

Guess Mel Brooks was wrong. It's not good to be the king.

Harper pulled her mask down long enough to spit on the ground, full of contempt for the once-leader of the gang who murdered her parents and messed Madison up for so long. It didn't take a huge leap of logic to assume the radiation sickness, lack of food, lack of victims, boredom, or any number of things caused the Lawless to break up into factions and turn on each other. Like the morons they seemed to have been, they probably expected to be able to simply keep looting food and supplies forever without having to work.

The totality of the scene around her set off a storm of fury, anxiety, and disappointment.

There she stood, in what had been the main 'citadel' of the group responsible for her parents' deaths, the place she'd spent so many weeks terrified of... and found it empty. Not only empty, but verging on silly and ridiculous. In her mind, she'd made it out to be this fortress of steel, spikes, chains, cages, blood, and hopelessness. To be fair, it probably wouldn't have seemed so pathetic if a hundred violent men surrounded her, screaming and mocking her.

Now, though? In silent ruin? It simply looked moronic. Juvenile and moronic. The Lawless had been so stupid, so reckless... they cared more about building a 'throne' for their leader and a place to make 'the weak' people fight each other rather than affording any thought toward food, or even adequate shelter. Sleeping on cots under sun canopies like the ones people used for outdoor parties might've worked in the summer. But during a Denver winter?

They couldn't be that dumb. They had to go inside the stadium building for bad weather. Maybe the cots were for the radiation sick.

Curious about that theory, she advanced into the field, wandering around to examine the corpses. Approximately seven for every ten dead were men. Radiation slowed decomposition to the point the place became an eerie sort of museum to depravity. Most of the dead had no trace of hair left. The ones still in possession of hair appeared to have suffered bullet or stab wounds, some immediately fatal, others likely succumbing later to infection or blood loss. She recognized one man as a geometry teacher from her school, Mr. Palas. Everyone, Harper included, thought the guy weird and a bit creepy with his pocket protectors and offputting social awkwardness. Kids joked he'd show up to school one day with a rifle and go crazy.

Guess they were right about him. All this time, he'd just been waiting for an excuse to go nuts.

She wandered the cots, looking at faces, hoping *not* to see any of her missing friends. Harper sorta recognized a few more, but couldn't quite remember where she'd seen them. Workers at the supermarket, maybe. Perhaps a co-worker of one of her parents or something. One guy still wore a Walmart polo shirt. Another had a security guard uniform that fit him too well to have been scavenged. A dead, emaciated bald woman in her later twenties lay on a cot, wearing a spiked leather collar, no shirt, and camo pants. She appeared to have died to a self-inflicted gunshot to the side of the head. A 9mm Beretta sat in her hand, still pointing at her head.

Everything about this place and the Lawless is awful.

"They left them here to die." Harper exhaled, relieved not to have discovered anyone she really knew here.

"What else were they going to do?" Deacon shrugged. "You think these jackasses had a medic or something?"

"They didn't want to go anywhere near the radiation victims." Tyreek whistled. "Thought they'd catch it."

"Oh, they caught it all right." Cliff gazed upward. "Just not from their buddies. On that note, we should get going."

Deacon stooped to pick up a katana lying on the ground half under one of the cots. "Come to papa. And yeah, radiation sucks. Course, it would'a been worse a year ago. Much worse."

"Idiots." Tyreek looked around. "Damn idiots."

Harper gestured at the gauntlet. "This *Mad Max* shit was supposed to be movie nonsense. What the actual hell? Is this really where we're heading?"

Cliff laughed. "These guys probably got the idea from the movies."

"You don't think it's a natural course for humanity?" She gave the place one last look, then started for the exit. "Are we not heading for a future like those movies?"

"Nah." Cliff fell in step beside her. "I don't see why we would. Humans survived pre-technology eras before without turning into roving bands of murderous crazies."

Deacon laughed. "Dependin' on how far back you go and where, we definitely had roving bands of murderous crazies. Ever hear of the Huns? Vikings? Crusades?"

"What he said." Harper pointed at Deacon.

"Fair." Cliff shrugged. "But, we also have the benefit now of knowing modern society existed."

They entered the corridor leading away from the field, which seemed oddly dark compared to being outside.

"You're saying you believe people are inherently civilized and good?" Harper ducked a broken pipe hanging off the wall. A slow trickle of dirty water flowed out of it, splattering on the floor.

Cliff overacted a thinking face for a moment, until they reached the stairwell. "I believe people are inherently *lazy*. As a species, we want to get back to sitting on the couch watching TV as fast as possible. We want someone else to worry about making the food, keeping the peace, and keeping the power on."

"Not everyone." Deacon grinned. "Ya got fools like this lot and them Promise mofos been waitin' they whole lives for 'the man' to fall so they could take over."

"Yeah." Harper frowned. "Good thing they suck at it."

Cliff laughed. "See, it's easy for the weekend warrior MEAL team six dudes to fantasize about taking over. Now that it's happened, they're like 'holy shit this is a lot of work!' and 'What do you mean we need to worry about farming and can't just ride around with our guns and feel like badasses?' and 'What the hell is all this white shit falling from the sky?'"

Harper snickered.

Deacon and Cliff continued to trade joking insults about guys who thought there would be nothing more to life-after-nukes than opportunities to look tough on an outdoorsman's magazine cover. Harper kept her gaze down, thinking about what she'd seen in the stadium all the way back to the USPS truck. She settled in to sit between a stack of copper wire in small wooden crates and a mound of various machinery: pumps, compressors, motors, anything with spinning parts and wire inside it that Rafael and Jeanette took to cannibalize.

As the engine started, Harper looked out the back, watching the parking lot slide to the right until the stadium building came into view. The number of corpses on the field made it highly unlikely the Lawless, as a group, existed anymore. Some of them might've survived. If so, they hadn't stuck around Denver. Harper couldn't believe her emotions. Mostly, that she had none. As the anxiety of being in the place she'd most dreaded for so long faded, blankness replaced it.

She didn't feel gratified to learn the gang she'd elevated to near bogie-man status in her mind mostly died to radiation or internal politics. While she didn't mourn them, she'd expected a certain degree of righteous indignation at their misfortune... but it didn't happen. Her mood ended up somewhere between a sense of being freed from the obligation to stop them herself and the relief of no longer having to worry about them. The idea of a world without Lawless seemed crazy to imagine, but it evidently happened.

Huh... maybe I will remember how to relax someday after all.

OH, HELL NO

HOUR FOUR AND A HALF - JUNE 7TH

The route Rafael and Jeanette plotted had three more stops before they would exit Denver.

Harper didn't mind. As much as she wanted to get home sooner, these stops wouldn't take very long and it no longer seemed like they risked much more than radiation exposure being here. True, they didn't know with absolute certainty a small group of former Lawless didn't still lurk around somewhere. However unlikely it might be, she couldn't let her guard down.

She had to make sure Madison volunteered for extra farm work.

If Maddie, Jonathan, Lorelei, and the twins all make it to thirty in good health, I swear I'll sing Under the Sea *in the middle of town.*

Blush crept up her face at the mere thought of it. But… if this jinx thing had any power whatsoever, she'd subject herself to such embarrassment for her family's sake.

At the next stop, another electronics wholesaler, Harper once again took up a guard position out by the truck. It made sense for her, being the physically weakest of everyone present, to handle security while the stronger people lugged heavy objects. Even Jeanette made her feel a bit weak in the bicep department.

This area hadn't been hit as hard as the last one. The electronics outlet, a warehouse style building not meant for consumers to walk into, remained intact with only a few holes in the wall. It had no windows, only a few truck docks and steel doors. It didn't even have signs or labels on the outside beyond a small eight-by-ten sticker on one door. Only thanks to Jeanette finding the address in the business-to-business directory she'd found at the roadworks garage did they even know this building might contain useful materials.

Harper spent a while looking over the commercial buildings. While the buildings around here remained mostly intact, no windows or anything else made of glass survived the bombs. Box trucks parked in the area resembled enormous toys some giant child stepped on. The direction from which the blast wave originated showed clearly in the way everything had been crushed/smushed in the same direction.

Voices came from the alley at the end of the electronics warehouse, low murmurs, people talking to each other.

Shit. There it is. Guess they didn't all die off. Harper flicked the safety off the Mossberg and debated hiding before the surviving Lawless emerged from the alley and she had nothing between herself and them but twenty feet of open space plus one crushed Toyota.

The instant two men in body armor slathered in white paint walked into view, Harper blinked in surprise, having expected Lawless. Still, Templars weren't any better. In fact, the crazy fanaticism made them even worse. She raised her weapon at them.

Ugh. These morons.

"A foundling," said the man on the left.

Harper narrowed her eyes.

Ten more men walked out of the alley, also done up in 'Templar' armor ranging from only a bulletproof vest over white clothing to full police riot gear or military Kevlar. Every scrap of armor bore a coating of white paint and bold red crosses. More proof of their foolishness: none of them had dust masks or any face protection from radioactive particles.

Twelve of them. Holy shit. Uhh, crap. Not good.

"Hey there, sweetie," said the second guy. His short blond hair and forced smile made him look like an evil version of a young Superman. Total 'Chad face.' "What are you doing out here all alone? You need to come with us and be safe."

"I'm not alone," said Harper. "Lonnie. Bad guys."

A metal-on-metal squeak came from the turret chair.

The Templars angled their gazes up, finally noticing the man atop the USPS truck.

"This poor old soul should come with us as well." The fourth Templar stepped closer.

"No thanks." Harper aimed at him. "I have enough problems without joining a crazy cult pretending to be religious."

The men gasped.

"Heresy," whispered one in the back.

"How far our society has fallen." The lead man bowed his head. "This is why God's fire rained down upon us. We are the chosen he has spared for our thoughts carried the word true despite the iniquities of man. That you, too, have survived the great inferno is testament He has chosen you."

"I can't tell if you're really dumb enough to believe that… or lying to scare people into obeying you." Harper edged to her right, moving out from behind the truck so she could run away if need be.

"We can save her," shouted the third Templar. "Purge the heresy from the child's mind."

The lead man advanced toward her.

She snapped her aim to him. "Take one more step closer to me and I'm going to purge the stupid straight out of your mind with buckshot."

Most of the men readied improvised broadswords, axes, or spears. One lifted a rifle. The two men farthest from her snapped bolts into hunting crossbows.

The lead man stared into her eyes, not the slightest trace of fear in his expression. "We are more than willing to sacrifice one of our number to save the soul of a breeder. The greater good of humanity and God's glory must prevail."

"Breeder?" Harper blinked in disbelief. "Oh, hell no. You guys are way past crazy into seriously evil. Get the hell away from me right now!" She yelled, "Dad! Deacon! Need help out here!"

The man took another step toward her.

Harper shot him in the face, splattering the other guys in white behind him with gore. The five Templars with swords charged. In a quarter second, Harper shifted her aim and shot the next nearest man in the face. Lonnie's rifle went off, as did the two Templar crossbows. Harper snapped her aim point to the next nearest guy and drilled him in the mouth. All three men she shot tumbled backward off their feet, dead in an instant. She had no time for a fourth shot without being swarmed and overwhelmed, so she bolted.

Lonnie wailed in pain.

She felt horrible running and leaving him there alone, but what could she do? Stand there and let a bunch of crazy, armored men grab her? Anyone who referred to her as a 'breeder' was both psychotic and evil. Even more evil than the Lawless. Sure, the Lawless would kidnap and rape women, but at least they didn't pretend to be doing 'god's work.' The way these creeps tried to make what they planned to do to her sound like a noble act for the sake of humanity caused her skin to crawl. Of course, the screamed battle cries coming from them now could mean they'd become so enraged at her for killing three of them they no longer wanted to take her as a baby factory. Assuming he hadn't been bluffing, they expected her to shoot one guy before they could get to them, not three. But... if they were *really* into the whole religious delusion thing, they also might not care about their own lives.

As she had zero time to think, she ran for now.

Cliff, Deacon, Tyreek, and Jeanette all shouted in the distance behind her as she sprinted down the empty street, weaving around abandoned cars away from a group of sword-toting men coming after her. Gunfire rang out behind her, a rapid peppering of 5.56. Hoping to give the other militia a clean shot, she had to get out from in front of the Templars. She headed for a dead sedan crashed into the corner of a building at the end of the block. When she reached the wreck, she leapt onto the trunk, ran over the car, and jumped off the hood into the alley on the other side. Zinging ricochets chased the men around the corner after her.

Two Templars followed her over the car, the rest went around. One of the guys who went around yowled in pain, grabbed his ass, and fell over. The remaining five Templars continued after her like a pack of starving wild dogs pursuing a ribeye steak. She didn't have enough distance to waste time trying to take a shot, so she ran as hard as she could.

The men had to be former athletes or something... or maybe they trained hard. Despite being loaded up with heavy looking armor and gear, they more or less kept up with her. True, Harper had been an introverted kid who never did much physical activity before the war. She hadn't been overweight, but it mostly came from good luck, young age, and genetics rather than activity. However, surviving nuclear war whipped her into the best shape of her life. A run like this would've kicked her ass before. She'd have already given up and collapsed. Now, she didn't even notice fatigue. While the men kept up with her for now, she felt confident she could outlast them. All that armor and gear couldn't be light. Those men shouldn't be able to keep up the same pace as long as she could, while she only had to carry plain clothes, a shotgun, and a hip satchel.

At least they didn't have guns or crossbows. The three Templars armed with ranged weapons focused on Lonnie... and were probably dead now thanks to Cliff and the others. She didn't want to stray too far away from the rest of the militia, so she sprinted around the next possible right turn and rushed down an alley, intending to loop around the block in a big circle. The blast wave, or perhaps the wind in front of it, had thrown a bunch of debris against the wall of a three-story building on the right. It all fell into the alley, mostly blocking it off.

Harper jumped onto a dumpster, bounded over it, and leapt to run across a smashed miniature school bus lying on its side. The Templars followed, though much slower, having to climb. At the front end of the van-bus, she jumped down to open pavement, then sprinted to the end of the alley, rounding the corner to the right again.

She found herself in front of a supermarket. The dark interior looked like a veritable maze of aisles, collapsed displays, and register counters. Lots of hiding spots as well as cover. A place like that could let her go from mouse to cat. Rather than be hunted, she could do the hunting.

Perfect.

The clunking of boots on the school bus behind her kicked her into motion. She leapt through the giant hole in the front of the store where a window used to be and darted into the aisles. The Lawless had definitely been here. Most of the food not rotten in place had been taken already. She stepped over as much junk as she ended up unintentionally punting out of her way.

Five Templars scrambled in the window after her.

Harper stopped running, favoring stealth and quiet over speed. The store would not be an escape, but rather a deathtrap—for them. As long as she kept them at least ten feet away, she had the advantage. In a game of broadsword-paper-shotgun, shotgun won every time. *Five of them, six shells left in the pipe.* She crouched low, moving to the end of the aisle, darting around the end, and going down the second set of aisles.

The men did not care about being quiet, tromping after her.

"Submit to *His* will and know greater glory," yelled a man.

As tempting as it was to yell 'eat a dick' or something similar, she kept her mouth shut. They tried to bait her into revealing her position. If she made any noise, it would be a loud *boom.* Gunfire not far off outside told her the others caught up with the guy who took a bullet to the ass.

"I dunno, Jim," whispered a guy. "That girl blew Michael, Todd, and Timothy's heads off in like a second. That ain't normal."

"It's *James.* Do not call me 'Jim.'"

"Whatever. They're coming up behind us. This ain't a good tactical position."

She bit her lip to stop herself from whistling in disbelief.

James cleared his throat. "We do not ask why things happen. It was their time. As it is this young lady's time to serve our greater glory. Let us rescue the lost girl and take our leave."

Footsteps moved down the next aisle over. 'James' sounded as if he'd be the man closest to her. Harper scurried to the end and eased around, swinging the Mossberg up at two armored Templars walking toward her.

She snapped her aim on the left man's face, and fired. James—or so she assumed—careened over backward in mid-stride, falling down in a splits posture, blood spraying like a fountain from the ruin of his head. She pivoted her aim to the other man. He stood at least twenty feet away and brandished an axe to her shotgun. "I got your greater glory right here." She tensed her finger on the trigger, but hesitated when the guy screamed in terror.

He flailed, slipping and sliding in blood as he tried to whip around and run. "James is dead. Fall back! Get out!"

"Harper!" shouted Cliff from the windows at the front.

"Four left," she yelled. "Heading your way."

The clamor of armored men running pulled an abrupt swerve to the right. She couldn't see them through all the aisles and junk in the way, but it sounded as if they changed their minds about going to the front windows and now hauled ass toward the rear part of the store in hopes of finding a back way out. Harper hurried toward the register area at a light jog, taking care to make sure her footsteps made enough noise for friendlies to hear her coming. She also didn't really care too much if the Templars heard her either; they only had swords, and they'd already decided to retreat.

"Friendly coming in fast," shouted Harper as she neared the end of the aisle.

"I got'cha," said Deacon.

She practically crashed into the big guy at the end of the aisle. "Oof."

Deacon grinned. "You okay?"

"How's Lonnie?" Harper stared up at him. "I heard him yell."

"Crossbow bolt in the chest." Deacon poked himself in the left pectoral. "Ornery old bastard's real pissed off, but he'll be okay. He's more upset he only killed *one* dude. Gotta leave the damn thing stuck in him until we get back home. He ain't happy about it. What about you, kiddo?"

"I'm fine." She slouched, relieved to hear Lonnie didn't die. "More pissed off than anything."

Cliff and Tyreek ran down the open space between the row of registers and aisle endcaps, chasing the retreating psychos. Harper waited with Deacon, covering the windows in case the morons decided to try again after running around the outside of the building. A few minutes later, Cliff and Tyreek returned.

"Didn't hear any shots." Harper rushed over to hug Cliff. "Guess you let them go?"

"Wasn't worth chasing them into a potential ambush." His 'Terminator face' relaxed to an expression of relief. "You okay?"

"Mostly. Just angry. Bit freaked out at how crazy people can be." She flipped the Mossberg upside down, unzipped her hip satchel, and fed shells into the loading port.

"Crazy?" Cliff tilted his head. "More than bringing swords and axes to a gunfight?"

"I'm sure they thought all that Kevlar would stop buckshot." Tyreek grimaced.

"It probably would have stopped buckshot." Harper locked the loading mechanism and flipped the gun over. "They didn't have Kevlar on their faces. And I'm not talking about that kind of crazy. They wanted to kidnap me as a freakin' 'breeder.' Literally called me a 'breeder' to my face."

Cliff's expression hardened again. "Back in a little while."

"Man, we gotta get Lonnie to see the doc." Deacon clapped him on the shoulder. "Ain't got time to go chasin' idiots."

Grumbling, Cliff begrudgingly backed up and headed for the front of the store.

"Dammit!" Harper scowled. "Twice in one week! Well... I guess the other guys who tried to kidnap me didn't say anything about 'breeder.' They wanted food."

"What's the deal with those fools?" Tyreek jabbed a thumb backward over his shoulder.

Cliff jumped out through one of the giant missing windows. "Just another crazy pack of bandits. These just picked a theme."

"Yeah..." Harper stepped up onto the knee-high shelf along the bottom of the window, then hopped down to the sidewalk outside, her sneakers crunching broken glass and pulverized concrete.

She followed Cliff around the corner, back the way she'd come.

A man in white-painted armor lay dead on his back in a puddle of blood near the car at the opposite end of the alley. The bullets from Cliff and Deacon made such small holes in his vest she couldn't make them out from here except for the little blood trickles staining the otherwise white armor. She started to feel somber about yet again being involved in a fatal shooting, but remembering the word 'breeder' shoved all guilt out of her mind. If not her, they'd have grabbed some other young woman. No doubt, Melanie and Zoey Anson would've ended up being used as baby factories... once Zoey got old enough.

Grr. Her blood nearly boiled in rage.

She suspected they would have been slightly more civilized than a *Mad Max* gang of marauders and wouldn't have passed her around to every man there. Rather, they'd probably have given her to a specific guy as a 'wife' and she'd be expected to remain in a constant state of pregnancy until her body gave up or she died in childbirth.

Harper almost shot the corpse as they went by it, purely for spite... but decided not to waste the ammo. *Only have 174 left. Yeah, sounds like a lot... right up until another bandit army raids Evergreen. Could blow through all of it in twenty minutes.*

When they rounded the second corner and the USPS truck came into view, it didn't surprise Harper *not* to see Lonnie sitting up out of the hole in the roof. Three dead men in shorts and T-shirts lay in a row against the wall of the electrical supply outlet. One didn't have much of a head left, the other two appeared riddled with multiple torso wounds.

Lonnie got the rifle dude. .308 explodes skulls.

She didn't pay much attention to the dead, fast-walking behind Cliff to the truck. Deacon and Tyreek brought up the rear. Two crossbows, a semi-auto rifle she didn't recognize, and a pile of white armor sat at the front right corner behind the passenger seat.

Lonnie sat on the right side, back to the wall, clutching a neon orange crossbow bolt sticking out of his chest. The wound didn't look bad, more like someone stabbed him with a pencil. *Target arrows. No blade on the tip. Stupid. Or... it's all they have.* Pain showed through a sheen of sweat on his face, but his expression radiated pure irritation. Jeanette and Rafael both looked up at her, relieved.

"Damn, girl." Jeanette pulled her into a hug. "Good to see you're in one piece."

"Thanks. You, too."

Rafael held up a fist. She bumped it.

"Hey, Lonnie." Harper crouched beside him. "Don't worry. We're gonna get you to the medical center as fast as this overgrown lawn mower can go."

"Don't rush on my account," he wheezed. "I'll be fine so long as I don't move. Prob'ly ought not ta speak too much neither."

It's in his lung. She nodded.

The truck had become cramped with all the stuff, plus Lonnie in back instead of the hatch. Deacon simply could not fit in the 'turret' chair. Tyreek wouldn't be comfortable. Cliff could probably manage. Before anyone said anything, or could stop her, Harper climbed up to sit in it, chest deep in the roof.

"You sure you wanna be up there?" asked Cliff. "First one they shoot is the door gunner."

"Good thing this isn't a door, then." Harper peered down at him. "Also, which 'they'? There's no one out here anymore."

"For now." Cliff turned to face the open rear door. "Raf, give me a holler if the ride's gonna get bouncy so I can shut this thing. Otherwise, covering our six."

"You got it, boss," called Rafael from the driver's seat.

Harper played lookout, spinning in a slow circle as they drove across the remains of Denver. A haunting sense of familiarity came over her after a while. This area looked like a place she should know, but recognition hid under a foggy haze of damage and trauma. A tilting sign marked Independence St. shocked her as effectively as a slap.

Ahead, past the corner where the road they drove down met Independence Street, stood Lakewood High School. She almost closed her eyes to preserve her memories of it as it had been. With only seconds to make up her mind, she ended up staring at the building as they drove around the corner onto Independence since Eighth Avenue dead-ended into the school property.

Surprisingly, the place didn't look *too* smashed up. All the windows had been destroyed and multiple cracks crisscrossed the walls in places.

"Whoa," whispered Harper.

"What's up?" asked Cliff.

"We're driving by my old school. Lakewood High. It's kinda trashed." She exhaled. "Not gonna ask to stop. Nothing in there for me to see but a whole heap of sad memories I don't need."

He chuckled. "Fair enough."

"I'm going to have enough of that when we stop at my old house."

Cliff tugged on her leg until she looked down, then raised an eyebrow at her. "Are you sure you want to do that? And... Lonnie?"

She bit her lip. "Crap. Sorry. You're right. Stupid of me."

"It's fine," said Lonnie in a low but controlled voice. "Few more minutes ain't gonna make this worse. Girl needs to say goodbye to her folks. Can't take that away from her. Just... don't make it an all-day thing, huh?"

"Mr. Blanchard..." Harper dropped down out of the chair and crouched near him. "I can't. It's fine. There will be other trips."

"Into radioactive heck?" He flapped his fingers at her. "That's me laughing since it hurts a bit too much to do it the usual way. Listen, we all picked up some rads on this trip and it won't do us any good to come back here soon. We already here. You go on and make that stop of yours. Try to skip it and I'll yank this sumbich thing right outta my chest."

She exhaled, feeling like a selfish monster. "Really. It's fine. I don't..."

"You do. I can see it in your eyes, kiddo." Lonnie smiled. "Take a couple of minutes. Reckon it's on the way or not too far if we're goin' past your old school."

"Are you really sure you want to pick that scab?" asked Cliff.

Harper squeezed her hands into fists. "Yeah. I am. I want to let go of the past, but I can't do it until I at least say goodbye. I can come back. Lonnie is hurt."

"Nonsense. No more rads for you. Do it now and stay the hell away from this place for a couple years." Lonnie gripped the crossbow bolt as if about to yank it out of himself. "I ain't kiddin' about that. Take care o' yer business now, and don't come back."

Harper grabbed his wrist, holding his arm back. "Don't pull it out. You'll bleed to death. Okay. If everyone doesn't mind, I'll stop at my old house. I won't be long."

32

FINAL FAREWELL

HOUR FIVE - JUNE 7TH

Two ticking clocks hung over Harper's head.

In addition to radiation, Lonnie waited in the USPS truck with a crossbow bolt stuck in him. She didn't doubt he'd been serious about ripping it out if she refused to do this. Harper stared down at her sneakers and the road between them. They'd stopped right in front of her old house like a UPS truck making a delivery. She hadn't yet lifted her gaze off the ground.

I have to do this. Put everything I can't change behind me. This is where life starts anew, or some Hallmark bullcrap like that.

She took a deep breath and looked up.

The initial sight of her old home visibly crumbling sent an electric jolt into the back of her eyes. Charred siding, smashed windows, the front door still hanging open from when she and Madison ran for their lives, and the big hole in the roof on the left side—her bedroom —hit her hard.

She expected to be crippled with grief, drop to her knees, and start sobbing as soon as she laid eyes on the place. She did not expect an ephemeral cloak of melancholy she could tuck over her shoulder and wear gracefully. This place no longer felt like home, but it also no longer felt like the font from which all her nightmares welled up out of the void. She couldn't even think of this house as where she'd made the biggest error of her life—hesitating before the Lawless shot Dad. She'd *always* been super squishy (as Renee said). Madison didn't blame her for being unable to kill a person in the heat of the moment. And now, it seemed she'd stopped blaming herself, too.

Bad shit happened.

Harper tightened her jaw and walked up the little sidewalk strip to the porch, the path she'd crossed so many hundreds of times without thinking much about it. This would, quite likely, be the last time she walked on it. Perhaps someday, after the radiation in Denver faded away and civilization crept back in, she'd try to reclaim this property... even if only to build a proper memorial to her parents.

She stepped in the open front door, involuntarily cringing at the stink of mold. In the back of her mind, she remembered a voice on television talking about the dangers of 'black mold.' This house she'd once thought of as her sanctuary from the world offered no protection. It could tangibly kill her now. Despite having a filter mask on, she tried not to breathe too much. Other than the effects of weather and time, things looked more or less as she remembered them. Patches of dark, dried blood on the floor in the kitchen outlined where her parents died. The living room carpet squished under her feet, still damp from the most recent rain to blow in the front door. She went upstairs, hoping the creaks didn't mean she'd fall through.

Her old bedroom got the worst of the mold, being directly exposed to the sky thanks to the hole in the ceiling. A hunk of concrete the size of a cabinet freezer studded with rebar lay where it fell, having obliterated her bed, dresser, and part of the wall. Not a thing remained in there in any state even close to salvageable. Clothing in the closets turned black and furry. Posters disintegrated. Anything electronic would've been fried by EMP. Harper closed her eyes.

I'm going to count to ten, open my eyes, and realize the whole nuclear war thing was only an awful nightmare.

When she looked again, nothing changed.

Harper sighed. *Figures. Well, had to try, right?*

She backed out, glanced at the bathroom she'd gotten ready for school in every day of her first seventeen years of life, then peered into Madison's bedroom. The mold made it across the hall, though hadn't quite yet spread all the way around the room. Still, she didn't trust anything here to be safe. The only point of going upstairs, she'd accomplished: one last look, one last goodbye to a part of her life lost to time.

In her parents' bedroom, she broke her rule and took something. Two somethings... framed photographs. One from their wedding day, and one showing the two of them with Harper and Madison from about seven years ago. The family in the picture smiled back at her, having no idea what the future held for them. Grandpa took the picture back in a world where she would've been in college by now, likely dorming away from her parents and Madison, and not thinking the separation was a big deal.

Now, even five hours away from her little sister felt like she did something mean.

Harper tucked the photos under her arm and made her way downstairs, out to the backyard, careful not to step on any bloodstains.

The spots in the corner where Cliff and the others buried her parents remained obvious due to the torn-up lawn and simple attempt at grave markers made from wooden planks. She'd neglected to tell Cliff their names, so he'd carved 'Cody' on both, with smaller 'Mom' and 'Dad' under. She set the photos on the ground, took a knee, and pulled out her knife. Out of concern for Lonnie, she didn't take the time to carve as deeply as she might have otherwise, but still added her father's name, Patrick, and her mother's name, Meg, above the family name.

After she finished, she stared at the graves for a moment in silence.

"I can't stay long. There's a wounded man in the truck. I probably shouldn't even be here now." She exhaled. "Still don't believe in ghosts or afterlives or anything, but who knows, right? Maybe it's real. I just had to say goodbye... and I'm sorry, Dad. I couldn't do it then. Maddie is safe. We're doing okay. Crazy thing… I've kinda become a cop. Not exactly what you guys were hoping for, but I like helping people."

She waited for a few seconds, but nothing happened. No one replied. No Jedi force ghosts manifested above the graves.

"Maddie and I made it to Evergreen. The rumor was right. We're kinda safe there. Speaking of Maddie, I should really get back there before she gets too upset with me for being away again."

"Do you think she's really going to volunteer on the farm?" asked Cliff.

Harper almost fainted. She clutched her chest, barely holding back a scream.

"Sorry," whispered Cliff. "Wasn't trying to sneak up on you, just being quiet out of respect."

Once she could breathe again, she stuck her knife back in its sheath and stood. "It's okay. And I dunno. Maybe she just said it hoping I'd stay home."

Cliff flashed a conspiratorial smile. "You could tell her she doesn't have to do that jinx thing. Last thing we need is any more superstitious nonsense or witchcraft."

"I dunno." Harper glanced down at the Mossberg in her hands. "Twelve guys tried to kidnap, maybe kill me, and I'm standing here without a scratch. Maybe I should streak across Evergreen."

He coughed. "Where the heck did that come from?"

"What Maddie said about the jinxing. It's gotta be something that doesn't hurt anyone, and you *really* would rather not do."

Cliff pursed his lips. "Well, if you do decide to do something nonsensical like that, warn me so I can go inside and close the shades."

She smirked at him. "You don't get awkward at all when Darci walks around topless or… with nothing at all."

"Darci…" He turned his head, tilted slightly. "Is not my daughter."

"Heh." Harper hugged him. "Oh, Dad, meet Dad. Probably should introduce you guys. He's looking out for me now. I think you'd be proud of him. Anyway…" She glanced down at the graves. "Goodbye, Mom. Goodbye, Dad. I love you both."

A lump formed briefly in her throat, but she managed not to cry.

After a minute-ish of silence, Cliff rested a hand on her back. He meant it to be comforting, but she took it as a time warning. Radiation blanketed everything here still, and they'd about reached the end of the time they could be around it without elevating their risk for cancer or other problems.

"I'm ready."

Cliff nodded, then walked with her around the side of the house— past Madison's pink bicycle with white tires—toward the truck waiting for them. He abruptly stopped, backed up two steps, and snagged the bike.

Harper raised both eyebrows.

"Not in bad shape." He winked. "Seems a shame to leave it here."

33

THE FEELS

EARLY EVENING - JUNE 7TH

Harper curled up against the stack of boxes, arms wrapped around her legs.

Small wood crates made for slightly more comfortable seating than the steel floor. Lonnie's labored breathing, slow and raspy, rose and fell in volume, competing with the continuous growl from the little biodiesel engine. No one spoke, all jostling in time with the sway of the truck. Cliff pulled the rear door shut before they got moving, mostly so Rafael could drive as fast as the thing could go without anyone or any of the stuff they grabbed falling out.

She preferred not to see Lakewood receding off into the distance. The only visible signs of the outside world manifested as patches of daylight sliding over the walls. At this hour, the sun hung low over the western horizon, more or less directly in front of them as they drove toward the mountains. Jeanette sat beside Lonnie, who appeared relatively okay albeit in pain. He'd been fast enough on the draw, even with a sniper rifle at close range, to take out the Templar's only gun before the man could shoot anyone. Both guys with crossbows returned fire, only one scoring a hit.

Cliff, Deacon, and Tyreek rushed out of the building and shredded them before they could reload.

Harper didn't think much about the Templar attack beyond setting it aside as arguably less frightening than the red-and-blue guys trying to grab her. Both attacks took a backseat to her fear of radiation. Even the constant threat of what was or wasn't irradiated paled in comparison to the stupid warhead.

So much weighed on her mind she didn't dwell too much on her visit to the house in which she grew up. That feeling she thought she'd suffer, of wanting to stay, wanting to reclaim her 'home', never came. Even if it hadn't been destroyed by mold and water, she couldn't ever feel comfortable in there again, the place where her parents were killed. Seventeen years of memories, happy, sad, and in between blew away on the wind in mere seconds that day.

Bringing Madison's bike may or may not be a good idea. Could seeing it undo some of the progress she'd made in coping? Perhaps not. Madison knew Harper went to Denver. She might assume a stop at the old house would occur. The bike her kid sister got for her tenth birthday hadn't been a huge deal. Not like Madison begged and begged and begged for a new bike. She liked it, but loved her PlayStation more.

Nah, she'll be happy to have it back. Probably give it to Lorelei eventually. Definitely share it with the other kids.

Face squished into her knees, she stared down her legs at her sneakers. A trip to the place her parents died haunted her thoughts for months, built up into this great, traumatic—or cathartic—moment. Instead, it left her more blank than anything. Perhaps it's what freedom from her demons felt like. Neither sad, nor relieved, nor angry.

Cliff gave her shoulder a light squeeze. "It's okay to feel like you feel."

"How do you know what I'm feeling?" asked Harper in a quiet, toneless voice.

"I don't." He patted her shoulder, then let his arm fall back into his lap. "Whatever you feel, it's okay."

"Do you miss your house?"

"Didn't have one. Lived in a crappy little one-bedroom apartment. No, I don't miss it." Cliff shifted his weight, leaning more against the wall. "I do sometimes miss the house I grew up in. Think that's pretty much normal for anyone."

Harper lifted her head off her knees. "Yeah. I don't think I miss it anymore, and I'm not sure if that's weird."

"It's not weird."

"Can't go home again, right?" She swiped her hair out of her eyes and peered up at him.

"That's what they say." He brushed splinters from the crates off his fatigue pant leg. "Ain't so much the house itself I miss. It's the good memories, a time before I was old enough to know what responsibility or worry was. Sorry you got cheated out of that."

She shrugged one shoulder. "Meh. I was seventeen. Not like I lost my whole childhood. Just, like one year. It happened. Can't undo it. So, yeah. Fate kicked me out of the nest a little earlier than I'd have liked, but here I am. Best thing I can do now is help Maddie, Lore, Jonathan, and the others feel safe enough to still be kids."

"For sure," said Deacon.

"Yeah." Jeanette nodded. "You sure you're only eighteen? Girl, you sound wise."

"I'm not." She almost smiled. "I'm nineteen."

"Oh, nineteen. Good grief. Almost time for a cane," deadpanned Cliff.

She laughed.

"Did it help?" asked Lonnie. "Sayin' goodbye?"

Harper let her head sink backward until it touched a crate. She stared at the roof. "I'd built it up to be this big, gut-wrenching thing. It wasn't. Yeah. It helped. I think I've finally let go. Sorry, I didn't want to stop with you hurt. It could've waited."

"Meh." Lonnie went to wave dismissively at her but stopped short, wincing. "You're better off staying away from Denver for a couple more years."

"Don't move your arm." Jeanette helped him lower it.

"Got all your issues dealt with now." Lonnie grinned. "Leave the radiation chicken to the old folks."

She nearly laughed. "Radiation chicken? What?"

"You ever hear of 'playing chicken'?" Lonnie squinted. "Or are you too young to know what that means?"

"Kinda sounds familiar." She bit her lip.

"S'where two guys drive head on at each other and the first one to swerve away is the chicken, and loses." Lonnie winced in pain. "Damn. Can't make myself laugh for a while."

"That's... kind of insane." Harper squirmed. "People really did that?"

Cliff chuckled. "Maybe in the Fifties. It doesn't always involve cars. Playing chicken just means doing something stupid and risky."

"Oh. Yeah, I don't really want to go back to Denver again." Harper reached up to rub her face, but stopped. "We should probably decontaminate or something, assuming all this dirt is glowing. Thanks, guys, for helping."

"No big deal." Rafael clapped a hand on the truck twice. "Good workout for my baby here. And we needed all them parts for windmills. Got a nice big score. Kinda easy when you're not getting shot at the whole time."

Harper nudged Cliff. "Hope Carrie's not too mad at me for dragging you out here when you've got two babies at home."

"You didn't drag me anywhere." He smirked. "She's not exactly thrilled, but understands the world is more 'Old West' than *Mad Max*. Besides, it might be safer out here... away from that bomb. I almost took the boys with me, but she objected."

She didn't know whether to laugh or cringe. He might have been serious about bringing the infants. Then again, probably not with Denver being a radiation hazard. "When are we gonna get rid of it?"

"Couple days," called Rafael. "Now that we got these lead aprons. *Gran Hermano* is ready."

"Okay." She clenched her hands into fists, worried the MIRV might get pissy like a stray cat and 'scratch' when touched.

Would Mayor Ned warn people to take cover in case it did? Or would they all stay quiet and hope no one noticed? If it *did* go off, Ned wouldn't exactly have to worry about angry residents demanding an explanation. It didn't matter that Dr. Rowland said the 'tube was dented' so the mechanism couldn't possibly work. He hadn't taken it apart. He hadn't looked inside to know for sure, merely guessed based on the visible condition of the warhead. Even if he happened to be correct, a 'dirty blast' that scattered plutonium or whatever else happened to be in its core all over the place would almost be worse. So close to Evergreen, the radioactive material would cause all sorts of problems. An instantaneous death in a nuclear fireball beat going out like that National Guard man who had so much cancer the different cancers got into fistfights with each other.

"Try to relax." Cliff offered a hand. "It's been there for almost two years and we never even knew about it."

She gave him a 'really' stare. "It's easy not to be worried about something you don't know exists."

"True. Either way, in a few more days, you won't have to worry about it."

"Uhh." Harper blinked. "I could take that in a really grim way. Are you saying it might go off, or whether or not I choose to be terrified, it won't matter?"

"The second option. It's not gonna blow up," said Cliff in a completely straight-faced manner. "If it went off, it would hurt my kids. I'm not going to allow that."

As ludicrous as his statement was—that a nuclear bomb would be so afraid of him it behaved itself—she still found comfort in it. The last vestiges of thoughts about her old house faded way. She leaned against her new dad, eager to get home and be with the family they made for themselves.

PAYMENT

MONDAY, JUNE 8TH

Harper's skin still felt weird.

Once they'd brought Lonnie to the medical center, they decontaminated. Harper and Jeanette at least got a bathroom to themselves, so it hadn't been terribly embarrassing. Given the choice between remaining covered with likely radioactive dust, getting cancer, and dropping dead, or having to take a bucket shower in the same room as her adoptive father, she'd have needed to flip a coin to decide. She and Jeanette scrubbed down with a nylon brush, helping each other get the spots they couldn't reach. The brush hadn't been intended for use on people, but they had nothing better.

The worst part had been the twenty minutes or so the two of them spent stranded naked in the bathroom while someone ran over to the quartermaster's to get clean clothing for everyone. All the stuff— except the dust masks—the team wore into Denver ended up in a large tub. After several repeated washings, the Geiger counter didn't react *too* much. The rinse-water got taken out and dumped a mile from town. It hadn't been super dangerous, but gave off enough detectable radiation that they didn't want to simply drop it down the drain here.

Madison didn't react much to the bike beyond an 'oh, neat' and a brief thanks. She did, however, hop on it right away and zoom off down Hilltop Drive. Harper and Cliff suspected she'd been much happier about it than she admitted openly. Perhaps she felt guilty and didn't want to act overly excited out of fear Harper might go back to Denver to grab more things she'd learned to live without.

The day after the trip into Denver, Harper tried to get comfortable. She sat on the sofa at home in a loose, too-large T-shirt and sweat shorts. Unfortunately, as Renee joked, the shorts had been designed for someone who 'actually had an ass' and would've fallen right off her without the addition of a drawstring her best friend happily added for her. Despite technically being shorts, it felt more like wearing a skirt or having a bath towel loosely tied around her waist.

Still, it didn't annoy her brush-angered skin.

Now I know how cats feel when they're bathed against their will.

She settled in to read a novel Renee found at the library and loved —*Whirlwind in the Thorn Tree*, by S.A. Hunt. Some manner of apocalyptic western type thing. Renee compared it to the *Dark Tower* novels, so she figured it worth a shot. Since Carrie handled dinner tonight, Harper had a few hours of free time, which felt a little weird, almost as if she goofed off when she should've been doing something.

The controlled roar of the kids playing outside came from the combined backyard area, as well as the space between the house and Carrie's place. Everyone sounded happy, innocent, and completely unaware that a bunch of older people would poke a nuclear bomb with a metaphorical stick at any minute.

Being freed from any responsibility involved in transporting the device did kinda make her feel like a kid, but in this case, she tolerated it. Not that a mere mile would make a ton of difference in a worst-case scenario, but she'd rather not go near it again. Keeping it out of sight let her pretend it didn't exist. 'Why worry about something you can't possibly change' sounded great on paper, but proved challenging to pull off.

As far as feeling like a kid again went, Harper sat for a few minutes merely looking at the book's cover while feeling grateful to Carrie for letting her play the role of teen daughter instead of mom. She preferred doing the 'big sister' thing, mostly because she worried the title of 'mom' carried way too much responsibility for her to handle. Lorelei still mostly thought of her as a mother figure and Carrie as sort of a grandma. But the girl was so damn adorable, Harper couldn't bring herself to complain. If nothing else, it let her practice for the day she may or may not have one of her own with Logan.

At least I was basically grown up before it hit the fan.

Most of the younger kids here had to grow up a heck of a lot faster than Harper did. Thankfully, the majority managed to let their guard down a bit and enjoy being children again.

"Harper!" shouted Madison from the back yard. "Need you. Please."

She held the book up and whispered, "Are you my new *Secret Garden?*"

"Harp?" called Madison.

"Yeah. Coming." She dropped the book on the sofa, jumped to her feet, and ran through the living room to the kitchen.

Madison stood at the base of the little concrete back porch, looking like a child actress taking on the part of Huckleberry Finn... a child actress who got *really* into method acting. Her kid sister wore overalls without a shirt or shoes—and she looked as if she'd gone swimming in a mud pool. Dirt covered her everywhere except for the upper part of her neck and face, though smudges dotted her cheeks, forehead, and nose.

Jonathan, Lorelei, Mila, Becca, Eva, and Christopher played in the middle of the shared backyards, seemingly inventing a new game that combined soccer with Frisbee.

Harper stared at her sister in disbelief. "Wha... what the heck?"

"This is your fault, but I'm not mad." Madison looked down at herself, the mud still oozing in spots.

"What happened to you?" Harper hurried down the three steps but stopped short of grabbing her. Unless she palmed the girl's face, anywhere she touched would get mud on her, too.

Madison looked up. "Fell in the pig enclosure. This is not all mud."

"Ugh." Harper cringed back. "How are you not freaking out and throwing up?"

"I dunno. It's animal stuff. Touching pig poop bothers me less than the idea of eating animals. How did Mom pick up our puke without puking?"

Harper grimaced.

Madison raised and lowered her toes. "I require a bath before going inside the house."

"Seriously."

"Please get the yard tub ready... or at least dump a few buckets of water over me." She winced at the overalls. "I'd say these should be burned, but it's not like we can just go buy new ones, so I'll wash them."

Harper looked around. The big steel washbasin Cliff scavenged stood nearby, up on end, leaning against the house. She dragged it a little way out into the yard and set it down flat. "Did you lose your shoes in the pig pit?"

"No. I took them off first. Shirt, too. Didn't want to ruin them." After a brief glance at the other kids playing, Madison unclasped the shoulder straps and shoved the overalls to the ground. She appeared to brace for mockery and laughter, but the others barely even looked in her direction. Relieved, she faced Harper again. "They're still clean at the farm." She stepped into the basin and sat.

"Wait, you *willingly* went barefoot in pig poop?"

"Yes. Much easier to wash my feet than get pig crap out of sneakers. It's just poop. Not like acid or needles or something dangerous."

Harper grabbed a bucket. "Wow, you really do like animals."

"Please hurry. I don't wanna do the Lorelei thing any longer than absolutely necessary."

"On it." Harper started toward the well pump, then stopped. "Wait, you took your *shirt* off before getting in the pig wallow?"

"Yes." Madison sighed, giving her a 'hurry up' stare.

"Did you expect to go swimming? Shoes I get, but your shirt?"

"No. I didn't *expect* to fall over... six times." Madison grumbled. "But the shirt's white. You remember the Law of Photochromatic Attraction, right? Figured if I kept it on, I'd definitely fall. I didn't want it anywhere near pig poo. Which, may I remind you, is *all over me!* Water. Please. Hurry. I don't care if it's not warmed up first."

Harper laughed and hurried off to fill the bucket. Dad jokingly claimed that the lighter the color of shirt someone wore near potential messes, the greater likelihood of stains. Eat spaghetti in a white shirt, you all but guaranteed spilling some sauce on it. Wear a black shirt, no sauce will go astray. Never in a million years during their former life could she have imagined Madison covered head to toe in mud and pig waste—and laughing about it.

Her kid sister worked a few extra volunteer hours on the farm to satisfy the debt owed by her jinx bet now that Harper returned alive. That Maddie had done something so foul out of her desire to protect her—even if witchcraft and supernatural woo really had no effect on the world—meant so much, she almost cried from happiness.

Harper lugged the first full bucket back over. "Ready? It's going to be cold."

Madison closed her eyes. "Hit me."

"Keep your mouth closed so you don't get any in there."

"Eww," deadpanned Madison.

Harper poured the bucket over her sister's head, splattering it into the big metal tub. Mud peeled off Madison's body, forming a not-quite-inch deep brown pool at the bottom. She didn't look much cleaner.

Madison squealed out her nostrils, flapping her arms. When the pour stopped, she sputtered, then looked up. "Eek! That was cold."

"I told you."

"More!" shouted Madison. "I am still poop-i-fied."

"Okay. Did you really have to go through with that?"

"Yeah." Madison wrapped her arms around herself, shivering. "If I didn't, the bomb would go off. Jinxes get mean if you ignore them."

Kid logic. Right? Magic isn't real. Harper tossed a bit of remaining water from the bucket into Madison's face.

"That's not more. Three more buckets at least, then I'll dump the tub out and you can do it again... then soap." Madison squirmed. "Maybe I'll stop feeling slimy by the end of the week."

Chuckling, Harper jogged over to the pump.

UFO

WEDNESDAY, JUNE 10TH

Last night, Harper slept better than she had in at least a year.

Word came back that a team took '*Gran Hermano*,' the semi-truck cab Rafael converted to run on biodiesel, out to the house, connected it to the red pickup truck via a twenty-foot chain, and towed it away from Evergreen. They went north to avoid bringing the warhead any closer to town or the farm, heading for a mine Sadie and Willis checked out. It met all the requirements: had an opening big enough for a whole pickup truck, a long tunnel, and went deep. The semi wouldn't fit into the mine, but the team agreed to push the truck.

Volunteers on the last leg of the job would probably be exposed to radiation for longer than the safety intervals Dr. Rowland came up with, but not so much they risked immediate sickness. For whatever it was worth, they all had lead aprons and also didn't really care if they died. The entire team moving the bomb were sixty or older, and all willing to sacrifice themselves to get the nuke away from everyone else. The threat of developing cancer twenty or thirty years after exposure didn't hold much weight for people who didn't expect to still be around by then even in the best of post-apocalyptic circumstances.

The team hadn't returned yet, but no one expected them to be back for at least a day as they wouldn't be driving fast.

Harper reclined on one of the lounge chairs at the pool in her bright green bikini, feeling strangely content and happy. Rumor said this might be the last, or second-to-last year the pool remained in a usable state. The storeroom at the country club only had so much chlorine, and it didn't exactly rank terribly high on the priority list to go off in search of more. Go figure, attempting to order it from Amazon didn't work. Although, with Denver momentarily free of Lawless, maybe someone would make a trip to the city to search for more. Pool supplies couldn't have been a major priority of looters, so there would likely be some left somewhere. Some residential areas in suburban Denver almost had pools in every backyard. There *had* to be chlorine out there somewhere... if anyone bothered to go looking.

For now, it's a nice illusion of hope. Might as well enjoy it and have fun while we can.

Renee, Darci, and Grace occupied the lounge chairs nearby, Renee and Grace in swimsuits, Darci not. At least she'd tied a small sarong—former window curtain—around her waist. Baby Piper appeared indifferent to being free of a diaper, happily relaxing on the chair between Darci's knees atop a folded towel. A chorus of happy screaming came from roughly twenty kids in or around the pool. Some swam, others chased each other around playing tag or whatever.

Summer Vasquez perched on the lifeguard stand in a red one-piece with a white towel around her waist. She'd worked as a lifeguard while in college, so offered to help out.

A dull plastic *thud* came from the pool.

"Hey!" shouted Daxton. "Watch it!"

"What are you yelling about, Dax?" called his mom, Jen, from the lounge chairs on the opposite side from where Harper sat.

"Mila tried to take my head off."

Harper blinked in shock and sat up fast, dreading what she'd see.

"It's only a stupid Frisbee!" yelled Mila. "Sorry, I didn't mean to hit you in the face. I'm accurate with knives, not plastic discs."

Oh, whew. He's not being literal. Harper flopped back down, then cracked up at the idea she momentarily worried he'd been serious about Mila trying to kill him.

Daxton winged the Frisbee back at her, clearly trying to smash her in the nose. The overly hard throw made the disc swerve, skip off the water, and glide to a landing all the way at the edge of the pool area by the fence—quite well away from the pool.

Mila stared at him for a second before rolling her eyes and mouthing, 'idiot.' "I'll get it." She swam to the edge and climbed out.

It didn't surprise Harper to see her wearing only the bottom half of a black two-piece swimsuit. Some of the younger girls wore boy swim shorts or just didn't bother with tops yet. Mila's suit being black felt natural for her. Some people did 'goth' without even trying to, and Mila Cline happened to be one of them. Luck, fate, or whatever, always seemed to send black or grey things her way. However, the dive knife tied to her left leg *did* surprise her.

I shouldn't be shocked. Harper glanced at the .45 in its holster on the little table beside her. *I've got a gun on me. Can't really fault the kid for wanting to be ready if the shit hits the fan.*

Watching Mila pad off to where the Frisbee landed, wearing a military knife as though it were an ordinary accessory for a public pool, got Harper thinking about the Templars. There had to be more of them. They would totally try to grab any children they found… boys to train up as soldiers, girls for… eventual breeding.

She scowled at the thought. Those idiots didn't quite reach the same level of 'shoot without even talking' the Lawless did, but it wouldn't take much more to put them there. The one guy in the abandoned grocery store who decided to break his brainwashing and run away gave her hope they might not *all* be crazy. How nuts did someone have to be to be willing to die to kidnap a young woman? Did those morons honestly believe they had to forcibly breed humanity back into existence? They clearly thought women only had one purpose.

Harper bit her knuckle. *I need to stop thinking about those jackasses before I scream. Assholes. Backward, knuckle-dragging assholes.*

Mila ran back to the pool. She leapt into the water, throwing the Frisbee at a cluster of tweens at the height of her jump before splashing down.

Harper closed her eyes, trying to calm herself. *The Lawless are gone, but now there's Templars. Am I ever going to be able to truly relax?*

She opened her eyes in time to watch Lorelei going off the diving board.

Crap. She knows she's not supposed to be at the deep end. We don't have floaties. Harper started to spring off her chair, but stopped herself from diving into the pool once Lorelei surfaced and began swimming to the right, toward shallower water. Jonathan and Madison both swam as fast as they could to intercept, grabbed her by the arms, and dragged her to the shallow part. Madison appeared to be gently scolding her for going to the deep side. This, of course, got Jonathan started on making *Star Wars* jokes about the 'deep side' being evil and telling Lorelei about how she shouldn't succumb to the temptation of the 'deep side.'

Harper flopped down to sit, head in her hands. "I'm going to suffer a heart attack from anxiety before I'm thirty."

"Welcome to having kids." Renee whistled. "You sound just like your mom."

"Right?" Harper exhaled hard. "I think that's the way the world works."

Piper shot a stream of pee into the air like a little cherubic fountain. Darci, completely unfazed by this, merely pivoted the baby to aim the stream toward the ground out of people's way. "Stand back. This baby is loaded and I'm not afraid to use her."

Harper, Renee, and Grace burst out laughing at her blasé reaction.

A moment later, Lorelei zoomed by, squealing happily. She went all the way around the pool and jumped into the shallow end, feet first.

Harper fluffed her hair up over the back of the chair to help cool down her neck and shoulders. "Every time things feel this normal, I get worried something bad's going to happen."

"There's no sentient universe out there looking to punish people for being happy." Grace stretched.

"Ugh, I could really use a joint right now if we're going to start having *this* conversation." Darci sighed in fake exasperation. "C'mon, gremlin. Eat solid food already. Mommy needs some leaf."

Piper cooed.

"Wish it worked that way." Grace snickered. "Hey, you know what? Once the kid's no longer on the boob and we get around to resolving that dare, I think it'll be fun to try it. That teacher of yours is a rip. He's hilarious."

"Rock." Darci again made 'metal horns.' "Harp? 'Nee?"

"Uhh." Renee squirmed. "I dunno. Maybe if Harper does."

"Nah. Gotta keep my brain sharp." Harper raised an eyebrow at Grace. "Surprised you're going to do it."

Grace shrugged. "It's not like I have to worry about being drug tested for college anymore."

"But aren't you like training to be a doctor or something?" Renee stared at Grace.

"Yeah, but it's nowhere near as bad as they tried to make us believe." Grace raised her water glass in mock toast. "It's less harmful than booze, and it really does have genuine medical applications. Especially now when our options for medicine are so limited."

"You sound like Darci." Renee laughed. "She always says that."

Darci gave a low volume fake scream like a victim in a cheesy horror movie being devoured by a monster while holding Piper to her neck as if the baby tore her throat open. She pretend-struggled for a moment, then lowered the baby into position to start nursing. "The monster is voracious."

Harper, Grace, and Darci laughed.

"But yeah, weed is not dangerous." Darci puffed a strand of hair away from her eye. "I've been smoking or dropping edibles since I was like twelve, and I turned out just fine."

The phrase 'that's debatable' formed at the tip of Harper's brain, the standard teasing she and her friends always tossed back and forth. But... this time, she hesitated, worried Darci might not respond well to the joke. The war, the camp at Eldorado Springs, and everything took a toll on her. Not too long ago, she worried Darci might've been depressed to the point of self-harm. But, with Lucas and now Piper and Elijah, she seemed completely happy and at peace with things. Even if Darci would've laughed, she couldn't risk it.

A child's scream came from the pool.

Harper reached for her .45 and scrambled to her feet. Darci, Grace, and Renee all sat up to look.

The scream came from little Robin Wheatley. The eight-year-old tried to swim backward so fast she didn't go anywhere, instead splashing around. She kept shrieking, staring in horror at a suspicious brown object floating in the water not quite five feet away from her. Her efforts to get away from the thing seemed to be encouraging it to glide toward her like a small, foul torpedo.

"Unidentified floating object," yelled Jonathan.

"Turd!" shouted about six other kids.

More children, as well as a few adults in the water, noticed the turd and screamed, everyone scrambling to get away from it.

Daxton Oliver swam *toward* it. When he came within arm's reach of the suspicious floater, he grabbed it—making everyone scream again and Renee grab her mouth to hold back the urge to vomit. "Chill out! It's just a hunk of wood."

Calm spread over the pool. Some of the kids laughed it off. Robin crawled out of the pool and ran to her mother, sobbing.

Harper felt bad for her, but also couldn't help but laugh. The release of tension—not a serious emergency—plus a kid being so disgusted by a fake turd she burst into tears just hit her funny. The normality of it wrapped around her like a comfy blanket.

One of the older kids, a boy about fifteen, appeared to be laughing a bit too hard over the false turd. She smirked at him, certain he'd been the one who threw it into the water. Nothing to do about it, though. A harmless prank hardly warranted the effort of chasing him around. Besides, what teenage boy could resist the temptation of finding a perfectly turd-shaped stick in the vicinity of a pool?

She sat back down, reclined, and gazed up at the sky, feeling surprisingly content and... almost even safe.

A flash caught her eye.

Harper squinted, trying to focus on something drifting by overhead. When the glare subsided a few seconds later, she made out a shape that somewhat resembled an airplane, only tiny. "Whoa... second UFO."

Her friends looked at the pool.

"Where?" asked Grace.

"Not floating. Flying." Harper pointed. "Look up."

"I can't see shit. It's too bright out." Darci patted Piper on the back. "C'mon sweetie. Belch for mommy. Make it good and loud."

"You're so bad." Renee laughed, then gasped. "Holy crap. You're right. What is it?"

"If I knew what it was, it wouldn't be an *unidentified* flying object." Harper exhaled.

Grace shielded her eyes under one hand. "Kinda looks like a little airplane. It's too small to be real, but... too high up to be a toy."

"It's obviously *real*." Darci rolled her eyes. "Unless we're all hallucinating."

"Duh. I mean real like an airplane people get inside of. I think it's a drone." Grace squinted.

Darci leaned forward to peek out from under the sun canopy. "Wow. Yeah. Looks like Air Force markings."

"Eep." Grace whistled. "Air Force? That's either really good news or really scary news."

They sat in silence, watching the drone go overhead. It banked left, heading out toward Denver. After a few minutes, it disappeared into the haze, no longer visible. A working USAF drone could mean anything from the government and military hadn't been completely wiped out to some random person breaking into an old base and playing around with the equipment. It didn't shock her beyond belief to see a working drone. The military had tech civilians didn't even know about. EMP shielding had to be possible on military hardware, or perhaps it had been safe in an underground bunker during the strike.

If, in fact, the government managed to survive in some form, what could that mean for Evergreen, or any of the survivor towns? Would the military roll in and take over? If they did, would that be good or bad? What if the Templars found the Air Force base and used the drones to search for victims? Farfetched, yeah, but not impossible.

Harper eased herself back into a reclined position. "Fingers crossed it's good news."

---

fin

ACKNOWLEDGMENTS

Thank you for reading *The Threat Unseen!*

Harper's story will continue...

Additional thanks to Lee Sheridan for editing and Alexandria Thompson for the cover design.

ABOUT THE AUTHOR

Originally from South Amboy NJ, Matthew has been creating science fiction and fantasy worlds for most of his reasoning life. Since 1996, he has developed the "Divergent Fates" world, in which *Division Zero, Virtual Immortality, The Awakened Series, The Harmony Paradox, and the Daughter of Mars series* take place. Along with being an editor at Curiosity Quills press, he has worked in IT and technical support.

Matthew is an avid gamer, a recovered WoW addict, Gamemaster for two custom RPG systems, and a fan of anime, British humour, and intellectual science fiction that questions the nature of reality, life, and what happens after it.

He is also fond of cats.

Visit me online at:
    Facebook: https://www.facebook.com/MatthewSCoxAuthor
    Pinterest: https://www.pinterest.com/matthewcox10420/
    Goodreads: https://www.goodreads.com/author/show/7712730.Matthew_S_Cox
    Email: mcox2112@gmail.com

OTHER BOOKS BY MATTHEW S. COX

Divergent Fates Universe Novels

Division Zero series

- Division Zero
- Lex De Mortuis
- Thrall
- Guardian
- Harbinger
- The Shadow Fixer
- Neuroshock

The Awakened series

- Prophet of the Badlands
- Archon's Queen
- Grey Ronin
- Daughter of Ash
- Zero Rogue
- Angel Descended

Daughter of Mars series

- The Hand of Raziel
- Araphel
- Ghost Black

Virtual Immortality series

- Virtual Immortality
- The Harmony Paradox

Prophet of the Badlands Series

- Prophet's Journey
- Prophet's Mercy

Divergent Fates Anthology

(Fiction Novels - Adult)

The Roadhouse Chronicles Series

- One More Run
- The Redeemed
- Dead Man's Number

Faded Skies series

- Heir Ascendant
- Ascendant Unrest
- Ascendant Revolution

Temporal Armistice Series

- Nascent Shadow
- The Shadow Collector
- The Gate to Oblivion
- The Queen of Discord
- The Burning Alchemist

Vampire Innocent series

- A Nighttime of Forever
- A Beginner's Guide to Fangs
- The Artist of Ruin

- The Last Family Road Trip
- The Phantom Oracle
- How Not to Summon Demons
- Ordinary Problems of a College Vampire
- A Vampire's Guide to Surviving Holidays
- An Introduction to Paranormal Diplomacy
- A Vampire's Guide to Adulting
- How to Stop a Vampire War in Six Easy Steps
- Ancient Vampire Death Cults and Other Annoyances
- Hunting Vampires for Fun and Profit
- A String of Seriously Unlucky Events
- The Summer of Completely Usual Strangeness
- Demonic Crisis Management for the Modern Vampire

Standalones

- Wayfarer: AV494
- Axillon99
- Chiaroscuro: The Mouse and the Candle
- The Spirits of Six Minstrel Run
- Sophie's Light
- The Far Side of Promise anthology
- Operation: Chimera (with Tony Healey)
- The Dysfunctional Conspiracy (with Christopher Veltmann)
- Of Myth and Shadow
- The Girl Who Found the Sun

Winter Solstice series (with J.R. Rain)

- Convergence
- Containment
- Catalyst
- Catacombs

Alexis Silver series (with J.R. Rain)

- Silver Light
- Deep Silver
- Silver Quarrel
- Silver Crucible
- Silver Heart

Samantha Moon Origins series (with J.R. Rain)

- New Moon Rising
- Moon Mourning
- Haunted Moon

Vampire For Hire series (with J.R. Rain)

- Moon Master
- Dead Moon
- Lost Moon
- Vampire Destiny
- Infinite Moon
- Vampire Empress
- Moon Elder
- Wicked Moon
- Moon Blade

Maddy Wimsey series (with J.R. Rain)

- The Devil's Eye
- The Drifting Gloom
- Dark Mercy
- Primal Wrath

Samantha Moon Case Files series (with J.R. Rain)

- Blood Moon

- The Lucky Ones
- Nuclear Summer
- The Nuclear Frontier
- The World We Make
- The Threat Unseen

Progenitor Series

- Out of Sight
- Out of Mind

Diary of a Teenage Fey

(Short story series)

- Elder Horror
- The Hag of Barrow Falls
- Babysitter's Nightmare
- Lharakki
- Bauble for a Soul
- Simulacrum
- Amorphous
- Manticore

Standalones

- Caller 107
- The Summer the World Ended
- Nine Candles of Deepest Black
- The Forest Beyond the Earth

Middle Grade Novels

The Adventures of Ubergirl series

- My Dad is a Mad Scientist
- Aliens Ate My Homework
- The End of all Halloweens
- Dr. Infinity and the Soul Smasher

Tales of Widowswood series

- Emma and the Banderwigh
- Emma and the Silk Thieves
- Emma and the Silverbell Faeries
- Emma and the Elixir of Madness
- Emma and the Weeping Spirit

Standalones

- Citadel: The Concordant Sequence
- The Cursed Codex
- The Menagerie of Jenkins Bailey